A Question of Honor

By Charles Todd

The Ian Rutledge Mysteries

A Test of Wills
Wings of Fire
Search the Dark
Legacy of the Dead
Watchers of Time
A Fearsome Doubt
A Cold Treachery
A Long Shadow
A False Mirror
A Pale Horse
A Matter of Justice
The Red Door
A Lonely Death
The Confession
Proof of Guilt

The Bess Crawford Mysteries

A Duty to the Dead
An Impartial Witness
A Bitter Truth
An Unmarked Grave
A Question of Honor

Other Fiction

The Murder Stone
The Walnut Tree

A Question of Honor

Charles Todd

WM WILLIAM MORROW *An Imprint of* HarperCollins*Publishers*

This book is a work of fiction. The characters, incidents, and dialogue are drawn from the author's imagination and are not to be construed as real. Any resemblance to actual events or persons, living or dead, is entirely coincidental.

HarperCollins books may be purchased for educational, business, or sales promotional use. For information please write: Special Markets Department, HarperCollins Publishers, 10 East 53rd Street, New York, NY 10022.

FIRST EDITION

Library of Congress Cataloging-in-Publication Data has been applied for.

ISBN 978-0-06-223715-6 (hardcover)
ISBN 978-0-06-229786-0 (international edition)

13 14 15 16 17 OV/RRD 10 9 8 7 6 5 4 3 2 1

Especially for Bella and for Willow, with our love . . .

Friends can be four-legged too. These are scattered over a lot of geography, and many of them are rescues. The happiness they've given everyone who knows them is boundless. So this book is also dedicated to them, our special dogs . . .

Sammie and Hunter and Simba, Biedermann and Cassandra, Zeus, Smoke, Gus, Zeke, Gus Gus, and Angel in Hockessin. Zoey in Stanton. Ranger and Princess in New Castle. Miglo in Scotland. My Lady, Tippy, Jingles, Cocoa, and Buddy in Aiken. And of course Dax in Dallas, Jack and Wilbur in Houston.

You are very dear . . .

A Question of Honor

PROLOGUE

Northwest Frontier, India, 1908

THE LETTER CAME for Lieutenant and Mrs. Standish on an afternoon when the heat was at its height, and we had already retired indoors to rest until the evening.

As he was crossing the parade ground, Sergeant Murphy heard a scream. According to his report to my mother, he ran at once to the Standish bungalow to see what was wrong. He found the Indian servants standing in the sitting room doorway, uncertain what to do. Inside, Mrs. Standish was staring at a sheet of paper in her hand, her face as white as the cotton dress she was wearing. Her other hand clutched the sleeve of her husband's uniform. He had been just about to leave on patrol when the post arrived.

We were far enough away that we hadn't heard the cry.

Nodding to me as he came in our door, Sergeant Murphy turned. "Begging your pardon for bursting in like this, Mrs. Crawford, but I think you're needed at Mrs. Standish's." He described what had happened, ending with "She's in a rare state, and I couldn't make head nor tails of it. But the letter's from England. I saw the stamp. The envelope was lying there on the floor at her feet, where she'd dropped it."

"And you were quite right to come for me. Thank you, Sergeant. I'd say nothing of this to anyone else until we know what's happened. No need for gossip to spread and cause the family more pain."

He saluted and left, glad, I think, to be spared escorting my mother to the Standish bungalow. Sergeant Murphy had a long record of courage in the face of the enemy, but he was a bachelor, and domestic crises threw him into full retreat.

Mother took a deep breath, preparing herself for what she must do. "It's bound to be news of her girls, Bess. One must have taken ill. Stay here, and when your father comes in, would you send him across, please? He'll be able to make whatever arrangements are necessary."

"I'd like to go too," I said tentatively. I'd been friends with the Standish girls before Alice and Rosemary had been sent back to England to be schooled. I'd been lucky, my parents had decided to keep me with them. But quite a few children did go home, to give them a better education and to help them make friends in a country many of them couldn't remember or, indeed, had never seen. It was also a climate many of them had never experienced and they sometimes came down with winter chills that lingered into summer.

"I know you're worried too, darling, but just now Mrs. Standish needs to be reassured that the Colonel Sahib and I will do whatever we can to find out what's happened since that letter was written. To put her mind at ease. Later I'm sure she'll appreciate having you sit with her for a while." She picked up the hat I'd worn earlier in the day, and looked around for her fan. It was on the little table by the door, and I handed it to her.

"Thank you, my dear." She touched my cheek lightly, and then went out into the heat.

I waited several hours for her to come back and tell me what had happened. And the longer she remained with Lieutenant and Mrs. Standish in their bungalow, the more concerned I became. Nor had the Lieutenant left on patrol. I'd heard it ride out and saw Lieutenant Wade in command.

Bad news from England took several weeks to reach us out here. A child could be seriously ill when a letter was written and healthy again by the time her parents read the letter. Or dead . . .

I tried to study, but my mind wasn't on my books. I went out to oversee the evening meal in my mother's place, then set about tidying up my room—much to the dismay of our Indian staff, who kept trying to take the feather duster and the books and the tea tray out of my hands. There was a rigid hierarchy amongst the staff, and I knew better than to infringe on their duties. But sitting still was impossible. Waiting for news was unbearable.

Simon Brandon, our Regimental Sergeant-Major, stopped in, and I was glad to see him come striding through the door. Where most of our fairer-skinned troops turned a fiery red, Simon browned easily under the Indian sun, making it easier for him to assume a disguise when he traveled in unfriendly territory. Today he was wearing his uniform, his face and clothes gray with dust. It was often his mission to keep friendly tribes pacified, a seemingly endless task.

He greeted me with a smile as he always did, for we had been friends as far back as my memories went. He'd seen me through scrapes, taught me to ride and to shoot, and comforted me when my first pony had had to be put down. He'd talked me out of foolishness when I was feeling headstrong, and even commiserated with me over my first heartbreak, a schoolgirl's infatuation with one of the new Lieutenants just out from England.

"Hallo, Bess. I just came to tell your mother that the Colonel should be back within an hour or at most an hour and a half. I cut his tracks somewhere near the dry streambed."

"Thank you, Simon. She isn't here just now, but she'll be glad to hear it." My father had been away for nearly a fortnight. I added, "The Standish family has had bad news of some sort, and she's gone across to offer comfort."

"Standish, is it? I'll leave word for the Colonel, in the event he stops at HQ before coming here."

"Yes, that's a good idea. All quiet on your rounds?" We always kept an eye to the west. Between here and Afghanistan lived men who would cut a throat as easily as they stole a horse.

"So it would seem. With the tribes, nothing is ever certain." With a nod he was gone.

Not long afterward I saw my mother walking back toward our house, little puffs of dust marking each step as she crossed the parched parade ground. In the trees behind the single officers' barracks, crows called, angry over something lurking there. Snake? Mongoose? One could never be sure what had sought shelter wherever there was a tiny bit of shade under a tree or in the shadow cast by a building.

My heart went out to my mother. The Colonel's lady was often called on to help the wives of the regiment's officers. It was her duty to see to it that not only were they invited to dine from time to time but also that whatever problems arose were dealt with quickly and quietly, without troubling husbands who already had enough to think about. She also kept an eye on the wives of married private soldiers, for they often found India difficult to cope with.

She was close enough to the house now that I could see her expression under the broad brim of my hat.

Abiding sadness.

Had it been a death then, not an illness? But which of the girls? I felt a lump growing in my throat.

Meeting her at the door, I took her hat—my hat. Cool lemonade was waiting for her under the fans in the parlor. Men sitting cross-legged in the shadows of the veranda took it by turns to pull the fan ropes steadily, day and night. This hot season we hadn't gone up to the cool pines and hills of Simla—there was too much activity along the frontier with Afghanistan. The tribes there attacked at will, without provocation, real or imagined. My father had not had time to escort us to the hill station, and Simon was busy with new recruits. Promises of "perhaps next week" had been just that, promises.

My mother sipped her lemonade, putting off what she must tell me. "It's little Alice," she said finally, as if it was hard for her to form the words. "She has died of typhoid. She'll be buried in England. In fact, *was* buried before the post got as far as Suez. That's doubly hard for Mary Standish to contemplate."

Dearest Alice, a fair-haired little sprite with dimples when she smiled. I'd brought a doll back from England for her second birthday, one I'd found in London while we were on leave. Sweet-natured little Alice. Six years old last November. I wanted to cry.

"And Rosemary?" I asked quickly. She was eleven. Only four years younger than I, and so we had spent hours playing in our nursery or hers, sharing our dolls, our rocking horses, and our secrets.

"Apparently she'd had a milder case. She'll be all right. They hadn't told her about Alice, when the letter was written. They wanted to wait until she was stronger. Mary is determined to go to England on the next P&O steamer. She's asked her husband to find passage for them, but William's leave doesn't come up for another six months. And the way things are out here, he wouldn't have a ghost of a chance to bring it forward. Richard will have to tell him as much."

"Not even for compassionate leave?"

Mother shook her head. "Simon won't have the new recruits up to strength until next month at the very least. Still, Ellen Asbury also came over to sit with Mary. She suggested that Thomas Wade might be willing to escort her. His leave was approved before the latest outbreak of fighting. But that's Richard's decision to make. And William's."

The air was breathless, even with the fans over our heads and the wet sheets in many of the windows to cool what breeze there was. A small lizard ran up the wall and disappeared into the rafters. Mother finished her lemonade and said, "How do you comfort someone who has lost a child? I never know the answer to that."

Later, after the Colonel Sahib—my father—returned, it was agreed that Mrs. Standish would leave directly for Bombay. But sadly, without her husband. Thomas Wade was summoned and asked if he would consider escorting Mary Standish back to England.

I happened to be in the room writing a letter when he arrived.

And I saw the shock on the Lieutenant's face as he learned what had happened. "My God. *Alice?*" He couldn't seem to take it in. "She ran out in front of my horse when she was three, begging for a ride. Everyone spoiled her. She had the sunniest disposition—" He broke off, then asked, his voice different now, "Are they quite sure—is it certain that she died of typhoid?"

"She and her sister are with the Middletons. I don't think you were here then, but Captain Middleton was invalided home in '04 when he lost his foot to snakebite. He and his wife have taken in a number of Army children sent back to England. They live in the Cotswolds, a house near Shepton Mallet. They treat their charges like their own."

"That's all right, then," Lieutenant Wade answered. "Yes, I'll be happy to take Mary to England. I'll see she reaches the Middletons before I leave her. I'd like to meet them myself."

"Good man."

"I'd gladly pass up my leave, if Lieutenant Standish could go in my stead," he offered.

"That's kind of you, Wade, but Mary Standish wants to leave straightaway, and it could be weeks before permission to rearrange dates of leave can arrive from Delhi." He took a deep breath. "All right, then, that's settled. You might look in on her again before your leave is up. She could decide to stay in England with Rosemary or she might wish to come back here, to her husband. I'm sure she'd appreciate knowing she'll be well looked after, if she does choose to come home."

"Yes, of course, sir. That goes without saying."

And so it was agreed. It was something my father took immense pride in, looking after his regiment.

When Lieutenant Wade left, my father went to find my mother. She was sitting on the veranda, enjoying what little change in temperature there was after the sun had set. It was always a blazing ball until the very last moment, as if intent on keeping the earth as hot as possible for as long as possible. It was, in fact, very good at that.

I heard her say, "Mary is taken care of? He agreed?"

"Yes, she'll be well cared for. And Wade will bring her back, if that's what she wants to do."

Mother sighed. "So sad, Richard. I'm very glad we kept Bess with us. It's been a blessing for us. And she's as well educated as any young woman sent back to England."

"My love, I couldn't agree more. I'm going across to speak to Mary and sit with them for an hour. Alice was such a bright child. I think we've all been touched by her death."

"I remember when Alice was born. During that heavy monsoon rain that threatened to flood the cantonment. So tiny, but so determined to live. Amazing."

And then my father was gone. I could hear his footsteps as he walked around the veranda to the path leading across the parade ground to the married officers' quarters.

There was a lovely memorial service for little Alice. Her mother had already left for England with Lieutenant Wade, but everyone else was there, to help Lieutenant Standish through his own grief. He was a good officer, one of my father's best men. And he'd thrown himself into his duties, to keep from remembering too much. He said to me one day as we set out for a ride, "I owe Lieutenant Wade more than I can repay. Mary couldn't have gone alone. And Tom seemed to be eager to meet the Middletons. I can't think why, he has no children of his own."

In fact, Thomas Wade wasn't married, which had caused a flutter when he was posted to us. But he hadn't shown much enthusiasm for finding a wife, although he'd dutifully danced with all the single women when we had a ball and willingly escorted them wherever they wished to go. He'd even brought me back from the Maharani's, after I'd spent a week with her in Jaipur.

"Perhaps there's someone in England he's in love with," I suggested.

Lieutenant Standish raised an eyebrow. "You think so? I'll be the first to offer him my best wishes."

The time went by very quickly. We had several men wounded out toward the Khyber Pass while keeping the unruly tribes in order. They seemed to enjoy warring against each other, and then joining forces to war against the British, when they fancied a new enemy. But we were here to stay, and they knew it. It was just their way of saying, at the cost of many lives, that they held their own opinion on that subject. For a fortnight, Simon and my father were out nearly every day, guarding the passes favored by raiders and keeping what peace there was.

And then blessedly, the heat broke, and we were given a little respite. It was just about this time that Lieutenant Wade came back with the supply train. He looked very tired, having sailed from England through Suez and into Bombay, before taking the railway to Agra and making the next leg of his journey overland. His parents lived in Agra, and the final two weeks of his leave had been spent with them. His father was an official with the railway. I'd met them once, when we were in the city with my father. Mr. Wade had taken me down to the Yards to see the big locomotives, and Mrs. Wade had accompanied my mother to the markets. Nothing seemed to last very long in India, and there was always something we needed. The mender of pots and pans could do only so much, he couldn't work miracles, and bedclothes, towels, and tablecloths were frequent victims of Indian laundrymen. In Bombay, I'd seen where the wash was done, in stone basins attended by men whose lives were spent keeping the English and the Indian communities in clean linens.

Mother remembered to ask Lieutenant Wade how his parents were faring, and he said that they were keeping very well and sent their regards to the Colonel and his lady.

He reported to my mother that Mary Standish had had a very difficult journey to England, and that she had collapsed over her daughter's grave. We could see that this had moved him deeply. He had quiet praise for the Middletons, telling us that they had been distraught over Alice's death. When asked whether Mary was intending to return to India—she hadn't come back with him—Lieutenant Wade had shaken his head.

"She's decided to spend a year in England to be with Rosemary and to visit Alice's grave as often as possible."

"It's really hard to judge if she'll ever come back," Lieutenant Wade had told my father privately in our sitting room. "I suggested that her husband needed her too, but she was clinging to Rosemary, as if afraid to let her out of her sight. How has Lieutenant Standish coped?"

"He's carried out his duties in exemplary fashion," my father answered. "But I think he's taken to drinking in the evening. Look in on him from time to time, if you will. I'm afraid my visit might seem too . . . official. Perhaps you can persuade him that Mary's better off where she is for the time being."

"I'll do my best," the Lieutenant promised, and then was gone.

Mother, watching him walk across the parade ground, said, "That was a good idea, Richard. They're of an age, those two. They may do more for each other than you can do."

But we all knew that his wife's absence would be devastating for Lieutenant Standish. The question was, would his promising career begin to suffer?

A fortnight passed, and it seemed that my father's suggestion had worked. Lieutenant Standish stopped his drinking and took a renewed strength from the hope that Lieutenant Wade had given him, that his wife intended to return. A kind white lie. What's more, Mary Standish had sent back with Lieutenant Wade two photographs. One the Middletons had taken at Christmas of a smiling, happy Alice opening the gifts that her parents had sent to England for her, and another of Rosemary learning to play lawn tennis with the children of the neighborhood. Lieutenant Standish showed both photographs to my mother and me, and I could see how much the children had grown.

"It was thoughtful of Mary. I've decided to put in for leave as soon as possible. I think if I go to England, Mary will come back with me. Wade seems to think it's likely."

"A very good idea," my mother answered encouragingly. "Do speak to the Colonel about it." But we all knew it would be six months before he could go.

A week later, Lieutenant Wade took a company out on patrol, and they were late getting back. Hiding his anxiety, my father went to the lines just after dusk, to look over the new horses that had come in, and then went to confer with Simon on problems arising from a village that had been friendly until now.

My father and Simon had just returned to the house when we heard horses approaching. The Colonel Sahib, lifting his head to listen as he was pouring Simon a whisky, said, "Ah, that must be Wade at last." Then he put down the decanter and turned to Simon, who was also listening. "The numbers are wrong. Wade's run into trouble somewhere."

He and Simon raced out, crossing to the barracks. And then not fifteen minutes later my father was back. His face was grim. At his heels were two men in the uniform of the Military Foot Police.

They went directly to the Colonel Sahib's study, and there they stayed for three quarters of an hour. After they'd gone, my father came out onto the veranda where my mother and I were sitting.

"I think it might be best if you both went inside. There's likely to be some unpleasantness as soon as Wade's patrol rides in."

We didn't question him. We went to the sitting room, where my mother picked up her book and began to read while I played the piano.

Whatever had happened, it was a serious matter, and we both knew it. Young as I was, I'd lived with this regiment all my life, and I understood how it worked as well as the men who fought for it. As time went on I found myself listening for loud arguments, noisy chases across the parade ground, some indication that whoever the police were after had been caught.

It was two hours later when the Colonel Sahib came back again. He hadn't lost the grimness around his mouth.

"What's happened, Richard?" my mother asked, reading his expression from years of experience. "Something has."

He cast a glance at me—I was still sitting at the piano—then quietly answered my mother. "It apparently concerns Lieutenant Wade. But he hasn't come back from patrol. When he does, the MFP from Agra want to speak to him."

"Has there been fighting?" my mother asked anxiously. "On the Frontier?"

"No. The patrol ran into a raiding party but it retreated as soon as it saw our men. No," he said again, as if distracted. "It has to do with matters in Agra."

My mother opened her mouth to ask a question, thought better of it, and said, "I'm sure it will work out."

My father sat down, pretending to read the newspaper. About forty-five minutes later Simon Brandon came to the door. His face was as grim as my father's had been.

"He's taken a fresh horse and disappeared," Simon reported. "I've sent out scouts, but in the dark they haven't a chance of finding his tracks."

I knew better than to ask who it was they were talking about. If the Colonel wanted us to know, he'd tell us later.

My father said, "Keep me informed."

Simon saluted and was gone.

After several minutes of staring at the *Gazette,* my father came to a decision and tossed the newspaper to one side. Going to the window, staring out into the night, he said, "It will be all over the cantonment by morning. You might as well know the facts. Lieutenant Wade's parents were found murdered in Agra."

Shocked, my mother exclaimed, "How perfectly awful. Who could have done such a thing? Was it political, Richard?"

"The police have been trying to find the killer. The evidence, it seems, is now pointing strongly at Wade himself. Because of something that happened elsewhere, Agra has turned the matter over to the Army."

"Are they very sure?" my mother asked. "*Our* Lieutenant Wade? I find that hard to believe."

"Nevertheless. His parents' bodies were discovered the morning Wade left to rejoin the regiment. He'd stopped over to visit them, you remember, on his way back from England. The staff thought it odd that his parents weren't up to see him off at dawn. And they didn't come down later for their breakfast. Finally, the housekeeper went to their room and found they'd been shot. The sound had apparently been lost in a noisy marriage procession that had passed the house the night before. At first the local police wished to be sure the murders had nothing to do with Wade's military career—we all make enemies from time to time. And so they traced Wade's movements from the day his ship docked in Bombay. In Agra, they spoke to the servants and to the neighbors, even interviewed the staff at the railway office, in the event someone there had been out for revenge after being disciplined. It was at that stage when the police got word of trouble of some sort in England, Scotland Yard wanting information about Wade—"

My mother interrupted. "Scotland Yard? Surely nothing to do with Mary Standish, I hope."

"No, not at all. The Military Foot Police were sent here to question Wade, but when they reached Lahore, there was another matter requiring their attention before they could travel on."

The journey from Delhi or even Agra was long and arduous. Even so, the MFP had made good time.

My father turned to face us. "I find this as hard to believe as you do. But after my conversation with the MFP, I'm forced to change my mind."

"But you said—Wade didn't come back? Or he left as soon as he spotted the police? How could he have *known*—?" my mother asked.

"As far as we can discover, he rode in with his men, and at the lines he saw horses he didn't recognize. He asked one of the grooms about them and was told they were MFP and had come from Agra. Wade's Sergeant, Beckles, saw Wade starting in the direction of HQ, as he should have done to make his report. He stopped, came back to the lines, and said his compass was no longer in his pocket. He was fairly sure where he'd lost it. Beckles offered to send some men back to search, but Wade told him they were tired, he'd deal with it himself. He asked for a fresh horse and told Beckles he should be back in half an hour at the most. No one questioned his actions. They had no reason to. And so he rode off into the darkness and that was that. The police have gone after him, but they don't know the country. If they find him, it will be a miracle. I've sent some of my own men out to search for Wade, with Simon in charge. They might have better luck."

It was all but an admission of guilt, I thought. Disappearing like that.

We sat there in silence, digesting the awful news. I had known Lieutenant Wade, I'd ridden with him any number of times. He'd taken me to the spice bazaar in Peshawar, and even to call on the Maharani. The thought that he could be a murderer had never crossed my mind. As for killing his parents—just considering it was appalling.

I looked across at my own mother and father, and I found it impossible to believe that anyone I knew could walk into his family's house, kill his parents, then calmly get up the next morning and start back toward the regiment here along the Frontier. Yes, he'd had days on the road to put what he'd done behind him. But still . . .

How do you ever recover from the shock of murdering your father? Your mother?

It was unconscionable. What in heaven's name could they have done to make their son do something so unspeakable?

It took me several days to get over my shock. I didn't speak of it to my mother. I knew she too was trying to cope with the news.

Lieutenant Standish, remembering that this was the man who'd escorted his wife all the way to England, was beside himself when he was told. He refused to believe it. I heard him, his voice raised in anger, arguing with my father in the Colonel Sahib's study.

None of us could have guessed. Least of all, Mary Standish. The letter Lieutenant Wade had brought back to Lieutenant Standish had given such a glowing account of his care for her comfort and safety. Hardly what one would expect of a man about to commit murder. All the same, my father sent a query to London to be certain that Mary Standish, her daughter Rosemary, and the Middletons were safe.

It was a nine days' wonder. Lieutenant Wade had vanished. We heard speculation that he'd died in the desert. That he'd been seen crossing the Khyber Pass. That he'd been spotted in Lahore, and even in Jaipur. And then the first reliable report came in.

The Military Foot Police were told during one of their search sweeps that Lieutenant Wade's body lay deep in the Pass, where he'd tried to reach Afghanistan. It was impossible to verify that or to bring his body back.

I knew my father had sent word out to posts in the Punjab and in Rajasthan offering a reward for information about the Lieutenant. He would have to find fresh horses and provisions somewhere. The ports had also been ordered to stop him if he came through looking for passage. And so it made sense that Lieutenant Wade had tried the only way open to him. It had been a terrible risk.

He'd lost. He'd died. That was the end of the matter.

I asked my father, several months after word of his body had reached the cantonment, if he believed the report. If he was satisfied that Lieutenant Wade was dead.

"He has to be," he said slowly. "He hasn't tried to leave the country by ship. North, into Nepal or Tibet, holds nothing for him. He'd have to go west. Through Afghanistan into Persia. A long perilous journey, but it could be done, if he was determined enough. There have been no reports of him in any other part of this country. We made certain that every local police station had a description. What's more, he hasn't shown up in England, either. We even sent word to Australia."

But I could hear the tiny echo of doubt in my father's voice. He'd trained Lieutenant Wade. He and Simon Brandon. He knew how good the man was.

He also knew how difficult the terrain was, how fearsome the Frontier tribes were. Yes, Wade had had the courage to try. And yes, he'd very likely died in the attempt.

It was what the Army had been forced to accept, and we could do no less. As the Lieutenant had no family other than his parents, there was no one to notify.

The years passed, and there was no further news of Lieutenant Wade. Indeed, officially he'd been declared dead, and the Army doesn't do that lightly.

It was ten years later, in France, in the middle of a war, that I heard Lieutenant Wade's name spoken again.

It was like a visitation from the past, and not a welcome one.

This man had not only killed, he had left a stain of dishonor on the Regimental Lists.

And what touched the regiment touched my family.

Chapter One

England, Summer 1918

The afternoon sun was warm on my face as I stepped out the door of Rudyard Kipling's house in East Sussex. Simon Brandon, his expression unreadable, followed me, pulling the door shut behind him.

I wasn't sure why he wasn't his usual steady self.

As we turned to walk together around the house, toward the back lawns and the stream and water meadows beyond, I said, referring to our host, "He's still grieving. Poor man."

As soon as war broke out in 1914, Rudyard Kipling had urged his only son to join the Army. Jack had been killed at Loos barely a year later. His body had never been recovered. He'd been eighteen, still a boy.

"I remember Jack," I went on. "Once or twice he visited Melinda when I was there."

"You can't find a house in England that isn't grieving. We've lost a generation, Bess. The best we have."

I knew that all too well. I'd watched so many men die.

"Mr. Kipling is going to be on the Graves Commission. It's fitting, don't you think?"

"He'll know what words to put on the monuments," Simon answered. "That will matter."

Melinda Crawford had asked Simon to drive her down to Bateman's to call on Mr. Kipling. Worried about him, she made a point of regular visits. But this time her driver was suffering from a bout of malaria. Just home from France on a brief leave, I'd decided to come with them. I hadn't been to Kent in some time—it was where Melinda lived—and on the long drive down to East Sussex we'd enjoyed each other's company.

As we rounded the house and walked on to the gardens Simon commented, as if it had been on his mind most of the day, "She's talking about returning to India." I didn't need to ask who *she* was. "Once the war is over. She wants me to take her there."

Surprised, I stopped, staring down at the reflection of the summer sky in the quiet surface of the pools. "Is that a good idea? It's such a long journey at her age."

Simon was looking back at the house. "I don't know." I'd always had a feeling that Simon didn't want to return there. If anyone could persuade him, it was Melinda.

Her father, like mine, had been an officer in the Army, and she had grown up in India, just as I had, although of course decades apart. Indeed she had been something of a heroine as a child during the Great Indian Mutiny of 1857, for she and her mother had been caught in the dreadful Siege of Lucknow. She had married another officer stationed out there and later lost him to cholera. Afterward, alone but for her Indian servants, she'd traveled the world while she grieved.

I turned to look too, thinking as I had on other visits how really beautiful the Kipling house was. Someone moved past one of the upstairs windows, and I waved.

Mr. Kipling had told Melinda that it was love at first sight when he came to Bateman's. Born in India of British parents, he'd finally settled in England. The house couldn't be more different from those in Bombay or Delhi or even Simla. Like Melinda Crawford, he'd put down roots in this cooler climate, but a part of his heart was still in the East. It showed most clearly in his writing.

"Perhaps she wants to visit her husband's grave again," I suggested as we walked on. "Surely most of the people she knew are long since dead as well."

"It's possible."

I watched fluffy summer clouds drifting across the pool, almost as real as the ones in the sky above us. Then we walked on in a companionable silence, taking the path through the copse that led toward the high grass of the meadow. The hem of my skirt caught on the dry stalk of a spring wildflower, and Simon bent to set it free.

"Do you want to go back?" I asked him, curious. "To India, I mean."

"I don't know," he said again.

We paused on the bridge over the stream, looking down at the slow-moving water below. The sound of it passing over the stones in the streambed was a soothing murmur. But I could sense the tension in the man beside me.

I didn't press. Whatever Simon had left behind in India, he had never spoken to me about it. I wondered sometimes if my mother knew. Simon was devoted to her, and I'd always had a feeling that something had happened to him in India before my father's regiment had been sent home from that last posting. It would explain why he was in her debt.

At the time, I'd been considered too young to be included in family secrets, but had Melinda known? Was that why she wished to return to India? For Simon's sake—as well as her own?

Changing the subject, I said lightly, "I haven't had a chance to ask. Are you well enough to return to duty?"

Neither my mother nor I knew what services my father, the Colonel Sahib, and Simon Brandon performed for the Army. Experienced men, both of them, they would disappear for a day or a week without explanation. It often had to do with training and sometimes went well beyond training. I was certain that Simon had gone behind enemy lines more than once, but I'd said nothing to anyone about that.

Simon smiled. "I've been told I'm sound as a bell."

I was glad for his sake, but I was also worried. The war was certain to end before very long—the arrival of the American forces under General Pershing was helping turn the tide at last—but until it did, Simon would be in the thick of things if he could. Perhaps he wouldn't be as lucky the next time the Germans shot at him. I shivered at the thought.

We'd left the house for a stroll after our lunch with Mr. Kipling, to give Melinda time alone with her old friend. Among the books in Mr. Kipling's study were many of his treasures from India, small pieces in ivory or wood or silver, and when we'd left them, they were reminiscing about their experiences out there. A safe subject, when the war was too painful to speak of.

Simon took out his watch. "We have a quarter of an hour left. Do you want to walk as far as the mill? Or would you prefer to turn back toward the house?"

"The mill," I decided, and by the time we'd reached it Simon was himself again, chatting with the miller and inspecting the machinery.

Chapter Two

Back in France after my brief leave, I was sorting the wounded just coming into our forward aid station when one of the orderlies pulled at my sleeve.

"Beg pardon, Sister. We've got one over here we can't understand."

I turned to look in the direction he was pointing and said, "That's a Subedar. An Indian Sergeant. He should be able to speak English. But what's he doing in this sector? I didn't think there were any Indian troops in the line here."

"That's just it. There's no one about who can help us. Can you talk to him, Sister? I think he's dying. And he's trying very hard to tell us something."

I asked Sister MacLean to take my place and quickly crossed to where the Indian soldier was lying on a stretcher.

One look confirmed what the orderly had said. He was dying. The bloody froth on his lips told its own story, and his breathing was ragged.

I'd learned to speak several local languages in India almost as soon as I'd learned to speak English. My ayah, my nurse, had been a Hindu, the porter at our gate Muslim, and our majordomo, nearly as tall as my father, was a gray-bearded Sikh. I'd absorbed their culture along with their dialect without even trying, much to the horror of my proper English governess.

Kneeling beside the stretcher, I spoke to the man in Hindi, and his eyes flew open, gazing up at me with such relief, I was glad I'd come to him.

Clutching my hand as if it were a shield against the approaching darkness, he began to speak, rapidly and carefully, as though reporting to his English officers. I listened in dismay, then made a promise I hoped I could keep.

"I will find a way."

He thanked me with an almost imperceptible nod, no longer able to form words. And then he was gone. I closed those dark, pain-filled eyes as they went blank. Rising, I found that men were standing just behind me, watching.

"What was it troubling him?" the orderly asked. "He was that upset."

"His family at home," I said, lying, but knowing it was the safest thing to do. "He wanted them to know he died bravely. Who brought him in? I'd like to speak to the stretcher bearers."

"There weren't any," the orderly told me. "He must have crawled here. One minute he wasn't there, and the next he was lying where you see him, holding out his hand as if to beg for help. I went to him, got him settled properly on that stretcher, but I couldn't make out what he was saying."

I shook my head. "Poor man."

I went back to my duties. Wounded were still arriving by foot and by stretcher. As I worked, I wondered how that Subedar had reached us. Had he crawled from wherever he'd been shot? And who had shot him? A nervous sentry? Was it a stray bullet from the last German attack? If he wasn't in the line—and he shouldn't have been—how had he got that near to the Front?

And then the ambulances were coming in, first one and then the others in an irregular line. The worst cases were quickly loaded, and we went on treating the steady stream of wounded.

At seven o'clock I was relieved by another Sister coming on duty. I ate my dinner as usual, trying not to hurry.

And then in the privacy of my quarters, where there were no prying eyes, I sat down on my cot and began a letter to Simon. I stopped halfway through my first sentence. What was I to tell him?

These were matters I couldn't put into a letter.

Finally, I wrote to my father instead.

It's my sad duty to inform you that Subedar Shanti Gupta of Agra has died of his wounds. He was a good man, and he worried at the end how his family would manage without him. I am writing to ask that you look into his affairs and see if there is some relief for his wife and children.

Satisfied, I signed it and addressed the envelope to my father. When the next runner came through, I sent the message to HQ with him, to be forwarded in the military pouch.

Two days later, Simon was there as the last of the light faded and faces were hard to distinguish in the dusk. But I knew him instantly: his height, the way he carried his shoulders, his stride. After all, he'd been there, underfoot in our household since I was a child and he a very young raw recruit just out from England. Too well spoken to be a guttersnipe given the choice of gaol or the Army, he never mentioned his past. There had been whispers about him, and the chip on his shoulder was the size of a boulder. My father, already a Captain with a promising future, had taken Simon under his wing before he got himself shot for insubordination. First as a batman, to replace an older private whose enlistment was up, and then as the man he turned to for dangerous missions, because Simon had picked up the local languages so quickly. The Colonel Sahib's trust had proved to be justified. Rising to Regimental Sergeant-Major, Simon had left the regiment when my father resigned his commission.

"Your father passed your letter on to me. Can we talk somewhere?"

But there was scarcely any privacy here. I led him to the perimeter, and he stood looking back at the line of wounded still coming in. The shelling, for a mercy, had stopped, but we could hear the rattle of rifles and machine guns in the distance.

"Start at the beginning. Who was this Indian Sergeant?"

"He told me he was from Agra, and he gave me his name. At least he claimed it was his name. Beyond that, I have no idea who he could be," I said, keeping my voice low. "Let me tell you how this began." I gave Simon a brief account and ended, "He was dying, and he knew he was. He didn't have time to tell me what he was doing in this sector or how it was he'd been shot. His message was more important to him than either of those. And what I heard I was afraid to put down on paper."

"And quite right. The censors must read everything. Exactly what did this man say?"

We had fallen into speaking in Urdu, almost without noticing it.

"He claimed he had seen Lieutenant Sahib Wade. Simon, I believed him. Even though Thomas Wade is supposed to be dead."

"Your father was never comfortable with that report. Nor was I. But the sighting of his body was too close to the Khyber Pass to send men out to verify the information. Far too dangerous. Still, Wade hasn't been seen since then."

"If he had managed to get out of India, he could have thought himself safe. Until the war came along."

The conflagration had brought together people from around the globe. There were Chinese laborers, freeing the English to fight. There were Spahis from North Africa, New Zealanders, Indian troops, Australians, South Africans, Kenyans, Nepalese Gurkhas, Canadians—from every corner of the Empire and most of France's holdings as well. A man you never expected to see again because he lived in a far corner of the earth could be marching to the Front as you were retreating in rotation; he could be lying next to you on a hospital cot or bringing up boxes of ammunition to your sector. Or even carrying the stretcher you were lying on.

A matter of chance. A simple trick played by Fate.

I added, "Have you looked into the Subedar's background?"

"I didn't know what I was looking for. And there must have been half a hundred Guptas serving in France. It's not an uncommon name. Still, there was only one man in the lists from Agra, and as I remember, he was of an age to have been in the city when Wade came back from England. He might very well have remembered what happened then."

It had been in all the English language newspapers as well, the murder of Thomas Wade's parents.

We at the cantonment knew nothing about this until the MFP arrived on our doorstep seeking to question Wade. I was never given the full account of what he'd been accused of, but what I knew was shocking enough.

And what he'd done to the reputation of my father's regiment—I'd known that very well. I don't think anyone had spoken his name since the official inquiry had concluded. We had only wanted to forget.

"Do you think Wade shot the Subedar—that somehow they had recognized each other?"

"It's too bad the Subedar died. We might have asked him. Gupta was well away from his lines. That's another mystery. Had he followed Wade? Or escaped from him?" He looked around at the aid station. "You were very wise not to make what the Subedar told you public. It probably would have done no harm, but people gossip. The last thing you need is for Wade to come looking for *you*."

I shivered at the thought. I'd already had one brush with a stalker. I wasn't eager to find myself in the sights of another.

"Would you recognize Wade, if you saw him again?" Simon asked, curious.

"I'm not sure. I was fourteen at the time. But it's possible. Of course now that I know he's in France, I just might—because I'm expecting to see him. The question is, would he recognize me?"

"It's my recollection that he was twenty-four, nearly twenty-five, in 1908. He'd be in his early thirties now. Keep that in mind and watch your step." Simon started to leave and then stopped. "You do know that he'd already killed three people in England before he returned to India?"

"No, I didn't," I answered, surprised. "Only that something had happened before he left England that had worried Lieutenant Standish. Of course my parents tried to keep such things from me. But everyone was talking about the murders in Agra, and then there was the hue and cry in the garrison when Wade disappeared. If this is true, why didn't the police stop him in England?"

"There was very little to go on at first. In fact, the assumption was a robbery that had gone wrong. By the time Scotland Yard had turned its attention to Wade, he was well on his way to India. The Yard handed the matter over to the Army. By the time the full report reached the Colonel, we had every reason to believe Wade was dead. The Colonel notified the Yard, and nothing more came of it."

I could understand that. And it explained why nothing had been said to me about England.

"There was never any sign—looking back, I mean—that he was troubled?"

"He was rather aloof. Kept to himself. I suspected in the beginning that he was shy. Later I wondered if something was troubling him. I asked, but he shook his head and told me that he was quite happy. As men go, he was a good officer. Nothing on his record to indicate he was likely to become a killer. In the field he was steady, looked after those under him, and never lost his head when in a tight corner."

I couldn't help but think that those same traits had given Wade the courage to return to his duties after the murders, as if nothing had happened.

"Which brings us back to the problem of what set him off."

"I don't suppose anyone will ever know. All right, I'll find out what I can about this man Gupta. What sector he was in, what he was doing the day he died. Whether his word is to be trusted."

"There's something else. Surely Wade couldn't have enlisted in 1914 under his own name. But whatever name he chose, I should think someone would have realized he'd had previous military training. He couldn't hide that from an experienced Sergeant or career officer."

"The Army was desperate for men. He could have slipped through, if he was very careful."

I hesitated. "What if the Subedar was wrong? What if the man he saw wasn't Wade? Just someone who resembled him?"

"It's quite possible," Simon agreed. "We won't know the answer to that until we find out who shot the Subedar."

"Will you let me know what you discover?"

"If I can. And Bess—until we're sure, it's best not to involve your father. Let him take your message at face value, your concern for a soldier's family."

"I understand." The Colonel Sahib had taken Wade's betrayal of the regiment personally. He had done everything he could to bring the man back to stand trial, continuing the search long after the Military Foot Police had given up. A question of honor.

"There's one other matter to consider. If Wade was somewhere out there in the darkness, making sure the Subedar died, and he heard you speaking to the man in Hindi, he'd have known what you were being told. Just . . . be careful."

And then he was gone, vanishing into the night with the ease that had marked him since he was a young soldier on the Frontier.

I took his warning to heart.

We were shifted to another sector, where a fresh attack meant long lines of casualties and long hours attending them. We slept when we could, and I ran out of clean uniforms, with no time to launder the soiled ones. We fell into bed only when we were starting to lose our concentration. No more than a brief respite, but desperately needed.

Since the institution of helmets for the men earlier in the war, and then for the officers as well, we were seeing fewer head wounds. But machine guns and shrapnel could rend the body or take an arm or leg, leaving only the jagged stump. Gas burned the lungs and eyes, proximity to exploding shells burst eardrums, and even the occasional enemy aircraft strafing the lines or flying deep into Allied territory to fire on relief columns added to our burden. As the stretchers came in, or men carried their comrades to us, we did what we could, and then sent the worst cases back to base hospitals. But the number of men dying hadn't changed, and we had no time to weep for them.

Baron von Richthofen had been shot down in late April near the Somme—by an Aussie machine gunner, it was said—and more than a few German pilots, eager to fill his boots, had taken to wild stunts to make their own names. Indeed, one flew over our position on our third day here. With so many wounded, it was impossible to take cover, and we held our breath until he had gone past us, looking for other targets.

By the end of the week, the push that had cost so many casualties had ended, and the deluge slowed to a trickle. We took it by turns sleeping nearly around the clock.

Word came soon after that two of us were being sent back to a base hospital. It was a long jolting ride in an ambulance, but the first thing I did when I got there was to launder all my uniforms and, when I could, press them to meet the standards of the Service.

I'd been there only a week when something happened that gave me much to think about.

There was a mix-up in the roster of wounded. There were two patients with the same name but quite different wounds. As it turned out, they were both Welsh, both Taffy Jones, but not related as far as either of them knew.

It was when I was ticking off names on the roster, helping to sort out the confusion, that I saw we had a Captain Wade in one of the wards. The chart said *gunshot wound.*

It would do no harm, I told myself, to have a look at him. I was fairly certain by this time that the Wade we were seeking hadn't followed the Subedar as far as the aid station where the man had died. What's more, no one had shown an interest in us or our wounded, no one had come round asking questions. The explanation might be, he was here, wounded by the Subedar.

And so I carried in a pitcher of fresh water for the Sister in charge. She had had a busy afternoon and was grateful for my help.

But the Captain Wade in the last cot but one, suffering from a shattered elbow, brought back no memories for me. He had fair hair and blue eyes, freckles across the bridge of his nose, and looked to be no older than I was.

Certainly not the man I'd known in India.

But of course there must be a dozen men named Wade in the British Army.

The Subedar had recognized him. I'd believed him when he said as much. Still, he was dying when I got to him. It was entirely possible that the man had imagined the encounter. I'd sat with too many who were breathing their last, and sometimes they saw themselves safe at home in the arms of someone they loved. It was comforting and eased their passage. But more than a few had also relived the horrors of their wounding or the death of a friend.

I tried to put the matter out of my mind.

Which only kept it alive.

I was on duty when a new contingent of Sisters arrived, two of them experienced and one just finishing her training only two months before. But she was as capable as the other pair. I knew Sister Burke. We'd served together before, but Sister Hadley and Sister Morgan were new to me.

The second night after their arrival, Sister Burke had come to sit with me before going to bed, catching me up on her news. She was worried about her brother, and while she made light of it, passing it off as an elder sister's concern, I could tell how hard it was to keep her voice light.

"He's spoiled, of course," she said deprecatingly. "He's the only son in a houseful of daughters. We were delighted when he married Janet. That was the week before war was declared. And it settled him down so much I hardly recognized him. The responsibility, you see. He'd never had to look after anyone else before. Then Papa died—you remember that, don't you? We were outside of Ypres just then. I was sent home on compassionate leave—and Rob took Mama home to Janet, rather than leave her in her own home. She was so lost, it was heartbreaking to watch."

"Yes, I remember that. How is your mother now?"

"She'd been writing letters to Rob, telling him that his wife was seeing other men. That she walked out with them nearly every night, leaving Mama at home alone."

"Oh, dear," I said, knowing what must be coming. But I was wrong.

Taking a deep breath, Sister Burke said, "And then Mama died suddenly. Or at least it seemed sudden to us. Rob came home to the funeral, and the doctor was telling him that Mama appeared to be well one day and ill the next. He had something to say as well about Janet's care of Mama, and Rob knocked him down. The doctor. It was dreadful. A terrible scene on the steps of the church."

I could imagine it, and I said as much. "What did the doctor accuse Janet of? Neglect?"

"Not precisely neglect. She fed and dressed Mama, took her to the doctor, filled all her medicines as directed. It was just leaving her home at night alone, while Janet went out with other men. Just the way Mama had described. And she wasn't there the night Mama suddenly took ill in the night. By the time Janet found her, there was nothing to be done."

"When was this?"

"In May. In the midst of that influenza epidemic. But Mama didn't die of influenza. It was some digestive disturbance."

I quickly went through my knowledge of poisons, unwilling to believe it was possible, unable to stop myself from wondering.

I said, "And all is well still between Janet and your brother?"

"I'm afraid not. He's just been told that Janet is going to have a child. And my brother swears it isn't his. Couldn't be. I just don't know. What's more, I don't know what to do."

Janet Burke wasn't the first woman who had married one man and then had fallen in love with someone else. And wartime made it easier, it seemed. It had now become something of an epidemic as the fighting went on and on, without an end in sight.

"Where is Janet now? Still in Norfolk?"

"No, she's gone to live with her sister in Hampshire. The Norfolk house has been closed up. It hasn't been a comfortable pregnancy, she says, and she needs her sister's care and support."

Or she wanted to escape the gossip in Norfolk.

"I'm sorry," I said, and meant it. I just hoped Rob wouldn't do anything rash when next he had leave. It sometimes happened.

We worked together, Sister Burke and I, on two men who were shell-shocked, dazed and uncertain where they were, calling for dead comrades and fighting off attempts to dress their wounds because they were determined to return to their lines. We gave a sedative to one of them, he was so difficult, and finally persuaded the other to sleep. I felt deeply for these men, although some of the orderlies treated them with contempt, calling them cowards. The mind can handle only so much despair and horror. Killing didn't come naturally to most men, although they had to become proficient at it if they hoped to survive. Many blotted out what they couldn't face, and others buried it deep inside, where only they could see it. And some simply walked into a German bullet to stop the torment.

They slept, and the next morning got up and went back to the lines, unwilling to leave their men to face the enemy without them. It took tremendous courage.

And then one night when rain was coming down in sheets and we were trying to get a convoy through to the Base Hospital in Rouen, fighting the mud and the slick road and dodging columns of men moving up the line, the ambulance just ahead of ours slid into a shallow gully. Teddy was the driver, one of the best we had, but the vehicles ahead of him had turned the ground to treacle, and even his skill couldn't save him.

Half a dozen men were pulled from the column by a Sergeant and they put their shoulders into pushing the ambulance back to solid ground. I watched them struggle for a footing, one of them nearly disappearing under the spinning rear wheel.

Another two or three men came to the aid of the first half dozen, and as the ambulance slowly crept back in line, the Sergeant's torch flicked over it, checking the rear axle.

It flicked as well across the faces of the men still braced against the side of the ambulance. And as it did, for an instant before it moved on, I saw a face I recognized.

The torch was shut off, leaving us in the rain-swept darkness, and one by one the men who had helped push rejoined their column. It was nearly impossible to tell which one was which as they hurried forward, and then they were marching on, disappearing from view. The Sister in charge of the ambulance that had slid into the ditch signaled that all was well with her charges, and we were continuing toward the south. There was no way I could go after the column. No way I could find that Sergeant and ask him if he knew the names of the men he'd sent to our rescue.

But I'd have sworn it was Thomas Wade I'd seen. Under oath, if need be.

Chapter Three

Soon thereafter I was sent back to England with a convoy of wounded, and after they had been settled in various clinics, I was given leave.

I sent a message to Simon that I was in London, at the flat I shared with other Sisters, and waited to hear from him.

Instead of writing, he came to Mrs. Hennessey's house-turned-lodgings, and was standing in her foyer when I returned from ordering fresh uniforms to replace those too stained to be used again.

Surprised, I said, "Hullo. Fancy finding you here."

He grinned. "I've been kicking my heels for over an hour. And neither Mary nor Diana is present in London or I'd have taken her to lunch instead."

We went out to his motorcar, and as he helped me into my seat, I told him what I had seen the night the ambulance had slid off the road.

"Did you indeed?" Simon demanded, turning briefly to look at me. "And he held the rank of a private soldier?"

"Yes, I'm sure of that," I said. "But I have no idea what company or regiment he was with. There was no time to see anything, really. Except his face and the fact that he wasn't wearing an officer's uniform."

"Damn!" Simon swore with great feeling under his breath. "But there's a logic to this, isn't there? What better place to hide than in the ranks?"

"What are we to do?" I asked. "Should we take this information any further? There's so little to go on."

"We can't. If we're wrong, then we've stirred up the past for no reason. It will do the regiment no good."

"Did you discover anything more about the Subedar?"

"Nothing we can use. He did live in Agra, and it was a cousin's wedding procession that covered the sound of the shots that killed Wade's parents. He was interviewed along with everyone else in the wedding party, but of course they'd seen or heard nothing. What's more, there's no proof that he knew Lieutenant Wade by sight. Only the house belonging to his parents. Wade's father, on the other hand, was a familiar figure. The railway employed thousands of people."

"Then we're back to being wrong, aren't we? I wish I could discuss this with my mother, if not my father. But there you are. It's too painful a subject to bring up, even casually."

The impasse cast a pall over our luncheon.

Afterward I asked, "Is Mary Standish still in the Cotswolds, do you think?"

"Mary Standish?"

"Yes, I'd like to ask her how Lieutenant Wade appeared to her while they were traveling together. And didn't he come back to call on her before he left? She might have seen a difference in him. Something—" I broke off, then added, "Was she ever interviewed by Scotland Yard, do you think?"

"I doubt it. She wasn't directly involved in . . . anything that happened. Bess, you don't intend to pursue this business, do you?"

I took a deep breath. "I don't know, Simon. It's just—if we had only the testimony of the dying Subedar, I would let it go, because there was no corroborating evidence. Only one man's word that he'd seen Lieutenant Wade. But what did I see? Lieutenant Wade?

Someone who looked like him, there in the rainy night? I need to know. I watched my father deal with the shocking charges against one of his men. You were there, you know how we felt."

"Yes, I was there. All right, if I help you with this visit, will you let it drop if we see there's nothing to these sightings?"

"I promise."

We found Mrs. Standish not in Shepton Mallet but in a bungalow in the next but one village. Her garden was lovely, and as we walked up the path between the beds, I said to Simon, "I think it's the flowers people missed most in India."

"Your mother would agree with you."

Knocking on the door, we waited. After a moment, an older woman dressed in the uniform of a housemaid opened it.

We asked for Mrs. Standish, and we were taken to the back garden where she was sitting on a bench, a pot of water and a palette of watercolors at her side.

I recognized her at once, in spite of the ten years since I'd seen her last, only her fair hair was graying now, and she was wearing glasses.

She frowned when she saw me, then a broad smile spread across her face.

"Bess? Bess Crawford? And it's Sergeant-Major Brandon, isn't it?" She set aside her paints and rose to take my hand, kissing my cheek before shaking hands with Simon. "What a lovely surprise!"

"We are on our way to visit friends in the north," I said, the agreed-upon tale Simon and I had concocted, "and as we were a little before the time, I thought I would say hello."

"I'm so glad you did. Your mother visits from time to time. She's told me you are a Sister now. How very brave of you. But then you were brought up with the regiment, weren't you?"

We were offered chairs, which the maid and Simon brought out to the garden, and we sat talking for a time. I asked about Rosemary, who was engaged now to a young Lieutenant in the Black Watch.

"She's staying with his mother at the moment. She hasn't been well, and Rosemary went to Gloucester to be with her. She'll be sorry to have missed seeing you."

"I'm glad to hear she's happy," I said, wondering how I could, gracefully, bring up the past. Losing little Alice had been such a blow, and it was very likely that Mrs. Standish would prefer not to remember too much about that dreadful time.

But she brought it up herself, saying, "I still find it hard to believe that that very kind Lieutenant Wade went back to India and committed such a dreadful crime. I find it even harder to believe he'd killed three people after he came to ask me if I wished to stay in England or return to India with him."

I knew so little about what had happened in England. Just what Simon had told me in passing. But Mrs. Standish would have read whatever newspaper accounts there were. I could imagine how they must have affected her. I cast a quick glance at Simon, then said to her, "You spent a great deal of time with the Lieutenant on the crossing. Did you see anything that would give you the feeling that he was distressed or angry?"

"Not at all. He looked after me as well as if I'd been his sister. We talked a good bit about Alice, you know. It helped me, even though it was very painful at the time. He'd been fond of her, which made it easier. He told me that she reminded him of his own little sister. I hadn't been aware that he'd had one. But it must be true, because he understood just how I felt."

"What became of her?"

"She died, I think, at quite a young age. Lieutenant Wade went with me to see the Middletons, and he asked them questions when I couldn't—how Alice had come to take ill, how her last moments were, what doctors had been called in, the treatments they'd tried, about the care that was given to Rosemary, and so on. My own husband couldn't have dealt with matters any more thoroughly. And he stayed with me until I'd seen Rosemary for myself—she'd been taken to the seaside at Lyme Regis to help her recover her health. Mrs. Middleton had gone with her, bless her. They couldn't have taken better care of my children than I would have myself." Mrs. Standish took a deep breath. "It was such an awful time. I couldn't go back to India, and for the longest while, Rosemary wasn't up to such an arduous journey even if I'd wished to take her. You can't imagine how happy I was when my husband finally got his leave. But of course he had to go back. While he was here he told me about the hue and cry for Lieutenant Wade. I couldn't believe we were talking about the same person, to tell you the truth."

"And you noticed no change in him when he came to ask you about returning to India? Nothing had happened during the rest of his leave to make you uneasy?"

"If it had, it didn't show in his manner toward me. He tried to persuade me to sail with him for my husband's sake, and I've wondered, you know, if my going back then would have changed what happened in England or Agra. Surely he wouldn't have killed his parents if I'd been staying there too."

Or she might have died with them, I thought, then changed my mind. Perhaps she was right; if she'd been present, Lieutenant Wade wouldn't have killed anyone.

It was such an odd contradiction in the man. Gentle and considerate with Mrs. Standish, and yet capable of killing his own parents.

Mrs. Standish shook herself, and said, "Well. That's best left in the past, isn't it? But it disturbed me for years. I couldn't reconcile the man who had looked after me with the reports of what he'd done in apparently cold blood."

"Are the Middletons still alive?" I asked, appearing to change the subject.

"Yes, in fact, they live on the other side of the village. I see them often. I thank the heavens that my children found such caring people to live with."

I had already asked Simon about Mrs. Standish's husband. He

hadn't resigned his commission; he'd stayed with the regiment and was at present serving in Egypt. I'd liked him immensely, and I was glad he was safe. If anyone could be called safe, in this war.

As if she'd overheard my thoughts, Mrs. Standish pointed to the small watercolor she'd been working on when we arrived. It was a view of the house and the back garden. "I was just finishing this to send to William. He says he has nothing to look at but desert."

"It's lovely," I told her, and it was. She was quite talented, capturing the colors and the peaceful air of the gardens.

We left soon after, although she offered us tea, and as we drove away, I said to Simon, "No one told me there were other murders. Not until you did, there in France."

"It was thought best. At the time."

I was angry, but I could also understand why my parents had wanted to spare me.

"But who did he kill, Simon? It was here in England. Did they have anything to do with his leave?"

"It appeared to be random. There was a family. Father, mother, and daughter."

Chapter Four

"Dear God." I'd gone riding with Lieutenant Wade. I'd danced with him. We had won a croquet tournament not six months before he went to England on leave, escorting Mary Standish. So many people dead—I couldn't quite take it in.

We were about to turn south, but I touched Simon's arm, and said, "While we're here, I'd like to speak to the Middletons. Would you mind? We could speak freely to them, couldn't we?"

I could see that he thought it unwise, but he reversed the motorcar, and after asking someone in the local pub for directions, we found the Middleton house on the outskirts of the village.

They were so much older now than the husband and wife I remembered as a child. Their hair was white, their faces lined. They recognized Simon at once, welcoming him into their home, and then turned to me.

"This can't be our little Bess?" Captain Middleton asked. "But I believe it must be—you look so very much like your mother. And how is she, and your father? I haven't seen them in—well, it must be six months now."

I hadn't been aware of how my parents had stayed in touch with so many former officers and men and their families. It was a measure of their feelings for the regiment, even now.

Mrs. Middleton took my arm and said, "Come into the kitchen with me, dear, while I make tea. We were just talking about it, and I've a lovely lemon cake we've been looking forward to."

She whisked me out to the kitchen while Simon and Captain Middleton sat down in the parlor, already talking about the progress of the war.

"The Sergeant-Major looks pale. Has he been wounded?"

"Yes, it was a training accident," I said, not wanting to tell her how Simon had come by that wound or where. "But he's well now."

"That's good. Albert—Captain Middleton—has been regretting not being young enough to fight for King and Country again. Never mind the loss of his foot. But to tell truth, I'm just as glad. I'm too old to worry about him the way I did in India. What brings you to our door? I hope it's not bad news about your mother or father!" She was filling the kettle with water and taking out the tea things. I offered to help but she refused. I was the Colonel's daughter and so I must not be put to work.

"Not at all. We were driving down from the north, Simon and I, and we stopped to see Mrs. Standish. I thought you were living in Shepton Mallet?"

"We were, my dear, but the house held too many memories. All those children we took care of. Grown now, and some of their names already in the casualty lists. It's heartbreaking."

I could understand. I'd seen the names of too many of my own friends there.

"I missed Rosemary," I said. "She's staying with the mother of her fiancé. I understand her future mother-in-law hasn't been well."

"That's so like Rosemary. She's grown up to be quite a lovely girl. Sometimes I wonder how dear little Alice would have looked now, and if she'd have found someone to love." She sighed. "It was like losing our own child. I couldn't sleep for the longest time, thinking I could hear her calling to me from her sickroom. But there you are. Children die, don't they, no matter how much you love them." The teakettle began to sing, and she poured a little of the hot water into the teapot, rinsing it.

"I remember when Lieutenant Wade volunteered to accompany Mrs. Standish to England. It was such a kind thing."

"Yes, and I was never so surprised than when I heard he had killed five people. I couldn't believe they'd found the right man." While the tea steeped, she set about cutting the lemon cake. "Cakes aren't quite the same these days, with all the shortages. But we make do."

All of Britain was making do.

"There was nothing about Lieutenant Wade that seemed—different—between the time he brought Mrs. Standish to you and when he returned to escort her back to India?"

"Absolutely nothing."

She set the slices of cake on the tray, added the cups and saucers, the individual plates, forks, and spoons, the sugar and a jug of milk, and lastly, the delicately embroidered tea napkins that she must keep for guests.

I moved to pick it up for her, but she smiled. "I've done this all my life. I'm used to carrying in the tea tray."

And we walked in procession to the sitting room, where Simon rose at once, took the tray from Mrs. Middleton, and set it on the tea table.

We enjoyed our tea but ate sparingly of the cake, knowing how hard it was to find the sugar and flour and eggs to make such a treat.

Captain Middleton, reminiscing about India, said, "It was a hard life, there on the Northwest Frontier. But I missed it when I had to leave it. Missed the men I served with and had to leave to the charge of others. I even missed the heat, when I came home to England." He chuckled. "It rained for a week, as I remember, and I thought I'd never sleep on dry sheets again."

Simon, laughing with him, asked about his former charges.

"Ah. The girls are well, all of them. The lads are another story. We've lost too many of them. I've kept an album, you know, photographs of all of them. Would you care to see it?"

And he reached behind his chair, taking a leather-bound photograph album out of the bookcase there.

I moved my chair closer, so that I could see while he showed Simon the contents.

I knew most of the faces, of course, and I watched the children who had been sent home to England to be educated grow into young adults.

And here on one page was Alice, lovely little Alice, and Rosemary. On the next page were Mrs. Standish, and just behind her, Lieutenant Wade, standing by the little grave of her daughter.

"It was the worst day of my life when that child died," Captain Middleton was saying. "But the doctors could do nothing. Writing the letter to Alice's mother took all the courage I could muster. No one wants to be the bearer of such news. But it had to be done."

I looked closely at Lieutenant Wade in the photograph. Could I have been mistaken when I thought I'd seen him in the rain in France? I couldn't be sure. Does murder change a person's face? Or was it only that ten years had passed?

I said, as if just discovering it, "That's Lieutenant Wade."

Captain Middleton peered at the photograph. "He was a good man. I'd have sworn to that. But we can't always be right in our judgments, can we?" And he turned the page, shutting off that part of the past.

We left soon afterward, thanking the Middletons for their hospitality.

On our way back to London, Simon asked, "Are you any more certain now than you were before? That photograph. Did it help or not?"

"I don't know," I told him truthfully. "I wish I did."

The next day I sailed for France.

Simon saw me off at the railway station.

"Let it go, Bess. Lieutenant Wade died in the Khyber Pass. Let his bones stay there."

"I'll try," I said. And at the time, I meant it.

Chapter Five

I reported to my post, which was again a base hospital, but I soon found myself sent to a forward aid station. The German Army was fighting to hold on, and it was a bloody business.

As I worked with the wounded, sorting them, trying to stabilize them for the uncertain transport to a base hospital, I had no time to worry about England or Lieutenant Wade.

But as I was lying in my cot each night, trying to erase the images of the day and relax enough to let sleep come, I thought back to the journey I had made with Simon to the Cotswolds and the conversations I'd had with Mrs. Standish and the Middletons.

Such a different picture of the man had emerged, more like that we'd had of Lieutenant Wade before the Military Foot Police knocked at our door. It was very difficult to imagine him as a cold-blooded killer. If he hadn't chosen to risk running for the border, if he'd decided to take his chances standing trial, what would have come of it? What could that trial have shown us about him as a man? Was there another side of his personality, one he'd kept well hidden? Or was he what he seemed to be, with no secrets to hide or tell?

If he hadn't run, could a trial have cleared his name? More than one person accused of being a murderer turned out to be nothing of the sort. It was easy to point a finger at Wade, coming as he did from his parents' home in Agra, leaving their bodies to be found by servants.

But what was the truth?

Night after night I fell asleep without finding any answers to my questions.

And there was Simon. He had taken me to see Mrs. Standish and to speak to the Middletons. But he had not wanted to do it. He had wanted to leave the past in the past, to accept the fact that Lieutenant Wade had perished. He hadn't wanted to put my father and my mother through the anguish of reliving that week in India. And I rather thought he didn't want to relive it either. He'd been Regimental Sergeant-Major. My father had been Colonel. How had they gone so very wrong in their reading of one of their own?

I could understand that.

At the same time five people had lost their lives because of this one man. And if he had survived the Khyber Pass and made his way across Afghanistan's very difficult terrain, there was still his debt to society, unpaid.

Of course it wasn't my responsibility to bring him to justice.

On the other hand, I dealt every day with life and death. I'd watched men die who would have given everything they owned to live one more week, one more month, one more year. There was the young Corporal who had just learned he was the father of a son. The Lieutenant who had just had word that his brother had been killed, and now he was dying as well, leaving his parents with no one to care for them. The Sergeant one day away from his leave who was planning to go home and be married. And none of them had seen the dawn. It was heartbreaking, it was real, it was impossible sometimes to forget.

Who were the three people in England? And why had they deserved to have their lives cut short?

I found myself thinking about them more than once. A father,

Hecror McDonald *MD FRCSC*
revisage surgical centre
1655 Kilborn Avenue, Ottawa, ON. K1H 6M7
Tel 613-739-5437 Fax 613-739-5432
enquiries@revisage.ca

Name ....

Appointment/s

DAY DATE TIME

1. Friday Oct 16/15. @ 805

2. ....

3. ....

4. ....

If you cannot make an appointment please give us 48 hours notice

a mother, a daughter. How old was that daughter? Ten? Fourteen? Twenty? Had it been a matter of unrequited love? Had Lieutenant Wade wanted to marry her and been turned down?

The doctor at our station commented that I had circles under my eyes, and he sent me back to my cot to sleep another two hours. I knew it wasn't a matter of enough sleep. The war was crammed into a corner of France, and broad as the Front was, most of the activity funneled down to Calais or Rouen. It was not unlikely that I'd encounter Lieutenant Wade again. As a patient, as one of a column of men moving up or falling back, whatever the tide of fighting brought in its wake. He could so easily see and recognize me before I was even aware he was there.

I had to put him out of my mind and get on with what I had come to France to do, save as many men as I possibly could. What's more, we had learned so much about treating wounds since I'd gone into training, and I was learning still more. It mattered more than a ten-year-old murder.

We fought a losing battle with the numbers being brought in, and then just as quickly as they had multiplied, they dwindled. This was something we had come to expect in trench warfare, where first one and then another sector felt the brunt of an attack. And then the probe moved on, always testing, always trying to find a weak point where an attack could succeed. It was done on both sides of No Man's Land, of course, but we only saw the outcome on our own side.

One afternoon we found ourselves with barely enough wounded to support continuing to keep the aid station open. In fact, the fighting seemed to have moved well beyond us, and we tried not to feel too cheerful about this, for fear the tide would turn. But accustomed as we were to an ever-changing Front, to see it static for even a few days lifted our spirits. A sign of hope.

I was sent back to the Base Hospital with a half-dozen ambulances, the last of our severely wounded, and because they needed more hands, I was kept on there. There were a large number of amputees in the recovery wards, and I had some experience working with them. Not long afterward, I was on the move again. The worst of our cases had stabilized to the point that we could send many of the men back to England for extended care. I was given charge of the convoy.

Amputees were difficult cases both medically and emotionally. For many of the men it was worse than dying. Keeping them alive was a matter of tending to their bodies and ministering to their minds. We took a chaplain back with us, and he comforted many of the patients. I held others while they cried.

These men had marched off to war taking into account the fact that they might not come back. When their wounds were such that they had a fair chance of full recovery, they were often impatient to heal and rejoin their men or their comrades in the trenches.

And while an amputation was a ticket home, in the eyes of the men, it was also failure. They could no longer fight. They had to leave behind friends who were still in the thick of the struggle. Their greatest fear was what they would read in the faces of parents or wives or children who remembered them whole and now saw them shattered. Many of them could never return to the work they had done before the war began. And charity—pity—was something they could not tolerate. The suicide rate was high, and constant vigilance was necessary

We reached England without losing anyone. And that was only because these were recent amputees who had neither the strength nor the means to kill themselves. Still, there were three who worried me to the point that I gave instructions at the clinic they were sent to for a twenty-four-hour watch over them.

I left my charges with a heavy heart, knowing the battle still ahead of them, and I was grateful to be given five days of leave before returning to France.

I longed for home and something to take my mind off war. And so without even letting anyone know I was coming, when I reached London, I took the next train to Somerset. There I cajoled one of the farmers just leaving the town market at the end of the day to give me a lift to the house.

Iris opened the door to my knock and stood there exclaiming in surprise.

"Oh, Miss, and never a word—I can't believe my eyes!"

She took my kit from me and, still flustered, stood aside to let me step inside. "And your parents off to Oxford only this morning. They'll be that upset. But I have the number here where they're to be staying—it's a funeral, Miss, another one, and your father to deliver the eulogy for the poor Captain—"

It was clear she expected me to rush to the telephone in my father's study and try to reach my parents at once. But I couldn't. The Colonel Sahib never refused to speak for one of his men or anyone in the regiment. The present Colonel was in France, and so my father took on many of the formal duties for him. This meant so much to grieving families. The regiment was a family too.

"And the Sergeant-Major? Is he in Oxford as well?"

"I can't say, Miss. But it's very likely. It was Captain Saunders who died of his wounds. That's the name your father left on his desk. Mrs. Saunders, The Beeches, Oxford."

He'd been a Lieutenant, Robert Saunders had, who rose quickly through the ranks. His care for his men had been legendary, and he'd been mentioned in dispatches countless times for bravery under fire. I felt his loss myself.

"We'll say nothing, Iris, agreed? It would be wrong to interfere with their plans. I need to sleep more than anything, and I can do that here as well as in London."

"Yes, Miss," she said doubtfully.

"I'll just go up to my room, and perhaps you could bring me a light tea in a while? I'm starving."

"We have fresh eggs, Miss, and there's vegetable marrow and leek soup that Cook made for dinner. And the last of the red currant jam with scones?"

"It sounds heavenly."

She insisted on carrying my kit up to my room, assuring me that there were fresh sheets on the bed as always, just waiting for me.

I tried to sleep. Truly I did. But by the next morning, I was awake before the sun came up, lying there trying to will my eyes closed again. Finally I got up, put on a dress from the wardrobe rather than my uniform, and walked down to the kitchen, where I found a heel of bread and some honey. With that in hand, I walked through the wood and down the path to Simon's cottage.

But I could tell, as I always could, that the cottage was empty. I was tempted to go inside and leave a message, and then I decided against it. Instead I turned back the way I'd come. It was when I was passing the shed where my own motorcar lived when I was in London or France that I was suddenly possessed with the idea of going to call on the Middletons again.

I hurried to the house, changed again into a fresh uniform, surprised Cook just blowing up the fire to set the kettle on to boil, and made a quick breakfast sitting there at the freshly scrubbed table as I used to do when I was a child and home and looking for a treat.

It was only seven o'clock when I opened the doors to the shed and pulled out the crank to my motorcar. It turned over easily, for Simon kept the vehicle in good repair. And I was on the road before the heat of the day.

I realized afterward that I should have asked for a Thermos and a picnic basket to take with me, but traffic was very light and I pressed on. There was the occasional herd of sheep filling the road or dairy cows making their way in single file from the milking barn to the pastures. Once I followed a hay wain, so overladen it seemed to wobble from side to side, for a quarter of a mile before it turned off into a farmyard. There was no military traffic to speak of, and I was grateful.

And then I was into the Cotswolds, through them, coming into the village where Mrs. Standish and the Middletons lived. I saw no reason to disturb Mrs. Standish, and instead drove on to the Captain's bungalow.

They were as surprised to see me as Iris had been, but welcomed me as warmly as they had before, offering me a cool lemonade after my long drive.

We made conversation about the war as we'd done when I was here with Simon the last time. Captain Middleton was eager for any scrap of news that the papers had not printed, and I told him what I could about the situation in France.

Mrs. Middleton went off to set the table for lunch, and that was my chance to ask the Captain more about Lieutenant Wade.

"Something that has stayed with me after my last visit was your comment that he'd killed three other people in England before returning to India. My parents never spoke to me of those deaths. I expect they felt I was too young. Could you tell me a little more about them?"

"Lass, are you sure you want to know? It's not pleasant."

"It's more harrowing to imagine than it will be to know," I told him.

He got up from his chair and limped to the hearth where there was a small stand of pipes on the mantel shelf. He chose one, filled and tamped it, and finally lit it. When it was pulling well enough to suit him, he came back to sit down.

"We only heard scraps of the story. I learned later that it was widely covered in Hampshire. Especially the hunt for the killer. The family lived just outside of Petersfield, as I remember. It was the afternoon off for the staff, and they had gone into the town to celebrate the birthday of one of the maids. When they came home again some time after five, they found their master, their mistress, and the daughter of the house shot dead in the sitting room. Someone went for the police, but of course nothing helpful was found. It was thought that the house was being watched, and when the staff left, whoever was out there assumed it was empty and came in to take what he could. And so the hunt was up for anyone who had been passing through the town or who had anything in his past that might explain why he would do such a thing."

I sat there, shocked and trying not to show it. "How did they finally come to the point where they suspected Lieutenant Wade?"

"Apparently someone in the village remembered seeing him that same day. On the road out to the house. Later it was discovered he'd taken the train on to Southampton where his ship was waiting to sail with the tide. But sail it had. And so there was nothing for it but to send word to India that he was wanted for questioning. The upshot of that was, his own parents were found dead, and so it was assumed that Lieutenant Wade must have killed the family in Petersfield as well."

"But why should he do such a thing? Was there a reason for him even to know them? Had he just walked in an open door and murdered three people?"

"It was said he'd known them before. Before he joined the regiment. But I never heard just how."

"It's horrifying," I said. "And I find it very hard to square that with the man I knew in India."

"That's what everyone seemed to be saying. Scotland Yard came here to interview us and Mrs. Standish, but we couldn't tell them anything useful. And so they went away. What distressed us both was the fact that the man had been in our house twice, and not very long after he'd left it that last time, he killed. Dolly couldn't sleep for a fortnight, thinking about it. It could have been us, she said. But not by the hand of Lieutenant Wade. Surely not." He frowned, and I could see that he was trying to convince himself that he believed wholeheartedly in what he'd said, that the Lieutenant would never have harmed them.

We could hear Dolly Middleton calling from the dining room,

and the Captain rose to escort me to the table, tacitly bringing the conversation to an end.

Over the meal, no mention was made of murder or the Lieutenant. Instead I told them about Captain Saunders, and Captain Middleton shook his head.

"We've lost so many of the officers and men we knew," he said, sadness in his voice. "War's a terrible thing. It's been my profession since I was a lad, being a soldier. But watching the young ones die is hard."

Mrs. Middleton changed the subject, and we enjoyed our lunch. I was sorry to leave them, but I had a long drive back to Somerset and I needed to start out as soon as possible. They offered to put me up for the night, which was kind of them, but I knew the roads I'd be driving as I neared home, even though it would be well after dark by then. And so I thanked them for their hospitality and their offer, and set out.

With me I carried the scent of Captain Middleton's pipe tobacco and the disturbing thought he'd left with me. That one of our own had killed before, and might well kill again.

Thinking about what might drive such a man to murder, I drew a blank.

That was when I decided to go to Petersfield myself and see what I could learn that would explain his conduct.

How had he managed to conceal his deeds from us? From my mother and from me, and most of all from Simon and my father?

Was it a cold-bloodedness that he kept so well hidden we had no inkling it was there? Or something else none of us had ever fathomed?

Driving along in the gathering dark, I felt a shiver that had nothing to do with the balmy night air.

I was glad to pull up in the drive and leave my motorcar where it was, hurrying into the lighted hall and hearing Iris's voice calling, as she came out of the kitchen passage, "Oh, Miss, is it you? And have you had your dinner?" And then as she reached me, she frowned. "You look unhappy, Miss. Is anything wrong?"

I couldn't tell her how sane and safe the lighted hall seemed, and how familiar and comforting her plain, concerned face was.

"I'm a little tired, that's all. I think I'll have a little soup or a sandwich, then go up to bed."

"Yes, Miss, and Cook has set aside a nice chop for your dinner. You'll come and eat it, won't you, and make her happy?"

And so I did, putting aside everything else that was on my mind.

Chapter Six

THE NEXT MORNING I was walking out to my motorcar—still sitting just where I'd left it last night—and there was Simon leaning against the nearside wing.

He hadn't come to the house for breakfast. And I couldn't read his face as he watched me approach.

"You didn't tell me you'd come home. I could have met you in London."

"I didn't know just when I'd be arriving. There was no point in keeping you standing around the railway station. They sent me home with another convoy of wounded. It was unexpected—and I was very tired. Amputees." It was the truth, every bit of it, but I felt guilty, as if I'd lied to him. But he knew something about amputees. He'd nearly lost his own arm.

When he said nothing, I added, "I went to the cottage yesterday morning. You weren't there."

"No." He considered me for a moment. Then he asked, "The motorcar performing well enough? It's been sitting for some time. I hadn't got around to giving it a run for several weeks."

"It ran beautifully. Thank you." I stood by the driver's door, uncertain what to say next. "I went back to call on the Middletons, yesterday. I stayed for lunch. And so I was late coming home. That's why I didn't return the motorcar to the shed."

I felt myself slowly flushing.

After a space he said, "You could have asked me, Bess. Rather than speak to the Middletons."

Exasperated suddenly, I reminded him, "You weren't here. Simon, I went to the cottage. You could have been away. For a few hours, for a week. And I have only five days. Didn't you go to the Captain's funeral service with my parents? I thought you might have done."

He straightened. "I was called to London. I just got in."

"Then you've no right to interrogate me, as if I were a German prisoner," I retorted.

Simon smiled then.

Coming around to open my door for me, he asked, "What did the Middletons tell you?"

"In fact they knew very little more than we'd learned on our last visit. They did tell me the three murders took place in Petersfield. In Hampshire."

"And that's where you're intending to go now?"

I lifted my chin. "Yes, of course."

"All right. Let me drive. I haven't been there myself."

And that surprised me. So I got out of the motorcar, went round to the other side, and got in there, leaving him to turn the crank.

We set out, leaving the village by the road to the south. He said nothing for a time. Finally he asked, "Have you seen this man again? The one who might be Wade?"

"I have not. I expect I've been trying to understand, that's all. Why someone I thought I knew well was very different from my experiences with him."

"We've all asked ourselves the same question."

"And yet no one pursued it."

"We pursued him. And were told he was dead. There was no need for your father to travel to England to go into the matter. He was needed there at the time."

"Yes, I expect you're right." I fell silent, thinking it through. "I was shocked when the Subedar told me who he'd seen. I would probably have left it there if I hadn't seen the man for myself. Or believed I did. We could both have been wrong, you know. Still, I remember my father's face when he got the news. I remember how *everyone* felt, even though I didn't know about the other murders. If we did see the Lieutenant in France, then I want to get to the bottom of it for the Colonel Sahib's sake. I think what bothers me most is that we assumed, the entire regiment, that Lieutenant Wade was dead. If he's escaped justice, then my father will feel responsible. He called off the search, you see." I smoothed the fingers of my driving gloves, not looking at Simon. It was the first time I'd really put my feelings into words. Even to myself. "I don't want him blamed. I don't want him to feel he should have done more. Because I don't think he could have done."

"Then you're going the wrong way about it. You're bringing it all back again. For all of us."

"No, I'm trying to lay the Subedar's words to rest. There must be someone out there in France who bears a resemblance to Wade. If it isn't Wade—then he's dead, his bones already dust in the Khyber Pass. Where they ought to be."

Simon turned to look at me. "Then why are you going to Petersfield?"

I gave that some thought. "I want to know something. Did Lieutenant Wade go to the Khyber Pass hoping to make it to the other side and then cross first Afghanistan and then Persia and even Turkey? To escape? Or did he go to the Pass knowing it would be a better death than hanging?"

It was Simon's turn to be silent. "A very interesting point. He knew enough of the languages of the Frontier. He might have passed himself off as a native. But it would have been an odyssey, that crossing. I don't know many men with the fortitude even to try."

"We aren't the only ones who served in India with Lieutenant

Wade. If the Subedar recognized him, if I did, then someone else will eventually. What happens then?"

"We must hope it doesn't."

"If we can find out why he killed the family in Petersfield, we just might learn why he killed his parents. Did he do it to keep them from learning what he'd done, what he'd become—what was surely going to catch up with him in the end? If that's true, then he died out there in the Pass. And whoever we think we've seen in France, the Subedar and I, it's been ten years."

"You're very persuasive."

"I'm just trying to explain all this to myself. And why it has disturbed me so much."

He reached out and touched my hand for a moment, then concentrated on his driving as we came into another busy town, motorcars and carts and wagons filling the street, and villagers crossing haphazardly from one side of the road to the other.

We paused for lunch along the way, then arrived in Petersfield just as the market was closing. The square in front of St. Peter's Church was filled with stalls and barrows and tables offering everything from sausages and cheese and bread to cloth and dried flowers and secondhand goods. In the shadow cast by the equestrian statue of William III, a man had a litter of puppies tumbling over themselves in a box, the mother watching anxiously beside it. Fat tummies and flailing tails and overlarge feet waiting to be grown into. I stopped to watch them while Simon made inquiries at the next stall.

"You'll like one to take home," the man said, smiling at me. "Which one catches your fancy, Sister? The little brown and tan? The one with the white face? Or the little 'un with the white paws?"

I could have taken every one of them, but I thanked him and moved on as I saw Simon signal me to follow him.

"The house we're after is outside the town. Not far, I'm told."

"How on earth did you elicit that bit of information?" I asked.

"Deviously," he replied, and we went back to the motorcar.

We drove past the market and a black and white Tudor inn, then followed the road to the outskirts of town, where we quickly picked up a low stone wall that led to gates into an overgrown park.

"This is the house?" I asked, surprised.

"It's on the market. Has been since 1914 when the previous owner died. His nephew is selling up."

"But how did you know?"

Simon grinned suddenly. "The old man selling brooms and patching pots and pans was garrulous. It didn't take me long to find out what I needed to know."

I was reminded again that Simon was a master at interrogating prisoners and suspicious camp followers. We'd had enough of them in India, from musicians to traveling buyers and sellers of every imaginable goods, from mendicants and holy men to beggars and thieves, scoundrels and snake charmers.

We left the motorcar by the gates and walked up the drive to the house. It was in a better state of repair than I'd expected, given the overgrown park.

"I think," I said warily, "someone must be living here now."

"I shouldn't be surprised."

The house was foursquare with smaller wings set back on either side. The center block was early Georgian, I thought, while the wings had been added later.

We were about to turn and leave when a woman came to the door.

"Can I help you?" she asked, peering out at us. "Are you the couple the estate agent was sending out? We weren't expecting you until tomorrow."

"We were driving past and stopped to have a look," Simon said. "Before speaking to the estate agent."

"I don't know if that's quite proper," she said, wringing her hands. "We asked not to have strangers coming by. The estate agent agreed."

"Then we'll be on our way," Simon told her, taking my arm.

She stopped us, asking anxiously, "Were you really interested in the house? I'll take your name, if you like. And give it to the owner."

Then she wasn't the wife of the owner. I'd thought she looked more like a housekeeper, but she was wearing a dark lavender dress, not the usual black.

As if she'd heard the thought, she said, "I'm housekeeper to my cousin."

"We have several other properties to look at," Simon told her. "We'll ask the estate agent to contact you if we decide to return."

Her expression was apprehensive, as if she was of two minds, letting us have a look around in case we were serious buyers, and keeping to the rules. But in the end, she nodded and closed the door.

We walked back up the drive and had nearly reached the gates when a man came striding up the road from Petersfield.

He was wearing the uniform of a chaplain, and one arm was in a sling.

"We don't care for trespassers," he said sternly when he was close enough not to be shouting.

"We weren't trespassing." Simon held his ground.

"We've had enough of curiosity seekers. I thought it had stopped. It drove my uncle mad, made his last days unbearable. Ever since that article in the Sunday papers."

"I've been out of the country," Simon replied easily. "I haven't seen an article about the house."

"Then why are you here? The property isn't listed locally. I was quite firm about that." He paused. "You aren't Mr. and Mrs. Davies, are you?"

"I'm afraid not."

Simon had his hand on my elbow and ushered me through the gates to the motorcar. The chaplain stared us off the property and watched to see that we did indeed go away.

He was still watching as we reversed and headed back to Petersfield.

"A warm welcome," I said. "But what article, Simon?"

"From time to time when there isn't any other news, London editors dig up sensational crimes. It sells papers."

We drove back to Petersfield and found the marketplace nearly empty, the stalls and carts and barrows all but gone.

"Let's go into the churchyard," I suggested, and we left the motorcar by the shops. It was only a short walk up to St. Peter's.

The handsome old church was not facing the square but set sideways to it. We made our way around to the west door and from there we went in different directions. I found myself near the enclosing outer wall and saw to my left a small plot with three stones on it. I glanced down at the names and dates, then called quietly to Simon, who was bending over to look at a stone in another part of the churchyard.

"Come see this."

He joined me, then whistled under his breath.

There it was. The graves of Lieutenant Wade's first victims.

It had to be. The year was right, 1908, and the dates matched as well.

Harvey Caswell, his wife, Isabella, and their daughter, Gwendolyn. They had died on the same day.

I looked again at the dates.

"But I thought she was a child, Simon. Everyone said, 'Mother, father, and daughter.' She was nineteen."

"That's right." He did the sums in his head. "Her parents were fifty and fifty-two."

I heard the sound of the heavy church door closing as a man stepped out. He started toward the square, saw us in the churchyard, and halted. Then he came our way. I don't know why, but I had a feeling he was the rector, or failing that either a church warden or someone else in authority. His expression was rather cold, and my first thought was, *He knows which graves these are.*

"Can I be of assistance?" he asked.

"Are you the rector?" It was Simon who put the question, before I could speak.

"The sexton," the man replied.

"We had just happened to noticed that three members of this family—the Caswells—died on the same day," I said.

The sexton frowned. "It was cholera, I believe," he said shortly, as if used to prying questions. "Are you looking for a member of your own family? There are records in the church, I can help you find their graves."

He was urging us away from this particular plot.

"We were passing the time until tea, wandering here," I said. "It's a lovely church."

"Then you must look inside. I recommend it."

There was nothing to do but follow him to the church and go inside. He held the door for us, and busied himself at a table, straightening up the literature there while we looked around. It was indeed a handsome church with a beautiful old wooden ceiling. We walked down toward the altar and then turned.

The sexton waited for us, and accompanied us to the square. I had the feeling that he was shepherding us, even though he was giving us information about the church as we went. Once he was certain we were heading for my motorcar, he bade us farewell, and then stood watching us until I got in and Simon went to turn the crank.

He was still there, in front of the gates, when we drove away.

We decided to stop for tea in the pretty inn just off the square. I was grateful for the quiet table Simon commanded that overlooked the road. There was a small group in the lounge that came through shortly after we'd sat down, choosing a table nearer the cold hearth. It was clear they knew one another, and I thought they must have met up in the square during market day, for I heard them catching up on family news as they sat down. Someone's daughter was to be married soon, and that occupied much of their conversation.

Our tea had just arrived, along with a dish of thin sandwiches made with the bread I'd just seen in a stall in the square—a lovely farm loaf—when the door opened and the chaplain we'd seen earlier as we'd left what must have been the Caswells' house at one time came into the room from the street.

He cast a glance around, spotted us, and came at once to our table. I could see that he was red in the face from suppressed anger.

"Just who are you?" he demanded. "First the house, then the graves. Are you down from London looking to bring up the whole sorry business again? Isn't the killing in France enough for you?"

Simon stayed seated, eyeing the chaplain mildly. But it was deceptive, that mildness. Simon was nearly as angry himself at being attacked this way in a public place.

"My name is Brandon," he said. "I have nothing to do with newspapers or London. And I've had enough of your rudeness."

"Have you indeed," the chaplain said. He hooked a chair with his foot and brought it around so that it stood at the table between Simon and me. Sitting down, the chaplain said, "I'm trying to sell that barn of a place. And bad publicity just now will put paid to any chance I have. Whatever you're up to, I won't let you do this. I'll have the constable in here and see what he has to say."

"Is the house yours?" I asked before Simon could speak, trying to prevent an unpleasant encounter between the two men. "Do you have the right to tell people what they ought and ought not to do, like this?"

He was taken aback. "Of course the house is mine. Ask anyone, it was left to me by my uncle."

"Have you ever lived there?"

He blinked, staring at me. "Of course not. Until the war I was rector of a church outside of Bury St. Edmunds. What business is it of yours?"

"Then you can't possibly tell me how well the plumbing works or if there's worm or dry rot in the attic. Or if the chimneys draw without smoking so badly it chases everyone out of a room. And there are the drains. Do they smell, in the servants' hall? Not to mention the state of the roof, which I can see for myself. How do you expect to sell a house you yourself consider to be a barn of a place?"

The poor man didn't know what to say. Out of the corner of my eye I caught Simon trying to smother a grin.

"I never met the Caswells," I went on. "I didn't even know their names until just before the sexton bore down on us and nearly drove us from the churchyard. Did he tell you we were staring at the graves? I happened to notice that here was a family who died on the same day. You don't often see that unless there's plague or cholera or typhoid. I couldn't have told you the name of the previous owners of that house of yours. But now I know it. Because everyone is behaving as if Simon and I have come here to make trouble. Well, we haven't. So go away and let us drink our tea in peace."

I'd succeeded in reducing the tension between the two men. I wasn't sure that a chaplain would have resorted to his fists, but I wasn't going to chance it. Tall as he was, he was several inches shorter than Simon, and his reach was shorter as well. Simon could have floored the man without turning a hair.

The chaplain stared at me, mouth open, uncertain what to say.

"Since you've insisted on joining us," I said while he was still at a loss for words, "you might as well have a cup of tea."

I nodded to the man who had just served us, asking for a third cup. When it arrived, accompanied by a wooden expression on the server's face, I poured three cups of tea and passed the honey as well as the small jug of milk.

By this time the chaplain didn't know where to look. He had come here with artillery and cavalry in his eyes, and now he was discovering that he and they were in full retreat.

"Tell me about these people, the Caswells," I said. "Are they related to you?"

"I—no—that's to say, not directly. The house went to my uncle when they—er—when the Caswells died. I'm his late wife's nephew."

"But you've been trying to sell the house, without any luck."

"I can't afford to live there. I hope to return to my church in Bury, when the war's over. Or to one like it. What I earn wouldn't keep that house for a month, much less a year. I tried to have it turned into a clinic, but even the Medical Board refused to accept my offer. That was at the start of the war. My uncle died in August 1914, just after the Germans marched into Belgium. My aunt had died the year before. She had never liked the place, not after what had happened there. And when I came to stay for a school holiday or the like, she always insisted that I lock my bedroom door. She'd come, after she thought I was asleep, to test it." He drank a little of his tea and grimaced. It was still too hot. "Why am I telling you all this?"

"Because you haven't been able to tell anyone else," I suggested. "Not if you wanted to sell the property. How did they die, the Caswells? Was it illness, as I'd expected?"

"They were murdered. All three of them. In cold blood, in what my aunt always referred to as the drawing room. It was shut off. I wasn't allowed to go in there. I doubt *she* ever used it. But then she was elderly when she came to Petersfield, and she probably had no taste for curiosity seekers. They came in droves the first few years, she said. And then the story was half forgotten. Until July, before the war started. One of the London papers brought up sensational murders. Jack the Ripper, that sort of thing. And they included the mysterious deaths at The Willows. There's a brook across the back of the property with willows along the banks. Very pretty in the spring. Long pale green fronds dipping down to the water. There were horses then, and they spent much of their time in the meadow across the brook."

"Were the deaths so mysterious?" Simon asked.

"The man who killed them got away. Scot-free. He was never found."

"And there was no motive?"

"The Caswells were upstanding members of the community. You could ask anyone and they would tell you the same."

"Was it a random killing? Or did the murderer know the family?" I asked.

The chaplain absently took one of the sandwiches when I passed the plate to him. He was a lonely man, tormented by a responsibility beyond his powers to cope, and there was a permanent frown between his eyes. I wondered if the house really disturbed him so much or if it was a means to put aside what he'd seen in France. But that was a question I couldn't ask.

"God knows," he replied. "I don't think anyone else did, even at the time. I asked my uncle once if he knew anything about what had happened, but he didn't. They were shot, point-blank range. They didn't have time to duck or run out of the room. My uncle said that even after he'd moved in, you could still see the stains in the carpet. He got rid of it. Burned it in the back garden."

"Yes, the only thing to be done," I agreed. "I'm surprised he was willing to live in the house."

"He had just retired. And he wanted to leave London. I don't think he asked my aunt what her thoughts were in the matter. But then he was a doctor, he'd seen death firsthand. As have I. My aunt hadn't. I think she must have been afraid every day she lived there."

I thought of the housekeeper, his cousin, who was there now. "Does someone live in the house full-time? If you're selling up, surely you'd need to have someone to answer the door and show prospective buyers around."

"My cousin is here for a month. I gave the estate agent a month to sell it. Then I have to go back to France. My leave will be up."

"Were you wounded?" I asked, gesturing to the sling.

But he shook his head. "Not—wounded."

I guessed then that he'd been given leave before he broke under the strain of his duties. Chaplains saw men at their worst—frightened, in pain, panicked, facing death or amputation. They comforted and they supported, and they must have struggled to hold on to their own faith while they were about it.

I had finished my tea, and Simon rose to order a fresh pot. But our uninvited guest seemed to come to himself as Simon moved.

"I'm so sorry," he said, stumbling to his feet as well. "I shouldn't have come here. I shouldn't have told you all that I have. It was wrong of me. I don't even know you."

Simon had given his name when we encountered this man by the house gates. Now I said, "My name is Crawford, Elizabeth Crawford. And you are—?"

But he was staring at me again, this time as if I'd suddenly grown two heads. "Crawford?"

"Yes—"

"That was the name of the officer who wrote to my uncle. From India. He told my uncle that the man Scotland Yard was searching for had died in some pass or other out there. That there was nothing more to be done. I found the letter in my uncle's desk, after his death. He always believed that the Army had lied about what happened to the murderer. I've seen it for myself, they protect their own. If you're any relation of that officer, then you ought to be ashamed of what he did. That killer should have been brought back, tried, and hanged. That would have finished the matter in everyone's eyes. It would have gone a long way toward lifting the cloud from that house. And from my family."

He knocked his chair over as he turned to go, and it clattered loudly in the quiet room, shocking the people sitting at the other tables. They stared, I could see their gaze turn from him to me and then to Simon.

Simon, infuriated by the man's outburst, started after him as he marched self-righteously toward the door.

I caught Simon's arm. "Let him go," I said quietly. "It doesn't matter."

But I knew it did. The man had assailed the Colonel Sahib's honor, and by extension, the honor of the regiment, and insulted me as well.

The door to the inn slammed shut. I could just hear footsteps walking unevenly away, as if the chaplain were drunk.

I could feel the muscles in Simon's arm where my fingers held him back. They were taut, hard as iron. I didn't know what Simon might do to the man, cleric or not. And so I held on.

And then he was sitting down, after lifting the fallen chair from the floor and setting it back where it belonged at the other table.

By that time Simon had himself under control again. "Your great-great-grandmother couldn't have sorted him out any better," he said, smiling. But it hadn't reached his eyes, that smile.

My great-great-grandmother had danced the night away in Belgium, keeping up a pretense that all was well, while her husband and his regiment marched to stop Napoleon at a place called Waterloo. Keeping the townspeople and any spies from guessing where the English had gone.

We didn't linger. After a moment Simon got up and paid for our tea, his face grim. There was a brief exchange of words with our waiter, and then Simon was back, collecting me.

And we walked out of the inn, back to the motorcar.

Simon didn't speak until we'd been on the road north for nearly an hour.

"Gates," he said then. "His name is Gates."

And that was all he said until we had reached Somerset and he had seen me safely inside the house. I heard him drive my motorcar around to the shed, and then could follow him in my mind's eye, through the back garden, along the path that crossed the wood, and down the lane to his own cottage.

But I couldn't help but wonder if that's what he did. As angry as he was, he might have walked until he was calm enough to sleep.

It had been at my request that we'd gone to Petersfield. I hadn't left well enough alone.

My sensible self reminded me that I could hardly have anticipated running into Reverend Gates.

Still, I went to bed carrying a large case of guilt with me.

Chapter Seven

THE NEXT MORNING, before I was quite awake, Simon was at the door, asking Iris to tell me that he was waiting for me.

I threw on clothes and went down, expecting to find him in the same dark mood of last night.

But he wasn't; he was standing in the dining room, lifting the covers on the sideboard, then helping himself to eggs, toast, and a rasher of bacon.

"Good morning," he said with more cheer than I felt.

"Good morning," I answered, pouring myself a cup of tea.

"I'm here to apologize. I was hardly a pleasant companion yesterday."

"It was hardly a pleasant journey," I retorted. "I spent most of the night wishing I'd never set foot in Petersfield."

"Yes. I understand. But it's done, Bess. We must close the door and go on."

Perversely, given the opportunity to do just that, I found myself resisting. I said, "I don't know what more we can do."

"Precisely my point."

And so we spent my last day taking a picnic to Glastonbury Tor.

We had finished our sandwiches and were putting things back into the basket when Simon said, out of the blue, "Bess, do you remember when you were a little girl and Cinnamon went missing?"

I was instantly transported back to that moment of discovery—when I came down the stairs to find my little spaniel not in his bed, not in the house, not even in the garden. Nowhere, in fact, that I looked. Frantic, I went to Simon, for my father was away, and we searched everywhere. I was convinced that one of the grooms had taken him, out of spite for a dressing-down he'd incurred on my account. In the end, we found the dog in the stables, cowering in a dark corner, terrified of the mare looming above him. She was an even-tempered mare, not at all likely to hurt him, but he didn't know that. He knew only that he'd wandered where he didn't belong and was now about to get his comeuppance. When Simon brought him to me, the spaniel lavished kisses on my face until my chin was red, and never strayed out an open door again. Afterward that groom came to me and swore he had not touched the spaniel, and even when I told him I believed him, he didn't believe me. Six months later he left our employ and went to work for a neighbor.

"I do, very well." I shielded my eyes from the sun and looked up at Simon. "What on earth brought Cinnamon to mind?"

"Petersfield," he said slowly. "Those murders were ten years ago, Bess. They should be ancient history as far as the people involved are concerned. But the sexton went to find Reverend Gates to tell him that we were poking around in the churchyard. And Gates was almost beside himself because he was afraid our raking up of the past would surely put paid to any hope of selling the house."

"Yes, I remember."

"Scotland Yard came to Petersfield and scoured the town and the outlying houses and farms looking for the Caswell family's killer. With no luck. Then someone reported seeing Wade in the vicinity, and the Yard went after him. But Wade had already left for India, and the inquiry was passed on to the Army. The Yard could do no more, Wade was beyond their reach."

"That's true." I nodded, quick to see where Simon was going.

"And so as far as the village is concerned, there was no conclusion to the case. The inquest most likely ended with an open verdict, person or persons unknown. Wade was in India, fled from the MFP, and was never brought to trial. Whether he was guilty or not was never determined. The case was simply closed. And that village was left to wonder if the Yard had got it right—or if there was still a murderer lurking in their midst."

"Scars that haven't healed," I agreed.

"Yes. Exactly that. I found myself wondering if Gates even suspected his uncle might have had a hand in it. A man looking to leave London for the country, and here's the perfect house, suddenly handed to him in a will. It would be interesting to know just why the uncle was eager to retire. I expect Gates must be aware of something in his uncle's past that he doesn't want to examine too carefully."

"I remember when Cinnamon went missing, I was ready to blame the neighbors' mastiff, to accuse that groom, to be angry with the maid who left the door to the gardens standing wide, even to blame the bustards down in the wood on the other side of the village. Anyone. Anything. Because imagining what had happened to my pet was more horrible than finding out the truth."

Cinnamon had lived to a ripe old age, of course, none the worse for his adventure. But I could understand the fears and suspicion that must have swirled around Petersfield in the aftermath of such a terrible crime.

Simon carried the picnic basket to the motorcar while I shook and folded the picnic rug.

"And then when a newspaper brought it all up again four years ago, it just served to make everyone anxious again," I added as I handed him the rug.

"All the more reason not to go wandering about there on your own. Promise me."

"Yes, that makes sense," I said. "Since it will probably have spread through the town that I'm a Crawford, and my father was responsible for losing Lieutenant Wade. At least in their eyes, not knowing the whole story."

"Absolutely."

I sighed as I settled myself into my seat, glancing back over my shoulder at the long shadow the Tor cast over the hillside. "I'm glad my father doesn't know. He did all he could."

"I was there," Simon said harshly as he turned the crank. "I know it for a fact."

I left for London the next morning, with Simon driving me to the station. In my kit I had freshly laundered and pressed uniforms, thanks to Iris, and a small jug of honey for my tea, which Cook had tucked in the basket along with sandwiches to speed me on my way.

"I've missed seeing my parents," I said as we waited for my train to come in.

"They'll be sad they missed you."

And then my train roared into the station with vast clouds of steam hanging in the damp air. Simon put me aboard and I was soon on my way back to France.

It was happenstance. My sharing a cabin with a Sister from Haslemere on the crossing. I'd met her before—in fact we'd worked together in 1917 for about two months off and on. Her name was Molly Fullerton, the daughter of a doctor. She was a very fine nursing Sister, and I'd shared a tent with her for a fortnight.

We caught up on news, asked each other about patients we'd attended, and talked about our recent leave. Hers had been longer than mine, and she had seen her younger sister married to a solicitor who had just been invalided out of the Army. The bride had contrived a sling for his arm that matched her wedding gown, and he had come down the aisle to applause.

"They'll be very happy," Molly told me, smiling and nodding. "I couldn't be happier for her myself. I've never seen two people so in love."

It wasn't until we were about to disembark, our kits already collected, that I thought to ask.

"Haslemere isn't far from Petersfield, is it?"

"No, not far at all. We sometimes went there on market day. My mother likes one of the farm loaves the baker there makes."

"I was in Petersfield two days ago. A friend was interested in a property for sale just outside the town, only he was told there was a mystery about a triple murder in that very house some ten years earlier. You were too young to remember anything about it, I'm sure. But your father might, and I could set my friend's mind at ease. The present owner was evasive about it—he hadn't lived there at the time, of course, that might explain his unwillingness to discuss the past. He probably knew as little as anyone did."

"That's intriguing," Molly exclaimed. "I knew nothing about it. What was the family's name?"

"Caswell, I believe. The house is The Willows."

"Next time I write I'll ask Papa about the murders. Three people, you say?"

"So we were told."

"I shouldn't care to live in a house where murder had been done." She shivered. "I can understand your friend's reluctance to proceed."

I had lied to her, although a part of what I'd told her was true. Enough to support the lie. As we disembarked, I found myself hoping she'd forget my request before she wrote next to her father.

After that I was too busy to dwell on Molly or the Caswell family or anything else. People were beginning to think that an end to the war was possible. After so many years of fighting, of wounded and dying and dead, no one seemed to trust the rumors. And certainly the fighting as far as I could tell was still as heavy, and we were seeing as many wounded as ever. I couldn't help but think that if there was to be peace anytime soon, how cruel it was for men to go on suffering and dying unnecessarily. It was depressing, and I couldn't shake that sense of waste as I tended my patients.

I wasn't prepared to encounter the Reverend Gates again. Late one evening as dusk was falling I saw him at a distance, speaking to the wounded still lying on stretchers at our forward aid station, and I wondered why he had been sent back to France, given his troubled state of mind. Had he felt he had to be here, drawn by the need to serve, to prove himself, or had the Army deemed him fit, looking only at the outward man? His sling at least was gone.

When I saw him again half an hour later, I noticed his face was haggard, his eyes tormented. But his voice was steady as he offered comfort to the men, as if it belonged to someone else, not the exhausted man going from patient to patient.

And then I lost track of him, distracted by the severity of the wounds I was seeing—shrapnel—and then by a familiar voice coming out of the darkness.

It was Sergeant Larimore nursing a sliver of shrapnel in his hand. It had festered, and it was hurting. He must have seen me working with several of the walking wounded, for the first inkling I had of his presence was the soft but distinctive cry of a kookaburra bird. I turned toward the sound, and with a grin he came to take his place in the line before me, to wait his turn.

I was always happy to see this cheeky Australian. He had helped me once when I needed help desperately, and I was fond of him. Dangerous to care about anyone in wartime, but still . . .

When I'd finished with the patient before him and turned his way, Sergeant Larimore smiled. "No one told me you were at this aid station. I'd have come along two days ago."

"You should have come anyway. Look at that hand. It must be twice its normal size. And swelling like that is dangerous. Here, let me see." As I took his large hand in mine, I could just pick out the black speck that was the shard of a shell, and all around it the flesh was puffy and red. It was a very good thing, I thought, that he was a big man, or this wound could have passed through the palm and the back of the hand as well. He could even have lost the use of it, if nerves were damaged, muscles torn.

I found tweezers and brought out the bit of shell, showing it to him. He hadn't made a sound as I worked, but now he whistled. "All because of that tiny mite? I shall have to give up all hope of a VC."

"A Victoria Cross is only given for gallantry above and beyond the call of duty. Not for a wound, however swollen," I told him as I cleaned out the infection and shook septic powder over it.

"I was mentioned in dispatches a fortnight ago," he said buoyantly, that irrepressible glint in his eyes.

"Oh, yes? As the biggest troublemaker this side of Adelaide?" I asked, bandaging his hand.

He laughed. "You're a lass after my own heart, Sister."

I was sorely tempted to ask him to help me find Lieutenant Wade—if he even existed. Sergeant Larimore had come to my aid before when I needed to find information quickly. The battlefield had its own way of passing news, as people's paths crossed behind the lines. That could have been how the Subedar had been found out and killed. I didn't want Sergeant Larimore to meet the same fate on my account.

He looked down at me. "What's the matter, lass? Is there anything I can do? Shoot a few dozen Hun for you? Win the war single-handed so you can have a good night's sleep?"

I had to smile. "Yes, win the war. It's lasted far too long."

I left him there while I went to empty the basin full of bloody water, and that's when I came face-to-face with Reverend Gates.

He saw me first, and before I could even greet him, he said, his voice shrill and carrying, causing heads to turn, "Are you pursuing me?"

I'd already taken note of how worn down he was, and I realized now that he was living on nerves alone.

"I've been at this station for some time," I answered him. "How are you, Chaplain Gates?"

"Well enough, no thanks to you. The people who wished to look at The Willows backed out. Did you talk to them? Did you tell them anything?" As he finished, his gaze traveled beyond me, and I was aware that someone had come to stand just behind me. But I didn't turn.

"No, why should I? I didn't even know their names. How could I?"

"But you did," he said vehemently. "Mr. and Mrs. Davies."

I remembered then. He'd mistaken us for someone else when he saw Simon and me coming down the drive from the house. It had completely flown my mind.

"I have no reason to prevent you or anyone else from selling your own property. I only came to Petersfield because I was never told precisely what happened there."

"No, you wouldn't have been. It was hushed up, wasn't it, to shield the regiment? I tell you, I don't believe that Lieutenant died in the Khyber Pass. I think he's still in the Army, protected by your father."

I stood very still. That was far too close to the truth, that Lieutenant Wade was still with the Army. Only not with our regiment.

"I can't imagine why you should think so," I answered finally, testing the waters. "Surely the killer was someone closer to Petersfield."

"His body was never brought in, was it? For all the world to see."

"You don't simply ride into that part of the Frontier and retrieve a body," I said sharply. "You'd take your life in your hands, and very likely end as dead as he was. One man isn't worth the lives of an entire company."

"If it was so bloody dangerous," Gates replied, "then why did *he* go there? He would have been committing suicide, wouldn't he? And he wasn't stupid enough to do that. No, it was covered up, the whole business. An excuse you thought everyone back in England would find easy to believe."

Behind me Sergeant Larimore spoke, his voice stark, cold. "Reverend or not, you don't speak that way to Sister Crawford. Not in my presence."

Gates went pale. "You can see how the Army protects its own," he said in a low, tense voice. "I've proved my point, have I not?"

And he was gone, hurrying toward the ambulances collecting to take the most severely wounded to the base hospital. He didn't look back.

Sergeant Larimore watched him go. "Are you all right, Bess?"

"Yes, I'm fine. Just—put out with his intransigence."

"And who is he, when he's at home?"

"He thinks the regiment covered a murder long ago. Or he's afraid, if the man everyone thinks was the killer really and truly isn't, then he'll have to look closer to home."

"Aye, he appears to be a man in torment. Where is this house he's so bent on selling?"

"Just outside Petersfield, in Hampshire. His uncle inherited the house after the family there was killed."

"Convenient, I'd say. Send me word if he gives you any more trouble. I've never knocked down a chaplain before. But that one would tempt me sorely."

Someone was calling to me, and I turned to see Sister Milton beckoning me.

"I must go. Not to worry, Sergeant. I'll be all right."

"So you will," he said without smiling. "I'll pass the word."

And with that he was gone. In the distance, when I could no longer see his tall, rangy figure, the call of the kookaburra came drifting back to me in a brief silence along the lines at the Front, one of those unexpected lulls that spell regrouping and respite.

Word reached me a few days later that the chaplain who had only recently passed through our aid station had collapsed and been sent back to England for care.

Had my presence here at the station precipitated his collapse? Seeing me here when he was already on the verge of breaking down?

On the whole, I thought not. He should never have been returned to duty. But I knew how it was. The doctors asked questions and evaluated the answers. If Gates had been afraid to admit just how ill he was, for fear of being forced to seek treatment, he could have collected himself well enough to lie to them. And the doctors, pressed to get as many walking wounded back to France as possible, might have turned a blind eye to shaking hands or strain around the mouth. Perhaps they had even thought he might be better off returning to France. So many wounded—so many Captain Barclays—had lied about their condition in the hope of being sent back to their men, where they felt desperately needed.

Captain Barclay, with a severe knee wound, had hounded the doctors, assuring them he was fit long before he truly was. When they relented and sent him to France at my father's request, he'd learned that will wasn't enough, however determined a man was to show he was fully healed.

Whatever had happened, I was just as glad not to have to keep an eye out for the chaplain. Breakdowns like his could turn violent. Most particularly, my father's regiment was serving here in France, and whispers made the rounds far too quickly. . . .

We spent part of the next three hours working with wounded German prisoners.

They were not as cocky as they had been two years ago, when the war seemed to be going their way. Tired, dispirited, short on reinforcements, they fought with the same fierce tenacity, but I could see in their dark-ringed eyes how much it had cost.

One, a young private who couldn't have been more than seventeen, slept nearly around the clock. The Lieutenant in charge of the prisoners looked in on him once or twice, but let him rest.

I happened by as the Lieutenant said to another Sister, "I've a brother about that age. Eager to fight, threatening to enlist, worrying my poor mother to the point of exhaustion. I just hope this damned war is over before he is eighteen."

"When is his birthday?" Sister Milton asked.

"November. Twenty-six November."

She shook her head. "I doubt we'll see it ended by Christmas. Whatever the Yanks are saying."

"Pray God you're wrong," the Lieutenant replied and went to look in on the more seriously wounded men. When the last of those was stable enough to be sent back for processing as prisoners, they were put into ambulances and lorries, with those able to walk bringing up the rear and often getting ahead of the vehicles lumbering through ruts and sliding toward holes. I found myself thinking they were well out of it, and would live to see the end of the war.

And what about our own men? More than one friend from before the war had been taken prisoner.

The shelling began again, and we were hard-pressed to keep up with the influx of wounded.

The attack that followed the shelling pushed the Germans back behind their own lines, and I was working with our only doctor, trying to stop bleeding in a leg wound.

An orderly came up on the run, breathless and covered in blood. "Sir? There's a Lieutenant down in one of the German trenches. We're not sure how long we can hold that sector, sir. He needs to be taken out as soon as may be."

"I'm needed here, can't you see that?" Dr. Reid snapped, his eyes on the leg he was trying to save. And then, satisfied that the bleeding was slowing down, he looked up. "Sister?" he said to me. "Are you game to go find a rat down a hole?"

"In the German trench, sir?" I asked, surprised. We'd never sent a Sister into the German lines. I thought briefly about Simon, who had been behind those very lines.

"Indeed."

"What should I take?" I asked the orderly.

"It's his arm and shoulder. Pinned under one of the bulwarks that hold up the trench walls. He was going down to be sure we'd routed all of them." He hesitated. "We might have to take that arm off. Morphine for the pain, something to brace that shoulder, sticks for wrapping the arm . . ."

He was still making the list as I led him to where we kept what stores we had. We made a quick survey, chose only what was necessary, and set out.

I'd been caught close to the lines before when the sectors lost ground. I'd almost been overrun by German forces a time or two. The orderly had insisted that I remove my cap and cover my hair with the cleanest helmet he could find. I had visions of lice in my hair and down my back as he pulled an officer's abandoned greatcoat over my uniform.

"It's for the best," he said as we hurried on. He was carrying the bundle in one hand and helping me over the rough, uneven ground toward the nearest trench on our side of the wire.

It was the most appalling sight. Mud, thick with unspeakable, mercifully unidentifiable bits and pieces. I thought I saw a boot with part of a foot still inside, and the body of a dead rat in a puddle of what smelled suspiciously like fresh urine. The walls were haphazardly shored up, sloping toward the top, and above my head was the barbed wire strung all along the top several feet out. What appeared to be caves dug out of the earth with flaps of burlap over them held the effects of officers in two I glimpsed, and in a third, a man bent over a field telephone, giving coordinates. I realized that he'd had to do it as quickly as possible or our own guns would be shelling our own men.

The smell was overwhelming on this warm afternoon. I'd smelled it before on the filthy bodies of wounded men and the orderlies who brought them in. A miasma of everything from stale cigarette smoke to the sweat of fear to urine and unwashed clothes, to something that I couldn't quite identify, the sweetness of rotting things.

We came to a ladder, flat against the dirty wall.

"Can you manage that, do you think, Sister? I'll look the other way."

And before I could think about it too long, I climbed up on the firing step and scrambled up the ladder.

The barbed wire was flattened, had been for the attack, and I saw a landscape that was as bleak and destroyed as anything I'd ever set eyes on. One or two tree stumps were the only things to give it any sense of reality, and I glimpsed what might have been the foundation of a farm building where a shell had blasted the earth away. There were dead men in the shell craters and littering the ground, and my guide said, "Best not to look, Sister. There's been no time to collect them."

I walked on, not able to imagine what was sticking to my boots as I went, and some seventy yards away, we came to the first of the German trenches, a shallow one where a machine gun had been set up. The men manning it were dead. I'd heard that very few machine gunners or their crews from either side wound up as prisoners. I could believe it now.

We reached a second line of trenches, and my orderly, casting about, found a reasonably sturdy ladder leading down. The rolls of barbed wire on this side of No Man's Land had already been pushed to the far side of the trench line, to protect against any surprise attack. But the Germans were quiet.

I was astonished by what I saw when I reached the end of the ladder and could look around.

It was so different from the British trenches that I could hardly take it in. It was as if ants had built a human-size world here, with trenches, latrines, rooms for men and officers, rough stairs down to even lower levels. A veritable city.

And the dead were here too, but not the mud, not the dead rats or bits of men. There were boards to walk on, doors into the cubbies, and down below were dormitories, mess rooms, planning rooms—I couldn't quite believe my eyes. And below that, according to my guide, was the bunker, which protected the German soldiers from the shelling. Our men, standing in their open trenches, had nowhere to go. And it explained to me why so often an attack after heavy shelling could be met with such fierce resistance on the part of the Germans.

All this while the orderly was leading me down another set of stairs. I saw almost at once that one of the supporting beams had come down, bringing a part of the upper portion of the trench down with it, and under all the debris, hardly visible, was an English officer.

I knelt in the wood splinters and dust and torn earth and called out. "I've come to help," I said just as someone on the far side of the debris field switched on a torch, followed by two more.

I could see him then, grateful that he wasn't someone I knew. His face was lined with pain and streaked with sweat, which had plastered his fair hair against his forehead.

"If you take my arm, I'll shoot myself," he said raggedly. "I mean it."

He moved his other hand, and I saw his service revolver, drawn and ready to use.

"I can hardly judge how bad it is, Lieutenant," I said briskly. "Not from here. So we'll have no threats at this stage."

"Just so we understand each other," he said through clenched teeth.

A disembodied voice, with the thick accent of the north of England, came from the other side of the debris. "He won't let us give him morphine. He thinks it's a trick."

"Yes, well, he may soon regret that," I replied, and began moving some of the smaller bits of wood in front of me.

"Careful, Sister," someone shouted from the other side. "It's like skittles, touch one and the lot goes down."

I worked more slowly, but it was necessary to get close enough to deal with the wound. The orderly beside me said, "Here, let me," and moved into my place, working with care.

"I was a miner once," he said, just as a part of the flooring above came down over us, like a roof fallen in. "But this is the best we can do."

I took his place again and slid as close as I could to the wounded man. It was then I could see what no one else had, a pointed shard of wood pinning the officer's arm to the wall, for all the world like a spear.

"What's your name?" I asked as I sat there judging what to do next.

"Graham," he said, biting off the word.

The way the shard of wood was angled was making it hard for Lieutenant Graham to breathe, jamming that arm tight against his chest. And there was no room on his other side to escape from it.

"I'm going to work now," I said calmly, more calmly than I felt. "Put down that revolver, Lieutenant, if you want any hope of salvaging your arm. I refuse to be shot by accident."

He didn't move at first, and then he cried out as he lowered his other arm, inadvertently pulling against his shoulders.

I thought, *If I can remove that shard—or have the orderly with me do it—there's a good chance he'll lose his arm with it. But if I can dig around the point, we might be able to pull out the Lieutenant and that spear with him, and let a surgeon finish the task.*

"I need something sharp—a heavy spoon, an entrenching tool, something."

The orderly scrambled away, and just as quickly he was back with a bayonet and a large steel spoon of the kind used to cook for great numbers of people.

"That should do the trick," he said.

The spoon was too dull, the bayonet too heavy, but I managed to get it where I wanted it, and then began to dig.

The orderly touched my arm. "Clever, that. Let me."

I moved away, holding the bayonet in place until he could take it. He went to work with a will, but Lieutenant Graham cried out with each stroke as it jarred the piece of wood and the arm sliced by it.

"I told you, you're going to regret not taking the morphine," I said.

"Shut up," Lieutenant Graham answered rudely.

We worked for half an hour before we freed the point of the

wood shard. And then we had to work around so that we could bring it and the Lieutenant out together.

We had just started that when someone up above shouted, "*Gas*."

We dropped everything and dug in our pouches for our gas masks. I was able to reach the Lieutenant's and hold it in place. He was breathing shallowly as it was, and I was relieved when another voice called, "*False alarm*."

We had to take the risk of dismantling more of the jumble of wood supports, and as I was helping on my side, I caught a glimpse of one of the men on the far side, a brief one as he turned to fling part of the flooring from above out of the way.

I said nothing, looked quickly back at my patient, so that no one could read my expression.

One of the men who had been helping me all afternoon was Lieutenant Wade.

I shut my eyes for a moment, trying to remember exactly what I'd seen. Yes, it was Wade, except that he had a long-healed scar across his jawline. Not where it distorted the features but where he must have once been shot in the face.

It hadn't been there when he served under my father. And in the dark and rain the first time I'd seen him, I hadn't noticed it.

The orderly with me said, "Are you all right, Sister?"

I opened my eyes and nodded. "Yes, just a little tired, that's all."

"No surprise there, Sister."

In the end we got Lieutenant Graham out. On a stretcher, he was carried up the set of stairs and then somehow up the ladder at the side of the trench.

It was nearly impossible, jarring that piece of wood jutting like an arrow out of his arm and shoulder, but somehow we managed. By that time the morphine I'd given him against his will had taken effect. Crossing No Man's Land, our little party moving at a jog, despite the cost to Lieutenant Graham, but in a hurry because he'd already lost so much blood, I made a point of not looking directly at any of the stretcher bearers until we were nearly to the flattened barbed wire on our side.

Then as they jockeyed for position lowering the Lieutenant down into the trench and turned the stretcher so they could move along it, I cast a quick glance at their faces.

There were two of them, one at each end of the stretcher. And neither one was Lieutenant Wade.

There had been half a dozen men on the far side of where the roof collapsed. They had helped us get Lieutenant Graham out of the German trenches. It would have been easy enough for one of them to stay behind as we started across No Man's Land.

I looked over my shoulder a last time before descending in the trench before me. Other men were coming back from the German lines, sliding into the British trenches as fast as they could, and beyond them I saw that the German artillery was opening up.

We'd got Lieutenant Graham out of there in the nick of time.

It took another half hour, the sun trying to set in a heavy bank of dark clouds, to reach the aid station.

The doctor saw us coming, and straightened, a needle and sutures still in his fingers.

"What the hell—"

I could almost read his lips. It must have been a strange little parade, the stretcher bearers, nearing exhaustion, stumbling along with a man lying on the canvas between them, and a slender arrow of wood sticking up out of his shoulder.

Men ran to relieve us, and a ragged cheer went up as others recognized Lieutenant Graham. I cast off my coat and helmet as soon as I could, shaking my head and dusting my skirts in a vain effort to rid myself of lice, if there were any, and then went ahead to meet the doctor coming toward us.

"He wouldn't come without his arm, sir," I said brightly. "And so we brought it with us."

Dr. Reid went to work at once, and with the help of two orderlies he was able to remove the shard of wood from the wound. It must have left behind God knew what in the way of splinters and filth, but I found myself thinking as I looked at the gash, if Lieutenant Graham didn't die of infection, he stood a very good chance of keeping that arm. Stiff and painful it might be for the rest of his life, but it would be there.

As the stretcher bearers turned to go, I said, offering each of them a drink of water, "Thank you for your help. And the other men with you over there on the other side—who were they?"

"Sappers," one of the stretcher bearers told me wearily. "Looking for traps. They never said their names."

I shivered. I hadn't thought about the possibility of mines or explosive traps in that multilevel trench. But it was most certainly possible. The threat of gas was bad enough, moving across the ground, seeking the lowest point, filtering down into the trenches and hanging there on its way to the open bunkers no one had had the time to close off.

I fell into bed that night, too tired even to write to Simon.

Three days later, a runner brought messages, and among them was one from my father, included in the military pouch.

"I thought you might like to know," the Colonel Sahib wrote, "that you were mentioned in dispatches. Your mother and I are very proud of you."

The only problem was, Lieutenant Wade, or whatever he called himself now, had probably learned my name as well. If he had recognized me as easily as I recognized him.

I hadn't written to Simon, and there was no message from him in the pouch. This very likely meant he was away.

It didn't matter. There was nothing he could do but hope to find a name in the list of sappers that might be the one Wade was using. But he might not have been one of the sappers. He might have simply been a witness to the floor coming down on the Lieutenant and stayed on to help in any way he could. A nameless Samaritan.

Chapter Eight

Before telling anyone about what I'd seen—or believed I'd seen—there in the German trenches, I gave the matter serious thought.

It would be fairly easy for my father to discover which companies had been in that sector on that day. From there it would be a matter of sifting through names and looking into backgrounds. And then sending someone who knew Lieutenant Wade to spot the man. More than likely that would be Simon.

And it would be finished.

Why then was I so hesitant to act?

Except for the dead Subedar, I was the only other person who had seen—or thought she'd seen—Lieutenant Wade. Still, my father would take my word for that, and open a door into the past.

Such a search was bound to stir up all the old gossip, all the acrimony. How had Lieutenant Wade managed to reach England? That in itself would be news. Many would believe that such a trek across Afghanistan and Persia was impossible, and there would be speculation about the role my father played in getting Lieutenant Wade out of India some other way.

Of course if we did find the man, the truth would come out at his trial, proving that he'd managed to escape on his own. Even so, there would always be doubters.

But if I were wrong, if the man wasn't Lieutenant Wade, just someone who resembled him, then we would be dragged through the past again for nothing.

I owed it to my father to be certain. . . .

I was still facing that dilemma when I heard from Sister Fullerton, whose family lived in Haslemere.

I asked my father about the murders you spoke of. Here is his reply. I'm sorry there isn't much information to pass on. But if I were your friend, I'd choose some other place to live.

And she had enclosed a page from her father's letter to her.

These murders happened before you were old enough to be told about such things. I don't care to speak of them now. But I would not advise your friend's friend to purchase The Willows. It was not a happy house to begin with, and the deaths only support that fact. I know this to be true, as the doctor at the time was a colleague of mine, we'd studied together, and he had told me that for many years he'd had his suspicions that all was not well there. But he could prove nothing. The mortality rate among the young is appallingly high, as you know from your own training. And speculation is harmful where there is no evidence to support it. I shall say no more in this matter.

I read the page a second time. There was nothing about Lieutenant Wade here, or whether the murderer was local, as some people would have it. Only the belief that the house was not a happy one and never had been. What had Dr. Fullerton meant by that? I didn't know enough about The Willows even to guess.

I'd hoped for something specific to be going on with. Something that might explain the murders. Something to explain how Lieutenant Wade had known these three people and why he had come back from India to kill them.

I asked for leave, and to my surprise I was given it. But first there was a convoy to accompany. We lost three patients in the crossing and two more on the train to London. We had hoped to get them safely back to England, but infection set in before we left France, and nothing could stop its spread. I worked for hours over these men, along with several other Sisters, and when we reached London, I felt drained, and full of sadness.

I went to Mrs. Hennessey's house and spent a restless night, wondering if I could have done more for any of those five men. But I knew even as I questioned everything we tried that it had been hopeless from the start.

I had sent word to my parents that I was coming home, but it was Simon who came to collect me.

On the way to Somerset, I told him what I'd seen in the German trench and what I'd learned from Sister Fullerton's father.

"Say nothing to the Colonel," he warned me. "I'll do what I can to make quiet inquiries." He paused, his attention on the traffic as we drove out of London. When the way was less crowded, he said, "I must go to Portsmouth tomorrow. You won't be satisfied until you get to the bottom of this. And that worries me."

I took this as criticism. "Do you think I should let it go? We could be wrong, you know, about this man in France. I'd be the first to agree there."

He was silent again, and we went through half a dozen villages before he glanced in my direction.

"There's something more. I looked at the background of that Subedar. He was part of a support company, not in the Front lines. He shouldn't have been where he was when he died. All there is to go on is that he came from Agra. I've written to someone I know in the city, to see what can be learned at that end."

"Perhaps he was following Lieutenant Wade. And he was spotted."

"It's possible. Which brings me back to Portsmouth. If you go with me, I'll leave you in Petersfield for a few hours. I shouldn't be long. You might be able to learn something about the Caswell family without getting yourself into any trouble in broad daylight. I'd feel better knowing you weren't on your own."

"I can try. I shan't wear my uniform."

And so it was that after spending the evening with my parents, I left the next morning for Portsmouth with Simon.

My mother, ever sensitive to my moods, asked, "Is anything amiss, Bess, dear? You seemed to be a little distracted during dinner."

The talk had turned to India, as it sometimes did, and I'd been tempted to ask my father about Lieutenant Wade. But Simon had warned me off, and I could see for myself that my father was tired. I didn't want to add to his burdens. That meant I couldn't confide in my mother either. I couldn't ask her to keep such news from the Colonel Sahib.

Simon was waiting for me when I came down the next morning. I was wearing a very becoming summer walking dress, which had been hanging in my closet for nearly four years. Iris had kept it fresh and nicely pressed.

As I got into his motorcar, Simon nodded approvingly. "I don't often see you in anything but your uniform. I remember the last time you wore that dress—it was to have lunch in London with Edward Lessing and Tommy Broadhurst. "

Edward had died at Ypres, and Tommy on the Somme.

"Yes, and you drove me up to London. It seems like a hundred years ago, doesn't it?"

We made good time to Petersfield, and I saw that it was market day again.

"Will you be all right?" Simon asked, having second thoughts.

"Of course I will. Don't worry."

I got out of the motorcar and watched it drive away toward the Portsmouth Road. Then I strolled into the square, looking at the display of meat and cheeses and breads.

There weren't nearly as many foodstuffs as there had been before the war. Our own village market had suffered a similar depletion. A few chickens, some sausages, and only local cheeses, nothing from as far away as Cheddar or the north of England. Eggs in plenty, for everyone had hens, and they must be laying again. No butter, some honey, and only simple farm loaves on the bread shelves. But there was a profusion of cut flowers from local gardens, and a charity stall with bits and pieces on sale to help war widows and orphans.

I paused by that stall to see if there was anything I could buy to help the cause. There were souvenir cups and dishes from Lyme Regis and Portsmouth, one of them bearing the likeness of Lord Nelson's ship *Victory,* lengths of lace and ribbon for refurbishing children's dresses, and a few old books. I saw a lovely little porcelain shepherdess, which I bought for Mrs. Hennessey, and as I was paying for it, I asked if the woman behind the till knew anything about it.

"I'm afraid I can't tell you," she said. "It was in a box of things from The Willows. They were clearing out the attics, and they donated it to us along with a rocking horse that's been sold, and a child's chair, pretty little thing, trimmed in white and gold. It's behind the table here. You could always paint over that ugly elephant."

I leaned forward to have a look, saw the chair, and realized that it had come from India. The "ugly elephant" was the elephant-headed Hindu god, Ganesh.

What was the connection between India and The Willows?

I asked the woman, and she looked away toward the church. "I have no idea," she answered, and I had the strongest feeling that she was lying.

"It doesn't matter," I said lightly. "Are there any other treasures like this shepherdess?"

"That leather-bound Testament," she said, "and this mirror." She took out a very pretty child's mirror, and held it up. I realized that the back of the mirror was actually silver, black with tarnish.

"There's a bracelet here too somewhere—" She poked about until she found it, and then added a box that held a child's tea set, cups and saucers and plates, and small teaspoons to go with it. "I've had to price that a little higher than the rest, because it's complete."

"I'll take them all," I said, smiling. "For—for my goddaughter." It was obvious to her that I wasn't married, and it was the best excuse I could offer.

"How old is she?" the woman asked.

Oh, dear. I had to come up with a suitable age. "Er—six her next birthday."

"Then she'll enjoy all of these."

As she packaged them in scraps of newspaper and old toweling, I asked, "You said they were from The Willows. Is that a house here in the town?"

"On the outskirts, really. The owner has put it on the market, which is why they've been looking through the attics."

"You said the rocking horse had sold. Anything else?"

"Most people are—superstitious," she said reluctantly. "They don't want anything that comes from a house with a history of trouble. It was a man who bought the horse. I don't think he cared either way. But women are a little more wary."

"Don't tell me the house is haunted?" I asked, trying to appear enthralled with the idea of ghosts.

"No such thing," she answered with asperity. "At least I've never heard of any such thing."

She finished wrapping my purchases, and I retired to the nearest inn, ordered a cup of tea, and took a better look at my finds.

The bracelet was round, the size of a small child's wrist, and engraved with flowers in a pattern of entwined rosebuds. It was very likely gold, I thought, and had been an expensive gift. But the woman behind the counter had been happy to be rid of it at any price. I didn't think she relished the idea of taking the contents of a box from The Willows home with her when the market closed.

The tea set was small, doll size, white with hawthorn blossoms, white on white, set among green leaves, a small bouquet tied with pale yellow ribbons.

The mirror was silver backed, and there had once been a comb to match, I thought, and possibly a brush.

Were these the treasures of Gwendolyn Caswell? Mr. Gates, the chaplain, and his housekeeper might not have recognized them as such. But there was no date here to help me identify when these might have come into the family's possession—they could have belonged to Gwendolyn's mother, for that matter.

I set these aside and opened the Testament.

There was an inscription on the presentation page, and the name there leapt out at me.

Presented to Thomas Edward George Wade
on the Occasion of His First Communion.

Beneath it was the date and the name of the church.

St. Peter's Church
in the Parish of Petersfield, Hampshire

What was Lieutenant Wade doing in Petersfield as a boy? His family lived in Agra, and I'd believed that he had grown up there. Something he'd said on one of our rides had led me to think that he had, for he talked about seeing the Taj Mahal from an upstairs window of his house, and how it changed color with every variation in light. A cool distant blue in moonlight, opal in the first warm light of dawn, pink and gold at sunset, and the purest of whites at noon.

And yet here in my hands was the proof that he hadn't been in Agra when he was twelve. Because of the date, it couldn't have been his father—or even an uncle.

A cousin?

I thumbed through the tissue-thin pages, looking for anything else that might tell me more about who had owned this Testament.

There was nothing. Not until I came to Romans 12:19. And here a line had been marked through with a pen so viciously that two of the following pages had been scored through as well.

I couldn't remember what this verse said, although the passage sounded familiar. Paul's letter to the Romans . . .

Where could I find a Bible?

The church. The lectern.

I finished my tea, packed away my treasures in the box that I'd been given for them, and paid my account.

Carrying the box with me, for at this stage I dared not let it out of my sight, I walked through the marketplace and into the churchyard.

I had to set the box down to open the heavy door.

There was no one else in the church, and I left the box in the corner of the last pew before walking down the center aisle, listening to my footsteps echoing against the high stone walls and praying that the sexton didn't find me here before I'd done what I came to do.

The Bible on the lectern was quite large, and a brocade bookmark embroidered with blue and gold thread lay in last Sunday's lesson. I turned the richly colored pages with great care until I found Romans, and finally located the verse that I was searching for.

I read it with shock.

What the owner of the Testament had marked out with such force was a very familiar quotation indeed.

Vengeance is mine; I will repay, saith the Lord.

As I stared down at the words, I felt cold.

If it was young Thomas Wade who had marked through this

passage with such fierce anger, signifying his vehement disagreement with leaving vengeance to God, then it could explain the murders of three people in 1908.

But what was he so angry about? And why had he nursed that anger until he was a grown man, until he could come here to this town and finally do something about whatever was driving him?

Here was proof of murderous intent, even at this young age.

A KC could make much of this evidence if Lieutenant Wade was ever brought to trial. If this Testament had indeed come from The Willows, it showed premeditation and motive.

I heard someone pushing at the west door, and I quickly turned the pages back to the lesson of last Sunday, moving hastily behind the pulpit where I was not immediately visible.

But it was only two women, walking together down the aisle. I could hear them chatting as they came toward me, discussing a christening service.

I moved around the pulpit and went up the side aisle, nodding to them as they turned, startled to see someone else in the church when they'd believed it was empty.

I collected my box and slipped outside into the warm sunlight, feeling it on my face as I walked quickly back to the square.

Just as I was passing the charity stall, the woman in charge beckoned to me.

"You might be interested in this," she said as I came nearer. "Someone bought it earlier and brought it back. You can always take out the photograph and use just the frame."

And she handed me a tarnished silver frame with velvet backing.

I turned it over to find a formal photograph of several children standing together in a parlor, their eyes wide, their faces tentative, staring up at the camera. Five boys and three girls of different ages.

"This was from the box you mentioned before?" I asked, trying to sound curious rather than excited.

"Yes, it was the only other thing I'd sold, besides the horse. But the woman who bought it said she didn't want it after all, not even as a charity item."

And so I took the frame as well, and as an afterthought, bought the pretty little chair with Ganesh reigning in the peak of the back.

For I had just glimpsed it in the background of the photograph.

"My goddaughter will be spoiled," I said as I paid her. "I shall have to give these to her a few at a time."

"You aren't from Petersfield," she said. "I know most of the people who live here."

"Actually, I'm visiting in Midhurst. The family had other plans today, and I decided to explore a bit. They were going to a christening, and I didn't know the people." I realized that I was babbling, and smiled. "Have you tried any of the sausages for sale over there? I might take some back for our dinner."

"They're very good. Try the fatter ones. My husband is very fond of them."

I thanked her, and knowing she was watching me, I stopped and bought two pounds of the sausages, then added a slice of cheese from the next tent.

And while I smiled and talked to the farmer's wife about the cheese, I prayed that Simon would be coming back very soon. Or I'd be wandering around with my purchases long after the market closed at three, standing out like a sore thumb.

Retiring to another pub, I ate my lunch at a table in the back, my box stowed against the wall beside me, out of sight, along with the chair and the sausages and cheese. I'd had to buy a large basket, but still the chair didn't fit.

As I remembered, the chaplain, Mr. Gates, had been sent to England again to recover. I didn't know if he'd been allowed to come here and rest or if he was in a clinic somewhere. I just didn't want him to walk in and spot me. Most of the tables were taken, which was a good thing.

I made my meal last as long as I could, pretending to dither over whether or not to try the pudding, and then letting the older man who had served me persuade me to order it. When it was gone, I had no excuse to linger. As I settled my bill, he asked where I'd come from—like the woman at the charity tent, he must have known half the village—and I trotted out my earlier excuse, exploring on my own because my friends had gone off to a christening.

He accepted that without any question, and I was taking up my purchases and preparing to venture out into the square again when I saw a familiar face just coming through the door.

It was Janet Burke, Sister Burke's brother's wife. She was heavily pregnant, and there was an older woman with her, enough like her to be her mother.

We stared at each other, and I said, "Janet? You may not remember me. Sister Crawford. We met once when Sister Burke and I were leaving for France. Last May."

She nodded, clearly uncomfortable to encounter an acquaintance. I wondered if she'd come to Petersfield because she didn't know anyone here. Or perhaps the market had drawn her, as it had quite a few other outsiders.

"Yes, of course," she said politely, and then introduced her mother, Anne Reston.

"Won't you join us for tea?" Mrs. Reston asked, but in a tone of voice that indicated she'd prefer to hear me say I couldn't.

"Thank you, but I had a late lunch," I replied and watched her expression ease.

Janet said sharply, "What brings you to Petersfield?"

I could hardly use the same excuse I'd given the man who had served me. Janet had left her husband and was now living in Midhurst, where my imaginary christening was taking place.

"I'm visiting friends. They went to the dentist and I'm amusing myself meanwhile."

"Oh."

The waiter had come up behind us and was hovering, eager to seat the newcomers.

"We have just come from looking at a house near here," Mrs. Reston said.

For Janet and her lover—soon to be her husband as well?

"I don't know much about Petersfield," I said, "but I did hear someone say that The Willows was on the market."

As the waiter got their attention, Mrs. Reston changed her mind. "Do come and join us, if only for another cup of tea. I'd like to talk to you about that house."

And so I followed them to a larger table, deposited my purchases, and sat down.

"You've quite a collection there," Mrs. Reston said, eyeing the chair.

"A friend is setting up her nursery. I found a few odd bits she might like."

She signaled to the waiter and ordered tea, and as an afterthought, sandwiches.

"It's an ugly chair," Janet was saying. "I don't much care for that odd figure in the peak of the back. Enough to frighten a child, I should think."

"It will be painted to match the nursery," I agreed. "I was passing the time and it caught my eye. If she doesn't like it, then I shall give it away."

Mrs. Reston said, "We were just visiting The Willows. An extraordinary house. Quite Victorian, dark and grim. I doubt anything has been changed since 1890. Although I must say the wallpaper is still in good condition, which tells me there's no damp in the walls. But I just couldn't find it in me to like it. And it would cost a great deal to refurbish it. Still, the property is quite extensive, and the gardens could easily be brought back, with the proper gardener in charge."

She was fishing for something, I could tell that. It was why she'd invited me to join them, when it was clear she'd have been happier to see the last of me. And I was just as certain it had nothing to do with damp or wallpaper. They were merely the opening salvos of her campaign.

"I know very little about the house or its history," I told her truthfully. Our tea arrived and she poured my cup. "Thank you. I did hear that it was on the market. If you dislike The Willows, there must be other properties that would suit you better?"

She busied herself passing the sandwiches, an excuse for not answering me directly.

Was it a matter of money? Was that why she had looked at The Willows? Here was a house that was affordable, surely, having stood empty so long. Reverend Gates had said something about the house being handled by an agent in Midhurst, and that would explain how Mrs. Reston had come to hear about it. She lived there.

"The housekeeper who showed us around seemed very ill at ease. I asked her about the latest owner of the house, and she tells me that he inherited it from his uncle. They were both named Gates. But over the door to the garden is a scrolled *C*, and she couldn't tell me who that was. And there was a *C* above the mantel in the master bedroom as well. You'd think she would know something about the history of the place. The oddest thing was the nursery. Not a suite of rooms but an entire floor. Were there that many children? A rector's family, do you think?"

"I couldn't say," I replied, not wanting to bring up the Caswells or murder. "It does seem rather odd. Perhaps if you spoke to some of the local people, they could answer your questions." And good luck to her there, I added silently.

"We tried. I did call on the rector of St. Peter's. He told me that he didn't know the history of The Willows, that he had come here in 1910, when the incumbent requested an exchange of livings, in order to be nearer his aging mother."

"Then it might be best to speak to the estate agent handling the property," I said.

"We shall have to. I'm annoyed with him, I can tell you." She finished her tea and the last of the sandwiches. "Well. This has been a wasted journey. I dislike being misled. The description of The Willows left much to be desired." She rose, and I followed suit, collecting my purchases.

Janet got to her feet with some difficulty, her hand pressing the small of her back.

"Are you all right?" I asked in a low voice, moving to her side.

"It hasn't been an easy pregnancy," she said, glancing at her mother, who was already waiting for us by the door of the inn. "But I shan't have to wait too much longer."

"I'm sorry you had to travel this far for nothing. I'm sure you'll find a happier house, one that suits you better."

"I hope so."

As we turned toward the square, I thanked Mrs. Reston for my tea and said my farewells. Out of the corner of my eye I saw Simon just arriving from the Portsmouth road. He was searching the thinning market day crowd for me. He spotted me with the two women, and then his gaze moved away, giving me the opportunity to finish my conversation uninterrupted.

Leaving Janet and her mother, I walked on, thinking how awkward that encounter could have been if I hadn't already spoken to Sister Burke. I'd have assumed that the child Janet was carrying was her husband's and asked after him.

I stopped at one of the stalls, choosing a bouquet of late summer flowers for my mother, and then went on to where Simon was waiting.

He got out of the motorcar to open the door for me, taking the little chair, the basket of cheese and sausages, and the box from my hands. "This is an odd collection of purchases," he said as I carefully set the flowers in the rear seat.

"I'll tell you about it later," I said. "The people I was with—Mrs. Reston and her daughter—have been looking at The Willows. They found it very old-fashioned and rather dreary inside. And the housekeeper, who took them round the house, denied any knowledge of the Caswells when Mrs. Reston asked her about the ornamental *C*s she saw in several places. These didn't match with the Gates name, and she was curious. She would have lost all interest if the housekeeper had given her a name. But she didn't." I went on, describing what Mrs. Reston and her daughter had seen.

"Victorian, dark, and grim? I'm surprised the uncle didn't renovate the property. Gates told us he was glad of the chance to leave London. But then he could have been in financial straits and managed just to maintain it in good repair."

"Yes, that's possible. Which would explain why the nursery floor was unchanged. There was no need. He didn't have any children, and the Caswells had only the one daughter. I wonder who had had such a large family. Which reminds me." I went on to tell Simon how I'd come by the little chair and the items in the box, and when we stopped for dinner along the road, we took the box inside the inn with us, and spread the contents out on the table between us.

Simon went through them, ignoring the shepherdess and concentrating on the photograph and the Testament. "This proves that Wade knew the Caswells many years before he came there with murder on his mind. So it wasn't a random killing or even murder by mistake, walking into the wrong house. But how did he know them?"

"I've no idea."

Our food had come, but Simon ignored it, feeling for the four latches that held the photograph in its silver frame. Finding them, he opened them, removed the velvet backing, and carefully took out the photograph.

There was nothing on the back, no names, no dates. But on the reverse of the velvet backing there was a stamp, pressed into the heavy paper.

Simon held it up to the light.

"Hard to read, but I think it says GESSLER'S FINE PHOTOGRAPHY."

He passed it to me, and I nodded. "Yes, you're right. And under it must be WINCHESTER. There's *W-i-n,* and then it's rubbed away, and it ends with *t-e-r.*"

"Could very easily be." He glanced at his watch, then returned it to his pocket.

"Shall we make a detour?"

"Mother will be worried, if we're late. She'll think you forgot to retrieve me in Portsmouth."

"Yes, we ought to look for a telephone."

But the village had no telephone, and it wasn't until Winchester that we found one.

It was set in a grilled closet, the seat buttoned velvet and very comfortable.

Iris answered the telephone, told me that my parents had gone to dine with the rector, thinking that Simon and I might stop along the way for our dinner.

"Yes, that's right, we have," I said. "Tell them not to wait up for us. It could be late."

"The Colonel must be in London tomorrow afternoon."

"Thank you, Iris, I'll pass that along to the Sergeant-Major."

Simon frowned when I told him. "That means I'm probably wanted as well. But we're here, we'll search out Mr. Gessler if we can."

We found the shop on a side street just off the square where Alfred the Great stared down the hill toward the town gates.

The shop was on the ground floor, living quarters on the two above that. The window, dusty and uninteresting, gave the impression that the shop was not faring well. Or possibly even had been sold up, the name left on the glass.

Simon knocked once, then twice, and after a time, a light came on in the passage by the stairs, spilling out through the fanlight above our heads.

A middle-aged woman opened the door, staring out at us in the gathering dusk of evening. "Yes, what is it?" Her voice was tired.

Simon asked simply for Mr. Gessler, the photographer. "Is this his shop? The sign in the window leads us to believe it is."

"My father or my son? If it's my son, he's in France somewhere."

"What we're interested in is an old family photograph. We were hoping your father was still alive and could tell us something about it."

"He's taken hundreds of photographs. How would he be able to identify any of them now? He's close on ninety."

"Still," Simon told her, "it would be worth a try. And worth his while."

Her face brightened at the mention of money. With her son in the war and her father too old to work any longer, she must be in need of it.

Stepping back, she let us precede her into the passage, and she motioned toward the steep, carpeted stairs. "The room to your left, at the top," she told us.

We climbed the stairs, listening to the squeak of age on tread after tread, and then at the first-floor landing found ourselves in a large room overlooking the street. It was simply furnished, with well-polished early Victorian pieces, heavy and dark.

An elderly man sat by the window, wrapped in blankets in spite of the summer heat, his hair thinning and his hands blue-veined with age. But his eyes were still a very bright blue. He greeted us with pleasure, turning his chair slightly so as to face us. I realized that it was on wheels.

Simon introduced himself as Brandon, without his rank, and gave my name as Miss Crawford.

"We're trying to identify a photograph," he said. "One that's been in the family for some time, but there's no one alive now who can tell us when it was taken or by whom. Your label was stamped on the backing. We wondered if you had any records of the photographs you've taken, where they were taken, and for whom, or even who had paid for them."

Mr. Gessler held out his hand and Simon gave him the photograph, now back in its frame.

The old man bent his head over it, studying the images. "It was a very long time ago," he said. "I don't recognize the faces. But perhaps there is a way."

He opened the back with ease, drew out the photograph, and looked at the stamped name of his shop.

"This was taken just after we came to Winchester." He turned to his daughter. "Bring me the red box," he said, then turned back to us. "We used the red ink when we first arrived, but it proved to be difficult. See here, where the middle of the word *Winchester* is missing. And so we tried a dark green, and it was more reliable. That's why I can tell you the photograph was taken exactly twenty-three years ago. There's no doubt of it."

His daughter came back carrying a narrow drawer with a row of cards from back to front and set it down before her father. As she did, I could see that the upper left-hand corner of all the cards in the tray had been marked with a red triangle.

Mr. Gessler's gnarled hands were unsteady as he went through the long rows of cards, moving backward in time as we watched. But his eyesight was still very good, for he found what he was searching for, and drew out a thick packet of cards.

He handed them to Simon as if they were rather large playing cards, and I leaned nearer so that I could look over Simon's shoulder.

He went through the cards quickly, scanning the names elegantly printed in black ink. These apparently represented orders, for they listed the name and address of the person who was the client, the number of poses taken, the number of final prints purchased.

A great many of the orders appeared to have been bridal photographs or christenings, for in each case the name of a church was written in. A parade of people's lives, and the events they wanted to remember. Attached to one card was a newspaper cutting, showing a horse that had come in second in the Derby. Ears pricked forward, he stood there like a champion, a smiling owner holding the bit. Mr. Gessler must have taken the photograph used in the cutting.

Each order had a line for the price to be written in, and another line showed the date paid. Below these was a box at the bottom of each card to check if a frame had been selected.

Simon had nearly reached the end of the packet when he stopped, and held one of them up so that I could read it.

Caswell, Mrs.

Reading on, I saw that she had ordered four poses and had settled on one of them. And she had arranged for ten of her final choice, asking for each of them to be framed.

"But what did she do with ten of the same photograph?" I asked. "And where are the others?"

My question was directed to Simon, but Mr. Gessler held out his hand.

"Let me see."

We passed the card to him. He frowned, staring at it, and then the memory came back.

"Yes, the children, as you see. She paid for copies, a frame for each. Seven of the frames were ordered without glass, as I remember. See? *NG7.*"

But the one I had bought from the charity booth was protected by glass.

"All these children were hers? There isn't much of a family resemblance, is there?" Mr. Gessler's daughter asked doubtfully, looking at the photograph we'd brought with us. "Perhaps it's a church school class."

Mr. Gessler scratched his chin. "It's too long ago. I don't remember. If it hadn't been for the ink, I couldn't have told you anything about your photograph. It's too bad, but there you are." He was fiddling with the card he was holding, and it slipped from his fingers, landing facedown on the floor.

Simon picked it up, then passed it to me.

And there it was, on the reverse. In the same crisp black hand.

Special requests: Seven frames packed in cotton wool and sealed in oiled cloth for posting to India and Ceylon.

But there were no addresses. No way of knowing where the photographs had been sent.

Simon spoke to me, saying only, "The Middletons."

And I knew at once what he meant. Hadn't Mrs. Standish sent her husband a photograph of Alice and Rosemary opening Christmas presents? One, surely, taken by the Middletons?

Had the Caswells fostered children of Anglo-Indian families, seeing to their education and their prospects for English parents stationed in India?

Fees were charged, of course. Schoolmasters and retired rectors or vicars sometimes augmented their income in this manner. Or householders with impeccable social standing and thin purses.

It would explain the overly large nursery that Mrs. Reston had mentioned, as well as why this photograph had been taken—to assure anxious parents at Christmas that their offspring were alive and happy in their surrogate homes.

I looked closely at the photograph before Simon returned it to its frame.

The row of young, unformed faces stared back at me. But if one of them was Lieutenant Wade, I couldn't see the likeness.

Chapter Nine

We were silent, Simon and I, most of the way back to Somerset. It was very late when we reached the drive up to the house. A light shone from the downstairs windows, left burning for me. Most likely Simon would be on his way to London tomorrow with my father, and I knew he was tired, with not many hours left to him to sleep.

"I'm sorry," I said. "It seems that the more we learn, the less we know."

"Don't apologize, Bess. Go to bed and put this behind you for tonight. Shall I carry your box and the chair to the cottage? You can offer your mother the sausages and the cheese as a sop for being late."

He was smiling, I could see the flash of white teeth in the reflection of the headlamps. I could also see the lines beneath his eyes.

"Yes, please." I reached out to touch his arm. "Thank you," I said, and then he was coming round to my side to take the sausages and cheese while I got out. I walked up to the door, knowing he would wait until I was safely inside, even here in the peaceful quiet darkness of Somerset. But there had been a time when this house had held danger. I remembered it too well.

I closed the door and stood there, listening to the sound of the motorcar reversing and going down the drive.

My mother's voice startled me. "Bess?"

She was standing on the threshold of the drawing room, no lamps lit.

"Is everything all right?"

"Simon was kept in Portsmouth longer than we expected, and then we had to go on to Winchester. I'm sorry if we woke you."

If it had been any other man keeping me out until this hour, my father would have been waiting in the drawing room as well. But this was Simon, and I was safe with Simon. My mother on the other hand had a sixth sense about some things, and her worry hadn't been for the company I was keeping. It had been for whatever had taken me so often from home on such a short leave. . . .

"I haven't been to bed," she said. "It's always hard for me to fall asleep when I know your father is leaving."

"Where to this time?"

I could see her shrug, the soft peach silk of her dressing gown rising and falling as she lifted her shoulder.

"When do we ever know? But he says, London."

I held out the basket I was carrying. "There was a market in the square where we stopped going down," I said. "I couldn't resist. Village sausages and cheese, and flowers too."

"I'll take them through to the kitchen. Thank you, my darling. Good night."

She kissed me lightly on the cheek and went through the door behind the stairs, on her way to the kitchen. I wanted nothing more than to follow her, make a cup of tea for both of us, and tell her everything.

But not yet.

Two days later when I took the train to London—neither Simon nor my father had come back—I left a little extra time and went directly to Somerset House. It was where all the birth and death records were housed.

I didn't know anyone there, but I was soon chatting away with an older man whose son had been wounded at Passchendaele. A Sister Hitchcock had stopped the bleeding from his leg wound and saved his life. I thought I could have asked for the moon and he would have tried to give it to me.

Instead I only wanted to look at the records for Lieutenant Wade's family. I wasn't really sure how this would help me, but I had known him just as an officer in my father's regiment and the son of a gentle man who had let me sit in the cab of one of the huge steam locomotives that ran across India.

I left Somerset House with a few bits of new information. Mr. and Mrs. Wade had had three children. A boy, Robert, older than Lieutenant Wade, who had died in Simla, India, at the age of eight. And a sister, Georgina, who had died at the age of six in Petersfield, Hampshire.

Had the Wades lost a child to the heat and pestilence of India, then decided to insure the future of their remaining children by packing them off to England where their chances were better?

They wouldn't have been the first family to do so. And still one of their children had died, in spite of all that could be done. Like Alice, in fact, in the care of the Middletons.

I tried to remember something that Lieutenant Wade had said to us when he learned of Alice's death. It had seemed odd at the time. But it was lost. My mother might remember, but I wasn't ready to confide in her.

I carried another bit of information away with me. Lieutenant Wade's mother's name had been Ferguson, and his dead brother had been named for her father—Robert Westin Ferguson Wade.

There was always a possibility that if Lieutenant Wade was alive and using another name, it could well be that of his brother. Who would think to look in the English cemetery in a hill station for a long dead child?

Hadn't Lieutenant Wade's parents arranged in their wills to be buried beside their child, in the cool mountain air that smelled of pines rather than dust and cow dung and the bare feet of thousands of people over the centuries? My parents and I had gone to Agra for the memorial service for the Wades, but I hadn't made the long journey north. Hadn't seen the small grave next to theirs.

I posted a letter to Simon before meeting my train to Portsmouth. I wondered what he'd make of what I'd learned.

Back in France once more, I had little time to think about Lieutenant Wade. Rumors of an armistice were traveling that invisible circuit that kept all of us informed or misinformed as the case might be. But the shelling was as intense, the attacks and retreats, and the lines of the wounded were just as long. I looked into the haggard faces of men who had been too long at war, and I prayed every night that if the end was in sight, it would come soon enough to spare as many as possible.

Twice I went to Rouen with convoys of wounded, and on the second journey there, I was given two days of leave. Not long enough to go home, not even long enough to go to Paris.

I found a bed in the Base Hospital run by the American doctors and nurses, and I heard more gossip there. But no one knew how much was true and how much was wishful thinking. The word *armistice* figured largely, but not *victory*.

One of the Sisters who had come to Rouen with me was celebrating her birthday, and we decided to go to one of the small restaurants in the older quarter. It was called La Poule Rouge, The Red Hen, and it was said to have the finest omelets in France. We set out just after noon, and as we passed by the Cathedral a funeral was in progress, the bell tolling the years of the dead person's life. Twenty-six. A soldier, then. And this was borne out by the caisson and trappings of the horses that pulled it. The son of someone important, to have a military funeral in the Cathedral or one of its chapels.

We hurried by, and soon found La Poule Rouge tucked between a wine shop with dusty windows and an apothecary. Its sign was old, a large wrought-iron hen that had once been painted red, and her beak and feet were a dull, worn gold that gleamed only in spots.

The restaurant was like so many others, tables arranged here and there in no obvious pattern but far enough apart to offer a little privacy. The floor was checked blue and white, and the wooden chairs were worn, but the cloths covering the tabletops were spotless. I could smell bacon frying, and my mouth watered. I couldn't remember when I'd last tasted it. At home, surely.

There were perhaps a dozen people at the other tables, all engaged in quiet conversation. In a corner at the back was a British soldier, a Corporal, seated with a young French girl at least fifteen years younger than he was. She was quite pretty, and it wasn't surprising that everyone glanced her way as they came through the door.

I noticed the sling on the Corporal's arm first, and the fact that the girl with him was cutting up his omelet for him, before I looked at his face.

"What is it?" Sister Emery asked me as I stopped short and she bumped into me.

"Nothing," I said, catching up with the middle-aged woman in black who was about to seat us. "Pardon, madame, but could we sit there, near the window?" I quickly asked as she started toward a table near the pair.

I don't think she was pleased with the suggestion, but she turned and led us to the table I'd pointed out.

Sister Emery was happy with the choice and sat down. I took the chair across from hers.

"The other would have done very well," she said. "But I'm glad you asked for this table."

"Yes, I always prefer to be near the window too," I told her, and took the menu being handed to me, opening it before she could say any more.

The Corporal was in profile to where I was seated, and I could see him over Sister Emery's head.

It had to be Lieutenant Wade. Ten years older, gray already showing at his temples, and I found myself thinking for a second time that the scar that marked his face appeared to be an old one, a narrow white line that looked as if it had been drawn in chalk. I could see it far more clearly here than I had in the German trench.

As if he felt eyes on him, he turned slightly, but I had already raised my menu. I glanced surreptitiously at the window glass, but I wasn't reflected there.

We chose the fine herb omelet with cheese, and a rasher of bacon. But there was no bacon, the woman serving us reported. Only enough to flavor the omelet.

Disappointed, we thanked her and asked for tea. But there was no tea, and in the end we had a glass of cider with the omelet.

It was delicious, steaming hot and still moist when it came. Sister Emery began to eat with an appetite, but I was distracted by the Corporal on the far side of the room.

Would he remember me from the German trenches? He couldn't have seen me the night Teddy's ambulance slid into the shallow ditch. I was behind the headlamps, and he would have been blinded by their barred glare.

The German trenches were another matter. If it hadn't been for that encounter I could have crossed to his table and pretended to have mistaken him for someone else. I might even have discovered the name he was using.

Frustrated, I tried to think of a way to learn the man's name. I could see that he was wearing the uniform of a sapper, just as he had been in the trenches. Dangerous work at the best of times. He must have been there to look for traps or mines before the British fully occupied the German lines. The general opinion was, the Germans set charges before abandoning their trenches. Not only to keep any secrets from falling into our hands but also to keep our side from digging in as they themselves had done and making it that much harder to retake the line.

When had he hurt his arm? And how?

Remembering that this was Sister Emery's birthday and that she was a long way from her family in Northumberland, I tried to make it a jolly occasion. We finished with a plate of cheese and biscuits and somewhere the restaurant had even found a stem of fresh grapes to add on the side.

We were almost finished with our lunch, sipping the last of our cider, when the Corporal and the young French girl rose to pay for their meal and leave. I wished with all my heart that I could follow them, but I couldn't very well walk out on Sister Emery.

I watched as they made their way toward the door. It wasn't ten feet from where we sat. And I had no menu to hide behind.

Should I let the man know I recognized him? Or should I keep my face down, looking in my pocket for the little gift I'd managed to find for Sister Emery?

In the end, I simply looked up as they came parallel with us, and smiled.

The girl smiled back, a dimple in one cheek, but the British Corporal ignored me. I knew then that he must have remembered me from the German trench.

But did he remember me from India ten years ago?

I rather thought he had.

By the time Sister Emery and I had finished our omelets and settled our own account, there was no sign of the Corporal or the young French girl.

I was back in a forward aid station when the messenger from HQ arrived just at dusk. Pulling off his goggles and his gauntlets, he went to the doctor who was scrubbing up for surgery. Dr. Patton nodded in my direction, and the messenger came across the slippery wet ground to hand a letter to me.

I thanked him, glancing at the handwriting. It was from Simon, and he had managed to send it by the military pouch. Avoiding the censors.

I opened it as soon as the messenger was on his way again.

There was no message inside. Only a cutting from a newspaper.

I unfolded it, and as I read it, my knees felt unsteady.

It was from a London newspaper, but the headline read:

Fire in Winchester Takes Life of Elderly Photographer and His Daughter

Scanning the article, I saw that the fire had occurred late at night, trapping the two inhabitants of the shop in the upstairs living quarters. Their bedrooms were said to have been on the second floor and the stairs were engulfed in flames before they could escape.

Mr. Gessler, it seems, had taken two well-known photographs in his career. One was the runner-up in the Derby, a horse named Parsifal that went on to win twenty other races before making a name for himself at stud. There was an impressive list of his offspring and the races they had won.

The second photograph was of Queen Victoria in her carriage on the occasion of her Diamond Jubilee. She had turned her head slightly and seemed to be staring directly into the camera lens. At the time of her death, according to the cutting, it had been carried in most of the newspapers of the day.

Except for these, Mr. Gessler had not been a famous London photographer, and from the dusty windows of his shop, it appeared that his business had failed as he aged. There was no reason to believe that his death was anything but a dreadful accident.

But the last sentence of his obituary was chilling.

> The Winchester police have not concluded their investigation into the fire and have not ruled out foul play.

I looked in the envelope to see if there was a later cutting, giving the final police report. But there wasn't. Which could mean that the London papers had not found it newsworthy—or that the investigation was incomplete.

Who would wish to kill the Gesslers?

More important, did it have anything to do with our visit?

There was one certainty, however.

The man I was nearly convinced was Lieutenant Wade must surely have been in France when the fire occurred. That arm in its sling wouldn't have earned him a transfer to England for further treatment.

As soon as I could, I wrote to Simon, but it was three days before I was able to send the letter off by the next messenger.

There was little I could say openly.

And so I wrote,

Our friend the sapper was here in France on the date in question.

The next time I was in Rouen, after turning over my charges, I went back to La Poule Rouge and sat at the same table by the window, ordering a coffee and an omelet, this time with cheese and onions. The same middle-aged woman in a dark dress came to take my order, and I thought perhaps she remembered me, for I had told her when we were giving our order that we were celebrating Sister Emery's birthday.

This time I chatted a bit about the weather and how the city had grown before bringing up the question I intended to ask.

She had just brought my omelet, and I said as she arranged the plate before me, "The last time I was here, there was such a pretty girl sitting over there, the table in the corner. She was with a British soldier. Does she come here often?"

She turned to look at the table, frowning, as if trying to remember. "She is young and very fair?"

"Yes." I nodded. "And such lovely eyes." I couldn't have said whether they were blue or brown, my attention had been on Lieutenant Wade.

"She should not give herself to that one, the soldier. It is wrong," she told me, dropping into French, and I knew then that she did remember the girl.

"Surely she has parents who would warn her to be careful," I agreed.

"*Ils sont mort,*" the woman told me. They are dead.

"A pity. Who then has the care of her?"

"An aunt. She is old, blind. And even if she were not blind, she can see nothing but the money her niece brings in."

A woman of the streets? Surely not! I felt a surge of sadness.

My expression must have mirrored what I was thinking.

"Not yet. But the soldiers, they are sorry for her, and give her money. It will not be long before a pathetic story is not enough. They will want more, these men."

"Where does she live?"

But the woman had said enough. She wished me a good appetite and left me to my meal.

I ate the omelet with pleasure and drank my coffee, all the time wondering how I could find out where the girl lived. If she took money from British soldiers, she might well know the name of the man who was with her that day.

But when I asked a second time, the woman's lips tightened in a narrow line, and I knew then it was useless.

But I was persistent. If she came here and brought the soldiers here, then perhaps she lived nearby. Somewhere in this quarter.

I walked for nearly an hour, up one street, down another, crossing over to look into café and shop windows, then crossing back to do the same on the other side. I had nearly given up—a sprinkle of rain was becoming a hard shower—when I saw her.

She was standing in the recessed doorway of a small church, and as I came closer, I saw that she was crying.

She must have realized I was staring, because she turned away, facing the wooden door and looking up at the tympanum of the arch and the array of stone saints carved into the stone there.

I stopped, speaking in French. "Mademoiselle, is something wrong?"

I had no way of knowing if she remembered me, if that was why she turned away.

"*Mais rien, merci, Soeur.*" Nothing, thank you, Sister. Her back was still toward me, and the stone saints appeared to hold her attention.

"But there is, if you stand here in the rain, crying. Let me help."

She broke down, her head going into her hands, sobs shaking her slim shoulders.

"I have no money."

I could hardly make out the words, she was crying so hard. I touched her hair gently, as one would a child's, and she turned, flinging herself into my arms.

It appeared that a soldier had befriended her, taking her to a restaurant for lunch, but instead of giving her money, as the others before him had, he wanted to take her to a hotel first.

"I am not that kind of girl," she whispered. "I am not. But sometimes they think I am, and they say very cruel things to me when I refuse to go with them."

"But who looks after you, my dear? Is there no one?"

"My aunt, but she is old, she needs medicine and food. We have no money, I must beg on the streets."

It was possible that, having failed to persuade the soldier to give her what she needed, she thought she could wring sympathy and a few sous from me. But I said, "And there is no one else?"

"No one. My parents are dead. My father was a soldier, my mother fell ill of the influenza. It took her but not my aunt."

"I think I know someone who can help you," I said briskly. "They have very little money themselves, but they will do what they can. For your aunt and for you."

She was skeptical. I could see it as she moved out of my arms and stared at me.

"They are nuns," I told her. "If your aunt is ill, they will help you nurse her. And they will feed you as well. You needn't beg."

It took me nearly a quarter of an hour to convince her to come with me, but in the end, I took her to a convent I knew of, knocking on the door, giving my name to the porteress, and sitting with the girl during the interview.

Her name was Claudette Miniere, after her father, and she lived two streets from La Poule Rouge. Her aunt had dropsy and could not walk or work. And she herself had no training. "Besides, I am too pretty," she told the nuns. "The shopkeepers turn me away, because men come around to speak to me but buy nothing."

It was true. Pretty shopgirls were vulnerable, and more than one had ended up pregnant and starving when she was no longer attractive. The older women who owned or worked in most of the shops saw trouble when someone like Claudette arrived on their doorstep and turned her away. It was not worth training someone who would leave as soon as she caught the eye of a man wealthy enough to keep her. Or who would believe false professions of undying love. War had not changed that fact of French life.

The nuns had seen many Claudettes, but she was young enough that I thought they would help her. And I was right. One of the nuns, Sister Marie Justine, agreed to return to their flat and have a look at the aunt.

Now was my chance, and I said, "Before you go, Claudette, I was in La Poule Rouge a fortnight ago, and you were sitting at a table by the back wall with a British soldier, a sapper. Do you remember him?"

I tried to describe him, his sling, his scar—but it was several minutes before we could agree on which man I was speaking of. I saw the elder nun's mouth tighten as she realized what the girl must have been doing. A decent meal for herself, a few sous for her grandmother. A desperate life.

"Do you recall his name? Did he tell you what to call him?"

"I think it was Walter. Yes, that's right, Walter. Corporal Caswell."

I sat there with my mouth open, I was so surprised. Of all the names that I thought Lieutenant Wade might be using, it had never occurred to me that he might have chosen the name of the family he was accused of killing in Petersfield.

I wanted to ask Claudette if she were sure. But Sister Marie Justine was eager to be on her way to see the aunt before the rain got any heavier, and I smiled, thanking her, thanking Claudette, wishing her well.

After they had gone, another of the nuns, Sister Marie Joseph, said, "This man is known to you?"

Again I was caught off guard.

"I don't know," I told her truthfully. "But I think he is someone from the past who has reappeared unexpectedly. From my family's past, not Claudette's," I added hastily.

"Is he likely to come back for her? Or harm her?"

"I don't know," I said again. "But I shouldn't think it's likely. When his arm is fully healed, he'll be back with his regiment."

"Just as well," Sister Marie Joseph replied. "There was a warmth in her voice when she spoke of this one. And that is unsafe for a vulnerable child who is on the streets."

"Perhaps because he was kinder than most," I said, almost against my will. But I was remembering that he hadn't touched her as they left the restaurant. He hadn't put his good arm around her shoulders or her waist, he hadn't held her hand. That could have been because he'd recognized me, but I thought not. What's more, she had given me a friendly smile, without anxiety or stress, as if not afraid of the demands that might come once they were in the street.

I reached the Base Hospital just in time to meet my convoy north. Teddy, driving my ambulance, nodded to me, and we joined the long line of vehicles and men heading toward the fighting.

Chapter Ten

When next I was given leave, I was grateful that it was Simon who met me as my train came in. I had already handed over my charges in Dover—to Diana, one of my flatmates. She had been there visiting her fiancé and had been ordered to see to the chest and abdomen cases I was bringing in. We barely had five minutes to catch up on news, and then she was gone.

I was just as glad because these cases were to be sent to a number of clinics in the north, and I was tired. It had been a long tour, and I slept most of the way from Canterbury to Victoria Station. By the time Simon walked up to take my kit from me, I felt a little more rested.

My parents, he informed me, had driven up to Chester to see an old friend who had just been invalided out of the regiment after major surgery on his back. They would return in two days, happy to spend the rest of my leave with me.

As we drove to Somerset, I told Simon what I'd learned.

He whistled when I gave him the name I thought Lieutenant Wade was using.

"Of course he could have lied to the girl," I added, "but somehow I don't think so."

"It's worth looking into. Meanwhile, the findings in that fire that killed the Gesslers are interesting. Arson, they believe, because the blaze began in the entrance to the shop, not in the back room where there still were chemicals for the developing process. As I remember, the lock on that shop door was a simple one. Anyone could pick it, slip inside, start a fire on the stairs, and see that it was blazing well before stepping out again."

I hadn't noticed, but it was typical of Simon to remember such details. It was one of the gifts that had made him a formidable Sergeant-Major.

"One good bit of news—they didn't burn to death. They were overcome by the smoke."

"I'm glad. It was hard to think of them trying to escape and finding no way out." I'd seen so many burn victims, mostly pilots. It was not an easy death. "Do the police have any suspects in mind?"

"According to the London papers, they don't. The inquest brought in a verdict of murder by person or persons unknown."

"Do you think it was connected in any way to our visit? I wish we'd never gone to see them."

"I don't know," he said, glancing at me and then back at the road. The late summer evening was already moving toward sunset, the days closing in. It would be dark before we reached home.

Rather than putting Iris to the trouble of serving dinner to one person, we stopped on the way and ate at a small inn just over the border into Somerset. The menu had once included a roast of apple and pork, but tonight there was only a bit of old beef.

"I want to go back to Petersfield," I said after we'd been served. "It couldn't have been Lieutenant Wade who set that blaze. And if he doesn't have an accomplice, then it must have been someone from the village. But why kill the Gesslers? We just went to see them about a photograph. We never asked them about Lieutenant Wade. I doubt that Mr. Gessler even knew his name."

"I don't think it had anything to do with our visit. You're making too much of it."

"If you truly believed that, Simon, you wouldn't have bothered to send me that cutting."

He looked across the room to where a family had come in to dine.

"All right," he said finally. "It was probably no more than a coincidence that they died so soon after we were there. But I don't particularly care for coincidences where you're involved. I wanted you to be on your guard."

"The Gesslers had lived in Winchester for twenty-three years or more," I said. "And no one had set fire to their shop. What's more, it's been closed for how many years?"

"Let's go back to the beginning. Did anyone take notice of what you'd bought at the charity stall?"

I tried to think. "The woman who sold the items to me seemed to be happy to be rid of them. She packed everything carefully in that box. Except the chair, of course. I carried that in my hand. For all the world to see. I took both with me to the inn. Janet Burke and her mother saw the chair, but that was all. Then you came and took the box and the chair from me and put them into the motorcar. Anyone might have seen me carrying those things. I wouldn't have been aware of it. And that chair identified me easily as the one who had bought the other things."

"No one could see the frame or the photograph in it?"

"No. But I'm reminded of something. The woman at the stall told me that the frame had been bought and then returned."

"By whom?"

"I don't know. At the time, I didn't think to ask."

"No, of course not." Simon had finished his food and set his knife and fork across his plate. "For all we know, we showed the Gesslers one photograph, and their killer was worried about an entirely different one. One we have no knowledge of. That makes more sense. Suspicion, even if unproven or entirely untrue, can still ruin a man or a woman. It's as good a motive for murder as any other."

I moved the small square of beef that seemed lost amidst the potatoes and the vegetables around my plate, my appetite gone.

"Bess. You aren't responsible. If anyone is, I am. After all, it was I who found the link between the frame and the Gesslers."

"I want to go back, Simon. I don't know precisely why, but I owe it to the Gesslers, and I want to know what this business has to do with Lieutenant Wade. If Reverend Gates is there, perhaps he can tell us more about the Caswells. My parents are in Chester. We could drive there tomorrow."

Simon was quiet for a time. "All right. I'll come by for you at seven."

I wanted to say that that was far too early, that I would have to be up by six. And it would be close on ten o'clock before we reached my house. But if Simon was willing to go with me, I was glad of his company.

The next morning, although the weather wasn't very promising, Simon was there and helped me into the motorcar. When he joined me, the motor ticking quietly over, I could tell that there was something on his mind. And I was right. He turned to me.

"I managed to find out a little more about the Subedar. His brother worked for the railway. And he was sacked for pilfering from the railway stores. Lieutenant Wade's father refused to hear any appeals."

The railway was an important employer in India. Not only could one work there all of one's life, but it was also possible to bring in brothers, sons, cousins. Security for an entire family for generations. To lose such a position was devastating, and it reflected on the entire family.

"That explains why the Subedar recognized Lieutenant Wade after all these years. He had good reason to remember the Wades."

"Yes. His brother could also have joined that noisy wedding party, slipped into the house, and killed Wade's parents."

"That's an alarming thought. Anyone could have known that

Lieutenant Wade was back from England, and about to rejoin his regiment. Simon, what if he *didn't* murder his parents?" It was a shocking realization.

"Don't jump to conclusions. The police investigation was thorough. The Colonel looked into that."

And he would have.

"Still . . ." I remembered the wedding processions I'd seen. Noisy, all the guests singing and dancing, music almost deafening as they passed. One man slipping out of the Wade house and joining in the celebration as the groom was carried to the bride's home, then disappearing into the darkness a little distance away would hardly be noticed. And when the police came, not one of the guests would want to admit to seeing anything out of the ordinary. That would be a poor reflection on the groom's family—and most of those people would be related to it in one way or another. The police would have no choice but to accept the truth of statements made to them, when so many tallied.

On the journey we talked about other things, among them our time in India and memories we shared. And then the first houses of the town came into view.

I said, "I'll walk to the square when we're a little closer."

"It isn't a good idea, Bess."

"If you follow me, you might be able to tell who finds my return interesting."

"Yes, I see. All right, then," he reluctantly agreed.

I came into the square from the church, having walked parallel to the High Street, past the police station and through a side gate in the churchyard wall. I caught sight of the sexton, standing beside a grave the gravediggers had just finished. One was climbing out of the pit, dusting his hands after setting aside his shovel. I was reminded of the Gesslers, dead in Winchester.

I ducked my head against the rising wind, and took the shortest way around the church, out of the sexton's sight. I had hardly stepped into the square when a woman hailed me from the far side. She was coming out of one of the shops, and I didn't recognize her at first. Then I realized that she had been in charge of the charity stall when I was here last. She was waving anxiously, as if afraid I'd not heard her.

Surprised that she remembered me, I waited for her. Breathless as she caught up with me, she said, her words spilling over one another, "I thought it was you. You bought that box of odd bits donated by The Willows, didn't you? I was so hoping to see you again. They need the items back, you see. The box shouldn't have been donated, it was a mistake, and the family is quite upset. Could we have the box back, please? Of course we'll return what you paid for it. We'll be happy to."

"I don't have it with me," I told her. "I'm so sorry. It's—" I started to tell her that it was in Somerset and thought better of it. "It's in London, you see. Surely there was nothing in it that mattered to anyone."

"The photograph has sentimental value, I'm told. Of course if you wished to keep the frame, I'm sure no one would mind. Really, you could even mail it. The picture, I mean. It wouldn't be a great bother, would it?"

"Has the Reverend Gates been angry with his housekeeper about the items being given to the charity stall?"

"Well—yes—that's to say, I don't really know. We were just packing away the items we hadn't sold, and someone came up and asked about the donation. He said no one had known the box was missing, and then there was a great fuss searching for it. I had to tell him it was sold. Gone. He was that upset."

"Was it the chaplain? Mr. Gates?"

"No, he said he'd been at the house, with an eye to buying it when the family noticed that the box wasn't where it should have been. He volunteered to see if it was by any chance in the charity stall while they went on looking. He wanted to know if I remembered the buyer, if there was any way to get the box back. Sadly I had no idea who you were or where you lived. I had to tell him that."

"Did he ask about the photograph? In particular?"

"No, just what was in the box. It was I who told him about the shepherdess, the photograph, and so on. He said that it was probably the photograph that the family was worried about. That's why I asked you if you could mail it back to me. Or to The Willows, if you prefer."

"I'm not going back to London just now," I told her, trying to seem concerned, putting off having to give her an answer.

"That's a pity. But you *will* look, won't you, when you are in London again? I feel so responsible, you see. It was I who picked up the boxes at The Willows, and it could have been my mistake. So easily."

"What was in the other boxes?"

"Linens. Tablecloths, some runners, pillowcases. Antimacassars and armrests for chairs. All hand embroidered, although not in my opinion by an expert hand. Still, there were no stains on the linens from being folded away so long. One could use them straightaway. There was one really lovely little piece. I kept it out for myself. That's to say, I paid for it, of course."

"What was it?"

"Just a child's sampler. It was sewn for her birthday, with a Bible verse and her name and the date, and wisteria all around it. Still such a pretty blue. I'm fond of blue." She caught herself, saying, "But that's neither here nor there. Could you give me your name, Miss? And tell me when you think you'll be in London again?"

But I didn't want to give her my name. I said, "That's not important. Just tell me where to send the photograph."

"To The Willows, attention the Reverend Gates. I'm sure that will do."

"Who did you say the man was, the one who came looking for the box?"

"He didn't give his name, and I never thought to ask. He wasn't asking for himself, you see. A rather nice-looking young man, I must say. Fair. Polite. He said he was from Peterborough. But I rather thought his accent was more West Country. My mother was from Cornwall."

I thanked her and went on my way. When I glanced over my shoulder, she was still there, that same anxious expression on her face.

I was all the way across the square when in a bakery shop window I was passing I could see as far as the church, and the sexton was just coming out of the churchyard. He crossed the square as I watched. But I needn't have worried, for he set off down the High Street. Two minutes more with the woman who had hailed me, and I'd have been in that man's path.

I waited until I was sure he was out of sight, and then turned and walked briskly back to the churchyard. The gravediggers had left too. The mound of earth had been covered with a tarpaulin.

It wasn't what I was interested in.

I quartered the churchyard as best I could, looking for an older grave. And I found it at last. It was in a corner, the stone sunk at an angle, but the name was clear enough to read easily.

Here lay Lieutenant Wade's little sister, Georgina. There were no pansies or other flowers planted here. She had been long forgotten. But it explained to me why Lieutenant Wade had been so upset over the death of little Alice Standish, why he had accompanied a grieving mother back to England and made certain she reached her destination.

He had been reminded of his own loss.

The question was, had Alice's death brought him back to Petersfield before he sailed for India, and had that renewed memory of an old grief sent him to The Willows with murderous intent?

There was no way of knowing.

I thought about the boy. Alone in England and far from his

parents in India. Losing his only sister must have been appallingly hard for a child. How had he coped? And had the Caswells given him the sympathy he desperately needed, or had they failed him?

The more I learned about Lieutenant Wade, the more confused I felt.

I left the churchyard and went in search of Simon.

But there was no sign of his motorcar or of him. He'd intended to drive out to The Willows later, to see if it had been sold. I couldn't imagine that he'd decided to do that while I was making my roundabout way to the church.

Where, then, was he?

I cast about in the streets leading out of the square. I even went back to the church and the side gate where I'd come in earlier. But he wasn't there.

It was unlike him to not be where I could find him. He'd been worried about me from the start. Then what could have delayed him? Had he encountered Mr. Gates and been held up longer than expected? It was very possible.

I started walking out of Petersfield in the direction of The Willows. I'd passed the last house before Church Street narrowed into the road that led west. Though the afternoon was warm and dry, The Willows was farther away than I remembered. I had at least another half mile to go.

And then around the bend came a motorcar, nearly sweeping me off my feet as it thundered past me, narrowly missing me.

Simon's motorcar.

But that wasn't Simon at the wheel. I'd swear to it.

I broke into a run. Something had happened, and I wanted to find Simon, to be sure he was all right. He could look after himself as well as any man and better than most. Then why was someone else driving his motorcar?

He wasn't by the gates into The Willows, and he wasn't on the drive. I cast about on either side of it, and the next thing I knew, the door of the house was flung open and Mr. Gates came roaring down the steps.

I turned to face him, thinking he was angry about the box I'd bought at the charity stall. But then he couldn't have known who it was, could he?

"What are you doing here? I find you everywhere I look, I can't escape you. Go away, in the name of God, and leave me in peace. I only want to be rid of this albatross about my neck, can't you understand that?"

"I'm so sorry," I said, standing my ground. I wouldn't have been surprised if he'd attacked me. "I was expecting to meet someone in Petersfield, and he hasn't come. But someone else was driving his motorcar just now, and I thought he might have come from here. I must find out if anything is wrong."

He stopped some five feet from me. "Why should he come here? What possible reason can he have for interfering in my life?" He was all but wringing his hands, his anger giving way to self-pity.

"He's not interfering. And I must find him. Won't you help me? If not, will you allow me to look for him here on the grounds? He must be somewhere."

"I don't care where he is. Get off my property or I shall have you up for trespassing."

The housekeeper came to the open door behind him, staring at us as we quarreled.

"What's happened? I could hear the shouting."

"We must send for the constable. At once," he said, turning toward her.

"My dear, there's no one to send," she said plaintively, and he closed his eyes, as if this was too much to bear.

"I'll leave," I said, angry with him now, in spite of what I could see was a very disturbed man. "But if I don't find my friend out there on the road, I shall come back, and I shall bring the constable with me, to sort it out."

I turned to leave and had just reached the gates when Simon stumbled toward them from the road, his face a bloody mask.

"Bess?" he said, and I ran toward him, catching his arm.

"What happened?" I asked as he leaned on me for a moment, shaking his head to clear it.

"I'm all right," he told me. "A little dazed still."

I looked around and Mr. Gates was staring at Simon as if he'd seen a ghost. And then I realized that it was the blood on Simon's face, almost obscuring his features.

I called to the housekeeper, "He needs help."

She hesitated, and I could see that she was torn between refusing me and helping Simon. Finally she said, "The kitchen. This way."

We walked past Mr. Gates, standing like a statue, his eyes unfocused as he looked into the past. Simon managed the steps somehow and walked into the house. We followed the housekeeper through the door beyond the stairs and down into the kitchen. What I'd seen of the rooms we passed was hardly what a potential buyer would find attractive. Janet's mother had been right, the wallpaper was old-fashioned and dark, the furniture heavy and depressing.

We reached the kitchen and the housekeeper pointed to a chair. "Sit there. I'll find water and some cloths." She disappeared down the passage as Simon sat down.

"I'd bent over to turn the crank. There was no one else on the road, I'd have sworn to that. I think he must have come from the small copse—I'd left the motorcar there where it was half hidden, and walked as far as the gates of the house. No one was about, and nothing seemed to have changed. I went back the way I'd come. I don't know what he had in his hand. I heard him just in time and ducked as he swung it, hard. Still, it caught me a glancing blow. I went down, and before I could roll, he hit me again. He got behind the wheel, and I managed to fling myself in the ditch before he could run me down. He tried twice, then gunned the motor and was gone. I think I must have lost consciousness—"

He broke off before I could ask if he'd seen the man. The housekeeper was coming down the passage, her heels clicking on the stone flagging. I went to take the basin of water from her, and she put the clean cloths down on the table.

Simon took one, dipped it the basin, and began to wipe the blood from his face. I could see the knot at his hairline and another on his cheekbone. He was lucky the bone wasn't broken or his skull fractured. He winced as he touched the torn skin. It was bleeding freely, the way head wounds can, and I looked up to see the housekeeper swaying on her feet.

I caught her and sat her down. "Mrs. . . ." I began, about to tell her to put her head between her knees.

"Miss. It's Miss Seavers," she answered weakly, her gaze still on the bloody cloths and bloodier water in the basin.

"No, look away. He will be all right. Please, put your head down, that's it, and keep it there for a moment."

She did as she was told. After a moment she said, "We left my cousin in the drive."

"He'll be all right." I hoped that was true. "I need to ask you something." Out of the corner of my eye I could see Simon holding a compress against his head, leaning back in his chair. "Have you been clearing out the attics?"

"Yes." She sat up too quickly, and I had to urge her to put her head down again. "We thought it might look—nicer. Cleaner and more inviting. I expect the Caswells never threw anything away. I sent several boxes of linens to the charity stall, and a box of children's things as well. I don't know how long they'd been up there. I wanted to keep the Dresden shepherdess, but my cousin wouldn't hear of it. Or the sampler. He wanted to be rid of them."

"Why?"

She sat up, shaking her head. "It brought back the past, he said. He wanted nothing to do with the Caswells. I've taken down the family portraits and put them out in the shed. A pity, but he said they were not by known artists, and worth very little."

"The sampler. Do you remember the name of the child who embroidered it?"

"Barbara, I think it was."

I felt a wave of disappointment. Simon was listening to the exchange, but he couldn't know what I did.

"It wasn't Georgina, by any chance, was it?"

"No, I don't believe so. The box holding the shepherdess had *Georgina, on her birthday* written on the outside. I threw that away, because the charity stall didn't care to have items identified. The sampler, of course, was different. But how did you know about these things?"

"I happened to see them at the charity stall," I told her. "Has anyone else come looking for them?"

"There was a man here. Some time ago. He was collecting children's toys and so on for the poor in London. I promised to let him have anything we didn't want, but the box got collected with the other items for the charity stall. It didn't matter, most of the items were not something poor children could play with very well. Like the shepherdess."

"Did you know this man?"

"I didn't. But he was very nice, and his concern for the London children was obvious even to me. He'd approached any number of people about this, he said. He was wearing the uniform of a wounded soldier, and his health wasn't the best, he said. But this was a cause dear to him."

I wondered about that. Miss Seavers was a kindhearted woman. A man appearing at her door could take advantage of that kindness. Proper housekeepers would have sent such a petitioner packing. Miss Seavers, a cousin acting in that capacity, was easier to appeal to. But what was this man really after?

Something from the past. Not the past of the Gates family but from the Caswells.

What was in this house that he wanted? I don't think Miss Seavers—or even her cousin—had any idea.

I could hear footsteps on the stairs. I turned to Simon, whose color was better now, his face and hair cleaner, although there were still stains on his uniform and his hands.

Mr. Gates came to the doorway. "I think we have done enough to help this man. Please leave." He was looking at me, not at Simon.

I thanked Miss Seavers as Simon put down the cloth in his hand and rose without a word. Mr. Gates stepped aside. I thanked him too as I left the kitchen and went up the stairs to the ground floor. I could hear Simon following me, but I didn't turn. We went out the main door, and it was firmly shut behind us.

"What the hell is going on?" Simon asked quietly, catching me up and walking beside me now.

I told him.

He whistled under his breath. "What have we stumbled into?"

"I don't know." I looked at him. "Are you up to walking into Petersfield?"

"Yes," he answered impatiently. After a moment he broke the silence that had fallen between us. "This doesn't mean that Lieutenant Wade didn't kill the Caswell family. There must be something else that would come to light if someone begins to look into the past."

"Then that's what cost Mr. Gessler and his daughter their lives," I said.

"Why does someone else want that photograph? Does he know what it shows? Or is he taking no chances?"

"Sadly we can't put names to those children. It might help if we could." I cast a sideways glance at Simon, but he seemed to be managing well enough. And we had reached the outskirts now. "But how to begin?"

"God knows." Simon put a hand to his head, and I realized it must ache abominably.

Why had he been attacked? What purpose would have been served if he'd been severely wounded—or killed? I didn't want to think about that.

"Do you remember anything about the person who struck you?"

"There was no time, Bess. A man. Not as tall as I am. Slim. That's about it. Could I recognize him again? I doubt it. I was too busy trying to stay alive."

"Well, it wasn't Mr. Gates, that's certain. The sexton?"

"I don't know." Simon stopped and turned to me. "Is it too obvious that I've been bleeding?"

"Yes. Your cheek is beginning to bruise—very red, and raw. The lump at your hairline—"

I found my handkerchief and tried to blot the blood. Finally I shook my head. "It's hopeless, Simon." I looked around. "Let me find an apothecary shop and buy some cotton wool and plasters."

"Yes, all right. I'll stay out of sight."

I hurried away, passed through the square and down the High Street until I came to an apothecary. I was just coming out with my purchases when I stopped short.

There was a motorcar parked not a dozen steps down from the shop, and I realized, looking more closely at it, that it must be Simon's. I could have sworn under oath that it hadn't been there when I went inside the shop. But then I'd been distracted. . . .

I turned and went to it for a closer look. I was right. And in the rear seat was a long cudgel.

Looking around, I could see no one watching. I set my purchases on the rear seat, then stepped around to the bonnet and turned the crank. Five minutes later, I was slowing beside Simon. He opened the passenger's door and got in.

"Well, well," he said.

"Look in the back."

He did, and I heard him swear under his breath. "He meant to kill me."

Would whoever it was have come next for me? Was that why the motorcar was left in plain sight, luring me to my own death? Or to frighten me into leaving? I felt angry suddenly. At Lieutenant Wade, at Mr. Gates and the Caswells, at whoever was behind this attack on Simon.

Picking up speed, I drove past The Willows, and as we came into the outskirts of the next village, where we could be seen by anyone looking out a window, I pulled to the side of the road and pulled up the brake. This was as safe as I could make it. As I retrieved the salve and the bandages, I asked, "Do you want to go to the Petersfield police? I think you should." Trying to interject a lighter note to conceal my worry, I added, "I don't know how you'll explain this to my father." I gestured to the bloody bits of cotton wool I'd been using on his face.

Simon ignored the last comment. "I'm not very clearheaded at the moment. And we don't know who's to be trusted in that village. No, much as I loathe retreat, it's wiser to go on to Somerset. But I promise you, I shall find out who is behind this."

His tone of voice warned me not to press.

He let me drive. I glanced his way from time to time, but his eyes were closed. I didn't think he was asleep. After an hour or so on the road north he stirred and said, "Bess. I don't like the direction this is taking. If Wade is in France, there's more to this than we could possibly have imagined."

I'd thought about that before, when I knew Lieutenant Wade had been wounded and at the Base Hospital in Rouen at the time the fire had been set.

"Simon. What if the photograph I bought in Petersfield is only part of the story? We showed it to the Gesslers. He couldn't remember it, of course. All he could tell us was when it was taken and for whom. Not who the children were. But what if, after we left, those faces stayed in his mind. A photographer deals in faces. Or places. And in a day or two, let's say, he begins to recall when he's seen one of the children before. But as an adult, someone he photographed in another time and place. Like the racehorse or Queen Victoria in her carriage."

"Go on."

"I don't know what happened next. Did he write to someone? Or did someone come to call? However it was, although our photograph was already beyond reach, there were still Mr. Gessler's files. And his memory. Something that would mean trouble if connections were made. Kill Mr. Gessler before he or his files become a source of interest to the police. Or to someone."

"You could be right. As long as that photograph was locked away in an attic, all well and good. But if whoever it is learned that the house was for sale, he would have a very good reason to worry that when the attics were emptied, the photograph and whatever else is up there might come to light. Even accidentally. As in fact it has."

"This takes us back to the Caswells and the children in their care. Among them Lieutenant Wade. Simon, do you think you could persuade Scotland Yard to let you see the files on the Caswell murders?"

"I don't know. It's worth a try. The Army might also have copies of those files. I'll have to come up with an acceptable reason."

"The Gessler fire?"

"No," Simon answered slowly. "Information that would have some direct bearing on the case. The Subedar is dead. He can't be questioned. We could use his sighting as our excuse."

"The Army might well contact the Colonel Sahib."

Simon grinned, and I could tell at once that he was feeling a little better. "I'll request the information in the Colonel's name. Pull over just there, Bess. I'll drive the rest of the way."

Chapter Eleven

My next leave was only forty-eight hours, too short to travel to London, and Dover was crowded, noisy, busy.

I found a telephone in the office of the Port Commandant, and called Melinda Crawford.

I was told she was staying with friends in Canterbury, and they were on the telephone. And so my second call was to the Russells.

When Melinda was brought to the telephone, she was excited at the prospect of seeing me, and promised to send her chauffeur straightaway to fetch me.

"I don't want to interrupt your visit," I said, trying to keep the disappointment out of my voice. I had hoped to ask a favor of her. I'd had a little time to think about matters while waiting for the connection to go through.

"Nonsense, my dear. I was leaving for home this noon. I'll just make it a few hours ahead of time. Jessica will understand."

"Cousin Melinda? Do you think we might call on Mr. Kipling? I have a few questions about India I'd like to put to him."

"I don't see why not. I'll telephone him at once. He invited me to lunch with him the last time I was there. I'll offer to take him somewhere for his tea."

And she rang off.

Fifteen minutes later, she called to say that she was on her way and would be in Dover as soon as may be.

Knowing how her driver handled the motorcar, I took that with a grain of salt and went to find breakfast. Afterward I walked along the shore and listened to the guns in France, across the Channel. They seemed to be pounding the sectors on both sides of the line, without regard to rumors of an armistice.

I had started up the hill to Dover Castle, where I hoped to find an officer I knew, when a motorcar came barreling toward me and slowed. A trunk and two valises were strapped to the boot, and I could see two other boxes in the seat next to Melinda's driver.

I greeted him in Urdu, for he was one of her Indian staff, and he returned the greeting as if I were a Maharani. He had always spoiled me.

Melinda poked her head out the window. "Well, this makes it so much easier, my dear. I thought we might have to scour the port."

Her driver was already opening the door for me. I got into the back beside Melinda and she gave me an enormous hug.

"It's so good to see you. Still, you look tired, my dear. I expect we all do, with this war going on and on, no end in sight. I did put through a call to your mother, to tell her that I was going to be seeing you. She and your father send their best love. And she wanted to ask what you might know about Simon's wounds. They didn't see him until after you'd left, and he refuses to talk about what happened. Your mother says they're healing but she's quite worried."

Simon had been least in sight after bringing me home from Petersfield. He'd left me at the door and disappeared into his own cottage. But he couldn't hide forever, and the bruises would have been there for much longer than my leave.

"An unavoidable accident," I said, and Melinda smiled.

"That's precisely what the Sergeant-Major told your mother. He's a dear man, our Simon. I hope he hasn't made any . . . unexpected enemies."

"I can promise you that all is well, and you can pass that on to my mother." I sincerely hoped that I was telling the truth.

Melinda had been as fond of Simon as if he had been her own. Childless, she had never remarried after her husband's death. I loved her as I would a favorite aunt, rather than a distant Crawford cousin.

We talked about the war most of the way to Bateman's. It was well past four by the time we got there, and Mr. Kipling was standing in his doorway, looking at his watch, when we came down the drive and pulled up by the front walk.

He was alone this weekend, as it happened, Mrs.Kipling and their daughter Elsie having gone to visit friends in Torquay. It was too late to think of going anywhere and so we sat on the terrace overlooking the lawns and drank lemonade while Melinda and Mr. Kipling chatted like the old friends they were. She was the only person I knew who called Mr. Kipling by his first name, Joseph.

At length he turned to me and said, peering over his glasses, "Well, Sister Crawford. You've been patient for three-quarters of an hour. What is it you wish to ask me?"

I had to smile. "How did you know?"

"You stare out across the gardens with that faraway look of someone only half listening. Not bored—therefore, waiting your turn to speak."

"I was never sent home from India to be educated. But you and your sister were. Can you tell me about that? What it was like—"

I stopped short. His face had darkened, his eyes narrowing in anger.

"I'm so sorry," I began, stumbling over my apology.

He turned to me. "Not your fault, my dear. You couldn't have known. And I can't talk about it. Let me only say that it was the most shocking experience a child can suffer, short of the death of a parent. Helpless, afraid, abused, and no escape."

I sat there, stunned. "I didn't know," I said after a moment, embarrassed to have given him such pain.

"How could you have? I have learned since that I was not alone in my suffering. There were good people who took in children to educate and promote. And there were others who did it for money, sadistic people who cared nothing for those committed to their care."

The Middletons, who had treated their charges as their own. And the Caswells? How had they treated the children?

Mr. Kipling was frowning. "What brought this to mind, my dear? Something must have done."

"There was a family in Hampshire. We think they also took in children. And it's possible that many years later they were murdered by one of their charges, at that time a young man. I wondered what could possibly have gone wrong."

It was his turn to be surprised. "I see. Rather drastic of him. Although to be honest I never spoke of what I endured. I knew that to do so would mean far worse suffering. There was my sister Trixie, you see. I couldn't take the chance of putting her at risk as well. They were kind to her, in their own way. I never understood why I was singled out for torment. Who knows? If they had touched her, I might have felt murderous myself."

I could see Lieutenant Wade's face as he learned of Alice Standish's death. And his question—*Are they sure?*—about the cause of death, and his insistence on traveling with Mrs. Standish all the way to the Middletons' home, when he could have put her on the next train, once they had reached London.

Had he been suspicious about the cause of his sister Georgina's death? There was the unopened birthday present, the little Dresden shepherdess. Had she died before she could be given it? Or had it been withheld maliciously?

I didn't have to remind myself that it was on this same leave that Lieutenant Wade had been sought as the killer of the Caswell family—mother, father, daughter.

My thoughts were in a whirl.

Mr. Kipling reached out and touched my hand. "It's in the past,

Bess. Let it go." And after a moment he said with false cheer, "You must come with me to the mill. I have sacks of flour the Army didn't take away. Wheat flour! Can you believe it? You'll take one home with you, Melinda."

And so we got up and walked through the gardens to the mill, as once Simon and I had done not so very long ago, crossing the little bridge over the noisy little stream.

I listened to the two old friends talking, made an effort to take part, as if I had indeed let the past go. And my performance must have outshone anything on the London stage, because as we were leaving, Mr. Kipling took my hand for a moment and said, "I'm glad you're all right. Don't stir up what's best forgotten."

"I wouldn't know where to begin," I said truthfully.

His eyes behind the glasses were sharp, like his mind. "There were nursemaids and doctors and housekeepers and gardeners. They too held their tongues. One must ask why . . ."

And then we were moving down the drive, through the late Sussex afternoon, dust motes dancing in the sunbeams that picked out the meadows and stands of trees. Mr. Kipling had invited us to stay for dinner, but it had already been a long day for Melinda, and we had had to decline.

"I had no idea," I said to Melinda in apology. "I would never have asked Mr. Kipling about coming to England as a child if I'd even dreamed he was—if such things had happened to him."

She took my hand. "I shouldn't worry, my dear. He knew that. We've been friends for many years, Joseph and I, and he's never spoken to me about his childhood. I understand now why he wouldn't. Or couldn't."

We were silent for a while as the motorcar reached the dusty main road and turned toward Kent.

After a time, Melinda said, "You're thinking about that young Lieutenant Wade, aren't you? What's brought him to your attention after all this time?"

"I didn't want my parents to know. You mustn't tell them until we can be sure. But a dying Subedar from Agra told me he'd seen Lieutenant Wade in France. I believed him. He had no reason to lie, as far as I can judge. I'd been told very little about what had happened in 1908. I've only just discovered who his other victims, the Caswells, were, or that it was very likely that they'd taken in children like Mr. Kipling and his sister. I expect I'm trying to understand why anyone would kill five people, two of them his own parents. This was a man I knew. That my mother and father knew and trusted."

"I read about the murders, of course. And the hunt for the Lieutenant. I keep up with any news of the regiment. It was in the London papers, but also in the Indian papers that are sent to me regularly. No motive was given for any of the murders, except perhaps that he'd killed his parents before the news of the Caswells' deaths could reach India. They were shot in their sleep, as I recall. They must have died instantly. It would explain so much if what you suggest is true."

It would. Drastic measures in the minds of most people. But for a man knowing that his time was short and that what he'd done would be catching up with him, and caring too much about how his parents would feel, shooting them in their sleep might have seemed to be a kindness.

Then why hadn't we seen any tension or other signs of distress in Lieutenant Wade between the time he had returned from Agra and England and the time the Military Foot Police came looking for him?

On the other hand, perhaps he'd felt no distress. Perhaps he'd held his parents responsible for sending their children to England in the first place.

How cold-blooded. Or perhaps it was not even that, perhaps he knew that if he showed nothing, his chances of escape if he was caught out would be better.

And that's precisely what had transpired.

Or appeared to have happened. Cold-blooded indeed.

I said, "Someone else appears to be worried about the past coming out. Someone who had nothing to do with the murders. But who stands to be caught in the publicity if there is a renewed interest in the Caswells?"

"Is that how Simon came to have his bruises?"

"I must presume so."

"Then you've awakened a sleeping snake, my dear. And you and Simon must take great care. A cobra strikes before you know he's there, curled up in the tangled roots of a banyan tree. Or lying quietly in the high grass before you come along and step on it. And then sadly it's too late."

It was a warning I took to heart.

I spent the night at Melinda's comfortable house in Kent, and in the morning, after breakfast, Ram took me to Dover and waited until my ship arrived in port before leaving. It was kind of him.

Before I'd slept that night at Melinda's, I found stationery and an envelope in the drawer of the desk in my room and wrote a long letter to Simon. I posted it in Dover before boarding. It would not have to pass through the hands of a censor, and so I could put on paper everything I'd learned.

I realized as I got out of the ambulance at the forward aid station where I was posted this time that we were all weary. Four years of war had taken its toll. The wounded men brought in to us, the staff, and the ambulance drivers, all were hollow-eyed. Even the vehicles were forever breaking down from overuse and from being maneuvered on what passed for roads, the ruts and ditches and pits sometimes covering half a mile in width. Tanks had been through one section, churning up the mud, and a caisson had bogged down in another stretch.

We saw quite a few Americans as they pushed hard to drive the Germans back. They reminded me of Captain Barclay, an American serving with a Canadian regiment. Polite but also very unreserved.

These men called me Nurse rather than Sister, and one or two asked if I was engaged or was walking out with anyone. I told them that I was engaged to the Prince of Wales and he would clap them in the Tower if they didn't do as they were told. They roared with laughter and took to calling me Your Royal Highness, much to the displeasure of Dr. Hilton, who thought them disrespectful in the extreme. But they also looked after their own and made no complaint when we had to cut a uniform off a shattered shoulder or a boot off a rotting foot. Many of them had never been more than a dozen miles from home before they enlisted—like so many British soldiers—and coming out of the ether they often called for their mothers.

And then the Yanks were gone and we were back to the Tommies, who demanded to know in mock seriousness if we'd given our hearts away to the enemy.

The next convoy I took to Britain came into Portsmouth in the middle of the night. I'd managed to find a telephone and called my parents to tell them I had no more than thirty-six hours of leave before sailing for France again, but that I was all right. The influenza epidemic of the spring had returned with a vengeance, just as predicted, and was more virulent than ever. Those who had escaped the first wave were falling ill now. Since I had survived the disease, and a very severe case at that, I had already been told I'd be returning to a base hospital to work with the latest victims. We had been warned that this was a deadlier strain, and there had been reports—none of which had been verified—that steam shovels had been brought in to some hospitals to dig mass graves. It had been good to hear my mother's voice, and then my father's, and be reassured that they were all right.

I went to the canteen and sat there over a cup of tea, wondering if I could find a room in a hotel, when Simon Brandon walked through the door. His bruises healed, he looked fit and preoccupied.

I don't know which of us was more surprised. He came across the room to greet me and sat down at my table.

"Good God," he said. "You do appear in the most amazing places!"

"I could say the same about you. What brings you to Portsmouth?"

"It's not for your ears," he said with a grin, and then he turned to look out the canteen window. A light rain had begun to fall, and the wind was pushing ships at anchor, making their running lights bob with the outgoing tide. When he looked at me again, he said more seriously, "I've been teaching infantry tactics to tank crews. A brave lot, those men. Shut into a metal coffin, only one way out. It doesn't bear thinking of. But since the Somme they've made tremendous strides in tactics."

I'd attended some of the men from inside those tanks, their flesh burned black as soot from the fire inside, their hands and faces and feet peeling red beneath the black.

"Are you on your way to Somerset or London?"

"Neither. I've spoken to my parents. I only have a few hours left."

"Then it's good I found you. Where are you billeted?"

"I'm not. I'll find a hotel and sleep a few hours."

"There's room in my quarters. I'll take you there."

I finished my tea and went with Simon. On the way I asked if he had read my letter, the one posted in Dover after visiting Melinda.

"Yes, it came while I was away. I retrieved it when I passed through Somerset some days later. I think it's very possible that the Caswells took in Anglo-Indian children. That photograph appears to confirm it, and the box you bought, along with the little chair, indicates Lieutenant Wade's sister was there, and it isn't very likely that he'd be sent to a different family."

Simon had taken rooms in a house near the center of town, and I sank down in the chair by the window in his sitting room.

"I think I could sleep for a month," I said, leaning back.

"Go ahead. But before you're beyond hearing what I have to say, let me tell you what has happened. The police in Winchester have been rather busy. They are looking for and interviewing everyone who called on the Gesslers in the past three months. The list isn't long—the shop has been closed for some time. But it appears that we're on it. It seems a neighbor across the street remembers a man and a woman who called rather late and stayed for about an hour. The neighbor had a toothache and couldn't sleep."

"We're suspects?" I asked, wide awake now.

"Apparently. The newspapers are carrying a request for this pair to contact them to help with their inquiries. At a guess I'd say we appear to be the last people to see the Gesslers alive."

"It's too bad the neighbor with the toothache wasn't at his or her window when the fire was started," I said.

"Quite."

"Should we contact the police?"

"And tell them what?" Simon asked.

I sighed. "I can't see that it would help them if we do. It will only cloud the issue."

"That was my conclusion." He walked away to fetch a blanket and then turned. "Burning two people to death is unconscionable. The killer must have a very strong reason for doing that."

"We've rather lost sight of Lieutenant Wade."

"Someone in Petersfield knows the truth. We need to find that person. If Wade isn't behind the fire, he may well know who is."

He was tired as well. I said, "Simon, go to bed. We've done all we can for now."

"When does your ship sail?"

"At ten tomorrow morning."

He nodded. "I'll see you're awake in time."

As my ship moved out into the roads and turned toward the sea, I thought about our conversation over breakfast.

Simon and I had agreed on one thing.

Whatever we chose to do in the future, we must make very certain that we didn't put anyone else in danger.

We had discussed taking what little we knew to Scotland Yard, rather than the local police in Winchester or Petersfield. But when we had listed what we knew, jotting it all down on a sheet of paper in black ink that stood out baldly against the white background, it was glaringly little.

As he was driving me to the port, Simon glanced at me, then said, "I'm going on to Somerset this afternoon. I don't have to be there at any particular time. It might be interesting to go by way of Midhurst and have a look at the estate agent who has put the property up for sale."

"Just be careful."

In France I spent long, exhausting days at the hospital to which I'd been assigned. They had tried to collect all their influenza cases in hastily constructed quarters where they could be cared for separately from the wounded. There was no surgical ward here. There was no need for it. Instead, long rows of cots held patients in every stage of infection. I was issued strong soap to keep my hands clean and face masks, then Matron accompanied me through the wards, giving me an overview. We hadn't learned much about the illness, but a little more about how to care for the patients.

Tired men, in the filthy living conditions of the trenches and jammed together using the same latrines and drinking the same stale water, were not fit enough to fight off the infection. Or perhaps infection was inevitable. Whatever the case, I worked to save as many as I could, and when that wasn't possible, I tried to make their deaths easier if I could.

One of the Sisters working with me watched the burial detail set out one cool, cloudy morning and said, "If a horse was that ill, or a dog, it would be put down as mercifully as possible."

I had to agree with her, except for the peculiarities of the infection. Sometimes those who had the least hope of surviving managed to pull through. As I had done. While those who appeared to be on the mend could relapse and die in a matter of hours.

A new convoy of patients arrived, were sorted, and carried to their cots. Three were dead before they reached us. One of them was an officer whose leg I had set at a forward aid station six months ago.

And almost on the heels of that convoy came another one. Another Sister was sorting this time, and some of the convalescent patients were moved to a makeshift ward to make room. I had just settled half a dozen men and was starting to work with another ten when I was called to help with a critical case.

He was in a bad way, and I did what I could to help him breathe more easily. It wasn't until I was gently lowering him to the cot once more that I noticed the fading scar along his jaw, that faint white line.

It was Lieutenant Wade. I glanced quickly at the tag that identified him, and saw in a hasty scrawl CORPORAL CASWELL.

There was not time to report his presence here, even if I wished to do so. And from his flushed face and difficulty breathing, it was unlikely that he would live.

But when I came back on duty in the early hours of the next morning, he was one of the men the Sister on night duty thought was showing a little improvement. I took around the cups of soup, all that some of the men could keep down in their paroxysms of coughing, and when I came to Lieutenant Wade, his eyes met mine.

Before I could stop him, he'd reached up and pulled at my mask, and it came down to my chin.

If he hadn't been sure before this, it was obvious he knew who I was now. I could read the expression in his eyes. Surprise. Certainty. Despair. For he could see that I had recognized him as well.

I set down the cup of soup and pulled my mask back into place. Then I held the cup to his lips and let him drink.

Busy elsewhere for the better part of the morning and then in the afternoon occupied with a new line of ambulances, I came back to the ward in time to help with the evening rounds, and Sister Whitby said, "I think we'll lose Caswell, bed sixteen. He showed so much improvement overnight that we were hopeful. Now—it's almost as if he's given up."

And that was my fault, although I hadn't said a word to him about the past.

Surely just my presence was enough.

I felt a surge of guilt, but there was nothing I could do about it. Matron assigned us where we were most needed, and most of us hardly had time to sleep.

I walked down the line of cots to bed sixteen. An orderly was just changing Lieutenant Wade's sheets, the sour smell of sweat lingering in the air. Helping to finish the task, I said to the orderly, "I'll sit with Corporal Caswell for a few minutes."

"Yes, Sister. It might be a good idea." The orderly's way of telling me that the end was near.

I drew up a chair close to the bed. Changing the sheets had tired the patient, and he lay there with eyes shut, his breathing labored. But I was fairly certain he could hear me.

"Corporal Caswell? You were much improved this morning. We had high hopes for you. And now this change. Won't you fight to live? You have survived much worse, I daresay. You must make the effort."

His eyes opened. I'd forgot how blue they were, and the fever racking him made them flash.

"Easier to die this way than hang." His voice was a thread.

"I'm a nursing Sister. I took an oath to save men."

"Not this time. Sorry." He closed his eyes again, stoically waiting for death.

"If I make you a promise," I said rashly, "if I swear to you that I will not hand you over to the Military Foot Police or anyone else, if you can walk out of here and return to your sector, it will be worth living, I think."

His eyes opened, and he stared at me. "You're Crawford's daughter."

And in his view, that was enough to condemn him. He knew,

better than most, what I must feel about the regiment even now, when it was no longer my father's responsibility.

"I'm Sister Crawford. I told you."

"Why would you let me walk away?"

I wasn't really sure of the answer to that myself. "It seems rather unfair to betray you now. But if you die, I promise you that I shall. To set the record straight."

"The record," he said, a world of bitterness in those two words.

I rose. "I'll leave you to think about it. You wanted to live badly enough that you took a terrible risk in 1908. I should think you'd be willing to do the same again."

And I walked away.

I went off duty half an hour later, but I didn't go back to look in on Lieutenant Wade. I had seen patients will themselves to die—most particularly the amputees. And I had seen others who willed themselves to live in spite of the medical prognosis. If I'd had to wager on the chances of Lieutenant Wade surviving until morning, I would have refused. The odds were impossible.

When I walked into the ward the next morning, I saw that bed sixteen was empty.

And I knew I'd lost. Lieutenant Wade—Corporal Caswell—had wanted to die, and so it had come to pass.

Chapter Twelve

As soon as I could spare a few minutes from my duties, I went to find Matron. She was in her tiny office, working on a sheet of paper lined with numbers. I saw the frown as she looked up, annoyed at having her concentration interrupted.

"I'm sorry, Matron. But there's a patient I need to speak to you about."

"Sister Crawford." She sighed. "I don't need to tell you we are being overwhelmed. I simply don't know where to put them all."

I could sympathize. We could have put two men to a cot, it was getting to be so bad.

"How are you holding up?"

"We're all very tired," I said. In the short time I'd worked under her, I'd learned she valued honesty. "But that's to be expected."

"I've asked for more Sisters. I doubt there are any to spare. One of our own has come down with the influenza. It must be the same everywhere else."

"Sister Browning?"

"Yes. How did you know?"

"She wasn't sleeping well last night. I heard her moving around. And then she began to cough. The orderlies came for her at six."

"I promised to look in on her at ten. Now then, what is it I can do for you?"

"It's about Corporal Caswell. There's something you must know." I took a deep breath. "He served some years ago in my father's regiment."

"Did he indeed? I expect he remembered you?"

"I'm afraid he did." I couldn't tell her that once he recognized me he'd willed himself to die. "You see, there was some trouble at the time, and I knew about it." Before I could go on, she smiled and interrupted me.

"I'm glad you brought this to my attention, Sister Crawford. I'll see that you aren't assigned to his ward. It will be more comfortable for both of you."

"But—I thought—his bed was empty this morning when I came on duty."

"Yes, he was much improved, and we moved him to the convalescent ward. I'm not convinced that he was quite ready for the change, but we needed his bed."

I stood there, rapidly reassessing what I had been about to say. I'd almost betrayed my promise—and Corporal Caswell too.

Matron was eager to return to her numbers. "Is there anything else, Sister Crawford?"

"I—no, Matron. Thank you."

I beat a hasty retreat.

Why had I been so certain that Lieutenant Wade had died? Perhaps because it would have been the honorable thing to do, in one sense. I could have reported his real name and his crimes, and the past would have finally been closed. The fact that he had escaped justice in India would have been expunged. The mills of the gods, and all that, but he had in the end been caught.

And I had nearly exposed him, breaking my promise to him.

With the feeling I'd been tricked, I went back to my ward and set to work again.

It was nearly nine o'clock in the evening when I went off duty. I could think of nothing but sleeping, because I'd be back on duty at six. But I took a moment to go to the convalescent ward and look for Lieutenant Wade.

He appeared to be asleep when I came down the row of cots and found him. His breathing was a little easier, but I could hear the rattle in his lungs still. In fact, when the light of my candle touched his face, he began to cough, waking up as he choked on the phlegm in his throat.

I held his shoulders and pounded on his back, helping him clear out the blockage, and he lay back exhausted when it was done.

"Now you can sleep again," I said, picking up my candle. He nodded, eyes closed. I waited for a few minutes to be sure he was asleep, and then I left. I didn't think he had known which Sister had come to his aid. He was far from out of the woods. But he had made up his mind to trust me, and he wanted to live.

As I made my quiet way up the rows, I thought his guilt had never troubled him before, there was no reason to believe he was repentant now. I could only trust to fate that somehow he would be found out, without my help.

When next I came to look in on him, I found him sitting up in his cot, drinking a cup of hot soup. He looked thin—most of the men in our care were terribly thin, thanks to the infection and the loss of appetite, the struggle to swallow and keep anything down.

I said as he finished it, "Would you like another? I'll bring you one."

"Feeding the fatted calf?" he asked, wary.

"Not precisely," I said briskly. "It's more a question of needing the beds. The more food you eat, the sooner you'll be well. And the sooner someone else can lie here."

He passed his free hand over his face. "I don't think I've ever felt so weak. Not even when I got this."

He meant the scar.

"How did you come by that?"

"I made it to Kabul before they found me out. Mostly moving at night, eating whatever I could find. They caught me and sentenced me to death. An infidel in their midst. I made a break for it, they shot me, and I survived. They decided that if God had wanted me dead, the bullet would have flown true. And so they threw me in prison instead. To tell you the truth, I think they forgot I was there. I escaped one night and got away. By that time I spoke the language with some fluency, and I was taken in by a family who thought I'd been set on by bandits and robbed. And so it went. I must have had an enormous store of luck, because I used up most of it. I was a shepherd, a beggar, a wandering holy man, a camel driver, whatever came to hand. I told myself it was an adventure, something I could tell my grandchildren about in my old age. I could write a book about my escape and be forgiven. Ridiculous, of course."

"You did what few Englishmen ever have."

"Yes, well, they didn't have my enthusiasm for the task," he answered wryly.

"Why did you enlist, when war came?"

"It was what I do best. Fight. Only this time I saw war from the point of view of the men in the ranks. There's another book, if you like."

I went to fetch more soup, and Lieutenant Wade drank half of that before setting it aside for later. I left him to rest. And then as the next convoy arrived, I had no time to think about him. For two days we worked with the ill and the dying, and more often than not it was the dying. As I looked at the rows of cots, I thought in despair that half the Army must be here or in similar hospitals. Who was left in the trenches? Would this bloody, all-consuming war end not in Armistice but in empty lines facing each other across No Man's Land? We had seen raw recruits who had never been to the Front die before they could fire a shot. The Germans must be suffering as badly as we were.

I had had two brief messages from home saying that my parents and Simon and the staff were well. But there had been no news from London of Mrs. Hennessey or my flatmates.

I discovered quite by chance that there were several men from the same sector as "Corporal Caswell," and I told them he was a patient, but recovering.

They were pleased to hear that bit of news. Ill as they were, all three of them had a good word for their Corporal.

"He'd have made Sergeant in a flash," one went on. "God knows we are short a few. But he didn't want to leave his unit. He said he'd see us through or know the reason why."

"I thought he was a sapper," I asked another.

"Aye, he was, and a good one. Never left a man behind. But he was transferred out into the line. He and his men. A tunnel went south on them, and he got the last two out, against all odds. He told the Captain he'd had enough of digging in the dark."

"Does he have a temper?" I asked.

Private Burton grinned. "If you aren't quick enough with an order. But he's not killed one of us yet." He broke off in a paroxysm of coughing, and I held him until it was over. After that he was too ill to talk.

Mary, one of my flatmates, had also survived the earlier round of illness, and she arrived one evening just before dusk, bringing in another thirty patients.

I saw her as she was handing her charges over to the Sister who was sorting the cases, and I called her name.

She turned, acknowledged me with an excited wave, and went back to her lists. As soon as those were done, she ran across the muddy ground to where I was waiting.

"Bess! How good it is to see you. Mrs. Hennessey sends her best love. She's missed you. And so have we."

"You're all well? Unbelievable."

"I have to go back with the convoy. But I'd love a cup of tea. Do you have five minutes?"

"Yes, of course." We went to the tiny canteen where the staff could find tea and something to eat at any hour of the day or night, and for a mercy, two chairs were available. Mary went over to them while I found the freshest pot of tea and poured two cups.

"No sugar, I'm afraid."

Mary smiled. "When last I was in London, Mrs. Hennessey had a jar of honey. Simon Brandon brought it to her, compliments of your mother. It was such a luxury."

I was telling her about Diana when the alarm went up. A patient had gone missing.

It was not unusual for someone in the throes of delirium to wander away from his bed, certain he was back in the trenches or somewhere at home. Such patients seldom got far, usually collapsing before a Sister could reach them. Someone stuck her head around the door, glanced about the room—there was nowhere even a mouse could hide—and said, "Not here, then." To us she added, "You'd better come. Bring a torch."

We gulped the last of our tea and hurried to join the search. Mary was saying as we came around to where the convoy was waiting, "It's one of ours. He's been out of his head most of the way here, shouting about the first wave of an attack. Poor man, we had to strap him down."

Someone handed us a torch, and we went to the far end of the convoy. Mary searched the rear of the ambulance while I looked in the driver's door.

Nothing. Before moving on, we each took a side of the ambulance and bent down to sweep the ground beneath the chassis. No one there.

We went to the next vehicle, and this time I searched the back while she opened the driver's door.

I could hear someone shouting from the wards, but then word was passed: *false alarm*. They hadn't found the missing man after all. We went on searching.

We had finished the interior of the fourth ambulance. I bent down to look beneath it just as my torch beam passed over a rumpled length of canvas. By now I was nearly convinced that our lost patient was out there in the dark somewhere. But the ambulances had to be cleared before they could leave. I swept the light over the canvas again. It seemed impossible that it could conceal a man.

"No one here," I called to Mary as I flicked off my torch. "Let's move on."

She reached out to open the back of the fifth ambulance, and the door shrieked, metal on metal. Here, where the guns were only a distant rumble, it jarred the nerves.

I heard the sudden movement almost at my feet, and stepping back, I flicked on the torch again. The beam caught a man's face, and for an instant we stared at each other, Lieutenant Wade and I. And then he was flinging away the canvas, rolling quickly to the far side.

I hadn't known who the patient was until that moment. And it wasn't delirium that had brought the Lieutenant here. He had been counting on escaping when the convoy left, climbing into the back of one of the empty ambulances and leaving it when he felt he was safe to do so. But his empty bed had been discovered too soon.

After all, this was the clever man who had crossed Afghanistan into Persia, and lived to tell about it.

I felt a surge of anger.

"Mary—your side." My tone of voice was enough, and she turned to shout for an orderly.

Lieutenant Wade made it out from under the vehicle, got to his feet, and began to run. But he wasn't strong enough. Mary's torch pinned him as he stumbled, but he regained his balance for another few yards before going down again. With a cry of despair, he struggled to rise, but his body wouldn't obey his will. By the time the first of the orderlies had reached him, he was pounding the hard-packed earth with his fist.

Another orderly was there on the heels of the first one, but in the end we had to send for a stretcher to carry Lieutenant Wade back to his bed. I followed it, and even in the dark I could feel his eyes on me. Accusing. Angry. I think it rankled more that I had been the one to stop him than being unable to escape.

As we settled him in the cot, I said, "You could have had a relapse, you know. A serious one. You can rejoin your men when you are well enough. You won't be much use to them now."

Mary, pouring him a cup of fresh water and holding it for him to sip, added, "You're still contagious. Did you think about that? Do you want to make your comrades ill too?"

He was racked by a coughing fit, then fell back on his pillows, exhausted, eyes closed, shutting us out.

When I came back an hour later, a cup of hot soup in my hands, he said curtly, "I'm sorry. For the trouble I caused."

"Drink this or your fever will come back. You're still too weak to survive it."

And I left him holding the cup.

I managed to send a letter to Simon, but I could say very little. I told him I'd seen Mary and that one of my patients was an old friend from our India days. He replied quickly: *For God's sake, watch yourself!*

I didn't need a reminder that Lieutenant Wade had already killed five people.

I was told by Sister Eliot that Corporal Caswell had been as meek as a lamb since the night he'd tried to rejoin his men. "Very silly of him, but very brave as well."

He had convinced everyone of his intentions. Except me.

I said nothing, just smiled, and kept an unobtrusive eye on the convalescent ward.

One night when the ward Sister was busy with one of the other patients, whose wounded leg was showing signs of infection—a worrisome state of affairs because the man had just recovered from the influenza and was very weak—I walked down the rows of cots and saw that Lieutenant Wade was awake, lying quietly with his eyes open.

"How are you feeling?" I asked, stopping at the foot of the bed.

"Well enough to be hanged," he said bitterly. "Rather useless for anything short of that."

I came round and pulled up a chair.

"I haven't decided what to do about you. I've spoken to several men in your company who are also patients here, and they tell me you're a good soldier. Smart. Steady. Dependable. My father believed you had the same qualities."

He looked away, not answering.

"You're accused of killing so many people. Including your own parents—"

He rose up so quickly on one elbow that I flinched before I could stop myself.

"What are you trying to do?" he demanded in a harsh whisper, his eyes blazing, galvanized by his anger. If he'd lashed out, he would have struck me. "Tell me that I broke my parents' hearts, because they believed I was a killer? I won't listen to this. Go away or I shall summon Matron."

Standing my ground, I said, "Your parents were murdered the night before you left Agra for the cantonment. They were found later that morning. Don't you remember?"

It could explain why he had seemed so normal when he returned from his leave. He had shut out what he'd done, walled it away somehow so that he could face the world.

"They were alive when I said good night to them. I was leaving at four in the morning, I'd told them they needn't get up to see me off."

"But they weren't," I said as gently as I could. "They'd been shot, a pillow over their faces to deaden the sound. That's how the servants found them. That's why the police came to the regiment to find you. Word hadn't come from England then. It caught up with the MFP when they were delayed in Lahore."

He stared blankly at me. I remembered what Simon had told me—that the Subedar's brother had been angry with the Wades over his dismissal. But that didn't make him a murderer, did it? It made just as much sense that Lieutenant Wade had killed his parents before they could learn their *son* was a murderer.

"I thought—" He stopped just short of convicting himself out of his own mouth. *I thought the MFP had come after me because of England. . . .*

But that wasn't what he was about to say. Slumping down onto the cot once more, he stared at the ceiling, such as it was. "I thought it would be best for them."

"To kill them?" I persisted, trying to keep the shock out of my voice at the admission.

"What good would it do if I swore I hadn't killed anyone," he replied wearily, "except in the war? You're Colonel Crawford's daughter. You won't believe me."

Stung, I retorted, "The Colonel has always been a fair man. You know that as well as I do. You could have stayed and faced the charges. If you were innocent, he'd have fought for you."

"Perhaps he would have done. But the evidence was against me from the start. It still is."

"Have you tried to contact your parents, to let them know you were still alive?"

"How could I, without giving myself away? Or putting them in an unconscionable position." He lay there, his face turned away again. "I didn't know they were dead," he whispered. "All these years, and I didn't know."

Did I believe him? Or was he cleverly using everything I'd said to him, twisting to it to suit his own ends.

I could hear Matron coming toward us on her nightly rounds.

"If you *are* innocent, tell me one thing that will let me believe it could be true."

He smiled grimly. "Ask the Caswells. Failing that—"

And Matron was there behind us. Had he timed his remarks so that she would appear to cut him off before he could answer my challenge?

"There you are, Sister Crawford," Matron said after nodding

to Lieutenant Wade. "I've been looking for you. Someone told me you'd gone off duty and were in your quarters."

It wasn't an accusation, although I felt that it was.

"I'm sorry, Matron. I thought I ought to look in on Corporal Caswell. But it appears that his—er—wandering away hasn't caused a relapse. He's very fortunate."

"Yes. Stubborn men often are, I've noticed," she said with a smile for the patient. "Good night, Corporal. I'll walk out with you, Sister."

We made our way out of the ward as the night medicines trolley was being brought around. When we were outside, Matron said, "Would you mind stepping into my office for a moment?"

"Yes, of course, Matron." I followed her to her cramped office and took the chair she offered. I had the sinking feeling I was about to be reminded that I should not take such a personal interest in a patient not my own.

"We've been really pleased with your work here, Sister Crawford."

She was searching on her cluttered desk for a sheet of paper, surely the complaint that had been filed against me. Ironic, I thought, that I should be suspected of an unprofessional relationship with Lieutenant Wade of all the men in France. Finding what she was after, she looked up at me again. "You're a very good nurse. And I must say I am very reluctant to lose you. There is a convoy leaving for England, and the Sister in charge has just fallen ill of this influenza. Because we are closer to Dover, I have been asked to spare someone who has extensive experience with wounds."

Stunned, I sat there, not knowing what to say. All I could think about was what I must do about Lieutenant Wade before I left. I could ask the MFP to come at once and arrest him. I should do just that. Promise or no promise. I opened my mouth to begin explaining my problem. And then I remembered the Gesslers. And the fire that killed them. If Lieutenant Wade hadn't killed them—who had? What did those deaths have to do with the Caswells?

We knew what name "Corporal Caswell" was using now. If he didn't go back to his company when he was discharged from the hospital, he would be hunted down and shot for desertion. He *had* to go back to his company. And if he did, my father and Simon could find him.

I could feel the long day dulling my ability to come to a decision. Before I could make up my mind, Matron nodded. "Yes, it's a shock, I'm sure. But we'll request your return to us, and I hope the request will be honored." She put the sheet aside. "My dear, there's nothing I can do. You must be ready to leave at five in the morning tomorrow. You'd better get some sleep. I'll see that someone wakes you in time. Are your ward reports in order?"

"Yes, Matron. But there's something else—"

"I'm sorry, Sister. There's nothing I can do. Sadly." Rising, she came around her desk. "Go to London. You're needed on that convoy."

I rose and accompanied her to the door. "There's Corporal Caswell."

"He's recovering, and I think he's aware that what he did was very foolish. You needn't worry. I believe you said before that he was in your father's former regiment?"

Avoiding answering, I said, "It's just that—he isn't what he appears to be."

Matron nodded. "I've suspected as much myself. He must be from a good family, well educated. Why he's not an officer is his business. I expect there's something in his background. The ranks needed men, and the Army was not particular about how it got them. I don't feel it's my place to inquire. If he's a good soldier, we can ask nothing more of him. Now go to bed."

"But, Matron," I protested.

She put a hand on my arm. "Are you—is there something between you and Corporal Caswell?"

"No!" I said at once, dismayed that she would think such a

thing—but then I had brought it on myself with my personal comments about a patient. "I—it's just that I have—it's a matter of responsibility to—"

"Then that does you credit. I shouldn't have doubted you. Go on. I must complete my rounds."

I thanked her and walked away, my thoughts in turmoil. If I went to see Corporal Caswell now, it would appear on my record. I had no business in that ward. If I said nothing, he would be discharged and returned to duty. Whether he actually arrived there was another matter.

I wished I could speak to Simon. But I knew what he would tell me.

Either call the MFP or walk away.

I went to bed. But I didn't sleep. When a Sister came to wake me in time to dress and leave for Dover, I was ready, my kit packed and closed.

I said, "Keep an eye on Corporal Caswell," as she walked with me to the waiting ambulance. "He—he's not to be trusted." It was as far as I could go without telling her the whole story.

"Yes, that's true enough." Sister Bailey laughed. "He's flirted with all the Sisters. Nothing serious, of course, just passing the time. He knows how charming he is."

I bit my lip. "Still, be careful."

"Always."

I got into the ambulance, thinking that I should have asked Matron to call the MFP after all.

But would anyone have listened to me? "Corporal Caswell" had seen to it that everyone believed he was a lovely man, while giving me nothing to be going on with.

After we reached London it required three days to escort all my charges to their destinations. Blind patients went to a lovely house in Essex, while those with shattered bones continued to Suffolk, where the care was extraordinary.

I discovered that the nurse I'd replaced was due a short leave, and

I was expected to take it in her stead, although I had volunteered to go back to France.

Paperwork, apparently, would be impossibly confused, so said the doctor in Suffolk. The lorries that had conveyed us there had no instructions about returning me to Dover, only to London.

I managed to put in a telephone call to Somerset before I left Suffolk, and so my father was there to meet me when I arrived outside the barracks.

He looked well, although the strain of this war had touched him too. Everyone was well at home, he assured me, although several friends had died of the contagion that was rampant. One of them was the mother of a girl I'd known in India.

After looking in on Mrs. Hennessey, the Colonel Sahib and I went on to Somerset. We were halfway there and had stopped for tea when my father said, "You and Simon have been busy. We've hardly seen you on your last few leaves."

I could feel myself flushing and looked down. "You've been away as well. And Portsmouth was so short a stay that I couldn't have come home at all. Fortunately Simon was there to rescue me and give me a night's lodging. The town is full."

"Yes, I'm glad of that. Your mother worries when you stay alone at a hotel."

That made me smile. "How like her to worry about that, when I crisscross France in the company of strange men."

He laughed but said, "Crime doesn't go away in wartime."

That sadly was true.

"Still, there's something going on, Bess. And you might as well tell me now, or I'll put Simon on the spot."

"No, he doesn't deserve that. All right, if you must know." I sighed as I looked around. The next tables were too close, we could be overheard. "It's a long story. And a confusing one. Wait until we're back in the motorcar."

We finished our tea and left. I tried to think how best to start my tale, and in the end decided to begin with the Subedar.

My father's face tightened as I described what I had seen, and how Simon and I had gone to Petersfield and even to Winchester. But I stopped short of telling him that I had treated Lieutenant Wade and then left him in a convalescent ward in France. Or that I'd learned the name he was using now. He would feel compelled to act on that information. Best to leave the Lieutenant's whereabouts vague.

"You should have told me. Straightaway," my father admonished me.

"We had nothing to be going on with. For all we knew, the Subedar had been mistaken. For all we knew, the man I'd glimpsed was someone who looked rather like how I believed Lieutenant Wade might look now. Perhaps if I hadn't spoken to the Subedar, I would never have seen such a likeness at all. Perhaps I was expecting to see what I saw."

It was jumbled, but my father nodded.

"And you didn't want to bring up the past when there was so little to go on. That's understandable."

He was silent for a time, and then he said, "There aren't many men who could have done what Wade did. And of all the men under me at the time, I'd have said that Simon was the only one who could have got through. His knowledge of languages would have saved him, and he didn't have Wade's lighter eyes to make people take a second look. But there are light-eyed Afghans and others in that part of the world who are fair. It would be interesting to know how Wade accomplished it."

"Did you think he was guilty, when the MFP came looking for him?"

"In 1908? I thought they were wide of the mark. I'd have backed him up if he'd stayed and stood trial. But then he fled. And I could see why—the proof I was shown was overwhelming."

"Still, it could have been overwhelming—but wrong. I rode with him any number of times after he came back from England. You always sent me out with an escort, and he volunteered if he was off duty. There was nothing—*nothing*—that could have convinced me that he'd killed his mother and father only nine weeks before. Surely that would have changed him in some fashion."

It was a theme I kept returning to—why hadn't Lieutenant Wade suffered visibly for what he'd done? It would have made him more—human—in my eyes. The answer was always, *He had to carry it off or betray himself too soon. . . .* Judging him by my own standards was useless.

"You said that Simon is pursuing the Subedar's past?"

"Yes. I was considering asking Mr. Kipling if his contacts in India could tell us any more."

"All right then, go ahead. But there remain the three deaths in Petersfield."

"I know."

He glanced my way. "I have met one or two men in my lifetime who could kill and show no remorse. I don't mean soldiers who must kill in the course of their duties. I'm speaking of someone who appears to be quite pleasant, and yet who could walk up to a stranger with no reason on earth to like or dislike him, and in cold blood kill him without turning a hair. One such man was in my command early on, and I had him discharged and tried for what he'd done."

I shivered even in the warm sunlight coming through the windscreen.

The description could very well fit Lieutenant Wade. Hadn't he charmed the other nursing Sisters, effectively spiking my guns if I'd broken my promise and betrayed him?

I had to ask. I wanted my father's opinion. "Do you think Lieutenant Wade is one of these men?"

He took a deep breath, and I knew he was finding it hard to be fair. "Ten years ago, I'd have said it was impossible. Now? I don't have an answer for you. Just—be careful, Bess."

It was an echo of what Simon had said to me already.

Chapter Thirteen

We talked of other things after that. But ten miles from home, I asked the Colonel Sahib, "Do you think we should tell Mother? About Lieutenant Wade?"

"We might as well," he said, resigned to the inevitable. "She'll find out sooner or later."

Before I went to bed that night, I wrote to Mr. Kipling. I told him what I could about the death of Mr. and Mrs. Wade, and about the Subedar's brother, and asked him if he could use his contacts in India to look into the matter.

Mr. Kipling had known so many people out there. In the newspaper business, in the Army, in the police. If anyone could discover useful information about that brother, it was he.

Simon was away, and so I spent several days enjoying being home, as much as I could, given what was happening in France, the war, the epidemic. Not to mention Corporal Caswell's whereabouts.

My mother broached the subject of Lieutenant Wade one afternoon when we were in the kitchen, putting up jars of plums.

"I don't know what to tell you about the man," she said, setting aside the jar she had been working with and reaching for another. "I was content when he volunteered to see Mary Standish safely to England, and I wasn't surprised that he took her all the way to the Middletons. That was a kindness."

But was it? I asked myself. Was he merely trying to be sure little Alice had died of natural causes, or to see if whatever had happened to his own sister had happened to her? After all, it was not until he knew for certain that Mary Standish was not going to travel with him back to India that he killed the Caswell family. Would they still be alive if Mary Standish had decided to return to her husband? I couldn't put that out of my mind.

My mother wiped her hands on her apron and stared out the window at the summer sunlight beating down on the gardens. "I'd always told myself that if I could have seen his face—Lieutenant Wade's—as the MFP took him into custody, I'd have known whether he was guilty or not. But of course that never happened." She picked up another jar and began to fill it with the fruit.

I had seen his face when I told him his parents were dead—and I hadn't been able to judge anything. Whether he was lying about not knowing or if he thought I would have doubts about his guilt if I was convinced he hadn't known about two of the murders.

"Well," my mother said, as we finished the last of the jars, "we aren't going to solve the puzzle of Lieutenant Wade this afternoon, are we?"

And we dropped the subject, walking out to the orchard to see how the apple crop was coming.

When Simon arrived at last, I had no chance to speak to him alone. It was the next morning before I could walk down to the cottage, just before breakfast.

He was awake, sitting in the back garden with a cup of tea in his hand and the pot at his elbow on a white-painted iron table.

"Hullo," he said. "There's another cup just inside the door. I rather thought you'd be coming over."

I smiled, but I still hadn't made up my mind how much to tell him. Would he and my father feel that they had no choice but to take measures to arrest Lieutenant Wade? I had a little time. I needn't make the decision straightaway, I told myself as I brought out the extra cup and poured myself a little of the tea. The milk in the jug was fresh, and there was a pot of honey beside it. I sighed with pleasure as I took my first sip.

"I want to go back to Petersfield. I know, there are problems with that. But I would like to go all the same."

"I looked into the estate agent who is handling The Willows. Nothing I learned about him seemed to be of interest. He's been in that same location for some years, his reputation is good, and because of a bad foot he's not in the war. Then I called on him. I'd put his age closer to forty than to thirty. When I mentioned The Willows, he showed no reaction whatsoever. I asked if he'd seen the property himself, and he said he had not. Nor could he tell me anything about the history of the house, only that it was far too large for the present owner."

"All the more reason to go back to Petersfield."

"I rather thought you would suggest that. The day is yours." He grinned at me. "What's this you wrote to me about a friend from our India days. Don't tell me you actually had Wade as a patient?"

"I haven't said anything to my parents. But yes, I did. He tried to make me believe he hadn't known about his parents' death—only about the three here in England. And he couldn't have known, could he, if he escaped before he spoke to the Military Foot Police?"

"Surely if he had tried to contact them, he'd have found out."

"He said he dared not try, that it would prove he'd survived. And he's clever, Simon, the men under him think he's a good soldier, the Sisters and even Matron thought him a lovely man. I tried to tell them they were wrong, but no one would listen. And I was sent away to bring another convoy across, while he was still a patient."

He turned to stare at me. "Are you quite serious? Yes, you are. You should have called in the police yourself."

"The fact that I was Colonel Crawford's daughter might have carried some weight. But the Army already knew him as Corporal Caswell, and I'm sure he had an unblemished record. Well, of course it was unblemished, he didn't dare step out of line for fear in any inquiry someone might stumble over his real past while looking into his background." I couldn't tell him about my promise—he'd have thought it mad.

"There's that dead Subedar, Gupta."

"But we don't know for certain who shot him. The Subedar could have seen him somewhere, just as I did. It doesn't mean he followed the Lieutenant to the Front. I think that if Thomas Wade had shot him, the Subedar would have said something about that, if only to reinforce his account of having spotted the man. It would have been a telling point."

"Then what was he doing so near the Front lines? Why would he have risked his life going that close to the trenches? He must have been tracking Wade."

"That's true." I took a deep breath. "Of course, there's his brother. If the Lieutenant had been caught and tried for the murder of his own parents, there was no reason for guilt to fall on the Subedar's brother. Perhaps the brother *hadn't* killed anyone—but the Subedar suspected he might have done."

"There must have been hundreds of other men at the Front who had served with Wade over his career. Why didn't they recognize the man?"

"Because he chose the sappers, not the infantry. It was only recently that he was posted to that regiment. And because in the chaos of trenches, people have more to think about than India ten years ago."

"Or because," Simon suggested, "he saw to it that anyone who might have begun to wonder or ask questions caught a bullet in the back during the next attack."

I remembered what my father had said about someone who killed without remorse.

"Well, it's not too late. He must still be a patient, he was too weak to return to his company. Have him taken into custody before he's discharged."

"We'll go to Petersfield, first, shall we?" Simon asked, setting his cup back on the tray.

"I'll tell Mother. Ten minutes?"

"Agreed." He took my cup from me and added, "Bess. We don't know if or how Wade and the Gesslers are connected. We can't afford to be rash."

"I know. I've thought about that too." I could still see the faint outline of the bruise on his cheek.

Ten minutes later, we were pulling out of the drive and on our way to Petersfield.

The day that had begun with a lovely summer clear sky was growing cloudy by the time we reached Hampshire, and by Petersfield, we could see black clouds gathering way out to sea, hovering on the far horizon.

By two o'clock, we were driving into Church Square in the heart of the village. It was quiet at this hour, for this wasn't market day.

We left the motorcar by a milliner's shop, and Simon had just come round to open my door when he saw Mr. Gates crossing the lower part of the square and disappearing down the High Street. Head down, the man looked haunted, and I felt pity for him.

"Let's go into the churchyard. Give him a head start," Simon suggested, and I agreed.

It was quiet too. I wondered if the sexton was looking out a window of one of the houses on the lane that ran on the far side of the churchyard, but there was no help for it if he was.

We paused by the Caswell tombstones, standing there busy with our own thoughts, when someone spoke from just behind us.

"Knew them, did you?"

We turned to see an elderly man standing there, leaning on a rosewood cane. He looked to be sixty-five, at the most seventy. It was hard to judge, for other than the cane, he appeared to be fit.

I realized that he'd been speaking to Simon, not to me.

"I'm not sure," Simon said. "The name is familiar."

"You're too young to be one of their lads," the man replied, squinting to look up at Simon.

"My elder brother." Simon had no brothers, but I said nothing. "Dead in the war, you see."

"Yes, well, a pilgrimage, like." The old man nodded. "I was sexton at St. Peter's when they were put into the ground. Another young gentleman was here not long ago—July, it must have been. Or just after I'd come from having my back seen to. Lumbago, they said it was. At any rate, he was standing by these graves at dusk, a lonely figure somehow. I came across to speak to him. He said he needed to see their graves. The way he spoke, I thought perhaps it made him feel better, knowing they were well taken care of in death."

I had the oddest thought—that he'd come to see they were indeed dead and buried. An exorcism . . .

I wanted to glance at Simon, to follow his lead. But when he said nothing, I asked, "Did you catch his name? He could have known our brother."

"If he told it, I don't remember."

Simon asked, "You must have seen the children at The Willows often. Attending church, coming into the village on market day or for an outing."

"They never came into Petersfield as a rule. Sometimes for Sunday services, of course, but even that was rare. The Caswells had a chapel in their house, and services were conducted there. But I saw the children from time to time. Out on the Common, or walking in the woods. Down by the stream. Never near enough to speak to."

"I have a photograph of them that my brother sent to us out in India. Perhaps you could put names to the faces there."

"Oh, I doubt it after all this time." He pointed across the churchyard. "Now that one I remember. The little Wade girl. Pretty as a picture. It like to broke my heart when she died. And such a small casket. She was the only typhoid case we had that entire spring. Sometimes it's the little ones who can't pull through. Too small, too frail."

"Was she frail?" I asked. "My brother thought she was in good health."

"They said she was frail. That's all I know. The doctor of the time could have told you. He attended her in her last hours."

"Where is he now?"

"He moved from Petersfield at the turn of the century, I think it was. Up to Lincolnshire where his sister lived. She was the widow of a doctor and he took over that practice."

That matched what we'd been told before.

"How many children did they have living there at a time? The Caswells. Do you know?"

"The most at a time was eight, as I remember. Mr. Caswell's money ran out, so rumor had it, although some thought it was bad investments. And they were gentry, they couldn't very well go out to work or take in boarders, could they? At any rate, they began to take in these children from India whose parents wished them to be properly educated. There was a governess and a tutor to prepare them for boarding school, with lessons in deportment and the like."

"Were they still taking in children at the time they were killed?"

"It had stopped by then. Well before then, in fact. After the governess died."

"When was this?"

"After your brother's day, I'd say. We were told she was never able to regain her spirits after her fiancé died in South Africa. Killed by the Boers, he was. Bloody business. She drowned herself in the little stream. But the doctor said he couldn't be sure she killed herself, she could have fallen and hit her head, then drowned before she came to again. I don't know. But that allowed her to be laid to rest in hallowed ground. She's over there, near the wall. She had wanted to leave, to find another position. She told me that herself. But she couldn't get up the courage. She said it more than once. Mrs. Caswell told me it was a great pity, that she'd tried to convince Miss Grant to go. But it was too much on top of her loss."

"Have any of the others come back?" Simon asked.

"If they did I'd have no way of knowing unless I was in the churchyard and seen them wandering about, looking at the stones. This is a favorite walk of mine. Most of my family and many of my friends are here, around me. Don't grow old. It's a lonely business."

"I'd have liked to learn the children's names. Perhaps they could tell me about my brother."

"You were too young to be sent to England with him, I daresay. Now Mabel Gooding might know. She was hired as a nursery maid, but it was usually Mabel who was present when the doctor was called in for an illness, not Mrs. Caswell or the governess. No training, you understand, Sister," he added, turning to me. "But if you were sick, now, and needed a cool hand on your brow or a soft voice in your ear telling you you were going to be just fine, there was no one like her. Even after she left the Caswells, she never lacked for work."

Many villages had such women, skilled in caring for the sick, sitting with them at the doctor's suggestion or just appearing on the doorstep when word reached them that a woman was in labor or a child had croup or a man had cut himself in the fields. Sometimes they were the only medical care for miles. But Petersfield had a doctor.

"Where can we find her?" I asked.

"She lives in that small cottage near the Common," he said. "Well, my back is tired, I need to start out for home." He nodded, and turned to walk away.

"Wait," I said, putting out a hand to stop him. "Who killed the Caswell family? We were never told. Does anyone know who it was? Was someone taken into custody?"

"One of the boys, that was what Scotland Yard had to say about it. But we knew better."

"How better?" I asked, trying to keep my voice calm and interested.

"It was bound to be someone who wanted what they had, but they wouldn't give it to him. And nobody has found it since then."

"What did they have?"

The old man smiled. "It was one of the lads who told the tale. That there was a statue or some such in the house. One of the children had brought it with him from India, and it was filled with diamonds."

"Who was this boy?"

He scratched his chin. "I couldn't tell you his name if my life depended on it. Besides, he called himself something foreign, and claimed he was a prince in disguise. Always running away from The Willows. We'd find him in the post office or the ironmonger's or even in the churchyard, telling anyone who would listen about this hoard. He was very earnest about it. Perhaps he even believed it. But most everyone thought he was taking us for fools. Well, then. Good evening."

And he was off, leaning heavily on his cane, and I felt guilty for keeping him so long. "An Indian idol filled with diamonds?" Simon was saying. "It's an old tale, old as the first Englishman's arrival in India. Diamonds in the foreheads of idols. Solid gold gods you could carry away in your pocket. Maharajah's rings or turban ornaments with rubies the size of hen's eggs. Many of them connected with a curse for good measure."

"But the boy's audience didn't know better. I wonder why he did it? For attention? Or was he trying to cause trouble for the Caswells in the only way he could think of?"

"He couldn't have been very happy there, if he ran away from The Willows so often."

While we'd been talking the wind had risen. I said, glancing over my shoulder at the advancing clouds, "Let's find Miss Grant before we go. There's time, don't you think?"

"If we don't have to search too long."

But we didn't. The headstone was low and without distinction, as if it were all the poor woman deserved. Just her name, Phyllis Anne Judith Grant. And the dates. No sentimental line of poetry or scripture, no *Beloved Daughter of* or *Promised Wife of.* Not even a rosebush or patch of pansies in the grass. Forgotten like the little Wade child. But then Miss Grant had possibly been a suicide. . . .

It was when we were hurrying back to the motorcar, the wind bringing drops of rain in its wake, that I stumbled over another low gravestone. Simon caught my arm to steady me. I reached down to massage my shin and as I did I saw the inscription on the stone.

"Simon. Look."

He bent down to clear away the grass that obscured part of what was engraved there.

GEORGE MURRAY ALBERT MAYFIELD, BELOVED SON OF HENRY M. A. AND MARGARET ANNE V. MAYFIELD, and then the dates. Hardly visible in the thick edging of grass below that was carved an elephant, of all things.

"Captain Harry Mayfield, by God," Simon said. "I didn't know he'd lost a son. It must be Captain Mayfield. Wasn't his wife named Margaret?"

"I'm sure of it. But Mother will know."

By this time rain was sweeping in a curtain across the fields and the rooftops. We couldn't make it to the motorcar, and so we scrambled to reach the door of the church, dashing inside and pulling it to just as a torrent burst against it. We could hardly hear ourselves think as it beat on the roof above us.

Simon handed me his handkerchief and I dried my face, laughing as I did so. "If we don't die of pneumonia from the chill in here, we should be all right." For the shoulders and arms of my uniform were wet. Simon gave me his coat, and I was grateful for the warmth.

Lightning lit the stained-glass windows and seemed to roll around the beautiful wooden roof over our heads. "It came up so fast. It shouldn't last too long."

But it was nearly forty-five minutes before the rain stopped and we could leave the sanctuary of the church.

Simon, pacing the flagstone floor, said, "If these children were neglected or abused, why didn't one of them tell the doctor or the rector?"

"Remember what Mr. Kipling said, when I went with Melinda to see him? He never told anyone how wretched he was. He was afraid he wouldn't be believed, and that would make life even more unbearable."

"You think this lad telling tall tales was Lieutenant Wade?"

"It's possible, isn't it? There's no way of guessing whether he was actually mistreated or simply hated being at The Willows, away from his parents. He might even have been having troubles with his studies and rebelled."

"I shouldn't think that would lead to murder."

He said something else that was lost in the next clap of thunder, which seemed to come from directly overhead.

"I'm sorry. I missed that."

"When this stops, we'll try to find that nurse. She ought to remember more than the former sexton does. She was in that house every day."

We sat there in silence for a time, listening to the storm move away, and after a bit the rain stopped hitting the roof like pebbles thrown against it. Simon went to look out, and stood there, a silhouette, holding the door open.

"Another five minutes," he said.

We drove out toward the Common, on the outskirts of Petersfield, and after asking at the first house we came to, we soon discovered where Miss Gooding lived. It was a tiny cottage, the front of it nearly overrun with wisteria vines and roses turned wild. All the same, I couldn't help but think how lovely it must look in the spring, when both were in bloom. There were flagstones leading up to the door, and I managed to keep my skirts out of the puddles that were everywhere and hard to see in the gray twilight.

The woman who opened the door was much older than the

former sexton, her hands gnarled and twisted, her back bent so badly she had trouble looking up at me.

"Miss Gooding?"

"Yes, my dear. What is it you need?"

"Just to speak to you for a moment, please? Sergeant-Major Brandon and I have come a long way and must leave shortly."

"Do come in, Sister Brandon," she said, and I didn't correct her. "Mr. Brandon as well. Is he your brother? Such a tall one. Mind that beam, sir."

Cozy was the word that came to mind as we stepped into the front room of the cottage. Chairs and a table, a work box filled with mending, and a low shelf filled with books and knickknacks, even a window seat where a gray tabby was curled up asleep gave it a peaceful air. A fire was burning on the hearth, and the room was very warm.

Turning to Simon, she asked, "Would it be forward of me, sir, to ask you to fill the coal scuttle for me?"

"Of course," he answered and carried it through the kitchen and outside to look for the coal pile.

She smiled at me. "That's very kind of him. Old bones feel the weather, and it's a struggle bringing it in. The coal. Now, then, what's troubling you, Sister?"

"I've come to ask you about the Caswell house, The Willows. I understand you took care of some of the children living there."

She rubbed the palms of her hands on her apron, looking away. "Best not to speak of the past," she said, her reluctance evident.

"It was the former sexton of St. Peter's who thought you might be able to help us. He told us where to find you."

"Did he, now? Well, then, it will be all right." Her gaze came back to me. "Mrs. Caswell didn't care to summon the doctor unless she had to. She left it to me to take care of them unless it was very bad. She didn't want him reporting what he saw there."

"What would he have seen?"

"Pinches and bruises mostly. A burn or two. Scratches. She didn't want the children there, cluttering up her house. She blamed her husband for making it necessary to take them in. There were other things you couldn't see the scars of. Miss Gwendolyn—the Caswells' daughter—would take something of theirs, then swear she hadn't. And the object would turn up in the most obvious place. The child would then be punished for a liar. Or Miss Gwendolyn would tear a page from their schoolbooks and claim she saw them do it. Hide letters or pictures. Steal food and swear it was one of the others. I told Mr. Caswell, but he wouldn't do anything to stop it. He couldn't see that his daughter was a spoiled, mean-spirited little girl."

"But the governess—someone—the tutor—must have seen what you saw? The other servants. And who else? The rector. The local constable."

"The other servants hated the extra work the children made for them. The rector never saw the children except when they were scrubbed and warned to keep their mouths shut. They were always well chaperoned if they went outside the gates. What's more, the tutor and the governess were browbeaten. They too had nowhere else to go."

"But surely interviewing parents saw what was happening. Saw that the tutor and the governess were worthless."

"Mr. Melvin had a First in mathematics. He had Greek and Latin. Miss Grant was shy, but she had been to the finest schools, paid for by her godfather. Parents didn't see how many days in a month Mr. Melvin was drunk, or that Miss Grant was afraid of her shadow. It was her first position. I think that's why she killed herself—after her fiancé died, she lost hope of a different life, for the Caswells would never have given her a decent reference."

"Where is Mr. Melvin now?"

"He was sacked when the last of the boys went away to school. Someone said he'd emigrated to Canada, but I heard later that he'd died of his liver. And that was good riddance. He enjoyed the cane too much for my taste."

"Tell me a little about the children."

"Every Sunday they would sit in the parlor and write to their parents in India. Those that could. They were told what to say, mind you, and the letter was read before it went into the post, to make certain there was nothing extra in there, like a plea for help. For the little ones, a letter was written for them, and they were taught to sign their names to it. Photographs were taken showing smiling faces. Or they went to bed without their dinner. During the week, they studied long hours. I'd find them asleep over their books and Mr. Melvin droning on. The other nursery maid left, not wanting to look after so many children. After that, I took over their care, saw that they bathed and had their tea and went to bed on time. It was such a dreary life for them. There was one little girl, pretty as a picture, and I enjoyed brushing her hair at night. Even Mr. Caswell made over her. It near broke my heart when she died."

She was talking about the Wade child. I was sure of it.

"How did she die? Of measles or scarlet fever?" I asked, one nurse to another.

"I never knew. They said typhoid, but I couldn't believe that. I went over it again and again in my mind."

"Instincts are often right," I reminded her. "Were there *other* cases of typhoid that spring? Trouble with the well? Of course if that was the source of infection, someone else would have fallen ill, surely."

Miss Gooding shook her head. "I've no call to speak ill of the dead."

"It will go no further," I assured her. "I've come here because I'm uncomfortable about the way the Caswells treated their charges."

She looked at me, and I could see that her eyes were beginning to cloud over with age.

"I don't mind telling you I've wondered the same. I did speak to the doctor about the child's illness when he came to sign the death certificate. He laughed at me, telling me I had no training."

"If it wasn't typhoid, what was it? This was the little Wade girl we're talking about?"

Miss Gooding didn't seem surprised that I knew the child's name.

"I even spoke to the constable. But he'd never been called to the house, had he, or seen the frightened eyes or the bruises? We only had one lad who was troublesome, and I heard the constable lecture him on being grateful to have such a fine family to give him a home."

I gently brought her back to what I was most interested in. "The little girl?"

"I did wonder if Miss Gwendolyn had given the child something to make her so ill. I kept telling myself that she couldn't have known what would happen. But I couldn't think what it could be. I saw her face when the doctor came out of the sickroom and told us the child was dead. She turned white as her nightdress, and she ran out of the room and up the stairs. I started after her, but her mother called me back and told me to leave Miss Gwendolyn alone."

"But what reason could she have had?"

"I thought about that as well. That she just wanted to make the child ill. The little one's birthday was the very next week, and there were already packages that had come from India. I couldn't help but think Miss Gwendolyn wanted to spoil it for her."

I remembered the shepherdess in the attic and the box that it came in.

"The Mayfield lad died as well," I said.

"Now that was a fall down the stairs. He said he was pushed, but there was no one at the top of the stairs when Mr. Caswell reached him. I was called because the doctor was at a lying-in, but I could see at once it was his spine. He lived another four and twenty hours before he died."

"How sad," I said as Simon came in with the coal scuttle, filled to the brim.

"It was that, and I cried when they put him in the ground. Such a promising lad."

"Was young Wade mistreated?"

She nodded her head. "But then he was trouble from the start, young Thomas was. Everyone said so. Still, the truth was, it wasn't until after his sister's death that he was difficult. They sent him away to Shaftsbury School as soon as they could. He told me as I was packing up his things that he would come back one day and make the Caswells tell him how his sister died."

And there was his motive for their murder, surely.

"Was there anyone else who made trouble?"

"Ah. The Bingham lad." She smiled at the memory. "He ran away as regular as clockwork. We'd find him in the village regaling anyone who would listen with his tales. He told me he'd seen a Maharajah with ropes of pearls that hung down to his feet, and elephants painted all over with pictures, and camels that bite when they're not pleased."

I could have told her that all those stories were true. I'd seen the ropes of pearls, and elephants decorated for Hindu festivals, and camels most certainly bit anyone who didn't have a care about how to approach them.

"What was young Bingham's first name?"

"He wasn't there very long. His parents died, I think, and someone came to fetch him. I can't seem to bring it back." She frowned with the effort. "Donald? Daniel? I do remember that he called himself a peculiar name. He showed me a picture once of this strange black creature with a red tongue and more arms than legs. Gave me a start to see such a thing. It wasn't normal."

I took a wild guess. "Was it Shiva?"

"That's it." She nodded. "How did you know?"

Shiva. The Destroyer. Not such an innocent little boy after all, if he longed for vengeance.

"I must have seen the same drawing somewhere."

"Then you'll understand why I remembered it all these years, because it truly sent a shiver up my spine."

She was tiring, we would be asked to leave soon. And so I put the last question baldly.

"I've always wondered. Who killed the Caswell family?"

"It was said that the Wade lad did it, but there were rumors that Mr. Gates, who inherited The Willows, had had his eye on it for some time. There were some thought Mr. Caswell owed him money and couldn't ever repay it. The day Mr. Gates first walked in the door, he settled our wages and dismissed the staff. And we were that glad to go. I couldn't step into the parlor without seeing them there stiff and dead. I wouldn't be surprised if ghosts walk in that house of a night. I've wondered if that isn't why The Willows is on the market. It's not a happy house. In my view it was never a happy house from the start."

Even if the elder Gates had killed the Caswells, he was dead now and could not be blamed for what happened to the Gesslers.

I rose to go, thanking her for speaking to me. Simon, who had been sitting across from me, got to his feet as well. I thought he was about to say something more, but he seemed to change his mind, and we took our leave.

As he turned the crank and got in beside me, I asked, "Why were you so long filling the coal scuttle?"

"Was it too obvious?"

"I don't think she noticed. Mainly because it would take her even longer to fill the scuttle herself and carry it in."

"I had a look around the cottage. And around the yard behind it. Miss Gooding is very trusting. She doesn't lock her doors or the shed out beyond the kitchen garden."

"That sounds rather ominous," I said. "What did you find?"

"Upstairs by Mrs. Gooding's bed, there was a picture frame like yours from the charity stall. I opened the back. There was a red stamp like that in your frame. Because the frame is heavy silver, I suspect it wasn't Miss Gooding's to begin with. Possibly it's one that the Caswells kept and she wanted it because of the children. She could well have decided, when everyone was sacked so precipitously, that the new owner would have no need of it. Or perhaps it had been relegated to the attics for years and she simply helped herself to it. At any rate, I expected the photograph to be very similar to yours. But it wasn't."

"Miss Gooding told me that every Christmas a photograph was taken of the children, to send to their parents. It could have come from another year."

"It was a more recent photograph of what appeared to be a group of children at a church outing or perhaps a private party. And it hadn't been taken by a professional like Gessler. I think it had been substituted for the original one in that frame."

"Perhaps that's what she wanted to put in there. That's why she kept the frame in the first place."

"That's possible." But I could hear the doubt in his voice.

I remembered Miss Gooding's clouded eyes. Once she would have known the difference if the photograph had been switched. By now she probably never really looked at it—*really* looked at it—at all. It was there, it was comforting, her children, and that was all that mattered. She knew their faces by heart.

I considered what that meant.

"Simon. We must turn around and go back to the cottage. There's one more question I want to put to Miss Gooding. But if what you're telling me is true, then her failing eyesight saved her life."

Chapter Fourteen

Miss Gooding was surprised to see us standing on her doorstep once more.

I apologized profusely, telling her that I must have left one of my gloves by my chair.

Trusting soul that she was, she held the door wide and said, "I don't remember seeing anything on the floor, but then my eyes aren't what they once were. Do come in and look, my dear."

I crossed the room to where I'd been sitting and said, "Oh, here it is." And I held up the glove I had just taken out of my pocket.

Miss Gooding squinted. "So it is. Well, I hope you hadn't got too far before you remembered it."

As I walked to the door again, I said, "Do you have visitors very often, Miss Gooding?"

"The rector calls when he can. And the former sexton comes to bring me the gossip. There was a young man not three weeks gone who had lost his way. I was just going to fetch more coal and he offered to do it for me. Very kind of him, wasn't it? But he said it was the least he could do after disturbing me."

"What did he look like?" Simon asked.

"He was not as tall as you, slender, I think, dark haired. I couldn't make out his face, but he had a kind voice."

"And a kind heart," Simon replied as she held the door for us.

"Yes, I'm sure of it." Miss Gooding smiled.

I thanked her again, and we left.

"How did you guess that he had come to the door, instead of slipping in the house?" Simon asked when we were once more on the road.

"Perhaps he wanted to see if she remembered him. Would he have killed her, do you think, if she weren't losing her sight?"

"That may have saved her, as well as being asked to fill the coal scuttle, which gave him the chance to look for whatever it was he came for. Something brought him here. If it was for the photograph, he was clever enough to switch it rather than steal it frame and all. She might have noticed if it went missing."

"Why did you wander around, Simon?"

He glanced at me. "To see if Miss Gooding had anything that would be worth burning down her cottage to destroy after we had returned to Somerset."

Before going to sleep that night, late as it was, I looked at the photograph again.

I was beginning to put names to some of the children, although I couldn't have said which were which.

The boys must be Thomas Wade, young Mayfield, and Bingham. That left two other boys unidentified. One of the little girls must be Lieutenant Wade's sister. Was one of the others Gwendolyn Caswell?

I studied the faces, trying to find something in them that would help me understand why this photograph mattered. But all I could really see was the unformed features of the young. Were they good children before they arrived at The Willows, and then shaped by their experiences there?

I remembered Mr. Kipling's tight mouth and hard eyes when he was asked about his own experiences in a house like The Willows. Whatever had happened to him was buried so deep inside that he couldn't bear to have it brought back again into the light of day. Even after all these years.

My father was already at breakfast when I came down the next morning.

He looked up from his newspaper and said, "Your friend Corporal Caswell has been discharged from hospital."

"Are you having him *watched*?" I asked, dismayed. "How did you find him?" I hadn't told him the name Lieutenant Wade was using. Or that he'd been a patient in the influenza ward. "Or—has someone been watching *me*?"

The Colonel Sahib smiled. "Nothing so dramatic, my dear. A postcard from Rouen."

He passed it across the table to me.

Sister Bailey had written it.

Took a convoy of weak and convalescent cases to American Base Hospital. Corporal Caswell discharged, everyone in mourning. Lucky you to get leave, we are overwhelmed as usual. Friend carrying this to England.

And beneath it in another hand I read:

Mailed in Portsmouth. Miss seeing you, Bess. Take care.

It was signed by the First Lieutenant of the *Mermaid,* a ship I'd taken back and forth from France I don't know how many times.

I felt my face flush. I'd assumed the worst. And now I would have to explain why I had said such things to my father.

"I'm so sorry," I apologized, setting the card down. "I didn't sleep well. But that's no excuse for being rude."

My father was astute. He got up and helped himself to more porridge and brought a bowl to me as well.

"Is Caswell the name he's using?" he asked gently.

"Yes. I didn't want to tell you that. I didn't want to put you on the spot, deciding whether to send someone to France to arrest the man or to wait and see what I could learn in Petersfield."

"Perhaps you should let Scotland Yard take over the inquiry now. Or the Army."

"What if they didn't do a very good job the first time round?"

"That's always possible," he agreed.

It was always hard to keep anything from my father. And so I told him about Corporal Caswell, the influenza patient brought in to our hospital, and how he had tried to escape, and how that had been perceived as trying to rejoin his men too soon. How he had told me a little about his escape from the MFP, but avoided telling me anything about the murders.

"But something happened in Petersfield," I finished. "And until I know what it was, I'm not comfortable with the view that Lieutenant Wade killed the Caswell family."

"You may have stumbled on something entirely unrelated to the murders, have you considered that? People have secrets, and a murder inquiry tends to bring them out into the open, guilty or not of the crime being investigated."

"Yes, I'm sure of that," I replied. "It's just—I don't know how to explain it. Except to say that it's rather odd that so many secrets seem to center around the Caswell family and their house."

The Colonel Sahib nodded. "Not so odd, given the fact that those children grew up and went on to lives of their own." He set his empty bowl aside. "I ought to send orders to have this Corporal Caswell picked up so that he can be questioned. Instead I'll see that someone keeps an eye on him. They needn't know why."

"He's clever," I warned. "He's survived this long."

Living with a regiment left me with no illusions about what would happen. And even if he escaped the MFP, where could Corporal Caswell go in the midst of a bloody, stalemated war?

The answer came unbidden. The smartest thing someone like

Corporal Caswell could do in the circumstances was to let himself be taken prisoner by the Germans. Whatever hardships he would have to face would be light compared to getting out of Afghanistan. And he would be out of reach until the end of the war.

My mother and I went to call on Mrs. Mayfield. She lived just thirty miles away, as it turned out.

I took with me the photograph of the children, and my mother carried with her several jars of the plums we had just put up.

I was shocked at how much Mrs. Mayfield had aged. Her son's death and then her husband's had turned her fair hair white before its time, and there were lines of suffering in her face that touched me deeply.

She welcomed my mother and me warmly, glad to have visitors. She took the jars of plums, embraced my mother in gratitude, ringing for tea to be brought in.

"I must tell you, the kitchen garden has been a godsend this summer. With so many shortages, it has meant some variety in meals. My cook does her best, but it has tried her patience to make do day in and day out."

My mother smiled. "So have we all. There was no sugar for the plums, of course, but never mind, it's a treat all the same."

They chatted about friends for a time until the tea tray was brought in by a middle-aged housekeeper. Mrs. Mayfield turned to me and asked how I felt, working with so many wounded, and whether I should continue nursing when—if—the war ended.

"I'm sure my work won't end straightaway. But after we have all the wounded and the returning prisoners safe, I shall have to consider what to do next."

"You're such a pretty girl, Bess, surely there's someone you care about?"

I smiled. "Not at the moment," I assured her. "I'm kept too busy to think about falling in love."

Across the room on the table by the window were framed photographs of Captain Mayfield, of the bridal couple when they were married, and then of their son, smiling in his mother's arms, in his grandfather's lap, riding a pony with an Indian servant leading it, and even the very one I had in my purse, along with another very much like it—but with fewer children—and what appeared to be a birthday photograph, for it showed their small son holding several toys and seated in the very chair I had bought.

I nodded toward the table. "Such lovely photographs," I said and felt ashamed of what I was about to do. "I remember some of them from India."

A shadow passed over her face. "My lads," she said, affectionately including her husband in the term.

Gesturing to those taken by the Gesslers, I singled out the copy of the one I was most interested in and asked, "Who are the other children there with George? Do you recall?"

She got up and crossed to the table. "This one? George is by the newel post, still so fair, just like Henry at the same age. And next to him I think is the Wade child, and his sister, just there. The older girl is Gwendolyn Caswell, and I don't remember who the younger one is. Josh Bingham at the foot of the stairs. George liked him, but I was told later that he was forever running away. Imaginative child, I thought him, telling his wild tales. I don't remember the other two boys. I don't believe they were there when Henry and I visited the house."

Disappointed more than she could possibly guess, I said, "Yes, I'm sure there were children coming and going much of the time."

"I was just so very grateful that those terrible murders took place after the family stopped taking in children. Just think what could have happened—what a harrowing experience it would have been for the children. Or they themselves might have been harmed. It doesn't bear thinking of."

"Why did they stop taking in children? Do you know?" my mother asked.

"I don't, really, but I seem to remember that Mrs. Wade told me the reason the Caswells offered was that their daughter was growing up and they wanted to give her more time than they could with a house full of little ones to look after. But then Henry told me he'd heard they had come into money. Still, it must have been quite a strain on young Gwendolyn to share her parents and her home with so many strangers."

My mother made noises of agreement, and then it was time for us to take our leave. We thanked Mrs. Mayfield for her hospitality, and my mother promised to come again soon.

A few minutes later we were on the road back to Somerset. I was driving, and my mother was silent for a time. "Did you learn anything useful, Bess?"

"I learned more about the others in that photograph. And I was grateful not to have to show her mine, or explain how I came by it."

"Yes, there's that. Poor woman. I can't imagine having to grow old without either you or your father there beside me."

"Captain Mayfield was close to the age of retiring from the Army. Why was he at Mons?"

"He'd gone over at once with the Expeditionary Force. They were outnumbered, sadly so. But they fought well. I don't think you could have stopped him from going if you'd tried. I lived in fear that Richard would be called back into the Army. But he was more useful in other capacities—how he must have hated that!—and I could sleep again."

I could imagine worrying about my father or Simon in the trenches. For both of them would have preferred active service to whatever it was they did when they disappeared for a day or a week at a time. I'd heard my father say more than once that he had agreed to it only because he felt his experience would save the lives of green recruits facing the German Army's best-trained men.

"Did they come into money—the Caswells?"

"Possibly," my mother said. "Or perhaps it suited them to let people believe it when they stopped taking in children. It must have rankled to be reduced to that."

"Yes," I said slowly, remembering Joshua Bingham telling the world that there was an idol in The Willows filled with diamonds. That was a little over the top, even for an imaginative boy. But one of the children could have left behind what appeared to be a trinket of no value, one that the Caswells discovered to be worth a small fortune. I wished I'd paid more heed to the toys little George Mayfield was holding.

What if somehow the Caswells came into money that wasn't theirs in the first place but belonged to one of the children? I couldn't quite see how that could happen. Was there another grave in the churchyard in Petersfield that we hadn't discovered?

Or worse, was there a grave that ought to have been in the churchyard but was elsewhere, to hide what they had done?

Was that the real reason the governess had committed suicide?

It was gruesome even to consider such a possibility, and I didn't mention it to my mother.

But my mother had already worked it out for herself. "It would be easy enough, wouldn't it, for someone to tell the world that this or that child was leaving on the morrow for boarding school in London or York? And even the child would be unaware of what was planned. Still, if the Caswells had helped themselves to a child's inheritance, surely there would have been a solicitor or guardian who would want to know where the child was?"

I shook my head. "I don't suppose we'll ever know. Whatever it was, they would take great care not to leave a record of it."

I set out the next morning for France, nothing resolved. Simon drove me to the train.

"I'll be gone for three days, Bess. I'm glad you've confided in your parents. That will offer you some protection."

"I hope protection won't be necessary. After all, Lieutenant Wade has been discharged from hospital."

"Still." He left it at that.

My train was late, and we spent the extra hour looking in on Mrs. Hennessey. She was well, staying close to the flat to be certain she didn't meet someone with influenza, and worrying about all of us. There was just time for a cup of tea, and then I was back at the station and Simon was seeing me onto my train.

He caught my hand as I was settling myself in the crowded carriage.

"Bess. If you want me to go to Scotland Yard in your stead, say the word. It might be better than turning Wade over to the MFP."

"I— Let me think about it, Simon." The whistle blew, and I could hear the carriage doors slamming shut. "All right. Speak to the Yard," I said hurriedly. "But please, don't tell them we know that Lieutenant Wade is still alive—or where he is."

Simon was forced to step back, and the guard was slamming my door.

He said something, but the train was picking up steam, and although I fumbled at the window, my glove got caught and I couldn't drop it in time. When at last I did, we were nearly out of the station. I couldn't read Simon's face as the locomotive's smoke roiled past us.

Had Simon agreed?

I didn't know. All I could do now was trust him.

Chapter Fifteen

Seven men had fallen ill on our journey and had had to be taken off in Dover. I watched them go in a pitiful line of stretchers moving through the early dawn hours toward the waiting ambulances. One of the young soldiers standing behind me swore softly.

"They never even saw a Hun," he said to no one in particular, his voice betraying his fear of an unseen enemy he couldn't shoot.

I was posted to the same hospital as before, much to Matron's delight, and it was as if I'd never left, although there were different patients lying in the cots, and three of our Sisters were in a small ward, fighting for their own lives. I admired their courage—they had come here knowing they didn't have immunity of any kind. I at least had a fair chance of survival. I'd been told I had a good chance of not being reinfected.

We worked long hours, endured the heartbreak of patients dying in spite of all we could do. Even Matron, dark circles under her eyes, seemed to be functioning on will alone. Soon I couldn't remember the comfort of my own bed, only falling down on my cot and sleeping without dreams, the sleep of the drugged. And my drug was exhaustion.

Sister Shelby came to find me late one afternoon, her eyes wide with shock.

"What is it? Matron?" I asked, for I'd worried that she couldn't possibly go on much longer without falling ill herself.

"You were here when Corporal Caswell was a patient, weren't you?"

"Yes, of course. He's—he's not dead, is he?"

"Nothing so final. But we have one of his men here, a Private Ball, and he told me Corporal Caswell has been taken prisoner. He—"

I didn't hear the rest. "A prisoner? Are you quite sure?"

"I was just trying to tell you. He was covering his men as they retreated to their lines, and he wasn't strong enough to keep up. I *told* Matron he wasn't ready to return to duty, but of course she insisted."

"I thought—Sister Bailey wrote me he'd been sent to Rouen to complete his recovery."

"That's true, but he wasn't himself when he returned to his men. Private Ball says he was different somehow. And there was nothing anyone could do to keep the Germans from taking him. By the time they could return fire, they feared hitting him."

She wiped her face with her hands. "We nurse them back to health only to send them out again to die."

I put a hand on her shoulder. "Sister Shelby—Louise—you need to lie down for an hour or two. I'll cover for you. It will be all right. And it isn't our fault that they are sent back too soon. Many of them do survive. Blame the war, with its endless hunger for men."

She smiled, but I could see the tears in her eyes. I walked with her to our quarters and saw her into bed. Pulling up the sheet, I said, "Did you know him well? Corporal Caswell?"

"Not *well.* He just had a way about him. He'd keep the men in the convalescent ward laughing and talking, picking up their spirits, and when he could, he'd help us, carrying linens or pushing the medicine cart. Reading to the other patients. We got used to him, you see. We'd succeeded with Corporal Caswell. It buoyed our spirits as well. A bright spot in the endless lines of new cases coming in and the dead being taken away for burial."

I could imagine how carefully he'd played his role. How he had gained the trust of the Sisters and made it impossible for me to declare him a murderer. Even after I'd gone, he kept up that role, and in the end, he was discharged. Free to go back to the lines and plot how best to get himself taken prisoner. It was a terrible risk. He could have been shot just as easily. But now he was safe from arrest.

I waited until she was relaxed, on the verge of sleep, and then I turned away. But she said, without opening her eyes, "He was the sort of man we hope will be waiting for us after the war, to marry and live happily ever after. Kind, caring, intelligent, and strong." She laughed, a light laugh, as if not taking herself seriously. "And rather attractive as well. One mustn't forget that."

I thought, this was the man who accompanied Mrs. Standish to England when her daughter died.

At what point had he changed into a murderer?

Because being taken prisoner was proof of his guilt.

Just as his flight from the MFP on the night they came to take him into custody.

I was Colonel Crawford's daughter, I'd been sent to England. And surely, once I'd told my father where to find him, the Army would come for him. He hadn't believed me. And so he had planned it well.

A letter came from Simon, brought in by a dispatch rider from HQ. There was no time to read it until I stopped for my dinner.

I spoke to Scotland Yard. The inspector I met with discussed what we know so far. He was interested but told me flatly that at this point there isn't enough evidence to warrant the Yard's time. Winchester is satisfied that the Gessler fire was the work of a known arsonist, and they are actively searching for him. They are also still looking for the two people who can help them with their inquiries. I've said nothing to the police in Petersfield. There really is nothing to tell them. Meanwhile, I've just seen the latest list of known prisoners of war. There is a familiar name on it.

A dead end. In every way.

I set the letter aside and finished my pudding.

Sister Murray was showing signs of recovering from the influenza, and Sister Shelby had become the latest victim among the staff.

I was doing their work as well as my own when a request came through to transfer me to a forward aid station where I was urgently needed. I spoke to Matron, telling her that I wished to refuse the request, because I was also needed here.

"The American base hospital is sending us two experienced Sisters to replace you and Sister Shelby."

"We could use six new Sisters and still not have enough hands."

"There's no doubt about that," she said in resignation. "But men are dying there because the last of the staff has collapsed. You must go."

My transportation was waiting. It was a motorcycle, all that could be spared, and the orderly in the saddle was impatient. There was no time for good-byes. I quickly collected my kit and went out to meet him. He helped me into the sidecar and handed me goggles and a helmet, then pulled a heavy canvas cover over me. We were away almost at once, roaring across the rutted excuse for a road, passing dead horses and dead men, bogged-down tanks, and a relief column moving up as fast as they could. The unspeakable black mud that had once been fertile farmland flew up in a bow wave as we sped on. Several times when we hit ruts, I could feel my spine jarring as I rose in my seat and then was slammed down again.

By the time we reached our destination, I could see nothing through those goggles, and the canvas protecting me was heavy with splatters of muck.

We came to a halt, and the orderly, grinning at me, white teeth in a face full of grimy black freckles and smears, hurried around the machine to help me out. I thanked him for the covering, and he nodded. "You'll be stiff at first," he said in a heavy cockney accent I could hardly decipher.

But it wasn't stiffness so much as weakness in my legs from the pounding that made me clutch his arm to keep from going down on my knees. He walked me about a bit, and the circulation returned quickly.

And a good thing, because I had no more than washed my face and hands than I was working on the next man in line, a severely torn arm. The guns were so loud I could hardly hear myself think, shell after shell screaming overhead or exploding amidst cries and screams.

I shut out the sounds and concentrated on what I was doing, hearing only the *clink* of bits of shell debris as I dropped them into the pan beside the patient's head. As soon as his arm was cleaned and ready to sew up, the doctor took him over and I went to the next in line, a mangled foot.

The pace kept up well into the night, and then there was a lull as the shelling stopped and both sides paused to lick their wounds. Someone brought me a cup of tea and a dry sandwich, and I was grateful for both. A little later, while I was sleeping, a cup of soup was set beside my bed. The aroma woke me up and I drank it down before falling asleep again. I didn't know where it had come from, but it tasted heavenly.

I awoke to more shelling, and a long line of wounded appeared before I could swallow my breakfast.

This went on for three or four days. I lost count. Teddy, one of the ambulance drivers, brought mail, and I was relieved to find letters from home waiting for me on my cot when I returned to my quarters late that evening.

My mother informed me that Iris, our maid, had had a mild case of influenza but was already on the mend. So far no one else at home had fallen ill, although there were ten cases in the village. My father was—presumably—in Scotland, for he had taken his greatcoat and gloves. She worried about him because he was tired. Simon was back in Somerset. Coming through London, he had looked in on Mrs. Hennessey and taken Diana—who was on leave—to lunch. Simon had asked my mother to include a message from him.

Joshua Bingham was a Captain serving in France, according to records at Sandhurst. Apparently there was a Sergeant who remembered him. The Bingham family had been civil servants first in India and then in Ceylon until their retirement in 1912. They had sent their only son to England to be educated, and until 1914 he had been a solicitor in Gloucester.

It seemed almost certain we'd tracked down another of the children in the Caswell household, although this one hadn't stayed as long as most. Because he was the runaway, telling wild tales to anyone who would listen? Only they weren't tales, they were what he'd seen as a young child in Ceylon.

But where in France was Captain Bingham serving? He could be anywhere, and the chances of finding him were slim.

If I could speak to him about the Caswells, I might discover the names of the other children in that household.

I couldn't just ask the wounded who their officers were. It was not done, and it would draw attention to me, leaving the impression I had a personal interest in finding this man. I did, of course, but not in the way it would be taken, and I certainly couldn't explain my reasons.

Nor was this something I could trust to the rumor mill.

And then one morning I heard a Corporal swear in what sounded very much like Sinhala, one of the languages of Ceylon. I didn't know any of them, but we'd had a soldier in our regiment who had served there, and this was his favorite word when he was angry. The pronunciation was all wrong, but I knew at once what he was trying to say.

I hurried over to where Sister Lee was probing for a bullet in a badly cut-up shoulder, and I told her I'd finish that while she dealt with the three new stretcher cases. She was glad to hand the probe over to me, and I said, careful not to make the wound any worse as I worked, "What's your regiment, Corporal?"

He told me between gritted teeth.

"Indeed." I located the bullet and began to bring it out. My patient was white as a sheet now, but grimly holding on. When I handed him the offending lump of lead, he smiled faintly and said, "I'll keep that, Sister. A souvenir."

A good many soldiers were superstitious, wanting to keep the shell fragment or the spent bullet that had wounded them. Almost a talisman against the future, in a way.

I rinsed it and handed it to him.

"Ta," he said as I set about powdering and then bandaging his wound. "I was hanging on the wire when the Captain saw me. I was praying to make it back to the lines, but I couldn't keep my balance, like. It seemed I was stumbling over my own feet, and the rifle weighed ten stone. I got to the wire, but couldn't stop myself in time. Went down into it, just hanging there, and a sniper trying to pick me off. I could see the spurts of earth at my feet. One of the men set up answering fire, and the Captain was clutching my good arm so hard I thought he'd come down with me instead of pulling me out. But he heaved me up somehow and I was flying headfirst into the trench where some other men caught me and let me down the rest of the way. And I still had the rifle in my hand. Like a death grip, the Sergeant said."

"Did the Captain make it?"

"Oh, yes, he came diving in after me, and they caught him too. They got the sniper, they told me. I must have passed out from the pain because I don't remember much else."

"A brave man, your Captain. What's his name?"

"Yes, he's all right." It was the highest accolade. "Captain

Bingham. We missed him when he went home on compassionate leave. His mum died. He took it hard. Well, so did I when my own mum was killed by a Zeppelin."

"When was he on leave?"

The Corporal cocked his head to one side. "That must have been the second week in August. Longest five days I can remember, while he was away."

"Why was that?" I was busy calculating just when Captain Bingham had been in England, and as far as I could tell, it was during that same week that the Gesslers were killed in the fire.

It proved nothing.

I realized that the Corporal was still talking. " . . . Have you ever seen a painted elephant? Or a mountain with half-naked women—begging your pardon, Sister—painted up its side, to keep the king happy while he climbs to his palace on the top? And a statue the length of five tanks in a row? And temples shaped like funnels turned on end, with snakes for railings up the steps? Gods with monkey faces?"

"I'm sorry, I was concentrating on closing up your shoulder. What were you saying?"

He chuckled. "I'm not surprised you don't believe me. But it's what the Captain tells us just before the whistle blows and we're over the top. All manner of wild tales. Not that we believe any of them, but it takes our minds off what's to come."

But they were real, all of the stories. My father had gone to Kandy for a conference, and he brought back photographs of what he'd seen while traveling around the island.

And that sounded very like the Josh Bingham we wanted to find.

"He has quite an imagination," I agreed, smiling. I finished bandaging the shoulder and told the Corporal that he'd be sent back to hospital so they could keep an eye on his wound. "If it becomes infected, you'll lose it," I warned when he tried to argue with me, telling me that his company had been decimated by the influenza and he was too badly needed to go to hospital. "You'll be an amputee, Corporal. You know what that means."

Still not completely convinced, he went to lie down until the ambulances came back. I had given him something for the pain, and he would sleep, waking up in hospital.

I went back to my duties, wondering how I was to manage a talk with Captain Bingham. It wasn't too surprising to find he was somewhere in this sector. British troops were sent where they were needed, then pulled back to regroup before being used to bring another company or regiment up to strength once more. The question was how long he'd be where he was now.

And then his company was relieved by reinforcements while I was taking another convoy of ambulances back to hospital.

I didn't recognize him then. I was in the last ambulance. We slowed to allow the end of an ammunition train to pass, when an officer of medium height opened the rear door and stuck his head in.

"The driver up ahead told me I must speak to you. We have five walking wounded. Any room for them?"

"Three can sit with the drivers. I can accommodate two more back here."

"Thank you, Sister."

His head disappeared and I heard him calling names, directing them to their places. The rear door opened again, and two men were helped inside.

One had trench foot, I could see that straightaway. The other had been shot in the calf and it was already inflamed.

The door was shut and the drivers pulled out again.

In spite of the horrid bouncing over ruts and sliding sideways where the ground was slick with mud, I managed to cut away the private's trouser leg for a better look.

"You're just in time, you know. Another day or two at the most, and gangrene would have set in. Once it does, there's no stopping it short of amputation."

The young private grimaced. "The Captain told me to go to the aid station. But I couldn't, could I? We needed every man who could walk."

"Yes, well, you were playing fast and loose with your leg," I told him. When I finished, I looked at the case of trench foot. I could smell it before I'd got his boot off.

Nothing I could do—it would have to be cleaned when we reached hospital—but at least the foot was open to the air.

We made better time as we came nearer the hospital. I said, "Your Captain seems to care about his men."

"He does that," the private answered. "Stands up for us regular. Cap'n Bingham is all right."

So that was the man I was after, sticking his head in the door!

But we'd left him far behind. And seeing him wasn't enough. Hearing about him wasn't enough, except to prove he was the right man.

I felt a surge of frustration.

When we arrived at our destination, there were three former British prisoners of war in the hospital, Matron told me, and I asked permission to speak to them.

They were weak, their wounds in bad shape. The Germans had left them behind during their last retreat.

One of them was sleeping, and from the way he was breathing, I could tell he was on morphine. The other two were restless, still suffering from the shock of suddenly finding themselves rescued. I watched one of them anxiously fingering the sheet pulled up over his chest, picking at it the way some men did in high fevers.

I spoke to the two who were awake, telling them I was grateful that they were home again and safe.

Then I asked if they had seen a prisoner by the name of Caswell, Corporal Caswell.

The man plucking at the sheet said, "They were sending us back when the attack came. I tell you, I thought we'd be shot by our own men before it was finished."

His comrade frowned over the name, then shook his head. "We never got sent back to where most of the prisoners were held. There wasn't time. Sorry, Sister. I'd give you news if I could."

I thanked them, wished them well, and went out to the waiting ambulances. I had had the foresight to write a short letter to my parents before leaving the aid station, and I posted it before we left the hospital.

The guns were opening up again as we made our way forward. And we found seven cases of influenza being treated, men too tired and weak from long days in the trenches to fight off the infection. We tried to segregate them from the wounded, but the influenza spread quickly to an orderly and two of the wounded.

One of the Sisters in the hospital had told me that France was also facing a losing battle with the Spanish influenza, and that she'd heard that Paris was a ghost city. I found that hard to imagine—it was always so bright and lively. With the cafés and wineshops, bakeries and charcuteries closed, along with the Opera and the theater, the museums, it would be as bleak as mourning.

We moved the influenza cases to the hospital where I'd served earlier, and scrubbed the vehicles well before returning for more wounded destined for another hospital.

The three former prisoners had been taken to Dover for transit to England, but one of Captain Bingham's men was still a patient here. The wound in his calf was inflamed and swollen. He was running a fever, his face flushed and his eyes too bright.

I stopped to look in on him, trying to cheer him up, but he couldn't remember who I was. I was turning away when an officer stopped by the man's bed. He nodded to me, and I saw that his left arm was in a sling, blood still staining the fresh bandage.

I stepped away to allow him a chance to speak to the Corporal.

"How are you, son?" the Captain asked.

"Not so well, sir." The Corporal's eyes tried to focus. "Captain Bingham, sir? Are you wounded too?"

I'd turned to leave, and I stopped where I was.

"Not as bad as it looks," he answered lightly, and I had a feeling he was lying. "The Sisters insisted on the sling. Best not to disobey them."

The Corporal made an effort to grin. "Yes, sir."

"Do your best to get better. I need you, your men need you. All right?"

"Yes, sir. I'll do my best, sir."

Captain Bingham reached down and gripped the Corporal's hand.

"I'm counting on you."

Turning, he grimaced as his sling pressed on his wound, and I could see the tension around his eyes. He smiled at me and started toward the ward door. I stopped him.

"Captain Bingham? Do you have five minutes? I need to speak to you."

"About Corporal Smythe?"

"About the past," I said, and we walked together in silence until we were outside the ward. A light rain was falling, and we huddled in what little shelter there was.

"Any chance of a cup of tea?" he asked, looking around.

"This way." I was heading for the canteen, ignoring the impatient blast of the horn from the ambulance driver eager to be on his way back to the forward aid station.

The tea was strong and bitter, but it was hot, and I could see as the Captain took the first sip that it was what he desperately needed. There were sandwiches as well, and I brought him one.

"Thank you. What's this about?"

"There's no time to explain, but something that happened in the past seems to be creating a problem in the present. You lived with the Caswells when you were sent back to England to be educated."

"Yes." His mouth was a tight line once more. "I was lucky, my cousin took me in charge soon after I got there. His wife had been very ill, and by the time I landed in England, she was dying. I was sent to the Caswells meanwhile, and tried my damn—my very best to make myself so obnoxious that they wanted to be rid of me. I hadn't counted on their greed. When at last my cousin came to see how I was progressing, I begged to be taken away. The Caswells told him I was only homesick, but he believed me."

"Was there treasure in that house?"

"I don't know. Gwendolyn swore there was, something one of the earlier boys had left behind. But no one could find it, although she had looked and so had several of the older children. I was delighted to spread the story. Anything to make the family as uncomfortable as I was." He started to shrug and at once regretted it. "I hated them," he finished, with such venom in his voice that I glanced up at him. "I meant that," he said, intercepting my glance. "I was too young to know precisely what hate was, but if God had struck them dead before my eyes, I wouldn't have blinked twice."

"They were murdered," I said.

"So I heard. I wasn't surprised." He finished the sandwich and was draining his cup. Setting it down again, he made to rise. "Is that it?"

"There's one more thing—" I began, but he interrupted.

"What's your interest in the Caswells? Are you related to them? If you are I won't apologize for what I've just said."

"I'm not related to them. It's just—I knew the man charged with the murders. And I found it nearly impossible to believe he had done such a thing."

"Believe it. They tormented us beyond bearing. I must say if I'd been on the jury, I couldn't have convicted him."

"There were photographs of five boys and three girls that were taken as a Christmas gift to all the parents in India. In your case, Ceylon. I happen to have one of them, and I can identify several of the children. George Mayfield, Thomas Wade, his little sister, Gwendolyn, and you."

"How did you identify me?" he demanded, his eyebrows raised in surprise and a rising anger.

"Mrs. Mayfield remembered you. But not the last two."

He nodded abruptly. "Yes, all right. The other two. I was seven when I left. I think the other lad's name was Sandy something. Sandy Hughes, that was it. I can't remember the other little girl. I'm confusing her with Wade's sister, I think. Ruth? Rachel? I'm sorry. Now I must go. And I see what must be your driver bearing down on us." He was standing now, and I rose as well.

"I don't know what this was about," he said. "But whatever it is, leave my name out of it. I'm a solicitor—or was. And a solicitor has no business being involved in murder."

And he was gone, striding back toward the ward where I thought he must be going for something to help with the pain. Why he wasn't in a cot I didn't know, but I rather thought he had talked his way out of it until now.

I went out to meet my irate driver, apologizing for the delay, but he was in no mood for excuses. I climbed into the ambulance, resigning myself to a lecture on punctuality as we made our way back to the aid station.

In an attempt to shut out the carping voice, although I knew I deserved the diatribe, I tried to decide if Captain Joshua Bingham was the murderer we were looking for.

Solicitor or not, he might well have killed the Caswell family. As soon as he could come after them.

Meanwhile, I would have to find a way to send the name of Sandy Hughes to Simon and my father.

Chapter Sixteen

When word came back from Simon, I had to wait until I was off duty to open the letter.

He had searched for an Alexander Hughes but had not found anyone by that name who was the proper age for the child in the Gessler photograph. He'd looked in Somerset House and Army records.

It was possible that the Sandy Hughes we wanted was born wherever his parents were posted. But that could be Canada, South Africa, East Africa, India, Ceylon, Egypt, the Near East, Gibraltar—the list was endless.

I could read between the lines of Simon's letter. We had done all we could, and even Scotland Yard felt that what we had uncovered was not enough to reopen the inquiry into the Caswells' murders. And it seemed that Simon had reluctantly come to agree with the Yard.

The only avenue left was to wait until the war was over and Lieutenant Wade was repatriated. He could be taken into custody then and tried.

That stopped me.

Someone would have to prove that Corporal Caswell was in fact Lieutenant Thomas Wade.

After all, he'd spent four years in France fighting for King and Country as Corporal Caswell. The Army could well refuse to honor an old warrant for another man, an officer at that, and simply demob him along with hundreds of others. If there was nothing on "Caswell's" record to stop them, they would be well within their rights.

It really was useless to go on.

And yet . . . and yet.

There was a question of truth. Of the regiment's honor. My father's pride in his men.

I'd come this far. Was I really about to quit?

I fell asleep still debating that with myself.

Two days later I was on my way back to England with a convoy of wounded, chosen because I'd had the dread influenza and wasn't likely to infect men who were terribly wounded and unlikely to survive if they fell ill.

Many were chest and stomach wounds, some were amputees, and three were manning the workhorse 18-pounder field guns when a defective shell exploded in the position next to theirs and shrapnel from the caissons left them barely alive. I couldn't help but think they looked more like the mummies I had seen in the Egyptian Museum in Cairo when we were on our way to India than living men.

It was very late when I reached London after all my charges had been safely transferred to their destinations. I walked close to a mile before I found a cab, and the driver was half asleep, jumping when I touched his arm to give him my direction.

Slipping past Mrs. Hennessey's rooms so as not to disturb her, I climbed the stairs, let myself into the flat, and remembered nothing almost as soon as my head touched my pillow. It was cool and rainy, perfect sleeping weather, and I didn't wake up until nearly eleven the next morning. I stumbled out to our tiny sitting room to make myself a cup of tea, and nearly fell over my mother, who had fallen asleep in the large chair by the window.

We were both startled, and my first thought was bad news. "Is everything all right?"

My mother sat up and rubbed her eyes. "Yes, of course, darling. I didn't mean to frighten you. But I reached London rather late, and I thought no one would mind if I stopped here. I'd been in York, you see. Another officer dead, the service in the Minster there. Your father delivered the eulogy and then had to leave straightaway for somewhere important. He put me on the train to London, and I wasn't up to going on to Somerset. The hotels were full. I must have got here sometime after three in the morning."

And I'd arrived shortly after two and had slept so soundly I didn't hear her slip in.

"I didn't know you had leave," she went on as I looked in the cabinet for tea and the pot of honey I'd brought here from Somerset on one of my last visits.

"There's no milk. I'll run down to Mrs. Hennessey's flat and beg some. But yes, I got in perhaps an hour before you. I think I needed this leave."

"You do look tired, my dear. All right, go fetch some milk and I'll put the kettle on."

Fifteen minutes later we were seated across from each other at the table.

"You're worried about the Colonel Sahib, aren't you?" I asked.

"Yes, he takes it upon himself to speak at the services, and it's hard for him. He knew so many men over the years, he watched so many of them grow up. Men in the ranks too. Like Simon, who was hardly more than a boy when he came out to India. Richard knew many of their wives, widows now. He might as well be back in the regiment, the way he works for the War Office. And he never says no."

I thought she seemed as tired as she believed I must be. It was the toll of war for those fighting and those at home waiting. Sometimes I wasn't sure which was the more difficult.

"I wish you had Father's motorcar with you," I said. "We could drive down to Somerset together."

"But I do. It's outside. We drove to London and took the train on to York."

"Well, then," I said, in an attempt to raise her spirits, "I'll drive us home."

She finished her tea before answering. "Bess. Would you take me to Petersfield? I know you and Simon have been there several times, but I think I'd like to see it for myself. Would you rather rest for a day or two? If you would, tell me so."

Surprised, I said, "But why would you want to go there?"

"I don't really have an answer for that. But I knew Lieutenant Wade, and the little Mayfield child. I'd like to see the house where these murders took place. Perhaps it will make it a little easier for me to accept the notion that he's a monster, a murderer."

"Simon, I think, has given up on proving him guilty or innocent. We really have struck a solid wall. I don't think there's any getting around that."

"Yes, but Simon has told me a little about what's been happening. That Thomas Wade is a prisoner of the Germans and you'd had the marvelous luck of finding Captain Bingham in France, who gave you another name. The Army will track down young Hughes sooner or later, if he's still alive. You only have two people left to identify, and one of them is that little girl. I think it's too soon to stop looking."

"It could be someone who wasn't in that photograph. A child who left before it was taken, or arrived afterward."

"That's very true. But it was *this* photograph that someone wanted. The photograph you bought at the charity stall. The photograph that might have got the Gesslers killed."

I had to agree with her logic. "But perhaps the person who wanted it actually didn't know which one it was—which Christmas—and therefore wanted to make certain."

"Will you drive me to Petersfield?"

"Yes, all right, I will. But Simon won't be happy if we go there alone."

She smiled conspiratorially. "But Simon is somewhere in Cornwall, I think. Or is it Devon?"

We cleared up the cups and saucers, I made my bed, and together we went out to the motorcar. It was larger than mine, but I'd driven it before and had no qualms about managing it now.

Once on our way, my mother asked me about Lieutenant Wade, while he was a patient at the influenza hospital.

"Very clever," I told her. "Or very much himself. I really don't know which." I went on to explain what had happened and how he'd managed to impress the Sisters and even Matron. How it had tied my hands.

"Did it occur to you," she asked after a moment, "that perhaps he was afraid of what choices you might make, and he set about spiking your guns before you made up your mind?"

"I don't know that he's *that* clever."

She smiled. "My love, he made it through Afghanistan and Persia. A man who can do that has to be very intelligent. He lived by his wits for months on end, and there's nothing like that to sharpen them. He joined the Army again under another name and hasn't been found out. And he had to be careful there as well, or an experienced Sergeant would have discovered that he had once been an officer. It isn't easy to deny years of training and experience. Little things give you away. Remembering to be subservient to an officer when you know he's wrong or stupid. The way you walk, the way you meet a superior's eyes like an equal. How you spend your free time. And with whom."

"Lieutenant Wade isn't the only gentleman who enlisted in the ranks."

"Very true. How many of them were once officers as well?"

"You could be right."

We rode in silence for a while. Then I broke that silence, saying, "You aren't known in Petersfield. Perhaps we can put that to good use."

"Whatever you say."

It was my turn to smile. "I really don't know what I'm saying. But we'll think of something."

The light rain that had followed us from London vanished a few miles from Petersfield. I pulled over at a muddy farm lane where we could stop for a few minutes.

"We can turn around. It isn't too late."

My mother took a deep breath. "We're here."

"So we are." I pulled back onto the road, and in a matter of minutes we were driving into Petersfield.

A funeral was in progress, the hearse standing to one side of the churchyard, the mutes just opening its rear door. But only a handful of mourners were there, and the rest of the square was empty. It was a forlorn picture, surely repeated many times over throughout England. My heart went out to the family.

"Another victim of this dread disease," my mother said, looking back over her shoulder. "We're all beginning to be afraid. Your father had a cough last week. It terrified me."

"You didn't tell me," I accused her.

"No, it was just the smoke he'd inhaled in some test or other on Salisbury Plain. But one's first thought . . ." Her voice trailed off.

We had reached The Willows, and I slowed down.

"Can you see the house, just there, through the trees?"

"Yes. Quite old, isn't it? And you said, early Victorian inside?"

"I don't think any changes have been made for decades. It's dreary."

"And that makes it harder to sell, surely? Here with the war still on—"

She broke off as someone came rushing toward the gates. I realized it was the housekeeper, red-faced and distraught.

My mother was already out of the motorcar, hurrying toward Miss Seavers. She had caught her arms by the time I reached them and was trying to penetrate the hysteria to find out what was wrong.

All I could really be sure of was that Mr. Gates had had an accident.

We didn't bother with the motorcar. I ran for the house, and as I got closer, through the open door I could see him crumpled on his side on the hall floor.

The first thing that met my eye as I dashed inside was the frayed length of rope that lay across his left arm, and then the improvised noose around his neck. Quickly glancing upward, I realized that there was a gap in the balusters where the stairs turned at the landing. Just beyond the body were two broken balusters with more rope still attached to them.

My hands were already busy at the noose by the time my mother knelt beside me, and with her help, I freed it and then put a hand to his throat to look for a pulse.

"He's alive," I said, and began to examine him. Miss Seavers was standing over us, wringing her hands piteously and crying in an uneven wail.

My mother said briskly, "He will need hot tea, you must go at once and make it. Do you understand?"

For an instant I thought she would fail to get through the woman's frenzy of worry, and then the housekeeper threw her apron over her mouth and ran for the door to the kitchen downstairs.

Blessed silence fell.

I could see the heavy rope burn along one side of Mr. Gates's throat, and it appeared that his right shoulder was dislocated. I kept working and discovered that his left leg was almost certainly fractured just above his ankle. He must have climbed on the banister. And if the rope had held, his neck would have snapped before he choked to death.

He was still unconscious, and there was the possibility of a concussion as well. But that would have to wait. I set about resetting the shoulder while he was out of his senses. I made certain that neither his collarbone nor his arm was broken, and then tested the use of his arm before putting it back into place.

Mr. Gates cried out with the pain and began to wake up.

My mother, rocking back on her heels, said, "Is there anything in your kit that would help him?"

"Until I'm sure there's no concussion I dare not. I can feel a large lump in his hair, above his ear where his head would have struck."

"Poor man," she said simply.

There was nothing I could do about the ankle, except to wrap it against the swelling. I sent my mother upstairs to find linens I could use, and while she was gone, Mr. Gates came fully to his senses and cried out as he tried to move.

"Stay still—please—you've hurt your shoulder and your leg and you mustn't try to get up," I urged, pressing him back.

But he surged to a sitting position, looked wildly toward the stairs, and saw the broken balusters.

"My God. I'm not dead—I thought—oh, dear God, *what am I to do*?"

I turned away from the anguish in his face, looking instead at the rope. He must have found it in one of the outbuildings, and while it was thick, it was also raveling in places where the strands had rotted with age. Tormented, half mad with whatever had driven him to hang himself, he had only seen what he wanted to see—a rope. His weight was too much for the balusters, and when they and the rope broke, he had fallen hard.

Mostly on that ankle and then his shoulder and head.

My mother came back down the steps carrying two sheets.

"These were in the linen closet. Help me rip them up."

Holding his arm and fighting against his pain, Mr. Gates frowned. "Who is *she*?"

"A friend," I said, not wanting to tell him that her name was also Crawford. We began to tear the sheets. It was easier than I'd expected. They were yellowed, thin, but clean. She must have found them, I thought, in the very back of the linen closet, but they would be far easier to manage than newer ones.

The door to the downstairs opened and Miss Seavers backed into the hall, the heavy tray in her hands. It held an entire tea service, not just a pot and a cup. She walked toward us, saw the strips of cloth, and exclaimed, "What are you doing?"

Mother rose and took the tray from her, setting it on a table by the stairs.

"Do sit down, my dear, and let me pour you a cup. We're making bandaging, that's all. Poor Mr. Gates has broken his leg. Do you know where to find the doctor?"

"Dr. Collins? Yes—yes, of course."

"Then drink this up and you can show me."

I said to my patient, "I'm going to wrap your ankle. It will keep the swelling down and that will make it easier for the doctor to set when he comes."

Mr. Gates wanted no part of having his ankle touched, much less bound. Perspiring from the agony, he shook his head. "I don't want you here. I don't want the doctor. Go away and leave me alone."

I got to my feet. "You can't walk, and Miss Seavers can't possibly carry you up the stairs to your bed. Or even into a sitting room," I said, in Matron's brisk voice. "You will do as you are told." But he shook his head. Turning, I gathered up the rope and the broken balusters. There was nowhere to put them, and in the end I opened the drawing room door and set them behind a chair. The doctor would see the missing balusters and the rope burn around the rector's neck and draw his own conclusions, but it was best to have the proof out of sight.

Mr. Gates refused the tea I poured for him, and so I set it next to him. Sitting awkwardly on the hard wood of the floor must be agonizing, for there was no way he could find a comfortable position.

I saw my mother set the housekeeper's empty cup on the tray. "Do you have a shawl, Miss Seavers? It's damp from the rain. I'll fetch it for you, if you'll tell me where to look."

"You aren't—you can't possibly leave him here alone?" she asked, staring from me to her cousin.

I was direct. "He can't go anywhere, and he needs a doctor. The sooner we bring him here, the better it is for Mr. Gates."

She got to her feet and walked over to her cousin. I thought at first she was going to try to help him rise and limp to a more comfortable place, but she surprised me.

"I'm heartily sick of your posturing, Harold. Let them bind your ankle while I go for Dr. Collins. You've just made trouble for yourself and much unnecessary work for me."

He turned to look at her as if the furniture had suddenly attacked him. It was the first time she'd shown any hint of spirit, to my knowledge, and from her cousin's expression, it was the first time ever.

And she set off up the stairs, hesitating only briefly at the spot where the balusters had broken away.

My mother raised her eyebrows in silent comment.

Two minutes later Miss Seavers came back with a shawl, her umbrella, and a pillow. She handed that last to me and said, "He might have to lie down while you work."

And then she was out the door, and my mother hurried after her.

But when I approached Mr. Gates, he still refused my help.

I sat down on the bottom step of the staircase, the ankle unbandaged, and Mr. Gates ignoring me. He was huddled into himself, biting his lip against the pain. He hadn't touched the tea. There was nothing I could do but wait.

"Please." His voice was just a thread. I turned toward him. His face was so pale I thought he must be on the verge of fainting.

I went to him at once, arranged the pillow to ease his shoulder, and still he couldn't lie down. I found more cushions in the sitting room, and with their help and mine, he finally lay back and put his good arm across his eyes, as if to shut out what I was about to do.

Easing off his boot, I could see that the swelling had begun in earnest, the bruising already extensive, but I wrapped the ankle to stabilize it as much as possible. From what I could tell it was a simple fracture some three inches above where the bone met the ankle joint. He couldn't bear to have me touch his foot, but he clenched his teeth and suffered in silence.

When it was done, I poured out his lukewarm tea and gave him a hot cup in its place. I was able to raise him enough to allow him to swallow a little, but his throat hurt, and after a moment I gently lowered him to the cushions again.

"Why did you want to kill yourself?" I asked quietly. "Is it the war? Or this house?"

I didn't think he was going to answer. But after a time he said in a voice that was weary and resigned, "I can't stand this house. I can't sell it, and until I do, there is nowhere else I can go. I was told by the Army doctors that I needed complete rest to heal. How can I rest here, in this place? I can't walk into the drawing room without seeing the dead sitting there staring back at me. I can't sleep in the master bedroom, it's my uncle's room, and I feel him there every time I cross the threshold. There's nowhere I can go to find any peace. I returned to France, and I was sent home from there, because I couldn't carry out my duties. I would be better off dead. Why did you cut me down?"

I realized that he was still dazed and confused enough to think we had somehow managed to save his life.

"This house isn't haunted," I said quietly, and then remembered that Miss Gooding had also believed it was.

"You don't know," he said savagely. "My God, you don't live here, you don't sleep here of a night. I can hear footsteps and there are voices too, only I can't make out what it is they're saying. I put the pillow over my head and they don't go away."

I could think of nothing to say. He didn't want to hear that it was just an old house creaking in the night or wind coming down the chimney or whistling around sashes that no longer quite fit the windows after all this time. Or perhaps the voices were in his head, and with them the sound of footsteps.

Without waiting for me to answer, he went on, this time talking mostly to himself. "I was always afraid that my uncle had killed the Caswells. Whatever the police said about it. He was quite capable of it, you know. As ruthless a person as I've ever seen. And now I'm no better than he is. I've got blood on my hands too. Murder must run in the family somehow."

Was Mr. Gates shell-shocked? Had something happened to him in the war?

"You were a chaplain, you couldn't have been guilty of murder."

"But I was. There was no time to send me back to the reserve trenches. It happened too fast. I picked up a dead man's rifle and shot two German soldiers at the edge of our trench. The wire was already down for our assault, and they beat us back, men dying everywhere I looked. I was angry and afraid—and so I shot them."

I understood now why he was unable to find any peace. It was sad, I'd seen so many like this poor man, and there was no cure of his affliction.

I could hear voices outside, and then the door opened to admit the doctor, with Miss Seavers at his heels.

He was a stocky man with graying hair, and he peered over his glasses at my uniform as I stepped forward to meet him.

"And who might you be?" he asked.

"Sister Crawford. My mother and I were driving past when Miss Seavers came running down the drive calling for help."

He made a sound that could mean anything from disapproval to disbelief. Getting down on one knee, grunting with the effort, he began to examine his patient. Mr. Gates lay there with his eyes closed, but I could see the workings of the muscles in his jaw. He wasn't able to face the doctor.

"While he was unconscious I took the opportunity to set his dislocated shoulder," I said, but the doctor ignored me. He pulled up one of Mr. Gates's eyelids, then ran his fingers over the lump on the side of his head. Reaching the shoulder, he ignored Mr. Gates's muffled cry of pain and continued down his body, checking the ribs and arms before moving to the patient's legs.

"Who bound the ankle?" he asked over his shoulder, as if Mr. Gates might have done that himself.

"I did, to reduce the swelling. It was ballooning."

"The leg is broken just there. You took a risk."

"Yes, I could tell it was broken. But it was not twisted, and I moved it as little as possible."

There was a knock at the door. I was sure it was my mother, and so I stepped forward to open it and let her in.

But it wasn't Mother on the doorstep. It was a well-dressed man and woman. They took in the scene before them, the doctor kneeling beside someone obviously injured lying on the hall floor while a nursing Sister was acting as housemaid.

I heard the woman gasp as her husband said, "There must be some—we were told that it would be convenient to call today to look at this—er—at The Willows."

I glanced toward Miss Seavers. She stood there with her hand over her mouth, staring from me to the pair on the doorstep. "I—I forgot—it flew completely out of my mind . . ." she said faintly.

"I must say," the man began, but his wife was already pulling at his arm.

"Please, I think perhaps we should go."

The man had seen the broken balusters now. Peering over my shoulder at the staircase and then at the man lying on cushions, he sniffed the air. "Has this man been drinking?"

I was glad I'd had the foresight to hide the rope. Even so, it was clear that this wasn't an ordinary fall down the stairs. Mr. Gates couldn't have slipped through the gap, and if he'd gone down the staircase, the balusters wouldn't have broken the way they had. I could almost hear the gossip starting.

"Get them out of here," the doctor said in a growl.

"Mr. Gates has had a very serious fall," I said, "while trying to make repairs to the staircase before you arrived. Now I'm afraid you'll have to arrange to visit at another time." And I politely shut the door in their faces.

Dr. Collins finished his examination and looked up at me. "I don't know that there's a concussion. His leg and that shoulder broke his fall, and then his head hit the floor as an afterthought. But we'll err on the side of caution." He got to his feet. "I'll have to send for a stretcher. He can't be left where he is, and I have no room for him at my surgery. There are influenza patients there. We've just buried one of them." He turned to Miss Seavers. "Get his bed ready for him, if you will, and I'll come back in the morning to set the leg. Meanwhile, I'll leave something with you to give him for the pain."

Then he prodded Mr. Gates with the toe of his boot, not hard but enough to get the man's full attention. And still Mr. Gates kept his eyes closed.

"We'll have no more of this, do you hear me? Whatever it is you've tried to do, I'll thank you not to be so stupid as to try it again any time soon. I have people who are dying who would exchange places with you gladly. And you've taken me away from them to attend you. Give me your word you'll be sensible."

But Mr. Gates lay there, tears squeezed out from behind his closed lids, and said nothing.

Dr. Collins considered him for a moment. "I will accept that as a promise on your part. Now I must finish here and go." Turning to me, he went on. "I take it you won't be staying."

I said, "No, sadly, I shan't be able to stay." And then instantly regretted it, for Miss Seavers could hardly be expected to take on the care of her cousin on her own, and I'd have been free to explore this house to find out what it was that had make it the scene of three murders, and possibly two suicides, those of Mr. Gates and a woman he never knew, the governess who drowned herself.

Dr. Collins was drawing Miss Seavers to one side, and opening his bag, he brought out a box of powders, giving her instructions as he did so. She cast a frightened glance in my direction, as if wishing I would change my mind and take over. But I didn't think the rector would want me here.

Miss Seavers listened, nodded anxiously, and then the doctor closed his bag, starting for the door. As an afterthought, he said to the housekeeper, "And keep those powders where he can't get to them. In your room, in the kitchen, I don't care which."

And then he was ready to go, holding the door wide for me to precede him, and then closing it behind us as we left. As it swung shut I had a last glimpse of Miss Seavers staring down at her cousin.

"What brought you to Petersfield?" Dr. Collins was asking. And I had a feeling that he might know more than he was divulging.

"I've been here before," I said. "And this time I brought my mother. I'm on leave, you see."

We had reached the motorcar. My mother was sitting there, waiting patiently. Dr. Collins heaved himself into the seat beside her, and I took the rear seat.

"Is that poor man all right?" Mother asked. "I thought it best not to come back inside."

"Better than he deserves to be. I have no patience with suicides when I have so many people who are fighting very hard to live." He lifted his glasses and ran a hand over his face. I could hear his palm brush across his chin where he'd missed a patch of beard. "Back to the surgery, if you please, Mrs. Crawford. I must find two men with stretchers to take that fool upstairs to his bed."

I wanted to tell Dr. Collins what Mr. Gates had told me, but it was in confidence and I didn't think the doctor would understand if I did.

And then he surprised me by adding, "Mr. Gates isn't suited to the cloth. It demands more than he can give. But then he's not the first clergyman to come back from France disillusioned and tormented by not being able to turn the other cheek." He sighed. "But then you've seen more of that than I have, Sister." We had reached his surgery, down a back street on the other side of the church, and he was opening the door, preparing to get down. "That binding of the broken leg was well done, by the by." And with that he was gone, striding briskly through the gate and up the walk to his door.

My mother watched him go. As the door was shut behind him and she was certain that she couldn't be overheard, she said in a low voice, "It was odd. Dr. Collins said something as we were coming up on The Willows. 'The house is up for sale, I'm told. It would be better to burn it down. There's been nothing but unhappiness there, according to my predecessor, and here's further proof he was right. If I believed in such things, I'd say it was haunted.' "

I said, "Then I'm surprised he had so little sympathy for Mr. Gates." I got out of the rear of the motorcar and moved up next to my mother.

"He's a rather brusque man, Dr. Collins. And just now he's overwhelmed. I did ask him who was handling the sale. Perhaps we should speak to them."

"Simon has called on the firm. But the agent couldn't tell him anything new."

She smiled. "I don't think Simon knew the name of the fourth boy when he went there. Hughes Estate Agents. Midhurst."

Chapter Seventeen

I SAT THERE, trying to take in what my mother had told me.

How often had I heard someone mention that The Willows was up for sale and that someone in Midhurst was handling the property. It was the reason Simon had gone there. He hadn't thought it important to tell me the name, and he hadn't connected it with the Sandy Hughes he'd been hunting. Most of the children had come from military or civil servant families, and the boys would have been of an age to serve King and Country when the war started. We'd concentrated our search in that direction because it was a reliable source.

Mother smiled at my expression of disbelief. "Of course we aren't sure he's the Hughes you're after. It really isn't an unusual name."

"But Simon was *there*," I said. "He's thorough. He would have remembered."

"It's possible the Hughes he spoke with was the wrong one. On the other hand," Mother asked thoughtfully, "what better way to have access to that house without arousing suspicion?"

I laughed. "All right, we'll go to Midhurst, shall we?"

As we drove toward the town, my mother asked about the man and woman who had come to the door of The Willows.

When I finished explaining, she shook her head.

"That was well done, covering up the rector's attempt. He'll find it easier to live down if it doesn't become the topic of the day."

"It was frightening seeing him lying there. I thought surely he was dead."

"Yes, it was amazing the fall didn't kill him." She took a deep breath. "And Lieutenant Wade—Corporal Caswell? Would Gates's death also lie at his door?"

We were silent the rest of the way to Midhurst. The estate agent's firm was halfway down the High Street. At first glance it appeared to be closed.

After we'd found a place to leave the motorcar we walked back.

"What shall we tell him? We can't just walk in and ask if he'd been one of the children at The Willows."

She had a good point. "We'll show interest in the house. That's the ticket."

I put out my hand and tried to turn the knob, but it appeared to be locked. I was just about to try again when someone on the other side opened it for me.

The man was tall and slim, and I recognized him at once. The boy was still there in the shape of his nose and the square chin. He was the right age as well.

"The door tends to stick when the weather is damp," he said, and stepped back to let us come inside.

It was small, as places of business went, but carefully decorated to give it an air of success and style.

There were chairs in front of a large desk, and the man at the door gestured toward them. "Do sit down, and tell me what I can do to help you."

"We're interested in a comfortable property in the vicinity of Petersfield," my mother said as she drew off her driving gloves.

But my attention was on the man who must be Sandy Hughes. As he closed the door and turned to come back to the desk, I couldn't help but notice that he was limping heavily.

I looked away at once, but he'd caught my glance at his feet and he flushed. "I do have a property in Petersfield, but I don't think it would suit you," he said, hurrying around his desk to hide his limp. "There are other properties that should be a better choice." Taking a sheaf of papers out of a drawer, he leafed through them, then chose one to hand to my mother.

Looking over her shoulder, I could see that it was a handsome property on the road to Haslemere, with a small pond fed by a stream.

Mother frowned. "Yes, that's very nice, but beyond what I should like to pay. Is there anything else?"

"Here is another house that might interest you. But you'll find that what it requires in order to bring it up to your standards more than makes up the difference in cost." He went on to offer her several more properties, one a lovely estate near Peterborough, but she managed to find a flaw in each one.

I said, now that we'd established our bona fides, so to speak, "Are you by any chance related to the Alexander Hughes who lived in The Willows during the time the Caswell family was in residence?"

He froze in the act of handing my mother another sheet of paper, staring at me in horror quickly supplanted by anger.

"I'm sorry if I've upset you," I said gently. "It's only because you look so much like one of the boys in a photograph I happen to have. And his name was Hughes. There are the two Wade children, the Bingham and the Mayfield boys, Gwendolyn Caswell, and another boy and girl—I'm afraid I can't remember their names."

"Is that why you've come here? Because of the past? I'm not this Alexander Hughes. I've never had anything to do with the family you've mentioned."

"You lived in India, didn't you? I did as well. That's how I came to know about the Caswells."

My mother was saying, "Yes, I was looking for just such a family for my daughter. That's how we happen to have the photograph.

Mrs. Caswell gave it to us. But in the end we decided to keep Bess with us instead of sending her to England."

"Get out," he said, rising from his chair. "Just—get out and leave me alone."

We had no choice but to go, and he followed us to the door, shutting it firmly behind us. And I heard the tumblers in the lock turn as well.

"Well." My mother walked to the motorcar, then looked up and down the street.

"I'm famished. We've missed our lunch, and I think we should stop for something."

I spotted a tea shop just a few doors down from where we stood, on the far side of the street. "That looks cozy. Shall we walk over there?" I glanced over my shoulder as we turned to go, and I saw Mr. Hughes at his window watching us. He stepped back when he realized I could see him there.

"Do you think we've found the right Alexander Hughes?" I asked.

"I'd say yes," my mother agreed. "But for some reason he doesn't want to admit it. Do you think he could have had anything to do with that fire at the photographer's shop?"

"It would depend on how much he had to hide, wouldn't it?" We reached the shop and went inside, choosing a table near the window.

A middle-aged woman came to take our order. My mother ordered for both of us, then turned to me when the woman had gone away. "We'll both feel better when we've got a little food inside us."

I had to agree. I was very tired myself and knew she must be as well. We sat in silence as we waited. And then my mother put out a hand to touch my arm. "Mr. Hughes has just come out of his shop. And he's locking up. We must have upset him more than we realized. Oh. Now he's coming this way." She watched him for a moment and then said, "I do think he's coming in here!"

"But he was watching—he knows we're here."

After a moment, the tea shop door opened, but I didn't turn around. Then I heard footsteps approaching our table. And the limp was pronounced.

"I'm sorry," Mr. Hughes said, and I looked up. His face was haggard. "I find it difficult—still, I need to know why you are here. Why you are asking questions about that family at The Willows."

I indicated the third chair. "Please join us, Mr. Hughes." I waited, afraid he wouldn't sit down after all. Others in the shop were staring, as if expecting a scene of some sort.

And then finally he did sit, perched on the edge of his chair, as if he was determined to leave as soon as he could. The woman who'd taken our order came over to ask if he would care to have anything.

He blinked as if he wasn't sure just what she'd asked. "I—yes, all right, tea, please, Mrs. Thompson."

"I'm sorry if we troubled you, Mr. Hughes," my mother was saying, keeping her voice down so that the others in the tea shop couldn't overhear us. "But you see, we do have that photograph. And we'd like very much to know the names of those children."

"Their murderer was found. The Caswells. There's nothing more to be said."

"And yet the man who took this photograph was killed in a fire that destroyed his shop—and with it all his negatives and papers. He was on the upper floor, asleep, when the fire started, and he never got out. Nor did his daughter. It happened just after my daughter and a friend went to see them to ask if Mr. Gessler could identify the photograph and when it was taken. He has aged, of course, and all he could tell us was that he had indeed taken that photograph. There was a mark, you see, that he recognized. But that was all. And so he died uselessly, and his daughter as well."

"You don't know that the fire was set," he told my mother, his voice tight.

"Indeed I don't. But the Winchester police believe it was. They called it arson."

He was silent for a moment. "We can't talk here. Come back to the estate office."

But before he could stand up, Mrs. Thompson was behind him with his tea and our sandwiches.

Sinking back into his chair, he looked cornered. My mother poured my cup and then her own, and began to eat one of the sandwiches. But I could tell that she was no longer hungry. It was mechanical. My own mouth was dry, but I got the sandwich down with dispatch, and finished my tea. I don't think Mr. Hughes had touched his. But as I watched, he gulped it down and got up.

"I'll wait for you in my office."

He turned and walked out the door,

"Do you think he killed the Caswells? Should we go back there?" I asked.

My mother put down her cup and said, "We really have to hear what he has to say. The two of us? I think we'll be safe enough." But as she rose and went to pay for our tea, I heard her say, "I do wish Simon was here."

We walked up the High Street and crossed over to HUGHES ESTATE AGENT.

The door stuck again, but Mr. Hughes opened it and stood aside to let us enter, just as he had before. We walked to the chairs we'd occupied earlier, but this time he stood by the door.

"I remember Mr. Gessler. He was quiet, gentle, and he managed to make us smile for him. He sent Mrs. Caswell out of the room and spoke sharply to Gwendolyn when she tried to make the little Wade girl cry. And so it was a suitable photograph of happy children preparing for Christmas." His mouth twisted with pain. "I had blocked that out of my mind. I'd blocked it all out."

"Do you remember the names of the other children? The two we don't know?"

He shook his head. "I'd shut that out as well."

"What happened to make that such an unhappy house?" I asked.

"They didn't want us there. They needed the money our parents sent them and they punished us in small spiteful ways and made certain we told no one what was happening. They warned us the house was haunted, and that if we left our rooms at night, something unspeakable was waiting out there for us." He broke off, looking down the street. "It's what I never wanted to do. Go back to the past," he said after a moment, and I saw the tears in his eyes.

"Why did you agree to represent The Willows?" I asked, when he had mastered his feelings. "If it hurt so much even to think about the past?"

"I've been ill, I had to ask an older cousin to help me for a bit. The truth is, I need the money." He shrugged, and something in that shrug spoke volumes about his pain. "I'm in the same boat as the Caswells. How ironic is that?" He left the door, limped to the desk, moved his chair, but didn't sit down.

"You've noticed the limp. I try to cover it up, but when I'm tense or anxious, it seems to get worse." He moved some of the papers around on his desk, but I didn't think he had any idea what he was doing. "I was destined for the Army. My father and my grandfather had been in the Army. It was expected that I'd follow them. But one day Gwendolyn brought around her pony and told me I could ride it. I was pleased, I'd always liked horses. But as I started to mount, she pinched it hard, and it threw me off. Only my foot was already in the stirrup, and the damage was done. They wouldn't call the doctor, they told me that I was making too much of what had happened. Miss Gooding did her best, but the foot was beyond her skills. So much for the Army. And I'm not fit for much else."

"There was the law. The church. Traditional alternatives."

"With this limp? Yes, I'm feeling sorry for myself. But the foot still hurts, and I can't bear the pity I see in the eyes of strangers as I hobble down the street. The people I deal with here? Our encounters are brief and transient. I sit behind my desk, except when it's damp and the damned door sticks. I talk to them, send them out to look at various properties, and they seldom see me do more than stand up to shake hands. Either I sell them a property or I don't. Either way I never have to see them again." He shoved the chair hard against the desk. "Even my parents were disappointed in me. My father was garrisoned in South Africa when I was born, and they stayed on when my father left the Army. I haven't seen them since I came down from Cambridge."

It was self-pity, but I could understand how hard it must have been for Mr. Hughes. And I could also see that festering resentment could have turned to murder.

"So there you have the life of Alexander Hughes," he finished bitterly.

"To say I'm sorry is not enough," my mother said. "I understand the pull of the Army. And I understand how you feel about your limp. But you walked into the tearoom."

"Yes, but they know me."

"Did they know you when you first came to Midhurst?"

"Well, no. But I had to find somewhere to have my tea."

"It seems that your shame is rather selective," my mother ended gently.

His face flamed with anger, and for an instant I saw a man who could well have committed murder. But he managed to get his temper under control and tell her to mind her own business.

I interrupted. "We must be going. Are you sure, Mr. Hughes, that you don't remember the names of the other two children in that photograph?"

"I remember one of the little girls. Hazel. Gwendolyn called her Witch Hazel. I haven't thought about her in years. She could give as good as she got, small as she was. And after a while Gwendolyn left her alone."

"No last name?"

"Simpson? No, Sheridan, I think it was. She came into a great deal of money when she was twenty-one. Poor as a church mouse before that. I saw in the *Times* that she married rather well. Her husband is—or was at the time—an equerry to one of the Princes. I forget which one." He passed a hand over his face. "You see why I don't want to remember. For God's sake, take your questions and go away."

My mother rose. "Thank you, Mr. Hughes. You were very kind to help us."

And we left. As I was cranking the motorcar, I saw Hughes at his window once more, but this time he was placing a discreet sign in it that said CLOSED.

My mother said as I got in beside her and took the wheel, "What a terrible legacy those awful people have left behind. I'm beginning to think that whoever killed them did Society a favor. If Lieutenant Wade is the guilty person, then I'm glad he escaped."

But there were his parents as well. It was a measure of how upset my mother was, to say such a thing.

We drove in silence for some time, then she said, "Mr. Gates's uncle. Lieutenant Wade. This Captain Bingham you spoke to in France. Mr. Hughes. Four people who had an excellent reason to commit murder. But why wait so many years?"

"Because," I suggested, "the Caswells stopped taking in children."

"Yes, that's likely. But something must have triggered the murders."

"There was Wade's little sister, who was thought to have died of typhoid because the Caswells didn't summon the doctor," I reminded her. "And then Alice Standish dying in England of what was said to be the same disease. Lieutenant Wade spent that long voyage home listening to a woman mourning her child. It must have revived memories he'd tried to push away, like Mr. Hughes. Perhaps he stopped by to confront them, and then things got out of hand. He'd have had his service revolver with him. It would be easy to kill three unsuspecting people."

"It's such a coincidence that Lieutenant Wade was traveling down to Portsmouth that same day. Who could have known he was there, or remembered him as a child even if he did come to Petersfield? But I can see that he found himself drawn to go back. Perhaps their intransigence, no sign of regret or remorse, angered him so much he had killed them before he came to his senses."

My mother took a deep breath. "I'm beginning to think we'll never know the answer, Bess. And that leaves the question of what to do about Thomas Wade."

"Yes, I know. I wish I'd never confided in the Colonel Sahib. I've just reminded him of what happened. And put him on the spot, now that he knows where Lieutenant Wade is."

"I don't think he's ever really forgot that night when Lieutenant Wade failed to come back from his patrol."

We drove the rest of the way busy with our thoughts. Rain caught up with us before we reached Somerset, and I was forced to concentrate on the road as the heavy squalls reduced visibility to the point that once I had to pull over under a tree until the worst had passed.

Simon was at the house when we returned. He'd brought some papers for the Colonel Sahib and was waiting for him.

Surprised to see me, he said, "You've been back to Petersfield, I take it."

"Yes, and we've learned a little more. I don't know if it's useful information or not," I added.

"Richard won't be back for a few days, Simon. Leave the papers in his study, if you will, and then stay for dinner. We could both use some cheering up."

It was Simon who drove me back to London and to the station when my leave was over.

My mother and I had asked him about his visit to Midhurst. But he had met a small, graying man who had introduced himself as Mr. Hughes. Was this the cousin Hughes had mentioned?

"He was hardly one of the Caswell children, and he could tell me very little about The Willows, just what was in the brochures that had been made up for prospective clients. What's more, he seemed uninterested in its past. I asked if he had a family, and he told me there was a son who died before he was two and a daughter who presently lives in Derbyshire. He himself had spent most of his life in London. At that point I thanked him for his help and left. He said nothing about taking his cousin's place."

He had never seen or heard of the man we'd spoken with.

We left home a little ahead of time because I wanted very much to see if I could find anything more about Hazel Sheridan.

That took us to Somerset House.

And there she was, the only child of the sister of a very wealthy merchant who had made his fortune in India but who had no one to leave it to but his niece.

She had married well, to a Sir Henry Campbell. They had a single son.

As we waited for the train to pull in, Simon commented, "I think your mother is persuaded that it was Lieutenant Wade after all. I think before she went to Petersfield, she had her doubts."

"It appears that way," I agreed. "But I'm glad I have delved into the Caswells and the children in their keeping. For one thing it has taught me how lucky I was that my parents kept me in India with them despite the risks. For another, I can better understand Lieutenant Wade. I couldn't fathom how the man I knew there in Peshawar could have killed anyone."

"It still doesn't explain why he killed his parents."

"Yes, there's that. Perhaps he blamed them for not taking him and his sister away from The Willows. For not seeing or believing the torment they endured. I don't think my mother would have been so easily deceived."

"Perhaps she would have been if you were too frightened to tell her what was happening to you."

"There's that."

"I don't think I'd have been misled," he said after a moment. "I knew you too well."

Before I could say anything more, the train came roaring into the station, wreathed with smoke and preventing any conversation at all.

Simon took my arm and helped me into the carriage, setting my kit on the rack. Shutting the door, he stood by the window for a moment, waiting for the bustle to die down.

"We have it on good authority," he said in a voice pitched for me to hear and no one else, "that Lieutenant Wade has tried to escape. Whether he succeeded or not, I don't know."

Astonished, I stared at him. "But why would he do that? He'd be safe in German hands until the end of the war." And why had Simon waited until now to tell me this piece of news?

"He was always a complicated man, Bess. Most of us are."

And the train was moving, leaving him standing there watching me out of sight.

Chapter Eighteen

The influenza epidemic hadn't abated. Nor had the killing in the trenches.

I was sent back to the same hospital where I'd worked before with the influenza patients. There were new doctors, new nurses, but Matron was still there. She greeted me warmly, and gave me news of those who had been here earlier. Of those who had fallen ill, three had died, but the rest were even now convalescing. And then I was back in the wards, tending the ill and dying.

I lost track of time. I ate when I was hungry and slept when I could. The days and nights were a blur. And then Matron came for me at dawn one morning as I was bathing a patient.

"You are being relieved," she said, "although I'm not sure how much relief there will be. You're needed again at one of the forward aid stations. The staff has fallen ill and the new nursing Sisters have just finished their training. An experienced nurse is badly needed. I have recommended you. You're steady and reliable, as well as accustomed to dealing with both wounded and influenza patients."

She helped me put fresh sheets on the bed and settle the patient again. "He's passed the crisis," I told her. "I'll place him on the list for broth tonight."

"Yes, that's good news."

I gathered up the basin and cloths while Matron collected the soiled sheets.

We walked together up the aisle between the cots. She said, "I lost my brother today. He was killed in the fighting. I'm glad he didn't suffer." She gestured around us at the men coughing or lying silent in the last throes of the illness.

"I'm so sorry," I said, knowing how inadequate that was.

"Thank you, Sister." She took a deep breath. "Go on and change. An ambulance will be here within the hour. I'll add the Sergeant's name to the broth list for you. Good luck, my dear."

And she walked away with the soiled linens and the basin, leaving me to make my preparations. The first thing I did was to have a cup of tea and a little food. It didn't take long to pack, and so I changed my uniform, bathed my face and hands, and was standing by the receiving area when my driver came up.

He looked tired, like the rest of us. I had known him for some time but hadn't seen him in months. So many people we knew disappeared. Wounded, killed, taken ill and invalided home.

"Hello, Teddy. How are you?"

"Well enough. It's rough going today, Sister."

I could hear the guns even now. "Yes, I expect it will be." I climbed in beside him, and only then did I notice the filthy bandage around his forearm.

"What happened?" I asked, catching his hand before he could drive on.

"It's not much," he said, shrugging it off as so many soldiers did.

"Serious enough to be bandaged once, and not seen to since," I said. "Come inside and I'll clean it for you."

"No need to make a fuss, Sister," he argued, taking his hand back. "It's healing well enough."

But when I touched it, he winced. I opened my door and got out. "We're not moving a mile until I've had a look at that arm."

Frustrated, saying something under his breath that I couldn't catch, he got out of the ambulance. "But you'll see to it here, Sister, if you would. I won't go in there." He nodded toward the hospital.

I had forgot about Teddy's reputation.

He was a conscientious objector. He had chosen not to fight but volunteered as a driver instead. Nor was he the first who had done that. It was by no means a safe alternative. Teddy had been wounded twice, and his ambulance had been strafed at least once and hit by shell fragments several times. He was a tall, rather attractive man but kept to himself to avoid comments about his views on war.

I hurried back inside and asked one of the Sisters for a tray. Cutting off the bandage, I saw that the wound in his forearm was rather deep and needed cleaning and stitches to close it properly.

"It's not going to heal like this," I said, and set to work. A quarter of an hour later, it was finished, the wound cleaned, stitched, and bandaged again. He really should have seen a doctor, but I knew I couldn't persuade him to do that.

He watched me work with stoic patience and said only, "You'd make a fine seamstress."

It made me laugh. Returning the tray to the hospital, I got into the ambulance and we set out for the aid station. It was in chaos when I got there, and I had no time to think. This was when training took over and experience was my guide. The Sisters here were willing and had worked with the wounded in clinics before being sent to France. But they had not dealt with battlefield conditions, where nothing was tidy and men were bleeding, not neatly bandaged. What's more, the sheer numbers of men coming in was overwhelming, with no system to follow for assessing their needs.

It took me the better part of the day to straighten out the tangle, and I had just stopped for my first break when the doctor arrived. I hadn't worked with him before, although I knew his reputation as a martinet. His name was Cunningham, and I thought he must be somewhere in his forties, for his fair hair was graying at the temples and deep lines were etched around his eyes and on either side of his mouth.

He made a brief tour, raised his eyebrows at the sight of me standing to one side with cup in hand, and said, "Are you enjoying your tea, Sister? I see others hard at work."

"Indeed, Dr. Cunningham, I am," I answered briskly. "Everything is running smoothly, and I've stopped to observe and look for room for improvement."

To my surprise he grinned. "You're not to talk back to doctors, you know."

"My apologies, sir, but you did ask."

The grin broadened. Then he asked, "You're the Sister that Matron sent up?"

"Yes, sir, I am."

"She told me you would have everything shipshape, Crawford, and by God she was right. Show me to my first patient."

Dr. Cunningham worked steadily until almost first light, and we sent a long line of ambulances back to hospitals in the rear. The shelling, which had been intense, had long since stopped, and the attack that followed was ferocious but blessedly brief. The endless stream of wounded had come down to a trickle, and I longed for my bed as I stood there in the cool dawn air and stretched my back.

Someone came up behind me. It was Dr. Cunningham with two cups of tea in his hands.

"Here. You've earned it. You didn't get any dinner, did you?"

I took the cup he was holding out and realized with the first sip how thirsty I was. "Nor did you."

"Never mind, the human body can go longer without food than without water. Although I understand one of the ambulance drivers brought up something hot as well as a letter for you." He reached into his pocket, balancing his cup in the other hand, and pulled out a much-traveled envelope. "He says to tell you that the forearm is no longer hurting as much."

That must have been Teddy. I wouldn't have been at all surprised if Matron hadn't given my letter to him, knowing I'd receive it faster than if it was left to the post to find me.

I took it eagerly, recognizing Simon's handwriting, but this was neither the time nor the place to read it. I shoved it into my pocket, and drank some of the tea.

"Simon Brandon. I know that name," Dr. Cunningham said, frowning. "Now from where? That's the question."

I said nothing. For one thing, I was surprised that he'd looked at the sender's name. Perhaps it was only idle curiosity. Perhaps his remark was no more than an attempt to discover if Simon was a member of my family—a cousin, perhaps—or my sweetheart. But it troubled me all the same.

"Well, doesn't matter, does it?" he said after a moment. "Go and eat something, Sister Crawford. I can't have you falling down in a faint over my patients."

I did as I was told, and as soon as I'd finished, I felt such a lethargy that I could hardly keep my eyes from drifting shut. I opened Simon's letter and lit a shielded candle, trying to concentrate on black lines that seemed determined to run together.

Your parents are well, as am I. Your father is in Cornwall, I think, and your mother has gone to visit Melinda in his absence. I have no recent news about Thomas and take that to mean he has either been recaptured or killed. I did discover one bit of information. Your mother wrote to the little girl you were concerned about. She denies that she was ever at The Willows. Did Hughes lie? She's often in the newspapers; he could easily have come up with that name in an effort to be rid of you.

I had to admit that this was entirely possible.

And yet I had been there when Mr. Hughes gave us the name. It was my feeling that he'd been too distraught to lie.

But then I'd been willing to believe him, all too keen on finding the children in that photograph. To tell the truth, I thought wryly, it hadn't occurred to me that when pressed, he might resort to a falsehood.

Or was he afraid that what the last remaining children might tell us would make it clear that he and not Lieutenant Wade had killed the Caswells?

I realized too that he had been in England from the start, unable to serve because of his bad foot and already in contact with Mr. Gates. He could have set the fire that killed the Gesslers and changed the photograph in Miss Gooding's frame. Of course Captain Bingham had been in England as well. But surely Miss Gooding would have said something about the man in uniform who had come to her house. On the other hand, she hadn't mentioned a limp . . . Wouldn't she remember the boy whose foot she'd tended?

I went back to the letter.

There was very little more to it.

I hope you are well and safe. I don't know which will happen first, the end of the war or the end of armies as we know them, from this epidemic. That will leave only the rats, and they have no loyalties to either side.

It was signed simply, *Yours, Simon.*

He sounded rather gloomy, as if he knew more than anyone here how the Army was faring. We saw only our small corner of it, and heard the gossip that ran like wildfire up and down the lines. Fresh troops, soldiers returning to the line, wounded, visiting staff officers, all brought with them new rumors.

Dr. Cunningham asked the next morning if my letter had brought good news from home, and I told him it had assured me that my family was well.

He nodded. "I was on compassionate leave, although my mother pulled through. Quite possibly because I was there." He finished his work on a leg wound and then said, "I still haven't placed Simon Brandon. But I shall. I never forget a name."

I smiled. "Shall I ask him next time I write whether he remembers you?"

Dr. Cunningham shook his head. "No, better to let sleeping dogs lie, until I've worked it out. We might well be lifelong enemies."

He smiled when he said it, but I noticed that the smile didn't quite reach his eyes.

The next letter was from my mother.

She wrote in haste, because my father had offered to put it in the pouch with dispatches so that she could write more freely.

After the news from home, she continued,

I spent the weekend with Melinda. She had asked me to come because she's had a letter from Mr. Kipling, in regard to that small matter in India that you wished him to look into. His contact has found it rather difficult to get to the bottom of what happened that night. Understandably the local people aren't eager to be drawn into what they feel is strictly an English matter. But the contact also feels that there's more to it than just ordinary reluctance to be involved. He went as far as to read newspaper accounts of the two deaths, to see what was being said at the time. One account indicates that when the MFP took over the inquiry, the only interest in our friend was as a witness, to discover if he had heard or seen anything that might help in the investigation. It wasn't until news caught up with them in Lahore that our friend was being sought in Britain for three other events that they concluded he must be responsible for the two in Agra as well. One of those two MFP has died, and so far it's not been possible to trace the other one. If this is true, it changes our perception, doesn't it? Mr. Kipling's contact is going to continue pursuing the matter, which is very kind of him. Mr. Kipling has told Melinda that his contact also has more curiosity than a cat and nearly as many lives. He won't easily be deterred.

Melinda is well and sends her love. She hopes you'll come for a visit the next time you pass through Dover.

I read the letter again. Discovering the truth about Lieutenant Wade was like watching a flag in the wind, twisting and turning on its ropes. When I had heard the Subedar's dying words, I was convinced that the Lieutenant was guilty as charged, that his flight had all but proclaimed it. And I wanted to see him taken into custody and tried, to remove the stain on my father's reputation and that of his regiment.

Now I wasn't sure of anything except that my father had done his duty at the time, regardless of the whispers outside the regiment. That I had never doubted.

But there was nothing I could do at present. And so I worked with Dr. Cunningham and I kept my thoughts to myself.

We sent sixteen men back to the influenza hospital, and two died en route. It was Teddy who brought me that news. "Nothing we could do," he added. "Nothing."

I could hear the distress in his voice. "People are dropping dead on the streets in England," I reminded him. "Unable to reach home or even hospital."

"It's like a visitation of the plague. Wasn't it the Black Death that killed over a quarter of the population of Europe in the Dark Ages? We haven't come very far, have we? We still can't save lives."

And he was gone, this time carrying wounded to the Base Hospital in Rouen.

Dr. Cunningham said very late one evening, "I'm heartily sick of death." Stalking off, he disappeared into the night. An hour later, when I went to look for him because one of the men just brought in was bleeding internally, I found him sitting with his back against a blasted, blackened tree. I could smell the whiskey before I reached him.

He looked up, and all I could see were the whites of his eyes as he gazed up at me.

"I've had enough," he said.

"I'm sorry," I replied, "but you must come. There's a machine-gun case, with internal bleeding."

"See to it."

"I can't. I've tried." When he didn't move, I added, "He's going to die."

"He'll die with or without me."

"You can't be sure of that until you've examined him."

"I really bloody don't care."

"He does." It was all I could think of to say.

After a moment he got to his feet. "I'll remind you of that when *you* break, Sister. Or do you care enough to break?"

He walked on, and when I reached the patient, he was already there, seemingly as sober as I was. I wondered then if this was a single instance or if he had problems with drinking and was accustomed to hiding it.

New men were moving into position in the trenches toward dawn. I could hear the shuffle of their feet and the occasional jingle of rifles against buttons or kit as they went. I thought about them, silent because they knew what was coming and could do nothing to change their fate. Many of them I was sure must be praying or remembering those back in England who were waiting for them.

Captain Bingham, as I learned later, was in command of those on rotation. He came striding toward us with a pair of stretchers in his wake. The stretcher bearers stopped just outside our perimeter, and he came in alone.

I hadn't seen him since we'd parted at the hospital. He nodded as he walked past where I was standing with Sister MacLeod and hailed Dr. Cunningham.

"I've two men with me who are coming down with this influenza. You must have ambulances coming in this morning."

"They're on their way. Or at least they're supposed to be."

"I'll wait."

Sister Ramsey brought him a cup of tea and then took more to the weary stretcher bearers squatting beside their charges. It wasn't twenty minutes later that I heard the hum of motors and looked up to see three ambulances coming toward us.

I said to Captain Bingham, "Take the lead ambulance for your men. There's enough room. We'll load the wounded in the others."

Going ahead to meet the first ambulance, I saw that Teddy was driving. I waved and leaned in the passenger window. "We've got two influenza patients," I said. "They're coming just now. If you'll take them in?"

He was looking beyond me and saw the Captain speaking to the stretcher bearers. Teddy was suddenly galvanized. "Sister—are those the ones?"

"Yes, Captain Bingham is just bringing them now."

"For God's sake, Sister, don't put them in my ambulance. I beg of you."

"But you've carried them before—" I began, mystified by his reaction.

"It's not the influenza. It's the Captain. Bingham. We have—there's a history between us. I don't want to see him."

I looked toward the Captain. He was twenty yards away now.

"Teddy—"

He was hunched over the wheel, his face turned away from me—and from the approaching officer.

"All right, I'll have Frank take them in." I hurried forward, calling to Captain Bingham. "There's been a change in plans, Captain. We'll use the last ambulance instead."

"Why not this one?" he demanded, frowning.

"Frank has more experience with influenza cases," I said, and without waiting for an answer I started toward the last ambulance in line. When the patients were on board and Frank was turning back the way he'd come, Captain Bingham thanked me curtly and set off with his stretcher bearers to catch the rest of his men up.

I watched him go and then went back to where Teddy was sitting. He looked ill, I realized, as he said, "Thank you, Sister."

"Is there something wrong? Anything I can do?"

"No. Just let it go." He shook his head. "I'm sorry, Sister."

"Never mind," I told him and went to the rear of the ambulance, opening the doors for the first of the wounded to be carried aboard. One of them was the internal bleeding case, and while he was pale and very weak, he was still alive.

As soon as the doors closed, Teddy was off, not waiting for the next ambulance to follow.

Dr. Cunningham saw Teddy's hasty retreat. "Was that the CO driving?" he asked.

"Yes. Teddy. He's not feeling very well himself."

"Well, I hope he doesn't pass the influenza on to those men," the doctor said, and turned back to his work.

It was after midnight when the storm blew up. It had been hot all afternoon and the sun set in a hazy sky half hidden as it went down in a bank of clouds.

We had had a surprisingly quiet evening. Dr. Cunningham went to bed around ten thirty, and at eleven, listening to the first distant rumbles of thunder, I left Sister MacLeod and Sister Ramsey in charge and went to my own quarters, aching with fatigue.

When the storm struck, it was accompanied by high winds and pelting rain that hit the ground like stones. It woke me up. I hadn't undressed, and throwing a coat over my shoulders, I hurried to be sure Sister MacLeod and Sister Ramsey were coping. There were only three patients, and all was well. On my way back to my bed, I heard muffled cries coming from Dr. Cunningham's quarters. With the thunder nearly overhead, my first thought was that he'd taken ill and was calling for help.

After a moment's hesitation as the rain soaked my cap and the shoulders of my coat, I went in to see what was wrong. He was thrashing about on his cot, and as I flicked on my torch, I realized that he was asleep and dreaming. The smell of whiskey was strong. He must have drunk himself to sleep, I thought as he cried out again, this time almost as if he were in pain. And then rearing up in bed, he shouted, "Don't leave me!"

I thought at first he was speaking to me. But his eyes, wide and wild, were unseeing, lost in whatever nightmare he was reliving.

The storm was overhead now, the thunder so close on the heels of the lightning flash that they seemed to be simultaneous. Dr. Cunningham screamed, and when I touched his shoulder to wake him up, he clutched at me as if I were a lifeline.

I shook him then, trying to bring him out of his drunken sleep, and almost as if he had never been dreaming at all, he said with perfect clarity, "What the hell are you doing?"

I broke free. "You were having a bad dream. I heard you screaming and came to see what was wrong."

In the light from my torch he peered toward the main tent. "Where are the others?"

"With the wounded. They're all right. The storm has been very bad."

"Then get out of here before they see you. And mind your own business in future." He lay back down on his cot, turning his back to me. His next words were almost lost in a crash of thunder. "And turn off that bloody torch."

I flicked it off and left. Back in my own quarters, I shook out my wet coat and hung it up on a hook. Drying my hair on a towel, I tried to remember what Dr. Cunningham had screamed, the only coherent word he'd uttered until he woke up.

It was *Mother.* Like a child who had been frightened of storms and called out for comfort.

I wondered what was tormenting him, why he drank more than he should. It hadn't affected his judgment, at least not so far. But a time would come when he made a wrong choice or failed to make the right one—sometimes two different things—because he was impaired.

I wasn't going to be there to find out. He must have asked for my transfer, for two days later I was on my way back to a rear hospital where the wounded were being treated until they were stabilized and could be sent on to England.

I hadn't worked with this Matron before. She was a fair-haired woman, trim and competent. She welcomed me the next morning after my arrival and asked if I'd settled in.

I told her I had.

"Good. I've assigned you to the surgical cases, given your experience. Dr. Cunningham wrote on your chart that you were capable of making decisions on your own and experienced enough to know what to do in emergencies."

I was surprised that Dr. Cunningham had given me such a glowing report. Not under the circumstances. But it occurred to me then that he'd wanted to be rid of me quickly because of what I'd witnessed.

"He's very kind" was all I could say in response.

My duties were familiar, and I was quickly at home here. When I was not occupied with the surgical patients I sometimes helped feed men who couldn't help themselves, those blinded by gas or shrapnel, amputees, and those with broken arms or damaged hands. That's how I came to meet Patient 3308.

"No one knows who he is," Sister Joyner explained. "He was emaciated, bleeding from several wounds, and unconscious when they brought him in. We're not even certain he's one of ours. He was wearing a German officer's uniform. He just lies there, he doesn't speak or try to help himself—exhaustion, Matron says. But he must eat."

He was swathed in bandages, over his head and covering one eye, wrapped around his chin where there was a neck wound, one arm in a sling and one leg in a cast.

I sat by his side and coaxed him into swallowing the sustaining broth we gave to men too ill to eat ordinary food. I'd put pillows behind his head and raised him enough that he wouldn't choke. He opened his mouth more by rote than by design, and swallowed painfully when he felt the gruel on his tongue.

It took half an hour to finish the cup, and I was on duty elsewhere by that time. I wiped his lips and said bracingly, "Count each cup as a step forward and you'll soon be fit again."

But I didn't think he understood what I was saying.

I was busy for the next two days, but returned to Patient 3308 when I was free. He accepted the broth as he had before, by rote, almost as if his brain was not aware of what he was doing, his body simply following commands.

Later I asked Matron if there was a head wound.

"There was, rather deep. He was probably concussed. Which must have made matters worse. Whatever he's been through nearly killed him, and it will be a while before he's truly sensible as opposed to being conscious. There's an officer missing in the Wilts. His name is James. Captain Stephen James. We believe it might be him—that he was caught behind enemy lines. Some three weeks ago. It would explain the exhaustion and the emaciation."

"Poor man," I said.

"Yes, there's a chance he will never fully recover. The mind can endure only so much before it withdraws completely."

I began reading to him when I had a moment. There were books in a tiny library that had begun quite by accident, someone leaving a book and someone else taking it but replacing it with another title. There were the poems of O. A. Manning on the shelf, several novels by Dickens, and a history of Rome, as well as Wilkie Collins's *The Moonstone.*

I chose that as less depressing than Dickens and more interesting than Rome's rise and tried to read at least half a chapter every evening.

I think Patient 3308 was soon responding to the steady tone of my voice if not to the words. It occurred to me that Matron was wrong, that he wasn't English. But it didn't matter. He was quieter, the fingers of his one good hand no longer restless on the coverlet. I couldn't imagine how much pain he was in, but Matron had been worried that sedatives might be too much for his body.

Dr. Cunningham came back with one of the ambulances, to have a cut in his forehead stitched. I wondered if he'd fallen while drunk, but Matron told me later that one of the head wound patients had lashed out, catching the doctor as he was bending over to suture the cut.

"He's a good doctor," Matron said, standing beside me as I watched him leave. "We could do with more like him. He asked how you were faring, and I told him you were working out very well indeed. Kind of him to remember."

I thought it was more likely he was making certain I hadn't told what I knew.

I also saw Teddy again, but he refused to discuss Captain Bingham. Had Teddy been one of the children at The Willows? I was reluctant to come right out and ask. He had said that he and the Captain had had "a history." And that could be the connection. It would be easy to jump to the wrong conclusions. Many people had no patience with conscientious objectors, although they did serve, only in other ways than the actual fighting. Some drove ambulances, many were orderlies, others worked in factories for the war effort.

I didn't press, and I could see the relief on Teddy's face when I smiled and changed the subject.

I wished for my turn to take a short leave. There was the little girl still to be interviewed, but it might be difficult to reach her if her husband was an equerry. My mother wrote again and this time gave me news of Hazel.

I was at a tea to raise money for the care of the wounded, and who should come in but one of the young Princes. His equerry was with him, and they stayed the obligatory fifteen minutes, while he made a short speech asking the people to give generously in gratitude for all the wounded who had given so much on behalf of King and Country. It was very affecting, and people responded as he would have hoped. I had an opportunity to observe Lady Campbell's husband. Haughty is the word that best describes him. Much more so than the Prince, who was very approachable. You'd have thought they had reversed roles.

There was a bit of gossip about Sir Henry. One of my friends told me he had been a Guards officer and had served in France before being wounded. He was in uniform, and I noticed that his right hand was still rather stiff.

At any rate, it was a lovely tea, and I'm glad I went. I had hoped Sir Henry's wife would come as well. I'd have liked to see her. I understand there's another charity event in honor of Princess Mary, and she could appear then. We'll see.

I had to smile. My mother was nothing if not inventive. And it was very likely that she'd attend the next charity event as well.

There were two spinal wounds, and we spent hours in surgery with them. I missed my usual hour of reading with Patient 3308, but the Sister in charge of the ward told me later that he was taking his gruel regularly and she thought he was slowly getting stronger.

"When I was changing his sheets, I saw the book by his bed. Is that yours?"

"It's from the little library. I thought it might help him escape from the memories that are too much for him. At least for a little while."

"A very good idea. I'll ask one of the other Sisters to take over when you aren't available."

But two days later Sister Bennett came to me and said ruefully, "Our blind Captain can distinguish between your voice and someone else's. Sister Higgins told me that when she began to read, the patient used his good hand and tried to force the book closed. Either you've made a conquest or 3308 doesn't care for Sister Higgins's Northumberland accent."

I laughed. "If he's German, he probably can't understand a word she says."

Sister Bennett nodded. "It's true. It took me a while to follow her myself. All right, we'll let *The Moonstone* wait for you."

I went back that evening, and when I picked up the book and began to read, I could have sworn that the patient sighed with relief.

If he could notice something as subtle as the difference in voices, it was a very good sign. But when I asked Sister Bennett how his wounds were healing, she told me they were taking their time. "That cut over his eye was infected when he was found. The clavicle is not healing the way we would like. There will be a knot where the bones had begun to rejoin crookedly on their own. The leg is making better progress. I'd like to see him up and walking next week. With a cane, if he can't manage crutches."

I said as much to the patient before I picked up the book the next evening.

"Sister Bennett would like to see you try to walk soon. With support, of course. The fear is, lying here so long you're likely to contract pneumonia."

There was no sign that he heard or understood me. The next day I asked if we had a German-speaking patient, and Sister Bennett found Julius Herring, whose parents, as it turned out, had been with the Foreign Office in Berlin before the war. He came limping down the row between cots and grinned at me when I rose to meet him.

"I hear you don't know if one of your patients is German or British. Shall I give it a try?"

"Please do," I said and gestured to the chair I'd just vacated

He sat down and began to speak, quietly and with assurance. But he got no response at all from 3308.

After a few minutes, Lieutenant Herring shrugged and got to his feet. "Either he doesn't know what I'm saying or he can't hear me wherever his mind is. The response I get is blankness."

"Thank you for trying. We might ask you again in a few days, if you don't mind. Depending on his progress."

"No, not at all. I'm supposed to be walking to strengthen this leg. I'll stop by on my own from time to time."

It didn't seem to worry the Lieutenant that 3308 was possibly a German officer. I'd noticed that in spite of all the posters and stories at home about how cruel and inhuman the Germans were, many men in the trenches seemed to see them differently, not as monsters but as soldiers like themselves.

I went about my work, reading to 3308 when I could. And then on a Tuesday evening as I was coming out of surgery, Sister Bennett called to me.

"We're taking the bandages off 3308 in a few minutes. Would you like to see what he looks like?"

I hadn't been there when the dressings were changed and so I was glad she had thought to tell me.

I washed my hands and changed my apron, then hurried to the ward. The sky was red with sunset, earlier each day as we moved toward autumn. I stopped to admire it, because as a rule, the sun had gone down before I had finished. By the time I reached 3308's cot, Sister Bennett had a tray before her on the bed with scissors and salves and fresh bandages as well as a bowl of water and clean cloths.

"Hello there," I said as I came up behind Sister Bennett. "I've come to sit with you while your bandages are removed. Would you like a mirror to see yourself—"

The patient had been lying back against a bank of pillows that Sister Bennett had piled behind his head so that she could work on his face. I had no more than said the word *mirror* when he erupted into violence, as unexpected as it was fierce.

The tray went flying, water splashing over the bed, bandages and scissors and pots of salve struck Sister Bennett in the face and chest, startling her so much that she cried out in alarm.

I turned to run for an orderly to help hold 3308 down, but he had subsided into his pillows once more, breathing hard. What I could see of his mouth was set in a hard line.

Sister Bennett bent down to retrieve the tray, the basin, and the other things. "I think we should let him rest for a while," she said calmly, regaining her composure very quickly.

And the two of us walked away.

"How odd. Why is he afraid of a mirror?" she asked me quietly when we were out of hearing. "Does he think he's been so badly scarred? He really isn't, you know."

"I have no idea. Perhaps he's afraid we'll discover he's German and send him to a camp for prisoners."

"There's that," she agreed. "He won't be pampered and read to there." She shook her head. "Perhaps he hates himself for letting himself be taken prisoner."

That made more sense than anything else. I'd treated prisoners, and they often saw their capture as a stain on their honor. A personal failure. I wasn't sure how British prisoners viewed it.

I went to my quarters for what was left of the half hour between surgeries.

It wasn't until I was sitting on my cot, wishing I'd stopped for a cup of tea on my way, that I understood what had happened there in Ward Three.

If I'd had that cup of tea in my lap, it would have gone spinning across the floor as I got to my feet and hurried back to the ward.

Chapter Nineteen

I HEADED DOWN the row. It appeared to me that 3308 was sleeping. He lay with his head turned to one side, his good hand slack on the coverlet. He couldn't see who I was, and I made a point of walking past his bed before turning to look back at him.

He didn't move, certain that the Sister who had come toward him had not stopped. I walked back the other way, moving at a steady pace as if I'd just come to be sure the patients were settled for the night. I opened and closed the ward door, and waited.

I could just see his bed.

Several men were already snoring or moaning in a drug-induced sleep. Fifteen minutes passed.

I thought I'd been wrong and was about to turn away and go back to my quarters when I saw 3308 tentatively sit up in his bed. It couldn't have been easy with his leg half healed and his shoulder still knitting. But he managed it. When no one said anything, he carefully lifted his arm out of its sling and flexed the hand. I couldn't see his mouth beneath the bandages, but I'd have been willing to wager he was grimacing in pain.

After a time, he swung his good leg over the edge of the bed and slowly brought the other leg after it. He was sitting on the side of the bed now, head down, catching his breath.

I was in the shadows by the door. He couldn't possibly see me there.

Finally he worked until he had unwound the bandages from his head and face. Again he sat there, waiting until the dizziness of lying in bed for days had passed. Then he got to his feet, holding on to the head of his bed, testing his legs. He nearly fell when he took his first step. Someone had brought crutches in for the patient in the next bed who had a broken foot. He reached out for them and again nearly went headfirst into the chair as he tried to grasp it to steady himself. But in the end he got the crutches and put one under each arm.

I wondered just how far he imagined he was going to get. He made a foray or two, getting the hang of the crutches, although it must have hurt his arm like the very devil while the cast on his leg must have pulled it down like lead.

After several minutes he stepped out into the space between the rows of cots. Slowly, painfully, head down, he came toward me, watching his footing and pausing every three or four steps.

I didn't move. But I knew he would see me very soon now, and I wondered what he would do.

On he came, a few steps, pause, a few steps. A patient cried out in his sleep, and 3308 froze, head up, looking to see if anyone would come. And still he didn't notice me there in the shadows of the doorway.

Finally, afraid that if I startled him he would go down, I stepped forward.

"Corporal Caswell," I said softly, "there's nowhere you can go. Not in your condition."

He swung toward me and nearly lost his balance. I sprang forward and caught his good arm, steadying him. "Let me take you back to bed before Matron sees you."

"I can't go back to England," he said tightly. "I won't. I can make it to a French town and find a way to stay there."

"Please listen to me. You can hardly walk. An orderly will spot you before you've gone ten yards. You have no clothing, no shoes, no money. What you're planning is impossible. Face it and go back to bed."

He stood there, stubbornly refusing to listen. "I can do it. I survived this long. It's only a matter of will."

"Yes, and if you damage that leg before it has fully healed, you'll be a beggar for the rest of your life." It was cruel but true.

I could hear voices outside the ward. I couldn't tell whether they were coming this way or only walking by. I had no choice now.

"If you leave this ward, I will call the MFP and have you taken into custody under your real name. And you'll hang."

"What does it matter? If I return to that bed they'll still come for me when you tell them who I am."

"All right," I said, hurrying because the voices were coming nearer. "A bargain. We made one before, if you remember. If you will go back to your bed and stay there, I promise I won't tell anyone what I know."

I thought he was going to refuse even so. And then slowly, with care, he turned. I helped him back to his bed, put the crutches where they belonged, roughly bandaged his head, and covered him with a sheet. When the door opened and Matron came in for her last rounds, I was reading from *The Moonstone* to Patient 3308.

She nodded to me then, and satisfied that all was well in the ward, turned and walked back the way she'd come. I waited to be sure she wasn't intending to return with a jug of water or medicines for the restless patients. And then I put the sling back into place and did up the bandages properly. When I had finished and he was settled, he turned to me.

"I don't understand you. But I'm grateful."

"Good night, Corporal. I think tomorrow you might let them know who you are, before they take you out and shoot you for a German spy."

The mouth beneath the bandages fought to conceal a grin. "It might be wise, yes."

* * *

The next morning, Sister Bennett came to inform me during my break that Corporal Caswell's mind had finally cleared. "He thought he was still a prisoner, that it was all a trick. Especially after Lieutenant Herring kept speaking to him in German."

"How miraculous," I said, trying to keep the dryness out of my voice. "I'm happy for him."

"Yes, I am too. I can't even imagine what he went through to escape."

And there it was again, that knack Lieutenant Wade had of making everyone around him believe in him.

I said, "If his bandages are off, he'll be able to finish that book for himself."

"Yes, I'm sure he'll be glad of that. He's a very attractive man. Too bad he's not an officer." And then with a laugh that belied any serious personal interest in Corporal Caswell, she was gone.

I wondered how she would feel if she were told he was wanted for five murders.

I took a deep breath.

Corporal Caswell would be reported to his company as back in British hands, wounded and recovering. That part of his masquerade would still be secure.

Later in the day, Matron told me that there would be a convoy of wounded bound for England very soon. "We need the beds," she added. "With the increase in influenza cases, we must move those who can safely be transported to clinics in England."

"Do you have a list of patients?"

"Yes, I've started one."

"Corporal Caswell," I said, "should go to a clinic in Somerset where I was once assigned. Longleigh House in Medford Longleigh. Dr. Gaines, who is in charge, is a marvel with broken limbs. And Matron does not suffer fools gladly."

"That's good to know. Thank you, Sister Crawford. I'd thought that particular clinic was for officers only."

"I believe exceptions are made. Indeed, Corporal Caswell is

probably a gentleman with his own reasons for enlisting in the ranks instead of going for officer training."

"Yes, I've noticed," she said, amused. "And so have my staff. It's been amazing how many Sisters have found an excuse to visit Ward Three."

I laughed. "All the more reason to transfer him to Somerset."

On my next break I wrote a hasty letter to my parents, asking them to arrange for Corporal Caswell to be accepted at Longleigh House.

I'll explain later. It's very important and I hope the transfer can be arranged.

I managed to waylay one of the motorcycle messengers from HQ and bribe him with cigarettes meant for the patients to add my letter to the HQ pouch for London.

"Sister Crawford, I'll be shot at dawn one of these days and it will be your fault," he said, slipping my letter inside his glove.

"Look at the direction. Colonel Crawford is happiest when he knows his only daughter is safe."

The messenger grinned. "And the court-martial will be glad to hear that, I'm sure."

And he was off with a roar, gunning the motor toward what passed as the road south.

I had no expectation of being asked to accompany the next convoy, but Matron had arranged it. "There are several very difficult cases that will need monitoring," she told me. "You've had the experience to see to them."

On the morning that we were to set out, we helped lift men from their beds onto stretchers while orderlies guided those who could walk.

In the midst of my duties I heard a frantic shout and turned to see Corporal Caswell calling my name. I finished giving orders to the next stretcher bearer and then went to speak to him. He looked haggard.

"Not to worry, Corporal," I said pleasantly, for there were too many ears within hearing. "I've seen to it that you'll be all right."

He frowned, uncertain whether to believe me or not.

"I promised, didn't I? And I keep my promises," I added.

There was too much to do to worry about one man. When the last of the ambulances was ready to pull out, I could finally sit down.

Teddy was driving. "I recognized that Corporal in Number Three," he said as we caught up with the convoy.

"You should," I said. "You brought him in when he was ill with influenza."

He shook his head. "I have the feeling I've met him before. Before the war, I mean."

Uneasy, because I didn't know just when Lieutenant Wade had begun to call himself Caswell, I said, "Well, if you work it out, let me know. Meanwhile, I'm going to close my eyes." It wouldn't do for Teddy to remember him by any other name. Not when the Corporal was a patient heading to England. I'd worry about Teddy later.

"Good luck there," he said as we hit the first of the ruts.

It wasn't until all my charges were on board ship for the crossing that I could really think about Corporal Caswell. After I'd looked at my serious cases, I found him in one of the wards. He saw me coming and put out a hand to stop me.

"You promised," he said in a low voice. "Now what the hell is going on?"

"I can't explain here. But you'll be safe. I've seen to it. You couldn't stay in France, they need the beds so desperately. What was I to tell them? The truth, that you couldn't go back to England?"

He cast a quick glance around. "I trusted you."

"And you must go on trusting me. There's no one else." I moved on, stopping to speak to a patient or talk to a Sister. And then I went up on deck, in desperate need of fresh air.

One of the officers was standing by the rail. As I stepped up beside him he said, "You'd better keep an eye on your charges, Sister. We're being shadowed by a submarine."

It was dark, cloudy. I couldn't see a thing but the motion of the Channel water, black and heaving beneath the railing.

A light flashed from one of the portholes and I heard an officer bark, "That man. Keep that curtain closed."

I couldn't help but think that if we were torpedoed, most of our patients would die. There would be no time to get them on deck, much less into boats. I found that my hands were gripping the rail so hard my nails were digging into the wood.

It brought back *Britannic*, and I shivered in spite of the warm night. We'd been so lucky then, so very lucky, that the ship was empty, traveling east to pick up wounded.

The officer began to walk around the deck, staring out at sea. I wanted to go with him, but I knew I'd be in the way.

How to save all these men? The question went round and round in my head and came back with the same answer every time. Most would die.

I went below and spoke quietly to each Sister, telling her that we could expect trouble. They nodded, then they turned to look around their wards. They knew as well as I did how many would survive.

Someone handed me a cup of tea, and I took it on deck with me, drinking it as I scanned the seas. It would be nearly impossible to see a torpedo in these conditions. Not until it was almost at the ship. I glanced up at the watch. All of the ship's officers were on duty tonight, all with field glasses trained on the sea. Ratings were posted around the railings as well, and more than a few of the orderlies on board.

I waited for that familiar judder as something hit the ship and for an instant threw her off her course before exploding down below the waterline. Even after two years, I would know it instantly.

I couldn't help but think about the many crossings I'd made and the many times a submarine had shadowed us. The ship was clearly marked as a hospital ship, but would that matter? Would the captain of the submarine even notice that in the dark, with the seas so rough?

All a torpedo needed to do was strike the rudder and the screws. It needn't strike amidships to stop us dead in the water. We'd lose way, and begin to turn in helpless circles. But that would still give us time to get some of the wounded to lifeboats, those who could be moved quickly without regard to their wounds. The more serious cases—it would be impossible. It would almost be more merciful to blow us out of the water and end it quickly.

I went below again, to be sure all was well, and found the Sisters going about their duties. But their gaze went immediately to my face as soon as I appeared. I smiled and shook my head. *Nothing so far.* And they nodded, their hands still busy.

We were zigzagging and the motion of the ship was already making some men seasick, adding to their misery.

I held buckets for many of them and carried the buckets up the companionways to throw the contents over the rail. The orderlies were needed elsewhere.

And then it was over. I could feel the engines changing speed, the ship losing headway in the water, and when I went on deck again, I could see Dover ahead, the castle a black menacing bulk on the cliffs above us.

I could hear the orderlies nervously chatting as they came down to their places, and my knees were weak from the stress of worrying.

The transfer to the waiting train went smoothly, from long practice. I overheard one of the officers making his report about the submarine to the men who had come aboard.

One said, "They've got two ships already, the bastards."

But not this one.

We loaded the last of the patients, I cleared the paperwork as quickly as possible, and then the train was pulling out, gathering speed.

I had a moment of alarm, wondering if somehow Corporal Caswell had managed to escape in the darkness. I couldn't imagine that it was possible, but I'd had no time to watch him or to warn the Sisters handling the transfer to keep an eye on him.

Making my way through the carriages, I found him at last. He was sleeping. Sister Waters smiled. "I gave him a little something. He was worried about the ship being sunk."

He had worried about what was to happen to him in Dover, I thought to myself, not about any submarines in our vicinity.

"Good work," I told her. "We didn't want him to alarm the others."

I spent the hours into London on my feet, most of my time with the serious cases. They had been jostled and moved and jostled some more, and I had to look for any bleeding that had broken through or stitches that had been pulled.

Finally, wishing myself a bed and an hour of sleep, I saw that we were coming through the familiar outskirts of the city. Our speed dropped and there was a bustle to get everything ready for what happened next. My serious cases were to go to hospitals in London, and I'd been told ambulances would be waiting. The others would be parceled out to another train or to lorries to carry them to their destinations.

When I had signed the last voucher and seen the last patient on his way, I looked around for my kit, intending to find a cab, go to Mrs. Hennessey's, and fall across my bed in a stupor.

Instead I saw Simon standing there, my bag in one hand.

"Welcome to London. I'm under orders to take you directly home. Your mother put pillows and blankets in the rear seat. She felt you might need them."

"Bless her! Yes, I do. But a cup of tea first would be wonderful."

"A fresh Thermos on the seat. She's thought of everything."

And five minutes later I'd turned in my ticket, walked with Simon the short distance to his motorcar, and was handed into the rear seat.

I remember the lights flashing by as we cleared the city, and then in the dark of the countryside, my eyes would stay open no longer. The next thing I knew, Simon had lifted me out of the motorcar and my mother's voice was saying, "Her room is ready, you know the way."

I awoke the next morning in my own bed, the draperies drawn and the room dark enough that I could have slept until noon. But I was up and dressed and down to breakfast by eight o'clock.

I was not surprised to find my mother, the Colonel Sahib, and Simon already there, just filling their plates.

"I didn't expect to see you for hours," Mother said. "Here, take my plate, I'll make up another one."

Sitting down at my usual place and picking up my napkin, I said, "I slept amazingly well. I must have been very tired."

"You were," Simon told me. "I don't think you spoke a word the entire drive."

"Just as well," my father said, smiling. "It will save her from having to give us the same account. All right, eat your breakfast, Bess, and then we'll talk."

Still sitting around the table fifteen minutes later, I began my explanation about Corporal Caswell. "And so I thought," I said, coming to the end, "it was better to keep him under our eye than let him go to a clinic in Essex or Derbyshire. Were you able to convince Dr. Gaines?"

"I had no trouble at all," my mother said serenely. "I told him that the Corporal was one of ours, a black sheep who needed looking after, whether he liked it or not, and Dr. Gaines was in complete agreement with me."

I suppressed a smile. Dr. Gaines was no match for the Colonel's lady.

"And what are we to do with him?" my father asked, in an interested tone of voice, as if I were about to describe the disposition of a new piece of furniture.

"I don't know," I said, being baldly honest.

"He's not a kitten or a puppy," Simon put in. "He could very well be a murderer five times over. Longleigh House doesn't know about that."

Which was very true. I had in fact put the staff there in danger.

"He may well try to escape," I said, "but he's clever enough to realize that if he harms anyone in the process, he'll be hunted down." I could only hope that was true.

"There's that," my mother agreed.

"How soon will it be before he can be returned to duty?" my father asked.

"A good six weeks," I replied. "At least."

"Then we shan't have to make any decisions right away," my mother said, always seeing the practical side of any problem.

"Just how guilty is Lieutenant Wade?" I asked. "According to Mr. Kipling's friend, there is some question about the murder of his parents. And even Simon, here, looking into the Subedar's past, thought there might be some question about the man's brother."

My father sighed. "God knows, Bess." And then as if the question were forced from him, he asked, "Has he changed?"

"He has learned to live by his wits," I said, taking my time to give a fair answer. "He can be utterly charming when it suits. And very determined when he is crossed. The odd thing is, I've never seen him really and truly violent. Yes, there was that incident of Sister Bennett's tray. But he did that deliberately to stop me from seeing his face." I couldn't help but think to myself that Lieutenant Wade might have taken a chance and killed me on at least two occasions, silencing the only person who knew who he now pretended to be and where he could be found. And yet he'd never laid a finger on me.

"Wade was always straightforward. No guile. That's why I could never quite believe that he was a murderer. That he'd worked with me for weeks and I never once saw anything that in retrospect I could consider an indication of his guilt. And yet all the evidence points strongly to him."

"If he didn't kill his parents, if the Subedar's brother had learned from the servants that Lieutenant Wade was leaving very early the next morning, he could have seen his opportunity to enact a little revenge and put the blame on the son of the house. I am almost willing to grant you that. Mostly because there seems to be no motive, except to spare them the knowledge of what he'd done in England. But there appears to be a very strong motive for killing the Caswells." Simon got up to refill his cup.

"He asked me if I knew how his parents were," I reminded the table at large. "Was that guile? Or did he truly not know because he'd thought he left them well, asleep in their beds?"

"If he wanted to throw off suspicion, he would have done just that," my father commented.

It was an endless circle. We talked for a little while longer. And then the Colonel Sahib said, "I'll give him a few days to settle in at Longleigh House. To feel safe there. But I think it's time I went to visit him."

There was a silence around the table. I had never wanted my father drawn back into the fate of Lieutenant Wade. And here he was, perforce, right in the middle of our dilemma.

Simon was saying, "That's a very sound idea. It's one thing to talk to Bess, here, and quite another to face you."

My mother had the last word. "In the meantime, I think we need to identify the last two people in that photograph. Who knows what we might uncover?"

Later in the afternoon when my mother came to find me, I was sitting in the garden trying to read. After more than an hour I was still on page two of the book when she sat down near me and looked out across the lawns.

"I think," she began, "it's just as well that this has happened. About Lieutenant Wade. It's upset the Colonel Sahib, I know, but like a festering wound, it needs to be lanced and given a chance to heal at last."

"I never intended to do more than find him and hand him over to the MFP. I can't even remember when the doubts began. I expect it was when Simon found out about the Subedar's brother. If part of the story was false, then why not the whole?"

"Bess, darling, if he's innocent, we need to know that too."

"I keep remembering how angry Captain Bingham was about the past. And even Alexander Hughes." That brought with it a new train of thought. "Teddy—an ambulance driver—tried to avoid Captain Bingham. And he thought he recognized Lieutenant Wade. I was too worried about getting my charges back to England to open that door. Now, it seems odd that he was afraid of Captain Bingham but not of Lieutenant Wade. You'd have thought it would have been the reverse, if he knew what the papers had been saying about the murder of the Caswells. But what if *he* was the other boy and he recognized the two men from growing up with them in the Caswell household?"

"Do you know his last name?"

"He's just—Teddy. I don't think I ever heard him called anything else."

"Let's go back to see Miss Gooding. And take your photograph with you this time."

"Wasn't there some charity event or other where we could meet Lady Campbell?"

"My dear, I'd forgot. It's today. This evening. We must hurry if we're to dress and make it to London in time."

As we went indoors, my mother suggested that I wear my uniform, as visiting hospitals was one of Princess Mary's interests.

Simon appeared just as we were going down the stairs, and Mother said, "There you are. I was hoping to see you. Could you possibly drive us into London?"

"Give me five minutes," he replied, and was gone.

"There. We'll arrive in style and won't have to concern ourselves with what to do with the motorcar."

We were fashionably late when we arrived, but Princess Mary wasn't there yet, though the hostess was expecting her at any moment.

She came in five minutes later. I'd seen her in photographs but never in person. She was close to my own age and very attractive. It was whispered that she was strong-minded, and she was close to her elder brother, Edward, who was also rumored to have a mind of his own. The Christmas Gift Box presented to all the troops in 1914 had been her idea, subscribed by a grateful nation. My parents had given generously to it.

She greeted our hostess and then was presented to the dignitaries before mixing briefly with other guests. Seeing my uniform, she came to speak to me, asking where I had served and how I had found my training.

"Difficult but useful," I replied, and she smiled.

"I admire all of you in the Nursing Service," she said and moved on to the next guest.

Turning to look for my mother, I saw that she was talking to a young woman with auburn hair, a high-bridged nose, and a strong chin. She was handsome in a very aristocratic way. She looked familiar. The chin, I thought, but I had no idea who she was.

I crossed the room and my mother made the introductions.

I found myself shaking hands—fingertips brushing briefly—with the former Hazel Sheridan. She was looking at my uniform with some disdain, as if thinking I should at least have made an effort to dress for the occasion. I was amused because Princess Mary, a King's daughter, had considered it a badge of honor.

"I've just come from France," I said with a smile. "I ran into Teddy there. He remembers you from your years at The Willows."

Her face froze. "I'm not acquainted with anyone called Teddy. What is The Willows? A restaurant? Should I know it?"

It was a quick recovery. She must, I thought, have steady nerves.

"I do apologize. I was certain you'd remember. I have the loveliest photograph of you as a little girl. It was taken with the rest of the children one Christmas." I was being impossibly rude, and I regretted it, but I wasn't sure I would have another chance to speak to this woman. She wouldn't be as accessible as Captain Bingham or Teddy or Sandy Hughes. Not given her husband's position. "I bought it at the charity stall in Petersfield. The one you were so anxious to have."

She darted a glance at my mother. "I don't know any Caswells. I'm sorry."

"And such a tragedy about Mr. and Mrs. Gessler dying in that fire. They did such fine work."

She opened her mouth to correct me, not the sort to suffer fools gladly. She knew very well it was his daughter and not his wife who had died in that fire. But she snapped her jaw shut just in time. For a moment we stared directly at each other. I could see the cold calculation in her eyes. Then she said in a low, harsh voice, "I have no connection with any of this. Now I'm walking away. Please don't follow me."

I could feel myself blushing, the blood rushing up into my face. I turned slightly so that no one else could see it.

My mother said soothingly, "Bess, that was very rude. But very effective indeed. I think it's time to pay our respects to the hostess and be ready to take our leave as soon as Princess Mary does."

It was not done to leave a function before royalty did.

We sipped the lemonade and ate one of the little cakes, and then Princess Mary was saying good-bye, thanking the guests for their generous contributions to the cause of caring for soldiers and their families in time of need. We had done our bit as well, which eased my conscience a little over my behavior. At least there had been no other witnesses to that conversation.

My mother and I were only a few minutes behind in our farewells.

Outside the hotel where the Charity Reception had been held, we looked for Simon. He saw us and brought up the motorcar.

"Is it too late to drive to Petersfield tonight?" my mother asked as he held her door and then mine.

"Better tomorrow morning, I should think."

"Then let's make our plans accordingly." Before he could ask what had transpired, my mother told him. "In ordinary circumstances I'd have been shocked and furious, but Bess found out what she wanted to know. And it was clear that the last thing Lady Campbell wanted was to make a scene with a member of the Royal Family present. But if looks could kill . . ." She let her voice trail off.

I said, "She recognized Teddy's name. She knew who I was talking about."

"Yes, she pretended otherwise, but I was watching her eyes."

I sat there, looking back to the arrival of the Subedar, playing it over and over again in my memory.

"Simon. The ambulances came in just after the Subedar died. First one, and then not far behind, the others. If Teddy was driving that ambulance, if he found the Subedar out in the middle of nowhere, he would be able to understand him, wouldn't he? Or even if he couldn't, the Subedar might have confided in him. It would explain why he wouldn't speak in English to anyone else, even to me."

"Do you think this man shot the Subedar? Bess, he's a conscientious objector."

"He doesn't want the past brought up again. He avoids Captain Bingham. He thought he recognized Lieutenant Wade, although he was confused about just where he'd seen him. And both times Lieutenant Wade had been very ill. But Teddy won't let it go. And in the end, he'll remember."

Simon commented, "There may be something else in his past that he doesn't want to remember. Not necessarily The Willows."

A slight change in his voice made me wonder if there were memories that Simon himself didn't want to recall.

But I didn't pursue the thought, and neither did my mother.

By the time we reached Petersfield the next day, the market was in full swing. This time in place of the charity stall was one decorated with bunting and flags, and behind the counter were two pretty girls supporting the same cause we had contributed to last night. We went over to put coins into the large earthen jar set between them, and we were told that if at the end of the day, anyone guessed the amount collected, he or she would win a prize.

The prize was sitting in the back of the stall for all to see. It was a rectangular lacquered box on brass feet with squared corners and trimmed in gold. Across the top galloped a hunt, beautifully etched in gold with a fine brush. High grass encircled the sides, and in it lurked the prey the hunt was chasing, well concealed and watchful—gazelles and tigers, deer and wild boar. Only these huntsmen were mounted on horses and elephants, followed by beaters and servants and musicians on foot. It was exquisite Indian workmanship, and I realized who must have donated it.

My mother said as she dropped a pound into the earthen jar, "What a lovely box that is. Could I see it?"

"We aren't supposed to let anyone touch it."

"Then perhaps you would lift the lid for me so that I could see inside," she said sweetly.

Reluctantly one of the girls lifted the top, and I could see that the inside was covered in what appeared to be gold leaf.

It was also empty.

Mother thanked the girls and we strolled on. "I was hoping there might be letters or some such inside."

"Someone must have emptied it before donating it to the sale."

"And tossed any letters into the fire. Worst luck."

Simon was waiting outside the square on Church Street, and we drove on to Miss Gooding's house.

She took to my mother immediately, as most people did, and while Simon was once more filling the coal scuttle, I made tea in the tiny kitchen. Remembering Miss Gooding's straitened circumstances, I had brought a little of our precious store of tea, a small jug of honey, and a tin of biscuits.

I could hear the conversation in the front room, and I knew when the framed photograph came out of the covered basket we had carried it in.

Miss Gooding was telling my mother that she had just such a one as that by her bed, and my mother said, "They were the dearest children. Here's Tommy Wade, and there's his sister Georgina next to Gwendolyn. That's such a pretty frock Georgina is wearing, isn't it? And that must be the little Mayfield child, who died so young. He's standing next to the Bingham boy, who joined the Army like his father before him. That must be Alexander Hughes, the one with the limp after hurting his foot trying to ride Gwendolyn's horse. The other girl is Hazel, isn't it? The children used to tease her and call her Witch Hazel. But she married a baronet, didn't she? He's an equerry to one of the Princes. She's quite fashionable now. And the last child—Teddy . . ." Her voice trailed off. "I do believe I've forgotten Teddy's surname. Isn't that awful?"

I peered into the front room. Miss Gooding had leaned forward to follow my mother's finger across the photograph. Squinting, she said, "That's Theodore Belmont. He was afraid of his own shadow, poor lad."

"Yes, that's right."

I nearly leapt out of my skin as a hand closed around my arm. In the same motion, Simon's hand closed over my mouth before I could cry out. Pulling me back into the kitchen, he let me go and beckoned toward the kitchen yard and the back garden. There were vegetables in a bed that was slowly losing ground to the weeds, and a pair of sheds by two old apple trees.

Following him, my heart still beating twice as fast as normal, I waited until we were out of hearing. “What is it?”

“I did a little poking around. You’ll never guess what I found.”

I followed him to one of the sheds. There were chickens penned next to a coop, and the rooster flew up at us as we passed. Inside the shed were tools from a generation gone, and cast-off household items from broken crockery to worn-out pans and a table that had lost a leg. A large vinegar jug with a crack running down to the base stood in the darkest corner. Simon reached down to lift the jug, and I thought surely it would break apart. But it was thicker walled than I expected. He turned it around and I could see that the back was out, as if something heavy had knocked against it.

But it was what was inside the hole that made me stare.

It was a revolver that appeared not to have been cleaned for years. It was standard service issue of the late Victorian era.

As I reached for it, Simon caught my hand. “It’s still loaded. Be careful.”

I leaned over, wishing I’d brought a torch with me. But as my eyes grew accustomed to the dim light, I realized that three of the cartridge chambers were empty. And three were still loaded.

“Simon—what on earth?” I straightened up. “Are you telling me—is this the *murder* weapon? The revolver that killed the Caswells?”

“Very likely.”

“But where did it come from? How did it get here?”

“Either the killer left it behind and Miss Gooding took it for reasons of her own or the killer has hidden it here. He couldn’t very well keep it, could he?”

“There’s the third possibility,” I said, not wanting to put it into words. “Miss Gooding killed the Caswells. While everyone else had the day off.”

"It's entirely possible."

From the house came the familiar whistle of the teakettle. "I must go. What shall we do with it?"

"I think it would be best if we take it."

I was already running toward the house as he answered me. I got to the kettle before the steam had reached fever pitch, and rinsed out the teapot before spooning in the tea and then setting it to one side to steep.

And all the while, the question was running through my mind. *Had whoever left the revolver in the shed also changed that photograph in the frame in Miss Gooding's bedroom upstairs?*

My mother's voice was coming from the front room, and I heard Miss Gooding reply, "Yes, that's true. But the money they'd come into didn't last forever. They had decided to take in children again. There were already two queries from their advertisement in the *Times*. One from South Africa and one from India."

There was a motive for murder if I'd ever heard one. Killing them before they took in more innocent children and turned their lives into wretched misery.

"But surely—"

"Who was there to stop them? I ask you."

I peered around the door again. Mother was putting the photograph back into Miss Gooding's blue-veined hands. "I should think any one of these children would have moved the earth to stop the Caswells from resuming their cruelty."

"Not Hazel Sheridan. She came back once. Did you know? After the murders were in all the newspapers, and she paid me to tell anyone nosing about that there was no such person as Hazel Sheridan who once lived at The Willows. I held out for more, because I'd lost my position, you see. And she paid up without a word of argument. I wouldn't have said anything now, but you already knew her name." She gestured around the room, indicating the cottage. "It made it possible to live here, you see."

"Did she indeed? Er—I understood that she was friends with the sexton. How did that come about?"

Simon had come in with the coal scuttle, and the tea was ready to pour.

We reached the front room, Simon with the coal scuttle and I with the tea tray in my hands.

Miss Gooding was saying, "Hardly friends. Barney Lowell? He was the gardener's son at The Willows. A troublemaker. The Caswells let him go, and his father set up as a nurseryman. They did well, much to everyone's surprise."

My mother glanced up at me as I set down the tray. I knew what she was thinking—that if Miss Sheridan bribed one person to remove her name from the list of children, why not two? I wondered if it was Lowell who had wanted to buy that photograph from me. It would make sense, if he'd intended to purchase it and I got there first. Still earning his keep from Miss Sheridan. He'd told Mr. Gates about Simon and me in the churchyard to cause more trouble. Had he put the gun in the shed?

Had he used that gun?

As I handed Miss Gooding her cup of tea, I said, "I can't remember just when Miss Sheridan was married."

"It was just before the Caswells were murdered. I know, because Miss Gwendolyn was angry about not being invited to the wedding. She'd written a letter to Miss Sheridan. I heard her tell her mother what she'd done. Mrs. Caswell laughed. But Miss Gwendolyn was set on going to a fashionable wedding." Miss Gooding chuckled. "She should have thought of that ten years before, and so her father told her, from behind his newspaper. If looks could kill, he'd have fallen dead where he sat. I had just come into the room to tell them Cook was better. She'd had an attack of gallstones."

She sipped the tea and smiled. "Honey. I don't know how long it's been since I tasted honey."

"The Caswells had lost their money," I said, taking my own cup.

"It's why they took in children in the first place. But then they came into money again. Where did that come from?"

"I don't know." She helped herself to another biscuit. "We talked about it sometimes, below stairs. The general view was that Miss Grant—the governess, you see—inherited a little money from her fiancé, and put together with what she'd saved, Mr. Caswell was able to make an investment, and it did well for some years. But he wasn't very clever with money, and in the end, he lost more than he was earning."

"He had no right to that money," I said before I could stop myself.

"Who was there to tell him he didn't? I ask you."

Servant gossip was often on the mark. They were invisible, and the family often talked in their presence without thinking twice.

Miss Gooding began to nod off soon after that, unused to company.

My mother gestured to the tea things and I took them to the kitchen to do the washing up. After a moment she joined me and helped dry.

"I've sent Simon out to the motorcar. When you've finished here, we'll take our leave."

"Did Simon tell you what he discovered in the shed?"

"He showed me. I gathered it could be the murder weapon?"

"Possibly. Simon remembers that was part of the evidence against Lieutenant Wade. According to the MFP, he'd taken it with him."

"Just so."

She returned to the front room. When I followed her there she was just saying farewell to a drowsy Miss Gooding, thanking her for the tea.

I thanked her as well, and she smiled. "Come again," she said. "I always enjoy having guests."

Simon had already cranked the motorcar and was standing beside it, ready to hold the door for my mother.

On our way into Petersfield, Simon glanced over his shoulder at me. "If I turn the revolver in to the police, I shall have to tell them where I found it."

"I hadn't thought of that. We can't have them descending on Miss Gooding, demanding to know how it got there, in the shed."

"I didn't think to ask her if there was a weapon in the Caswell house," Mother said.

"The police must have asked the staff at the time." Simon slowed, finding a place to pull over.

"True, of course. There's certainly no way to connect it to this man Lowell."

"I'd like to talk to him again," I said.

"It's too dangerous," Simon interjected.

"Not in broad daylight in the churchyard. He must live in one of the houses overlooking it. He always seems to appear without warning," I said.

Reluctantly Simon agreed, but only if Mother went with me. "And I'll find a spot where I can watch, unobserved."

When we reached the square again, Mother and I got down, and Simon drove on. We were to give him ten minutes to leave the motorcar and circle around behind the church. Meanwhile, Mother and I strolled through the market, looking at the wares for sale. When we came to the garden stall, which featured a wooden arbor that shaded the offerings from the sun, we paused to look at the healthy array of perennials.

It was then I saw the discreet sign behind the counter where a young woman was explaining to an elderly couple where and how to put in the wisteria they were buying.

LOWELL AND SON

Judging from the display, the former gardener's boy had done very well indeed. Certainly he or someone had a knack for growing healthy plants.

Had the money the former Miss Sheridan paid him helped him to build his business? Just as it had helped Miss Gooding live in her cottage?

The elderly couple walked on with their young wisteria, and we walked up to the counter in our turn. "You have such lovely plants," my mother said effusively. "Who has the green thumb?"

"Mr. Lowell," the girl said shyly. "He's a wonder with anything green, and his grafting is amazing. Ornamental trees, fruit trees. It's an art, you know."

My mother did know, because her grandfather had grafted grapes and apple trees and even roses, as a hobby.

"Yes, that takes a great deal of skill. I used to know a Lowell here in Petersfield. He had a son named Barnaby, as I recall."

"That would be Mr. Lowell's father," she said, nodding.

"Was the father by any chance in the Army?" I asked. "I seem to remember something about that."

"He was in South Africa until he was invalided out. My mother was his housekeeper and he had malaria something fierce. She said she'd never seen anyone sweat like that."

Another customer came up, a pot of pansies in her hand, and we stepped aside.

"He wouldn't have had a revolver as an ordinary rank," Mother was saying under her breath, "but he wouldn't be the first to pick one up as a souvenir."

She went back to the plants and found a pretty low-growing ground cover with lavender flowers. "I'll take this one," she told the young woman, and paid for it. "And that trowel as well. I've misplaced mine. Yes, thank you."

We paid for the plant and the trowel, and my mother said, "I think it's time we go to the churchyard."

I carried the plant while she took up the trowel and then at another stall she saw a pair of gloves for the garden.

Laden with our purchases, we went into the churchyard and I pointed out Georgina Wade's grave. My mother got down on her knees and, drawing on the gloves, took the trowel from me and began to dig in the soft earth by the headstone. "Poor child. She deserves something, doesn't she?" With my help we planted the ground cover in the center by the headstone. Patting the earth around it, she said, "There. We need a little water to settle it in."

I looked up. "Here comes the sexton," I said under my breath.

"Perfect. I thought we might get his attention very quickly."

She rose, and dusting her gloves, she pulled them off. Handing them to me along with the trowel, she looked around, and seeing the sexton apparently for the first time, she walked toward him, smiling.

"Just the man to help me," she said brightly. "I need a little water. Is there any to be had close by? Or must I ask at the pub?"

"You need permission to plant flowers on the graves," he said.

"Oh, surely not," she answered. "I'm a member of the family. And look at the other flowers there and there and even over there."

"What family?"

"The Wade family, of course. Cousins on my mother's side. That's why we're here, to remember that poor child."

He stared at my mother. "I don't believe you."

"Why ever not?" Mother asked sharply. "My daughter here found the grave for us, and I've come to take care of it." When he stood his ground, she added, "If you don't believe me, I have a photograph of Georgina. And a chair that was hers. They were being sold at the charity stall, believe it or not. I'd asked Mr. Gates to keep them, and someone made a terrible mistake."

I could see him taking in what she had to say. She gave him a moment. "Now about that water," she pressed.

"You'll have to go to the pub," he answered ungraciously.

"I understand your nursery grew the flowers I just put in. You must enjoy working with them. I was quite impressed with your stall. Did I see azaleas there? I'm sure I did. Was your father a plant man as well?"

His face was rigid, dark color coming up under his weather-roughened skin. "Leave my father out of this."

"I don't see why I should. Like father like son, only you chose not to go into the Army. At least that's what Hazel Campbell tells me. We saw her just the other night, in London."

"I don't know anyone called Hazel Campbell."

"But you must know her. She was one of the children at The Willows when you were the gardener's boy. Surely you haven't forgotten? Well, I don't have time to stand and chat, I need to find some water. Good day, Mr. Lowell."

And she walked away, with me in her wake.

"That should confuse him," she said as we walked out into the square. "But the question now is, what did Hazel Sheridan have to hide?"

"If she was marrying into Society, being drawn into the murder of the Caswells wouldn't endear her to her husband's family."

"I must have a friend who knows something about her background. It's worth pursuing. Let me think where to start."

We found the pub and went inside. The polished brass at the bar reflected the dark beams and the lamplight. My mother walked up to the barman, smiled, and said, "I should like to buy a little water for the plants I just put in by my niece's grave."

"Yes, of course, madam," he said. "There's no charge, but I'm afraid you'll have to bring the container back. I don't have a pail."

She agreed, and he went behind the bar, came back with a jar, and filled it for her.

Thanking him, she left and we started back toward the churchyard. "Marianne Thorndyke," she said.

"Sorry?"

"I can speak to Marianne Thorndyke. I'm sure she can tell me what I need to know about Lady Campbell. Or if she can't, she'll know someone who can."

I laughed as we walked back to the church. Depend upon my mother to know where to turn.

There was no sign of the sexton when we reached the churchyard and made our way to Georgina Wade's grave. We watered the little plant well and then my mother stood back. "There. Something good has come of this."

We returned the jar to the pub and went to look for Simon. He was standing near the Lowell nursery stall, and he looked up as we approached.

"What did you say to that man? He left the churchyard as if all the imps of hell were at his heels."

I told him.

"That was pushing rather hard, wasn't it?"

Mother shook her head. "If we don't, who will? And I knew you were close by."

"Have we finished here?" Simon asked.

"Yes, I think so," I answered. And he led us back to where he had left the motorcar.

When we got there, Simon put out a hand, telling us to wait while he went forward.

He came back to us and said, "Someone searched the motorcar."

"Dear God," I said, "did he find the revolver? Or the photograph?"

"Neither. I had them with me, in case."

It was late when we reached Somerset, and we fell into our beds, exhausted.

But the next morning my mother was dressed and ready to go. "The proper time to call is in the afternoon, but Marianne won't mind if I show up in the middle of the morning. Simon will drive us. She's always been quite fond of him."

And so it was we drove into Glastonbury to call on Marianne Thorndyke.

She had moved to the family home there when the Zeppelins began dropping bombs on London. Her husband was an under-secretary at the Foreign Office and couldn't very well leave. And so she was very glad of company, and Mother used the excuse that I was at home on leave to explain our early call.

Mrs. Thorndyke greeted me warmly and welcomed Simon like an old friend. She ordered tea and asked all the news.

When there was an opening in the conversation, I said, "We were in London for a charity event on my last leave, and Lady Campbell was among the guests. I'm sure I've met her before, but I can't think where. Who was she, before her marriage?"

"I believe her name was Felton."

"Felton." I frowned. "That doesn't sound quite right."

My mother said to me, "Wasn't her father something in the Civil Service in Delhi? Perhaps that's where you saw her, my dear."

"Yes, that's possible," Mrs. Thorndyke replied. "Her parents died quite young, in a cholera epidemic, and she was made the ward of Sir James Felton. They were related through her mother. Sir James wanted her to take his name because he had no children. I believe it was while she was living in London with him that she met her future husband."

I knew who the Feltons were; they had made their fortune early on in India under Robert Clive and had inherited the title from a senior branch of the family. I also knew that the Feltons were probably more Victorian than Victoria, upright to the point of rigidity. I wouldn't have been surprised to learn that it was Sir James who suppressed any connection with the Caswells. And Hazel Sheridan would have been happy to comply.

"What was her name before she was Sir James's ward?" my mother asked.

"You know, I'm not sure I ever heard it."

"Where was she schooled?" I asked.

"In Kent, I believe. The daughter of a friend was there at the same time."

An impeccable background, with no mention of her years with the Caswells. Or their murder.

"That's interesting," I said, trying to look perplexed. "I met someone in France, an English officer, who knew her in Hampshire, where she lived with a family until she was old enough to go to boarding school."

"Hazel Felton? He's mistaken, of course. There's a Hazel Gallagher who lives in Hampshire. Portsmouth, in fact. She's the daughter of a Naval officer in the White Fleet. The sweetest girl."

"Has Miss Gallagher ever lived in India?" my mother asked. "Or Ceylon?"

"No, her mother is an invalid, not up to traveling abroad."

"I'm sure I'll remember later," I said, smiling. Mrs. Thorndyke was my mother's friend, and I couldn't press her any further.

Our hostess turned to Simon, who was standing in his favorite place, by the hearth, asking if he believed that it was possible that the war would end before Christmas. "We'd thought," she added, "that when it began, it was sure to end by Christmas. And we were deeply disappointed."

Whatever he knew, Simon gave her a summary of the speculations in the London newspapers, and she was grateful for his opinion. And then it was time to take our leave. Mrs. Thorndyke politely asked us to stay for lunch, but we as politely thanked her profusely and said our good-byes.

As we left, Mother said with a sigh, "Well. I don't know that we've learned anything that's helpful, except the fact that Hazel Sheridan has erased her past very efficiently."

"She must have been infuriated when she received a letter from Gwendolyn Caswell, asking why she and her parents weren't invited to the wedding," Simon replied. "She could hardly explain to anyone why these people were asking to be included."

"A reason to kill three people? I'm not sure," Mother commented.

"It's odd that she was offering bribes to Miss Gooding and Lowell, the sexton, so soon after the fact. You'd think," I went on, "that she would be grateful the Caswells were dead and stay as far away from Petersfield as she possibly could."

It was Simon who made the most cogent argument. "I can see that she might bribe Miss Gooding, who had probably stayed in

Petersfield after the rest of the staff found employment elsewhere. The question is, how did she know to offer Lowell a bribe? If she wanted no part of being reminded of her past, then why seek out the gardener's boy?"

"Lieutenant Wade, Captain Bingham, this man Teddy, and Alexander Hughes. All of them had very sound reasons for killing the Caswells. Why not one of them?" my mother asked. "It doesn't seem unlikely."

"Because," I said, thinking it through, "each of them had more to lose than to gain from murder. While Hazel Sheridan had the most to gain."

"I think she's right," Mother said after a moment. "But did Hazel kill them or did she pay Lowell to do it for her? And how did she come by the revolver?"

"They were sitting in their chairs in the parlor," I pointed out. "Would they have received Mr. Lowell there? A tradesman would have come to the kitchen door."

"He could have done, the staff had been given the afternoon off. He could have walked straight through the house," Mother said, "but as soon as he showed his face, Mr. Caswell would have risen from his chair and asked what he wanted."

Simon spoke. "She didn't bribe anyone until after the fact, after the police were stymied. If they'd taken someone into custody straightaway, she would never have needed to come back to Petersfield."

"I think," I said, "it's time for Lieutenant Wade to tell us what he knows."

Chapter Twenty

We came home to find my father there. He'd been at Sandhurst for several days, and he was working in his study when we knocked and were admitted.

After telling him what we'd learned, we asked if he had had a chance to visit Lieutenant Wade at Longleigh House.

"No, to my sorrow, I haven't," he admitted. "This talk of an Armistice has kept all of us busy."

"Could we go this afternoon? You can see why we need to speak to him now. Or rather, to persuade him to speak to us."

"Bess, I don't think the four of us arriving on his doorstep would persuade him to tell us anything. I'll go alone."

"If you do, he'll think I've broken my promise and you're there to see to it that he's taken into custody. Let me go as well."

"All right," the Colonel Sahib agreed reluctantly.

And so it was that after lunch my father and I got into his motorcar and set out for Longleigh House.

"Does it bring back memories," he asked after a time, "this drive?"

"Yes. I haven't heard from Captain Barclay for over a month. I hope he's safe."

"He is. I've kept up with his career. A pity he's planning to join his father in the family enterprises. The Army could use his experience."

"I don't see him lecturing to recruits," I said dryly.

"No. But he's a good man."

As we approached Longleigh House and were about to turn up the drive, I said, "How shall we begin? This won't be easy, will it?"

"Let Lieutenant Wade—Corporal Caswell—make that decision for us."

When we arrived, we were taken directly to call on Matron, and she had tea brought in. After asking my father what he knew about the course of the war, she asked how my time had been spent in France. I told her about the influenza hospital, and she nodded.

"It hasn't spared us here, either, sad to say. But Dr. Gaines is recovering, and so are the three patients we have in quarantine."

As we finished our tea, she turned to the Colonel Sahib. "This isn't a social call, I'm sure, much as I've enjoyed our chat. Did you come about anything in particular?"

"We'd like to speak to Corporal Caswell," I said. "If that's possible."

She took a deep breath. "He hasn't had an easy time of it here, my dear. The officers shun him, of course, but Dr. Gaines had set up a special course of treatment before he was taken ill, and the Sisters have carried it out to the letter. He's in his room on the first floor. He takes his meals there. It might make his life easier if the others see Colonel Crawford calling on him." But there was doubt in her voice all the same.

"I'm sorry to hear that he's had trouble fitting in. I was more interested in the medical care he'd received," my father said as we rose to leave. "I can't think of anyone better at dealing with his wounds."

"I agree. But sometimes healing comes from within, as well."

She was about to summon someone to take us to Corporal Caswell's room, then shook her head. "You know the way, Sister. It might be better if you go alone."

Matron walked with us as far as the staircase and was still standing at the foot when I looked back from the landing.

We found the room without difficulty. I remembered it as fair-sized and sunny. I knocked and then opened the door, as one of the staff would. Lieutenant Wade was sitting by the window looking out on the garden. Some of the patients had taken it upon themselves to keep the flower beds tidy, but it was still a ghost of what it must have been. A book lay open in his lap, and he was in a wheeled chair, with his injured leg elevated.

"Hallo, Corporal," I said, coming into the room.

He knew my voice. Swinging around so fast that the book went flying, he saw first me and then, behind me, still in the open doorway, my father.

There was nothing he could do. I watched a train of emotions flick across his features and knew he felt cornered, and as a result, his anger spilled over.

"What do you want?" he demanded.

My father took a chair and brought it forward for me, then went to stand by the hearth, his elbow on the mantelpiece, the picture of a man relaxed and in no hurry. "To see how you are faring," he said mildly.

"As you see, still crippled by this leg," Lieutenant Wade responded harshly. "They put me on this floor purposely to make it impossible for me to escape."

"I had nothing to do with that," my father told him. "Bess here has served at Longleigh House before. Perhaps she can explain that decision."

I smiled. "Really, it's a matter of what room is available when you arrive."

A silence fell. Lieutenant Wade was still glaring at us.

There was nothing for it but to start somewhere. I chose what I thought would be the most roundabout way, to give the Lieutenant time to collect himself. "I was in London not long ago with my mother. A charity affair. And Hazel Sheridan came to it with Princess Mary. Lady Campbell, she is now. Her husband is a royal equerry."

His eyes were suddenly shuttered, and I realized he was about to lie. "I don't believe I know her. Should I?"

I had inadvertently touched a nerve, and I quickly shifted my approach, choosing the most charged answer I could think of.

"A summer's day in 1908. Coming out of the Caswell house just as you were arriving?"

It took all the skill he possessed to answer calmly, "Nonsense."

"And perhaps she told you how the Caswells were trying to ruin her chances of marrying the man she was very much in love with, and that she had come to plead with them to let her be happy."

An eyelid betrayed him. Twitching as he tried to keep any reaction out of his face. "If you want to make up fairy tales, go somewhere else."

"Did you believe her? Did she throw herself on your mercy? Did she cry and tell you they deserved to die for what they'd done to the children in their charge? Your silence allowed her to marry that man, to have a child, to be accepted socially in the highest circles. Did you think about that on the long cold nights in Afghanistan, hiding in the hills? Or crossing the mountains in Persia, when you were exhausted and friendless and lost?"

"You've taken leave of your senses, Sister Crawford. None of this is true."

"Did it occur to you that if you were taken prisoner and sent back to England for trial, you would have to sacrifice yourself or tell the truth about Hazel? Was that why you left the regiment without speaking to the Colonel Sahib, because you couldn't answer his questions without consigning Hazel to the hangman?"

"Stop. I don't want to hear any more of this. I don't have to listen."

I rose. "I'm so sorry. I'd hoped you might want to know that Hazel has tricked you just as she's tricked everyone else." I started for the door. "We found the revolver in a broken vinegar jug in Miss Gooding's shed. Now she's the chief suspect, not you."

"*Liar!*" he cried, and I looked back, thinking he was about to rise out of his chair. Instead he was pounding the arms in impotent fury.

My father wheeled on him. "Mind your tongue, Lieutenant. My daughter doesn't lie."

I was just crossing the threshold. I turned and said, "Hazel Sheridan wasn't your little sister, fragile and in need of your protection. She was nothing like Georgina. Don't you remember? And because you think you failed Georgina, you've protected Hazel all these years. Did you know, when I first heard that you were alive and in France, I wanted to see you hang, because of what you did to the regiment?" I could hear footsteps on the stairs, and I added hurriedly, "All the same, I shall keep my promise, Corporal Caswell. I have no desire now to see you punished for something you didn't do."

We were in the passage, the door shut behind us, on our way to the stairs when I heard him cry out. The Sister just coming up rushed past us, intent on going to his aid.

I put out my hand and smiled at her, saying, "It's all right, Sister. He's just had bad news."

My father said, "I'll go back to him, he won't care to have you see him cry."

And he turned, went to the door, and opened it, shutting it firmly behind him.

Still uncertain, the Sister went on her way, looking over her shoulder once to assure herself all was well. I waited where I was, at the top of the stairs. Below I could hear all the familiar sounds. Of crutches and canes tapping across the bare floors, of wheeled chairs squeaking as they rolled, men laughing, a Sister leading her charges in exercises to strengthen a limb and counting out loud. An out-of-tune piano was being played with more gusto than skill and men were singing to it, a rather bawdy song from the trenches.

A doctor was calling for an orderly, two Sisters were on their way out the door, their voices rising to where I stood, and Matron was giving instructions to someone.

It was odd to stand here and not hurry to carry out my next duty. I was about to find someone and ask if I could speak to Dr. Gaines when the door to Corporal Caswell's room opened and my father said quietly, "Bess."

I turned and saw that he was waiting for me.

I went quickly to him, and as he ushered me into the room, he said, "I think you'd better hear this."

Lieutenant Wade was sitting where I'd left him, his head in his hands. I couldn't see his face. I could only hear him clear his throat, as if he'd been crying and was trying to hide it.

"I'm tired," he said then. "I've run for so long. Changing identities, hiding in the shadows. I was going to stay on the Continent, but it wasn't my home. And I was homesick, I wanted to come back to England somehow. Finally I hired out on a small merchant ship trading up and down the coast. When we came into Whitby, I jumped ship and left there before I was expected back on board, well before the hunt for me was up. I had some money, so I changed my appearance and did whatever work I could find. I told most people that I'd lost my fiancée and had taken to a gypsy way of life to forget. They were generally sympathetic, but sometimes there was trouble, and I had to move on. When the war came, I enlisted. They were happy to have me, no questions asked, and for the very first time since I walked away from the garrison, I had a home. Even so, I was different, never really accepted, but when I rose to Corporal, I had a position of some authority and that was all right. I could manage. Sergeants and some of the Lieutenants asked me why I hadn't trained to be an officer, and I told them I was the black sheep of the family and preferred anonymity." He started to shrug and remembered his collarbone. "It's been a long road."

He wasn't asking for our sympathy. For the first time he was able to tell the truth, and it seemed to make him feel something I couldn't quite define. As if he were freed of a great burden, I thought, or could feel himself a man again.

My father was sitting in the only chair now, facing the Lieutenant, and I stood behind him.

"Welcome home, son," he said quietly, the Colonel to a wayward recruit.

At first he refused to talk about what had happened in 1908. But my father told him sternly that the time had come to do his duty. "Whether you choose to stand up in a courtroom and tell the truth, you owe it to me to clear up the past. The regiment was not to blame for your desertion, but it redounded on us all the same. Some thought we had deliberately let a murderer escape, that I had somehow warned you in time."

I don't think that that had ever occurred to the man before us, hunched over in his wheeled chair. He looked up, staring at my father with shock in his face.

"No one warned me. When I learned that the MFP had come, I knew that someone must have seen me leaving Petersfield. They couldn't have known who I was, of course, not after so much time, but eventually the police or Scotland Yard or someone would work it out that I'd been there. I'd stopped by my sister's grave, you see, before going on to the house."

"What did you mean to do there?"

"I only wanted to confront them. To rid myself of the demons I'd carried so long. When my sister Georgina died, I thought—I thought they had refused to call in a doctor soon enough because I was such a thorn in their sides. That it was my fault that my sister died. Gwendolyn said as much, she told me outright that I had only myself to blame. Little Alice's death brought it all back, you see—I thought the Middletons must be no better than the Caswells. I was wrong, of course, but how did I know? I wanted to make them pay for Mrs. Standish's suffering. I was going to unmask them as the monsters they were. Only they were as cut up by Alice's death as her parents were, and it was genuine grief I saw, not crocodile tears. That's when I decided to go to Hampshire and face the Caswells down. I should have done it years before, long before I joined the Army, but I couldn't. I had shut off that part of my life, and I didn't want to relive it."

"And that's when you saw Hazel Sheridan. She told you that the family was deciding to take in children again, and she couldn't bear it," I said.

He frowned. "Who told you they were starting up again? I thought no one else but the two of us knew. Hazel and I."

"Miss Gooding had seen the advertisement in the *Times*."

"Then it *was* true. Afterward I sometimes doubted it was. At any rate, I went into the house to see if they were wounded or if she had really killed them. They were dead, there was no doubt there. I walked out again, and by that time Hazel had left. I thought she might have gone to the police, that if I stayed, I'd be forced to give evidence against her as a witness. I walked away to protect her. But I saw the newspapers before I sailed, and the police had nothing to go on. There was some mention of asking Scotland Yard to take over the investigation. Several people reported seeing a stranger in the town. One described me as wearing the uniform of an Army officer. There was no mention at all of Hazel. I was glad she hadn't confessed. If anyone deserved to die, it was that family. I sailed for India satisfied that she was going to be safe."

"But *you* weren't," my father said.

"No. Scotland Yard was more thorough. They had only to find out that an officer had got down from one train and an hour later got on the next train south, heading for Portsmouth. When they looked into sailings, they could have come up with a list of names. It was only a matter of asking the servants if they recognized one of them. I hadn't considered that, you see. I wasn't used to having to hide my actions. I worked it out later, far too late to do anything about it."

"Initially the police only wanted you to help with their inquiries. When your parents were killed, it confirmed the fact that you were the man they were after."

"Bess—Sister Crawford told me they were dead. I still don't know how someone got to them."

"What I don't understand," I said, "is why the Gesslers had to die."

"The Gesslers? Who are they? Oh God, don't tell me I'm accused of more murders."

"Don't you remember—the photographer who came each year to take your photographs to send to your parents?"

"Is that his name? I just remember being told that if we weren't happy and smiling, we'd all be punished severely. Once I tried to say something to the photographer's assistant, a short, bustling little man. I was angry enough to risk everything, because Gwendolyn had pinched my sister and made her cry. But the man wouldn't listen. He told me not to bother him, he was busy. After that I was sure they were the Caswells' creatures, and I had no more to do with them. Don't tell me Hazel killed them as well."

"Someone burned the house down a few weeks ago. Mr. Gessler and his daughter died in the fire," my father told him.

"Then it couldn't have been Hazel, could it?" The relief in his voice was real.

It would take more than one visit to convince Lieutenant Wade that Hazel Sheridan Campbell was a cold-blooded killer. He had defended her too long. Had suffered too much on her behalf.

"You need to rest," my father said at that point, getting to his feet. "I think we've said enough. And my daughter is right. I am obligated to bring in the murderer of five people. If you are not this person, then I have no reason to call the police and inform them that you are here."

"My parents—who killed them? You haven't told me. It can't have been Hazel, surely."

"We're waiting to hear from India," my father said briskly. "Rest now. We'll come again. Nothing can be done until you are well enough. That's your first duty now."

But Thomas Wade's face was haggard as we went out and closed the door.

When we were back in the motorcar, I leaned back against my seat, suddenly exhausted.

"How did you know he was protecting Hazel Sheridan?" the Colonel Sahib asked.

"I didn't. I thought I was going around the bush when I mentioned her. Then it occurred to me that perhaps it wasn't a question of why he wouldn't talk about what happened but why he *couldn't*. He loved his sister, he fretted over Alice Standish's death. Perhaps he was protecting Hazel, believing she too was worth protecting."

"Well done. Poor devil. I can't begin to imagine what he's suffered. Still, he may have to continue to live as Corporal Caswell. I'll talk to Simon, and we'll find a way to take care of him. It mustn't be known that Wade is still alive. If it's true that Lady Campbell is guilty, there's no chance of our proving it, and that will result in a reinstatement of the charges against Lieutenant Wade. But I am more relieved than I can say to know my trust was not misplaced."

We told Mother and Simon what had happened at Longleigh House. Simon, standing by the window, said nothing while my mother was obviously very pleased.

"It was well done, Bess. Truly. And probably just as well for his sanity for Lieutenant Wade to confess to what had happened."

"You've accepted his story, then?" Simon asked, not turning from the window.

I knew what he'd left unsaid. *Or is it that you want to believe it?*

The Colonel Sahib glanced at my mother. It was she who answered Simon.

"Perhaps we shouldn't until there's more proof. That's the sensible thing to do. You're absolutely right. It might be a good idea for you to speak to Lieutenant Wade. He might find it harder to convince you."

Simon turned now. I think he wanted to see if my mother was serious or mocking him. Relenting, he said, "All right. I'll go tomorrow."

He said good night then and left. I walked to the door with him and put a hand on his arm. "What's worrying you, Simon?" I asked softly, so that my parents wouldn't hear me.

"Who shot the Subedar, Bess? It wasn't Lady Campbell."

I had lost sight of that. I should have asked Lieutenant Wade.

"Let me go back with you. It's important."

He didn't answer at first, and I thought perhaps he might not. Then he said, "He's lived by his wits. For ten long years. The Colonel doesn't want to believe he was wrong in his judgment of the man. But I worked under Wade during that month following his return from England. He appeared to be the same person who'd left us weeks before." He looked down the dark drive. "I don't want your father to be deceived, that's all."

And he was gone, disappearing into the black shadows.

Whatever my parents had been discussing while I was seeing Simon out, they broke off when I came back into the room.

Mother said, getting up from her chair, "I think I'll call it a night, my dear. Richard?"

"I'll be up shortly," he said, smiling at her.

We listened to her footsteps on the stairs and then my father asked me, "Are you very sure of your facts?"

"It's the only explanation. Short of Lieutenant Wade's guilt. I don't think he'd have faced the Khyber Pass for Captain Bingham or Teddy or Sandy Hughes. He might have lied for them when the police came, saying something like, 'I saw someone running from the house, but I couldn't identify him. Not after all these years.' "

"Why couldn't he have done the same for Hazel Sheridan?"

My father had a point. "I don't know," I said.

The Colonel rose. "I'll say good night. Sleep well, my dear."

I stayed in the drawing room for another hour looking for the answer to his question and still couldn't find it.

Lieutenant Wade had gone through a trial by fire that most men wouldn't have survived. Why?

Because he was innocent? Or because he felt the price wasn't too high in order to live to savor his revenge?

Why had Simon brought back all my doubts?

The day before I was to leave for France, I was helping Iris pack my kit when I heard the telephone ringing in my father's study. My mother had gone into the village to take a jar of broth to the innkeeper's daughter who was recovering from the influenza.

Thinking it must be my father, who had had to travel up to London, I ran to answer it.

But it wasn't my father. It was Simon. His voice tight, he said, "Bess, I'm at Longleigh House. How soon can you get here?"

"I don't know—what's happened?"

"No time. Just—come."

I didn't stop to change. I ran out to my motorcar and prayed that it would crank. It didn't.

There was nothing for it but to find my mother. My old bicycle was leaning against the shed wall, and I turned to it, got on, and pedaled as quick as I could to the village.

Mother was just coming out of The Four Doves, and I hailed her before she could reach her motorcar.

"Bess? What is it? You father . . . ?"

"Simon wants me to come straightaway to Longleigh House. He must have gone to see Lieutenant Wade. And something's gone wrong. He didn't have time to explain."

"Here," she said as I came to a skidding stop beside her, "I'll help you put that bicycle into the rear seat."

We just managed it, and I turned the crank while she got behind the wheel.

On the straight stretches, she let the motorcar run, the powerful engine roaring into life, taking the bumps and ruts in stride, my mother's hands firm on the wheel.

Her concentration made any conversation about what lay ahead impossible, but I couldn't stop my own mind from spinning reason after reason for this urgent summons.

Closer to Longleigh House the road twisted and turned like a tangled ribbon, shut in between the retaining walls, and we had to slow to a very sedate pace. Anxious to be there, I bit my lip to stop myself from begging Mother to hurry.

And then the park walls came into view, followed by the gates. My mother pressed on up the drive. When we arrived in front of the steps, an orderly appeared, and I feared the worst.

He asked if we would leave our motorcar near the stables, as Matron wished to keep the drive free.

We went round to the stables as he asked, and I led Mother in through the garden entrance and straight to the stairs, praying as I did that Matron would be too busy to feel that I had been disrespectful.

Someone called, but I didn't stop. I'd have taken the stairs two at a time as the Colonel Sahib did, if I could.

I knocked briefly at the door to Lieutenant Wade's room, then opened it.

He was sitting by the window as before, although his head had been bandaged again, and I had the sinking feeling that he had tried to escape and gone headfirst down the stairs.

Walking forward, I said, "Why did you do anything so foolish?"

He turned the wheeled chair toward me and at once my gaze went to his hands on the rims of the wheel.

"Simon?" I looked at his bandaged face, the arm in a sling, his bandaged leg. "What has happened? Dear God, where is Lieutenant Wade?"

"He's safely ensconced in the next room. I'm all right, Bess. There's nothing wrong with me." He motioned to the chair across from his. "Sit down. There isn't time to explain everything. But there's a party of visitors, come to inspect the clinic and lift the morale of the men. I was just leaving when one of the Sisters mentioned that Princess Mary and Lady Campbell would be among the guests. Apparently they had visited another clinic when Sister Milton was there. The Sister was not very complimentary about Lady Campbell. I asked if we might play a little trick on Lady Campbell. She wasn't very happy with the suggestion, but I pointed out that Lady Campbell knew Corporal Caswell, and it would be appreciated." He gestured to the bed. On it lay a pretty box tied with an elegant bow.

"What's in there?" I asked, frowning. Simon was a master at improvising, but I couldn't imagine what sort of gift he's managed to find on such short notice that was suitable for someone like Lady Campbell.

"Better if you don't know," he said, and I decided he was right.

From the window I could hear the sounds of a motorcade arriving.

"You made it just in time. All right, you're my dedicated Sister. Where is your mother?"

"Downstairs," I said.

"The patient screen is there. I'd like to have her stand behind it where she won't be seen. But she can hear."

"I'll find her."

But she was just coming up the stairs when I reached them. I said quietly, "Come with me. We're about to have guests."

She recognized Simon more quickly than I did.

"Are you hurt or is this an elaborate masquerade?" she asked.

"A masquerade."

We could hear voices at the door below, a welcoming committee including Matron but not Dr. Gaines, who was still recuperating.

The voices faded as the guests were ushered inside. I explained to my mother about the screen.

"Inspections are usually a formality," Mother said quickly. "The ground floor, the more presentable patients, a little speech about how fine the clinic is and the gratitude of the nation . . . I've done these visits before, with your father."

"She must come upstairs," I said. I could hear the progress of the tour, fading and then returning.

"I rather think Sister Milton will see that she does," Simon told me, just as there was laughter from the hall below.

Sounds of footsteps from the staircase. I held my breath. Then they were coming down the passage. Purposeful, impatient.

"I hope Sister Milton doesn't come to regret helping you," I said quickly, as Mother disappeared behind the screen and I reached for the book on the table.

There was a tap at the door, and I called, "Come."

It opened, and Lady Campbell walked in, smiling. "My dear man," she said, crossing the room to Simon, "I hear you are an old friend wanting to see me."

It wasn't until she was standing before Simon that she looked up and recognized me.

"I was right. It's Hazel Sheridan, isn't it? I wanted to be sure you were safe," he said. "I've worried these ten years."

There was stunned silence for several seconds. Then Lady Campbell said sharply, "Send her away. I don't want her here."

Simon didn't hesitate. "Sister, will you leave us for a moment?"

"Yes, of course," I said reluctantly, wishing I could step behind the screen where my mother was quietly waiting.

I marched out, but instead of slamming the door, I left it ajar and walked away. I got as far as the stairs, untied my shoes, stepped out of them, and moved on stocking feet back to the door, all the while praying no one caught me there and ruined whatever it was Simon was up to. Through the crack, I could just see the bed, the gift, and Simon's bandaged face in profile. But I could hear very well.

"Who are you?" she was asking. "And why was that Crawford woman here?"

"She saved my life in France."

"I don't like her. Who are you? I won't ask again."

"Didn't you think to inquire who was in room twelve? Whoever you were expecting to find, it surely wasn't someone who knew you had blood on your hands."

There was a long silence. "I thought you were dead."

"Everyone did. But now people are asking questions. I don't know how much more I can suffer on your behalf."

"I never asked you to suffer, did I?"

"No. But you knew very well I'd hold my tongue. Right now the staff here doesn't know that I'm wanted. It's a matter of time before the Yard or the MFP finds me. I'll need your help if I'm to escape."

I could just see his good hand making a gesture. I thought he must be pointing out his bandages.

"I'm not responsible for you. If you say anything, I'll deny I was even there. They'll believe me. I never knew the Caswells, you see. Everyone knows I was never in Hampshire. There's nothing to connect me with you."

"I still have one of the Christmas photographs."

"I was a child then. I'm very different now."

"You've become a very beautiful woman."

"Don't flatter me, Lieutenant. I'm leaving."

"Tell me why you killed that family? All of us had better reasons to hate them than you did. All of us had better reasons to kill the Caswell family than you did."

"Yes, of course, that was always my safeguard. As for my reasons, that impossible girl—Gwendolyn—wanted to be invited to my wedding. She wouldn't go away, I knew that. She was always a tenacious little beast. She would show up at my door one day, claiming acquaintance. I can't keep the Princess waiting. It's rude."

"I have something for you. A parting gift, as it were."

She must have seen the box on the bed. I glimpsed her as she crossed the room and reached for it. "For me? I don't trust you," she said. "I'll take it with me and decide later whether I wish to open it or not."

"I wouldn't do that if I were you. It's rather personal."

I could hear people in the hall below, taking their leave. Someone called up the stairs, "Lady Campbell?" and then the remark, "She must have met an officer she knew."

I was praying now that no one would start up to find her, half my mind on the distraction, the other half trying to hear what was going on inside that room,

The sound of someone opening a box. And then I heard Lady Campbell say, *"Where did you find this?"*

"You left it in that poor woman's shed. You left her to take the blame if I wouldn't."

I realized that the revolver must have been in that box. My heart was in my throat. Large as it was, the room wasn't big enough for a gun to be fired without hitting someone. Simon. My mother.

"Well, it never hurts to be prepared, does it?" Lady Campbell was saying. "I see it still has three shots left. A shame to waste them."

And before I could move I heard her scream, an ear-shattering cry.

In almost the same instant, the revolver went off. And again.

Chapter Twenty-one

People were racing up the stairs, someone shouting Lady Campbell's name. I was already through the door, my shoes forgotten.

Simon was on his feet, struggling with her, hampered by the unwinding bandages. He had just twisted her wrist, forcing her to drop the revolver.

Somewhere in a corner of my mind, I realized that if it had been Lieutenant Wade in that chair, he couldn't have moved as fast, not with the collarbone just healing, and his leg still fragile. And that was what she must have counted on.

I started to pick up the revolver but Simon shouted, "Don't touch it."

He had her hands behind her back, and now Lady Campbell was screaming for help. "He's run mad, I stopped him from killing himself, and *now he's run mad.*"

An officer came through the door ahead of the others, and he drew his own revolver.

"Let her go at once. Do you hear me?"

I stepped between Simon and the officer. "There are witnesses, Major. Perhaps you'd care to listen to them before you go any further."

My mother was just coming out from behind the screen. Lady Campbell, furious, exclaimed, "Shoot him, if you have to, just make him let me go."

Mother came up to the Major and put a hand on his arm. "I'm Colonel Richard Crawford's wife," she said, as if she were holding a regimental tea and the Major was an expected guest. "I was a witness to attempted murder. Only it wasn't the patient who was holding the weapon, it was Lady Campbell, and it wasn't the patient who fired, it was Lady Campbell. I could see her very well from behind that screen, as perhaps you'd care to verify."

The Major stared at her, frowning.

Mother looked over his shoulder. "Matron, how lovely to see you again. I'm afraid there's been a little confusion, but no one has been hurt."

The Major was shoving his revolver back into its holster. "I want to know what's going on here," he said.

"Sister Crawford, if you could settle the patient again, I'll see you, Major, and Mrs. Crawford, as well as Lady Campbell in my office." Matron's voice brooked no argument.

She turned and sent everyone else away, then waited for us to follow her.

The Major, almost as an afterthought, retrieved the revolver, and marched out the door in Matron's wake. My mother waited for Lady Campbell to precede her and then followed them.

"You took a terrible risk," I scolded Simon. "Her aim is good enough that she shot three people before they could move from their chairs."

"A timely reminder," Simon replied. "Now go after your mother while I change into my own clothes and bring Wade back into his room."

I caught up my shoes and hurried down the stairs, reaching Matron's office just as she was saying something to my mother. She broke off, adding to me, "Is the patient's leg all right?"

"Yes, Matron, I don't believe it was damaged in the struggle."

She nodded, then turned back to Lady Campbell. "I was unaware that this patient was suicidal. How in fact did he come by a weapon? We are very careful about that, you see."

"It was in a box. There on the bed. I can only think someone gave it to him."

"Sister Crawford, will you please retrieve the box she's referring to?"

"I'll go," the Major cut in.

I could only hope that Simon was ready for him.

We sat in silence, crowded together in the small office, waiting for him, and after a moment the Major brought us the box. He set it on the desk, and Matron opened it. Inside was a man's driving gloves, suspiciously like a pair Simon had bought some time ago when we were in London. There was a card under the gloves, and she slid it out.

"It reads *Thank you.* And it's signed *Colonel Crawford.*" She looked up. "I know the Colonel. In fact, he visited the patient only recently. He would not bring a weapon to any patient in this house. What did the patient say to you, Major, when you went up for this box?"

"He was sitting quietly in his chair. I told him I'd come for the box, and he pointed to it with his good hand." He paused. "I stepped behind the screen. I could see well enough through the cloth. The patient was seated by the window, and the light was good."

"I'm sorry, Lady Campbell, but it appears you've not told us the truth. You insisted on going up alone to see this patient, and shots were fired when you were in the room. I myself saw the holes in the ceiling. We were very fortunate that the staff works with patients during the day and so they were not in their rooms. I'd like to hear your side of this story."

She said, "I don't need to defend myself. I have told you that the man was suicidal, and I tried to take the weapon from him."

"It was lying on the floor," Matron said. "And the patient was holding *your* wrists, not the reverse."

"He was trying to prevent me from going for help."

"Sister Crawford was already in the room, and still the patient was keeping his grip on your hands. The revolver remained on the floor."

"They're all lying, I tell you. That man in room twelve is being sought by the police, Matron. When I arrived he knew that he would be facing the hangman."

"Corporal Caswell?" Matron asked, shocked. "How do you know this?"

"He's wanted—" She broke off in the midst of answering Matron's question, the name not registering at first. "What did you say?"

"I asked you how you could possibly know that Corporal Caswell is wanted by the police."

Lady Campbell sat there, boxed in. Anything that she could tell us about the man in room twelve would convict her as well. "I don't know any Corporal Caswell," she said finally.

My mother spoke then. "I overheard you calling the poor man by a very different name. You confessed to killing three people in 1908 in Hampshire, and you told him why. That you were marrying well, and they were threatening to claim acquaintance. An impossible family, and you didn't want them at your wedding. It's quite possible that that revolver is the same one you used to kill them. Three of the chambers were empty, and now two more are as well."

The Major, looking down at the revolver he was holding, said, "She's right."

Lady Campbell stood up, pushing back her chair. "This is ridiculous. I've kept the Princess waiting. I don't have time for this nonsense. These people have been badgering me, and I have had enough."

"Sit down," Matron said, in the voice that could calm a riot in the streets. "Her Royal Highness has already left."

Lady Campbell hesitated, then sank back into her chair.

"I think we should call in Scotland Yard. I don't believe this is a matter the local constable could handle well enough. Is there a telephone here, Matron?" the Major asked.

"Yes, it's there in Dr. Gaines's office. Sister Crawford, would you please show him the way?"

He laid the revolver on the desk, and I followed him out of the little office. As I was leading him to Dr. Gaines's office, he turned to me and said, "I'd like very much to know just what is going on."

"Actually, it's quite true that a mother and father and daughter were shot in their house, The Willows, just outside Petersfield, in 1908. As I understand it, there was a witness after the shooting, who claims Lady Campbell—Hazel Sheridan as she was then—came out of the house with the revolver in her hand. He went inside and found the bodies. When he came out, she had gone."

He whistled. "This can be proved?"

"The man who saw her there was in my father's regiment. He went missing on the Northwest Frontier before the police could question him."

"Is that why she brought the revolver with her today, to kill the only witness? But you say this witness is missing or dead?"

"*She,* it seems, thought he was the man in room twelve."

We had reached the doctor's office. "I would never have believed such a thing of Lady Campbell. She's always been a pillar." He picked up the telephone, preparing to make the call, when I heard a commotion in the passage.

My only thought was for my mother, in Matron's office with a murderer.

Without a word, I dashed out and ran toward Matron's office.

I got there in time to see Simon once more forcing the revolver out of Lady Campbell's hand, and in the doorway to the office, Matron's pale face, mouth open in surprise. Behind her was my mother, watching Simon.

There was only one shot left, but the rooms down here were filled with patients and staff, a revolver fired here would most certainly strike someone.

And Lady Campbell was fighting viciously, determined to keep control of the weapon.

Then, very quickly, it was over. Simon had the revolver, and he was once more pinning Lady Campbell's hands behind her back.

The Major—I still didn't know his name—was saying, "I'll take charge of that, if you please, Sergeant-Major. Matron, is there somewhere we can confine this woman until the police arrive?"

Half an hour later, calm had been restored. Lady Campbell was locked up in a linen closet, the Major had reached Scotland Yard, and my mother was taking tea with Matron, who had been speechless when Lady Campbell had taken the revolver from the desk and pointed it directly at her. The other patients had gone back to their usual occupations, and Simon had disappeared up the stairs to speak to Lieutenant Wade.

I was standing in the drive, where the cool breeze of late afternoon was beginning to soothe my own inner turmoil.

I wasn't sure what was going to happen. Whether Lady Campbell—Hazel Sheridan, that was—would ever be tried for the murder of the Caswells. But she had tried to shoot the man in room twelve, and she had pointed the same weapon at Matron.

Simon came down the steps to the drive and stood behind me, looking up at the sky. "You'll have a rough crossing tomorrow," he said after a moment.

"What about the Subedar?" I asked. It was the question he'd raised two nights ago.

"I don't know. It's likely he was trying to find Wade, to be sure, and was shot by a sentry who brought him as far as the nearest aid station. It happens."

"If you didn't believe Wade, why did you ambush Lady Campbell?"

"It was the only way I could think of to be sure. I never indicated I was Wade. When I told her I knew she had blood on her hands, she jumped to the conclusion I must be the Lieutenant. She must have wondered all these years when he'd show up. Perhaps that's why she erased her past in Hampshire." He reached out and put a hand on my shoulder. "Bess, it couldn't go on. Either Wade was a fraud or he was not. For your father's sake, we had to be certain."

"There's still India."

"I know. But I think Mr. Kipling will get to the truth, if anyone can."

"And the Gesslers?"

"When the sexton couldn't retrieve that last photograph, he must have sent word to her. And so the Gesslers had to die. We may not be able to prove that. But I rather think the sexton might be persuaded to talk, and that will point to Lady Campbell."

"That's terrible. I feel so guilty about them."

"Don't. You and I had no way of knowing what would happen. Lieutenant Wade was in France. We had no reason to think there was anyone else involved."

"Perhaps," I said, still unconvinced. I took a deep breath. "You took a terrible risk in there today," I said again. "At the very least, you should have removed the cartridges."

I could hear him chuckle deep in his chest. "To tell you the truth, I thought the gun would never fire. Given the condition it was in."

I was back in France and busy with influenza patients again when the final resolution came.

Mr. Kipling wrote to Melinda—and Melinda sent the letter on to me—to say that the Subedar's brother had been found in Delhi where he had gone to live with another cousin and had been taken into custody for the killing of Mr. and Mrs. Wade, driven by his anger over losing his position with the railways. He had, in fact, confessed, claiming he'd been drunk at the time. She had sent a copy of the letter to my parents. My father saw that the information reached the right ears at Scotland Yard and the Army, exonerating the late Lieutenant Thomas Wade.

I had an opportunity later on that week to speak to Teddy Belmont. Teddy claimed he knew nothing about the dying Subedar. I didn't know whether to believe him or not. But his desperate need to escape from the past made me wonder if perhaps he hadn't killed the man to prevent any search for Lieutenant Wade, either to protect himself or to protect the man who had done what he had never had the courage to do. It didn't matter—he was killed two weeks after I returned to France, when a probing shell made a direct hit on his ambulance.

As for Lady Campbell, she maintained throughout that she had had no contact with the Caswells. Miss Gooding swore she was in their care, as did Sandy Hughes and Captain Bingham. Barney Lowell refused to testify until he saw which way the wind blew, that his tidy little sum of bribes was finished forever. And then, for fear he would be charged as an accessory, he agreed to tell what he knew. He even confessed to attacking Simon by the motorcar, convinced that it was the only way to discourage us. I was certain Lowell had also been Miss Gooding's caller, but whether he was just looking to change the photograph or had come to look for the revolver with an eye to blackmail, I wasn't sure.

No one ever discovered where Lady Campbell got the revolver. It was possible that it had come from the house of her late guardian, Sir James Felton.

Simon swore—but privately to the family—that it had come from Barney Lowell.

To my surprise, "Thomas Wade" was never called to testify. Only Corporal Caswell—no relation to the family of the same name—was asked about his spurious attempt at suicide. With his scars and a limp as the leg healed, no one recognized him. And Lady Campbell dared not name him as Thomas Wade because to do so would have allowed him to tell the court about encountering her coming out the door of The Willows, revolver in hand.

As to why she tried to kill him at the clinic, it was alleged that bandaged as he was, she had mistaken him for someone else. That was all she would say.

I wondered what would happen to Corporal Caswell. With any luck the war would be over before he'd healed sufficiently to return to duty. He could start a new life anywhere in the world. My father told me that the Lieutenant didn't want to return to the regiment. There was a new Colonel now, and most of the men he'd served with in India were dead.

Was I happy about the way this had turned out? Justice had been served, honor had been satisfied. Thomas Wade was no longer a hunted man. Still . . .

It was my mother who put it best in a letter she wrote soon after I'd reached France.

You went into this for your father's sake, and the good name of the regiment. I was drawn in by the faces of those children. And Simon because in Wade's boots, he would have stood fast and fought to clear himself. Sad, isn't it, that no one was moved to seek justice for the Caswells? Hazel was the only child strong enough to withstand them, and in the end, even she was pushed too far by their greed, when it threatened her happiness. They decided their own fate, and in the end, it will cost Lady Campbell her life.

And, meanwhile, Simon was forced to buy a new pair of driving gloves. His had been entered into evidence.